The Rage of I

(Matthew Quinton's Journals - Book 6)

J D Davies

© J D Davies 2016

J D Davies has asserted his rights under the Copyright, Design and Patents Act, 1988, to be identified as the author of this work.

First published in 2016 by Old Street Publishing

This edition published in 2017 by Endeavour Press Ltd.

For Iwan, Efa, and Rhiannon Mullin

*The rage of fortune is less directed against the humble,
and providence strikes more lightly on the low.*
Seneca (cAD4–65)

*

Champaigne: The cause, My Lord, of this intestine uproar?
Marquis de Hauvrye: The cause is murder, misery, and death.
Anon., *Alarum for London*: *Or*, *The Siege of Antwerp* (1602)

Table of Contents

CHAPTER ONE	7
CHAPTER TWO	21
CHAPTER THREE	38
CHAPTER FOUR	51
CHAPTER FIVE	61
CHAPTER SIX	69
CHAPTER SEVEN	77
CHAPTER EIGHT	85
CHAPTER NINE	93
CHAPTER TEN	100
CHAPTER ELEVEN	107
CHAPTER TWELVE	117
CHAPTER THIRTEEN	127
CHAPTER FOURTEEN	134
CHAPTER FIFTEEN	140
CHAPTER SIXTEEN	148
CHAPTER SEVENTEEN	159
CHAPTER EIGHTEEN	168

CHAPTER NINETEEN	178
CHAPTER TWENTY	188
CHAPTER TWENTY-ONE	199
CHAPTER TWENTY-TWO	207
CHAPTER TWENTY-THREE	214
CHAPTER TWENTY-FOUR	221
CHAPTER TWENTY-FIVE	229
CHAPTER TWENTY-SIX	244
CHAPTER TWENTY-SEVEN	253
CHAPTER TWENTY-EIGHT	259
CHAPTER TWENTY-NINE	267
HISTORICAL NOTE	271
ACKNOWLEDGEMENTS	279

CHAPTER ONE

'*Francis Drake. Mm, well then. Sir fucking Francis fucking Drake. Did I ever tell you about my dealings with him, grandson?*'

'*No, My Lord. You died when I was five.*'

Beware of ghosts with too much eternity on their hands.

'*I did? So I did, young Matthew. But you bear my name, and you have heard my voice, have you not? You heard it through all those years that you commanded men-of-war for those worthless whoresons, the Stuarts—*'

'*Yes, grandfather. I heard it.*'

'*But I really never told you about Drake? That man—*'

'*Matthieu! Pas devant l'enfant, pour la grâce de Dieu!*'

'*As you say, my dearest. Francis Drake, then, grandson. Hero of England, my arse. That man was a liar, a villain, a coxcomb, an arrogant strutting rogue, who deluded Queen and country alike—*'

Rather, beware of old men with too much time on their hands. Very old men forced to take to their beds with a slight fever, which their doctors and servants are convinced will kill them at long last. Bored old men who know that it really is only a slight fever, *so leave me alone, you damnable vultures, I may be nearly ninety years old, but I will yet outlive you all.*

Old men who know it's not yet their time to die, but who would greatly prefer it if the fever-borne spirits of their long dead grandparents would permit them just a little sleep.

'*You know the story of Drake's Drum, grandson?*'

'*Yes, My Lord, I'm sure—*'

'*How it'll beat when England's in danger, to bring back the great hero to save us all? Satan's cock it will. Frank Drake's ancient history now, and he's not coming back, that much is certain. I saw him dead in his sea-bed, shrivelled and yellow from the bloody flux that did for him. I saw his lead coffin slip into the sapphire-blue Carib ocean. I heard that Christforsaken drum beat its lament for the dead admiral. I heard the thunder of the fleet's guns echoing round the bay. God help me, I even* raised my own sword to salute him. And I know damn well that at that moment I wasn't the only man in the fleet who was thinking "good riddance, you preposterous, preening old turd-sack".'

'*As you say, grandfather.*'

Oh Lord, why cannot I be granted a feverish dream of a nubile unclad wench? Why, instead, must my illness bring me a dream-visitation from my namesake, Matthew Quinton, eighth Earl of Ravensden, sometime admiral to the great Queen Elizabeth, sometime adventurer in the Carib ocean, sometime scourge of every Spaniard from Belize to Barcelona?

'*These journals that you scribble. Your so-called adventures. They are nothing compared to mine, of course. Tales fit only to amuse children, grandson. The Dutch as enemies? Christ's bollocks, in my day the Dutch had barely crawled out of their bogs for the first time. I had a decent foe, at least – Spain, by God! A vast empire that stretched around the entire globe, founded upon gold and silver beyond measure! The galleons! The armadas! That's what you should be writing about, grandson. The journals of Matthew Quinton, indeed. The journals of* this *Matthew Quinton, that's what you should be writing! Now, you can start with how I fooled Drake at Cartagena – or with my part in the fight against the Invincible Armada—*'

'*Tais-toi, husband! Pay no heed to his vanities, grandson. But he is right in one thing. You should write of our times, but of the days when your grandfather and I first knew each other. You remember, young Matthew, how you and Herry discovered the papers together, at Ravensden Abbey in 1651, when you were eleven years old? When the first gale of autumn brought down a chimney and, with it, the partition wall of the muniment room?*'

'I remember, *grandmaman*. I remember, and I promise I will write of your adventures. When I am well enough to leave this bed.'

I woke, still mumbling as my eyes opened, my wrinkled brow drenched in sweat.

I was in my bedroom, surrounded by the familiar oak panelling and the portraits mounted upon it. Above the fireplace, my mother and father. Between the windows, my grandfather, bold and bearded, just as he had been in my dream, and my grandmother, much younger than I remembered her. And even in waking, I could remember my first, astonished sight of grandfather's words upon paper, all those years ago –

'Francis Drake. Sir fucking—'

In truth, the ghosts that had come to me in my fever were the ghosts of words upon a page, words read avidly for the first time nearly eighty years before. And with the words came the memory of a youthful and well-loved voice –

'Maggot!'

September 1651, then. Dearest God in Heaven, what a time. Some weeks after what had seemed to be the final defeat of the King's cause – the Quinton family's cause – on the battlefield of Worcester. So many long years before this day, when I sat up in bed, called for claret, insulted my doctors, and remembered what had transpired all those years before.

Remembered the sweet face of my dear twin sister, as clearly as if she stood before me in that moment.

*

'Maggot! *Matthew*!'

Henrietta Quinton burst through the door of the muniment room, grabbed my shoulder and shook me. I was aware of the familiar sound of armed men dismounting, of boots and spurs upon cobbles, of orders being barked in harsh artisan tones. That, and only that, served to break the spell cast by my grandfather's words, and made me turn to look into Herry's wide, alarmed eyes.

'Soldiers, Matthew! Ironsides! An entire troop of them! They must have come—'

'To search for our brother. Very well. With mother and Lizzie away, it falls to us to welcome them, Herry.'

'*Welcome*? Soldiers of the army that killed our father? That killed our king? I would rather die, Maggot!'

My twin was a gangling creature, almost as tall as me but with limbs that seemed to fling themselves haphazardly in several different directions at once. Yet she had a fearless heart, and a good soul.

'Remember who we are, Herry,' said my eleven-year-old self. 'We are Quintons. We act with honour. Always with honour. By welcoming the enemy, we make ourselves better than them. That's what Uncle Tris teaches, and it's what our mother and brother would expect of us. What father and grandfather would have expected of us. But, sis, it might be wise if you didn't call me Maggot in their presence.'

Her response was grave. 'Of course, brother. Matthew. I swear I will not demean the heir to Ravensden before prating rebel scum.'

I stood to go downstairs with her, but turned for one more glance at our newly-discovered treasure trove. I could just remember him, a white-bearded, stooped, but still remarkably strong old man who delighted in lifting both Herry and me with each hand to balance us on his shoulders. I turned back again, and as I did so, my eyes fell upon another of the rat-eaten, mildewed fragments of paper that were strewn everywhere: fragments that appeared to have been written in three distinct hands, of which only my grandfather's was familiar.

There it was again: just a short passage this time, scribbled in his hand in the margin of his diatribe against Sir Francis Drake.

Drake's Drum doesn't need to beat. England still has a hero.
It has me.
It has Matthew Quinton, Earl of Ravensden.

*

In the dining hall of the Abbey, an Ironside captain – a stocky, nearly bald man with a ferociously pimpled nose – was remonstrating with old Barcock, the loyal steward of Ravensden Abbey. Half a dozen heavily armed, buff-jacketed, turtle-helmeted troopers lounged against the ancient, insect-devoured, Flemish tapestries, looking at once bored and menacing.

'...under orders of the Council of State, to search this house—'

'I know you, don't I?' said Barcock in his broad Bedfordshire accent, screwing up his eyes to study the face before him more intently. 'Yes, it's come back to me. Couldn't place where I'd seen your face before. Remember now, all right. Ezekiel Fensom, that's who you are. Miller of Willington before the war.'

The rebel officer bridled at that. '*Captain* Fensom to you, Steward. Acting, as I say, upon the authority of the Council of State of this Commonwealth of England—'

They both realised at once that Herry and I had entered the hall, and turned to face us.

'Well, then,' said Ezekiel Fensom, 'what have we here?'

I hated and feared the creature with every inch and ounce of my lanky eleven-year-old frame. But I was a Quinton and the man of the house, and I prayed that my voice would not tremble.

'I am Matthew Quinton, brother and heir to the noble Lord Charles, Earl of Ravensden. This is my sister Henrietta, and this is our home. Why do you interrupt our peace, Captain?'

The sometime miller of Willington looked down over the pimples.

'I do not deal with children,' he said, turning back to Barcock. I swore then that I would kill him one day. And, many years later, when I was a captain in the navy of the restored King Charles the Second, and Ezekiel Fensom was –

But no, that is not an episode which I recall with any great sense of pride, and I will gainsay recording it now.

'As I say,' continued the Ironside officer, 'I have orders to search for the notorious traitor and malignant Charles Quinton, believed to be wounded and to have fled from the Worcester battlefield after the recent glorious victory of Lord General Cromwell and God's chosen army—'

'Wounded?' Herry gasped. 'How badly wounded?'

Fensom turned back toward us, and examined my sister intently.

'Well, now. Perchance you are a good actress, girl, for if you have been sheltering him, you will know full well what his condition is. Standish, Gunn, Laurence, search the outbuildings! Remember we seek treasonable correspondence too, so search under floorboards and the like. The rest of you, go through this building—'

'No,' I said.

The russet-coated captain looked at me as though I were a dog turd upon the sole of his boot.

'What's that, boy? *No*? To a commissioned captain of the New Model Army?' Fensom drew his wheel-lock pistol from his belt, then turned it this way and that, as though he were studying it for the first time. 'Perhaps I should shoot you now, to stop you growing into as monstrous a traitor as your brother and father.'

He cocked the pistol, raised it, and levelled it at me.

Herry's mouth fell open and she gripped my hand, but I did not flinch, did not even sway in the slightest. In truth, I think I was paralysed with fear and anger: fear at the sight of the gun barrel pointing directly at my eyes, anger at this pretend-captain's insult to my father, who had fallen in glory at the Naseby fight after being the ninth Earl of Ravensden for exactly one hundred and eighteen days.

But there, high on the wall above Ezekiel Fensom, was the vast Van Dyck portrait of my grandfather, the eighth Earl, arms akimbo and formidably bearded, looking every inch the mighty warrior who had ventured out against the Invincible Armada. Wherever I was in the room, I always felt that his eyes were looking down on me, and I never had that sense more strongly than in that moment. And I remembered his words:

England still has a hero. It has me. It has Matthew Quinton.

'No, Captain Fensom,' I said, with all the authority that the living and distinctly unheroic Matthew Quinton could muster. 'My brother, the Earl, is not here. There is no correspondence in this house that you would find treasonable. You have my word of honour upon it.'

Fensom continued to aim his pistol directly at me, but after a moment, his hand began to shake. Then the rest of his frame followed suit. Finally, he lowered the pistol a fraction and began to laugh. His men joined in, uncertainly at first, then more confidently.

'Honour!' cried the erstwhile miller. 'Great Lord, an infant seeks to fob off a godly soldier with his word of honour!'

While the troopers continued to laugh, Fensom beckoned to them to be about their business. As ordered, three men went outside, the others made for the stairs to the upper floors of the ramshackle old mansion which had been converted from a dissolved abbey over a hundred years before.

Finally, Fensom's laughter began to subside. In its place came cold, unsettling contempt.

'Honour that tips over into arrogance, that tips over into the monstrous lie called the Divine Right of Kings. That is why you cavaliers lost the Worcester battle, and the war before that, and the war before that one too, and why we cut off your king's head in the end, for causing all that needless death. And I remember you Quintons, before the war, how you lorded it over this part of the county. Your grandfather there, boy—' he nodded toward the portrait, levelling the pistol at my head once again as he did so – 'he was the worst. Saw him riding by many a time, proud and arrogant as they come—'

'You, *monsieur*, will not dare to speak ill of my late husband, and you will not dare to point guns at my grandson!'

The unexpected voice came from the doorway that led from the kitchen range in what had once been the monastic refectory. Despite spending the best part of half a century in England, my grandmother's accent was still that of a Frenchwoman who had learned English reluctantly, suspiciously, and very, very, slowly, as if each word of the language represented a threat to her very Frenchness. Louise-Marie Quinton, formerly de Monconseil-Bragelonne, Dowager Countess of Ravensden, was now over seventy years old, but she still dressed as though she were attending a ball at the court of *le roi Henri le Bon*. She could no longer stand, but sat in her silvery satin finery within the wheeled contraption that had been invented for her by her younger son, the strangely-garbed man with a face like a gargoyle who now pushed it forward into the hall: my uncle Tristram, scientist, alchemist, and God alone knew what else.

Herry and I looked toward each other at exactly the same moment, as we often did, and I knew that exactly the same thought was in her mind.

Where had they come from? They were not here an hour ago. Our grandmother should have been at her dower property, Quinton Hall, the old monastic grange farm across the valley. She and Tristram should have been attending to –

Herry ran to *grandmaman* and hugged her, but I remained where I was, watching Fensom. He seemed utterly nonplussed by the new arrivals. His eyes moved from my grandmother to Tristram and back again, settling upon the silver crucifix boldly displayed at her bosom. I saw what I took to be untrammelled Calvinistic rage in his eyes. Finally, though, Ezekiel Fensom inclined his head very slightly toward the dowager Countess.

'My Lady Ravensden,' he said, decades of deference overcoming his Roundhead ardour. 'Doctor Quinton. I had not expected you—'

'Evidently,' said Tristram.

'My apologies, Doctor Quinton. But I have orders from the Council of State, to search for the malig– that is to say, for the fugitive, Charles, Earl of Ravensden.'

'You will not find my nephew here, Captain. My elder nephew,' said my uncle, neutrally. 'And your orders from the Council of State? How small, exactly, was the quorum when whatever Councillors remain at Whitehall signed it? When every honest man in England with a landed interest is upon his estates, bringing in the last of the harvest? Let me see your orders, Captain.'

Tristram thrust out his right hand. Fensom hesitated, then handed him the papers. I looked at my grandmother, and saw that her gaze was upon me, too. There was a pride in it – pride at my obstinate defence of our family honour, I hoped – but there was something else. Something I could not quite comprehend.

'As I thought,' said Uncle Tris. 'Three names. Three, out of a Council of State of forty-one men. But it does not need forty-one signatures, this document, does it, Captain Fensom? It does not need even three. It needs only this one, the one that signed first. "O Cromwell". How very modest of him. So the Lord General has returned to London after his victory at Worcester?'

'He has, sir. He—'

Two of Fensom's men came down from upstairs, their boots clanking loudly upon the stone steps. They each bore armfuls of paper. I recognised them immediately: they were the same papers I had been reading only minutes before. The soldiers cast them down roughly upon the long oak table in the centre of the hall.

'Grandfather's papers,' I said. 'We found them just now, in the collapsed—'

'Silence, child!' cried Fensom. 'Your grandfather's papers, you say. A likely excuse for treasonable correspondence, I say.'

Fensom looked at Tristram, as though for approbation, but my uncle said nothing, seemingly waiting for the Roundhead officer to make a decision.

'Well, Captain,' said my grandmother, 'you seek proof of treason. You seek proof of my elder grandson's whereabouts. Do you expect him to appear miraculously before you, surrendering abjectly to the omniscient Captain Fensom, or are you willing to make even the slightest effort to achieve that end? Look there, Captain. If my other grandson, here, is correct, you see before you private papers of a family of renowned Cavaliers, or malignants as you term them, who have had to endure compounding, sequestration and all the other exactions of this Rump Parliament. Go to it, man. Go through the papers. Prove my grandson right, or disprove him. Or, perchance, is it that you cannot read?'

Fensom's face seemed drained of blood. He no longer appeared a proud Parliamentarian officer, but the very image of a scapegrace village miller being upbraided by a great lady for the poor quality of his bread.

Finally, he took the half-dozen steps to the table and picked up two or three scraps of paper, then the same number again.

'Ancient scribbling,' he said. 'Unless it is in code, and the paper discoloured to make it seem old. I have heard of such things.'

'If it please you, Captain—'

One of Fensom's men: his voice unmistakeably that of Hertfordshire.

'Yes, Dunkley?'

'Have a look at that piece, sir. It was the one on top of the pile I carried down. The one with what looks like a wine stain.'

'A literate trooper of the New Model,' said *grandmaman*. 'Truly, we live in a new age of manifold wonders.'

Fensom took the paper, raised it to the light coming in through what had once been one of the ancient monastery's transept windows, and read aloud again; which, I suddenly realised, was the only way he could read. I, who was but eleven, was already a long way beyond that.

'*Francis Drake*,' he read. '*Sir fucking* –Y– your pardon, my lady!'

My grandmother gave him one of the thin smiles she usually reserved for the Reverend Jermy, our ancient vicar, or else for Goodwife Barcock whenever she undercooked the fish.

'You have it, Captain. I am entirely familiar with my late husband's opinion of Sir Francis Drake, and of the language in which he chose to express it. Indeed, the sentence you hold in your hand seems distinctly mild compared to some of the things the late Earl said about the late Sir Francis in my presence. And obscenity is the solitary field in which the English tongue might be regarded as superior to my native French.'

'Captain Fensom,' said Tristram, 'my father has been dead for over six years. I would respectfully suggest that you are unlikely to find proof of the current Earl's whereabouts, or of this family's treason, among these ancient papers of his.'

I almost felt pity for Ezekiel Fensom: he had to contend with those inexorable forces, my uncle and my grandmother, and even with the spirit of my dead grandfather. I thought I could almost detect the ghost of a smile on the visage in the Van Dyck portrait. Yet the sometime miller of Willington still rallied, perhaps remembering that he wore the uniform of an officer of the New Model Army and of the fledgling English republic.

'But still, Doctor Quinton, I have orders to—'

'I think it is time we spoke privately, Captain.'

Without waiting for a response, Tristram led Fensom away, out into the courtyard that had once been the abbey cloister. The New Model captain could have shot him, or arrested him, or simply said 'no'; but he did none of these things. He went with my uncle as meekly as a lamb. I went over to the window. The Roundhead soldiers looked at each other, perhaps wondering whether they should order me not to move, but *grandmaman* glowered at them, and I ignored them. Through the window, I could see the two men disappear into what had once been the undercroft of the monks' refectory: disappear with Tristram Quinton's arm upon Ezekiel Fensom's shoulder.

Long minutes passed. Herry sat upon the arm of *grandmaman*'s wheeled chariot, chattering to her in French, at which my twin was considerably more proficient than I. For my part, I went to the head of the table and sat in the Earl's chair, affecting to study my grandfather's papers.

At length, Fensom and Tristram Quinton returned. The former seemed at once abashed and furious, the latter merely inscrutable.

'Get the others,' Fensom barked at his men. Then he turned to my grandmother. 'My Lady Ravensden,' he said. 'My apologies for inconveniencing you.'

He bowed his head, albeit so little and so quickly that one could have blinked and missed it entirely. Then he turned on his heel and left. After a minute or so more, we heard hooves upon cobbles. Herry ran out to see them off, but I stayed where I was. I turned, and saw *grandmaman* staring up at my uncle, her head tilted slightly to the left.

'Ah, Tristram,' she said softly, '*qu'es-tu devenu*?'

'*Votre fils, maman*. Your son, and a Quinton. Nothing more matters.' Then Tristram Quinton turned to me. 'Well done, Matt. You were brave, if obstinate. You could have had your head blown off, and then where would we be, if your brother succumbs to his wounds at Quinton Hall?'

'Then you would be Earl of Ravensden, uncle.'

'Which I have no desire whatever to be, so if only to assure my own comfort, I shall have to teach you the arts of compromise and bending with the wind, methinks.'

'Is that what they are called these days, my son?' said *grandmaman*. 'We had other words for them, once. Your father certainly had words for them.'

'Ah yes, my father's words,' said Tristram. 'Let us look at them, shall we, rather than trying to put them into his dead mouth? Show us these papers you have discovered, Matthew.'

I arranged the papers upon the table. My grandmother picked up a few pieces, Tristram rather more. For a few minutes, they studied them intently, an act which ensured that they did not need to look at or talk to each other.

'The Earl's handwriting,' said *grandmaman* at length. 'There is no mistaking it. He had *écriture diabolique*, my husband. A mighty heart, but atrocious handwriting. This second hand, though – this must be Iles, I think.'

'Iles?' said Tristram. 'Who is Iles?'

The old Countess smiled. 'Ah, young Tris—' Her son was over forty years old at this time – 'I had forgotten that he was before your day, or that you would have been very young when he—'Her mind seemed to drift away, and she was silent for a time; something that occurred with increasing frequency. But then she was with us again, and all was well. 'Who was Nicholas Iles? Ah, now. That is a question, indeed.'

'And one that you do not intend to answer, *Maman*?'

'The old should not be asked questions, Tristram. But if they are, they should not be expected to give answers. Beyond a certain age, we have done with all of that. You will find that in your time, my son, and you too in yours, young Matthew. This third hand, though – this is difficult.'

'He writes in English, but I do not think it was his native language,' said Tris, staring at one of the torn pieces of paper.

'In which case it is probably the Hungarian.'

'Hungarian, *Maman*?'

'Laszlo Horvath. Or at least, that was the name he chose to call himself. For a time, at least. His, too, is a story.' Tristram stared at her intently, willing her to say more, but she was deep in thought, screwing up her eyes to study the difficult writing on the fragments. 'These pieces all seem to be from the time just before Queen Elizabeth died. The time when I met and married the Earl.' *Grandmaman* smiled, and closed her eyes. It was though she were transporting herself back fifty years, to the time when she was young, to the time when – 'And, of course, there was the conspiracy of Gowrie, and the rebellion of Essex. And the affair of the Invisible Armada—'

'Invincible, *Maman*,' said Tristram. 'The Invincible Armada.'

'When I say Invisible, *mon fils*, I mean Invisible. Do not assume that the old have lost their wits entirely. But look, here are papers about my husband's battle in the *Merhonour*, which brought him to me. And the battles at Kinsale and Sesimbra Bay. And the great fight with the Spanish galleys, that seems to be in these papers, too. And all the time, the certain knowledge that the old Queen would soon be dead, and the greatest question of the day – who was to succeed her?' She studied the pieces of paper in her hand. 'I wonder if any of them, even my husband, dared to write down the truth of all of that?'

In my eleven years of life, I had never seen my uncle Tristram shocked. But now, the rational, pragmatic man of science was clearly shocked beyond all measure.

'And you knew that truth, *Maman*?'

The old lady seemed offended that her son could even consider asking her such a thing.

'*Mais oui* – of course I did, *mon cher* Tristram—'

Herry ran into the hall, bounding like an excited hound.

'The Roundheads have gone! They're beyond the mill leet, riding down the Bedford road!'

'*Très, très bon*,' said the Dowager Countess, arching her hands and fingers in the eternal gesture of prayer.

'I did not blink!' cried Herry, triumphantly. 'You saw that, Maggot? When that vile captain said I must be a good actress, when I pretended it was the first time I'd heard that our brother was wounded? And I was! I was a good actress!'

'The best, sis,' I said, grinning.

Indeed she was. Perhaps my dear twin might have had a glorious career on the stage after the King returned, when women were permitted to tread the boards: might have, had she not been a noblewoman, the daughter and sister of earls, for whom such a vocation was inconceivable, and had she not been dead a little over two years later, just as she was blooming into the woman she was destined never to be.

Tristram rose from the table.

'Then it is time for me to return to the patient,' he said.

'When can I come and see him?' I demanded.

'Patience, Matthew,' said grandmaman. 'Your brother is still very weak, and must not be overly taxed. It is a miracle that Musk brought him back to us alive, after the wounds he took in the Worcester fight.'

'But I'm bored!' I cried. Herry rolled her eyes, as though, once again, her twin brother was behaving *so* immaturely. 'Although this, today, has been exciting – finding grandfather's papers, and pulling the wool over the eyes of that idiot Fensom—'

'Well, then,' said Tris, 'we must find something for you to do, young Matthew, to keep you out of mischief. For some weeks, at least, I will be too busy tending your brother to teach you, and you claim to have outgrown the school in Bedford—'

'They are dolts, Uncle! The master is a Welsh oaf, while apart from good Dick Norris, the rest of the students are lumpen simpletons. And what need does the heir to an earldom have of school?'

'We shall have that argument another time, nephew. Yet again.' Tristram shook his head. 'But in the meantime, it seems to me that there is something useful that you can do – indeed, something I'm sure you will enjoy. All these papers of your grandfather's, and of these other two men, Iles and Horvath – read them, Matt. Put them into order.'

'*Oui*,' said *grandmaman* emphatically. 'I would like that very much, Matthew. I would like to read of those times once more. I was young and beautiful then, and your grandfather and I had such glorious adventures. And if there are gaps, I shall do my best to fill them. Yes, you can write down my part in the story – I shall tell it to you in French, to improve your skill in my language. Your French will need to be very fine by the time the King comes into his own again. So go it, *mon cher*. Put our adventures into order, dear grandson.'

*

That I did.

So even as I despatch a footman to bring to my London house the old oak chest containing the papers, I remember the astonishing story that I learned from them. Determined to honour a promise made to a ghost, and ignoring my doctors' dire imprecations, I leave my bed and walk slowly, unsteadily upon sticks, to my desk by the window. There, I take up a quill, dip it in the ink, and put it to a virgin sheet of paper.

The Voyages, Battles, and Travails, of Matthew Quinton, eighth Earl of Ravensden, in the years between 1598 and 1603, during the Reign of Her Majesty Queen Elizabeth of Blessed Memory.

Down in the street, a drunken Jacobite is crying out for the Pretender, calling tipsily upon God to preserve His Majesty King James and his son Charles Edward, rightful Prince of Wales. He is set upon at once by a Hanoverian mob bawling 'God save King George!' I observe the forced departure of teeth from a bloodied mouth, and hear the crack of an arm being broken.

I smile.

'A plague on both your houses,' I mutter. 'King James. King George. If only you knew, you ale-sodden shit-for-brains simpletons. If only you knew.'

And then I begin to write.

'*Sir Francis Drake. Sir—*'

CHAPTER TWO

1598

Torn fragment from the Diurnal of Nicholas Iles, 23 November 1598

...just as I stabbed upward with my dagger and sliced open the balls of the Spaniard who was charging me, sword raised, yelling '*Para el rey Felipe y Santiago!*'

The man fell to the deck, screaming piteously as he tried to stop his life-blood pouring out of his sack. I heard a familiar growl behind me.

'Not a bad thrust. For a poet, at any rate.'

I turned, and there he was.

A tall, broad man of middle years, brown beard tinged with grey, clad in breastplate and morrion helmet. His face, clean shaven, weather-tanned and scarred: yet still possessing a youthfulness about the eyes, and a beauteous smile, that belied his warlike appearance. In his hand, a wide-bladed sword of middling length. The kind that was unfashionable at court, where the long, thin rapier now held sway. The kind that could still seem like a razor-edged feather as it lightly severed the neck of the unfortunate enemy pikeman who opposed Matthew Quinton, Earl of Ravensden, captain of Her Majesty's ship the *Merhonour*.

Truly, here was England's Hercules, her Agamemnon, her Alexander!

No.

I have sworn to eschew hyperbole, to eschew poetry itself, in this account. This is not a history: that low, cursed form which distorts and exaggerates to suit the malicious whims of the writer.

Away with fictions, short of our stout man,
The Poet must now turn Historian –
His fights, his fights, his fights, his victories
His conquests, his trophies, and yet no lies!

No. No lies, Nicholas.

What I write here is but the raw bone, the stuff from which those who come after me can write their lauded dramas and high-flown verses exalting the legend that is Matthew of Ravensden. Or perhaps it is the source I will use myself, if ever I return to writing for the stage; that is, if mountebanks like Dekker, Chettle and Shakespeare do not still monopolise all on the Southwark shore. And if I can obtain a pardon. But that is another matter, for another day.

So, then: facts, and facts alone.

The Spaniard that I had split open continued to convulse and scream, his blood spurting over the deck to form an ugly puddle around the Earl's feet. In that moment our great guns below decks bellowed again. I heard the solid balls smash into the sides of the galley that opposed us. The galley that had managed to manoeuvre close enough in light winds to pound us mercilessly with her vast bow cannon, and to get boarders across onto our forecastle. Scores of boarders.

'Write this, poet,' shouted the Earl, as he stabbed through the heart of another Spaniard who had managed to reach the quarterdeck. 'Write what you see here. Over yonder, in their disciplined ranks and gleaming armour, stand the invincible *tercios* of Castile. Look how they level their pikes and prime their muskets. They are veterans. They are the best, and they know it. These are the men that have conquered half the world, Master Iles. And look what stands before them.'

Merhonour's crew were in a great mass in the after half of the ship's waist, forward of the quarterdeck. Roughly clad, some bare chested or bare footed, all dirty, carrying a fantastical assortment of weapons, they resembled no more than a mob playing a particularly violent game of village football. They bunched together for protection, but cowered visibly as the mighty Spanish phalanx began to advance along the deck.

My Lord took hold of the rigging and hauled himself up onto the quarterdeck rail, defying the musket fire of the Spaniards and waving his sword boldly about his head. *Lo here, Great Ravensden, in whom do dwell both Mars and Mercury, gods stout and fell –*

No, Nicholas. His words. Only his words.

'Englishmen!' he cried. The sailors' eyes turned to him. 'Be not afeared, my brave English lads! Are we not Harry the Fifth's men reborn, the few facing down the massed thousands of the enemy? Are we not one with Dick Grenville's lads on *Revenge*?' Still the Spanish advanced, barely deigning to fire their muskets, confident that their pikes would finish us off. 'Aye, my lads, Master Iles, here, will write your legend into the history books! You have the words, do you not, Master Iles?'

'That I do, My Lord!'

'Then be ready with them, poet! Englishmen! *Merhonours*! On my command! Ready – ready—' Still the Spanish came on. Their first rank was now at the mainmast, the pike-points already stabbing toward the front rows of our men, who shrank back before them. 'Ready – *now*!'

Upon Lord Ravensden's command, the entire body of our men flung themselves flat upon the deck, like plague-corpses falling mown down by a summer pestilence.

And now it was time for my part to be played, as I had played it so often upon the boards of Southwark's shore.

'*Give fire!*' I shouted.

The quarterdeck shook, and I felt as though I were being launched into the air. Two monstrous blasts sundered the heavens. The entire ship seemed to move backwards. A cloud of thick smoke blanketed all, blinding me for a moment. Then I saw the dark shape of Lord Ravensden leap down from the rail into the ship's waist. I went after him, running into the midst of our men, who were rising from the deck, screaming defiance at the Spanish and charging toward the smoke-shrouded enemy.

'For God, the Queen and England!' the Earl cried.

'For Ravensden!' I shouted. 'For—'

I stopped, and said no more. We all stopped, the Earl and every man of *Merhonour*'s crew with me. The smoke was clearing, and we could see that we had no enemy to charge. What had been a proud regiment of Castile was now a mass of limbs, brains and blood. The deck was an ocean of black-red gore, studded with islands of flesh and armour. A few horrible remnants of shattered men still lived, particularly in the back ranks. Blinded men clasped at where their eyes had been. Four or five legless men heaved themselves piteously along the deck, as though still attempting to charge the English heretics. One fellow struggled frantically to staunch the blood spouting over the sides of his breastplate.

I was close to one with half a head, who was mumbling some Papist prayer.

'Despatch him, lad,' said the Earl.

'I cannot, My Lord—'

Lord Ravensden shrugged, lifted his pistol and fired, blowing out the remaining part of the Spaniard's brains.

'Best not write this after all, Master Iles. Too indelicate for the ladies in a Southwark audience, eh? Too grim for most of the men, come to that.' He looked up, at our men who were moving methodically through the ranks of mangled Spaniards, finishing off the wounded with daggers or pistols. 'Not much glory or honour in it, eh, poet? Having the men pretend to cower in a huddle while the gun crews turned the stern culverins and brought them forward, hidden from sight, then blowing the Dons to hell with grape, chain and bar shot – an old trick, by God, but I've never seen it work so well. And look yonder. The galley has had enough, especially as the wind's getting up and he thinks that'll give us the advantage. Thank the dear Lord in Heaven he doesn't realise that he's holed us beneath the waterline. Time for us all to man the pumps, Master Iles. Aye, lad, earls and poets alike are included in that dispensation!'

*

Paper written by the man named Laszlo Horvath, undated but evidently 23 November 1598

It is my first sight of how the English execute their traitors, and I hope it will not be my last. It is at a place called Tyburn, to the west of London. It is a cold, wet day. Although I have been in England but a month, thus far I have known only cold, wet days.

They have hanged the man until he is nearly dead, and now they have cut him down. They have laid him upon a pallet, and the executioner carves open his belly. The man screams – a terrible, unending scream. This seems to delight the crowd, for many of them laugh, especially the women and children. The entrails are pulled out, also to a great cheer. A youth faints, and there is more merry laughter at his expense. Still the condemned man screams, especially when his own guts are shown to him.

So I turn to my neighbour in the crowd, who is eating a pie that seems to be filled with blood. I ask him who this man is, and what he has done.

'You talk strange,' my neighbour says.

'I am from Hungary,' I say.

'Hungry? What you hungry for, then? This pie? Or are you a Spanish spy, perchance?'

There is a loud murmuring among the crowd. I see fear and hatred in dozens of eyes. Women whisper, and children point at me. I see men's hands going to the hilts of swords and daggers. I grip my own sword-hilt. The odds will not be good, but I sense there are few able swordsmen here. I have faith in my blade. And yet – perhaps in England, the slaughter of a dozen or so peasants might be considered a crime? I should confirm this before running a few men through, but with the angry growls of the mob getting louder, I have no time to do so.

A better dressed man steps forward. He is a small man, a little older than myself; thus I reckon him to be of perhaps thirty-five years or so. He has a thin, pointed beard of black, well mingled with grey.

'Hungarian? Subject to the Emperor Rudolf, or to the Voyevode?'

'To the Voyevode – the Prince of Transylvania. My name is Laszlo Horvath.'

And so it is: for today.

I am surprised to find an Englishman who is aware of the difference between the two Hungarys. Indeed, I have learned that very few Englishmen even know the name of Hungary. I often have to describe myself as German, else drunken men in taverns take me for a Frenchman. Or, as with this mob at Tyburn, a Spaniard. I have observed that in this strange kingdom, being of either nation is a sure way to an early grave.

The small man turns and addresses the crowd.

'The subjects of the Voyevode of Transylvania are good Protestants,' he says. 'This man is a friend to England.'

More murmuring, little of it friendly. I sense it does not matter if a man from another land is a friend of England or not: for these people, the very fact he is from another land is sufficient to damn him.

The small man hears the cries demanding to know who he is. There are whispers against him, too, although I do not understand why. I wonder what the term 'Welsh rampallion' can mean.

The small man waits for the murmuring to subside.

'I am John Trevor,' he says, 'the Surveyor of Her Majesty's Navy Royal. Lately secretary to the Lord Admiral. Is there a man here who will gainsay me?'

More murmuring: the English seem much addicted to this pastime. Then there is a shout – 'God bless Lord Admiral Howard, that put King Philip's Armada to flight! God bless the Navy Royal! God bless Her Majesty!'

With their eyes on us, few in the crowd see who it is who shouts. But I do. It is the hangman.

'Aye,' shouts John Trevor, 'God save the Queen!'

'God save the Queen!' cries the crowd, almost in unison.

I see the eyes of men and women on each other. Are they looking to see if there are some who do not acclaim, or if others are judging their own acclamation to be suspiciously unenthusiastic? I have witnessed this in London many times already. The shout of 'God save the Queen!' ends all discourse. Those who do not shout loudly and long are either swiftly arrested, or else are dead within the minute. Such was the fate of a man I witnessed being stabbed to death in a tavern, having responded to the shout with a drunken 'Damn the barren old Queen and all like tyrants to Hell!'

But this crowd turns back toward the spectacle before them, and the guards surrounding the scaffold stand easy.

'I give you my thanks, sir,' I say, and bow, for I have observed that the English are much taken with bowing.

'It is nothing, Master Horvath,' he says. 'The English, there, can be a querulous race.' I am confused: how is it that this Englishman claims not to be English? 'Ah, but look yonder,' says John Trevor, 'the right leg is severed. I believe that is the part destined for the gates of Warwick, whence the traitor hailed.'

I turn back to look at the scaffold. It seems that during the course of my squabble with the peasants around me, and my discourse with Master Trevor, I have somehow missed the moment of the man's death. This is a disappointment to me. The cutting of a dead man's corpse into quarters is a tedious affair, little different to a butcher carving a cow. One of the few good things that can be said for Popery is that burning at the stake is a so much more satisfying means of execution.

'What was this man's treason, Master Trevor?' I ask.

'His name was Edward Squire,' says my new friend; for I have decided that my friend he will be, by virtue of the remarkably convenient office that he holds. Convenient for my purposes, that is. And he seems equally keen to be my friend, for the age-old reason that I swiftly divine, his hand clasping my shoulder a little too tightly, and for too long.

John Trevor nods toward the scaffold, where this Squire is still being hacked into pieces, each cut being cheered to the heavens. 'Tried to kill the Queen, in the name of the Jesuits.'

'Indeed? I did not hear of any attempted shooting, as with the dead Prince of Orange, or stabbing, as with the dead King of France. I am surprised. News of an attempt on the life of the great and famous Queen Elizabeth would certainly have reached even Hungary.'

'He poisoned the pommel of her horse,' my friend says.

'This is a normal English way of murder?'

'Not normal. But the times are not normal.'

'Then he was a Jesuit, Master Trevor? We in Hungary have learned to hate the Jesuits. And even in the short time I have been in England, I have seen how their very name terrifies the people here.'

'He was not, although they made him into the vile regicide that he aspired to be. He was a mere scrivener – ah, you do not know the word? A scribe, Mister Horvath, a man who reads and writes documents for those who cannot do so. Then he served in the royal stables and afterwards at sea, under our greatest captains – Drake, Essex, Ravensden. That was how the Spaniards captured him, when he was at sea in one of our ships. And then, after the Inquisition had broken him, the English Jesuits in Spain turned him, and sent him back to the royal stables to carry out his heinous attempt upon Her Majesty's life.'

'Interesting, Master Trevor,' I say, 'most interesting. But you named the most noble and famous sailor, the Earl of Ravensden, whose fame has reached even the remotest villages in the mountains of Carpathia. Tell me more of him, sir, for it is his name that has brought me to England. Indeed, I think God must have ordained our meeting this day, Master Trevor, for perhaps you, a great man in this kingdom's Navy Royal, can help me to achieve my aim. I am a warrior, sir, and I am of a mind to go to sea. I wish to fight against the Popish enemy of both our peoples, and for the valiant Queen and navy that put the mighty Armada to flight. In short, sir, I wish to volunteer to serve under the noble Lord Ravensden.'

There is a cheer, and I see the traitor Squire's head and torso being skewered onto a pike, which is held up and shown to the crowd.

It is strange that I should utter the name of Ravensden in that very same moment.

Perfectly strange.

*

Fragments of a Journal kept by Matthew Quinton, eighth Earl of Ravensden, November and December 1598

I hate it when the Dons put up a fight. I hate it even more when they have a galley – a fucking *galley*, of all things – in the chops of the Channel in November. Even in the Mediterranean, those precious, fragile hulls are always safe in their covered docks by the time the first storms of autumn come along. But this one hadn't been fragile. This one had been out in one of the worst seas in the world. In November. Not skulking. Not running for port. She was there by design, and she was ready to fight anything that came her way. Even the stout *Merhonour*, a fine race-built galleon, deep in the water and narrow in the beam, which was built for those seas. And even in the heat of the battle, as I crossed swords with a particularly stubborn officer sporting one of those silly little waxed beards the Dons like so much – just before we blew most of his men to the world below – just then, I thought to myself, '*So why are you here, Diego? What the hell is it that brings you, and a mighty galley of Galicia, to be in this place, at this moment, when you should be no further north than the Tagus?*'

I hate those: mysteries, I mean. I hate them in the theatre, where I prefer plays that have clowns and dogs. And I hate them at sea, especially when they bring my ship to within an ace of foundering with all hands.

So there we were, holed below the waterline, carpenter's crew desperately trying to patch the holes in the hull with canvas, men on the pumps until they dropped like knackered donkeys, even the captain and his hired scribbler joining in. Iles and I stood side by side, and I told him then that he should write more scenes with clowns and dogs, especially in the play I'm paying him to write about me. He gave me the look, that one which poets put on when they're whining about how much they suffer for their art, so I went back to heaving upon the pump and thinking about Spanish galleys.

I thought back ten years, to the feast we had in the great cabin of the *Ark Royal*, when the fleet was at an anchor in the Downs after returning from the Armada fight.

Only Drake was miserable. Usually, I would have been unutterably delighted to see the vile old shit in such a condition, but for him to be miserable at this time of all times, when we had just saved England and put the supposedly invincible Spanish to flight, beggared belief. So I asked what ailed him.

'We were doubly fortunate,' he said. 'The wind blew, and they were scattered. But more fortunate still, the Dons didn't bring their galleys. If they'd had them in the fight off Portland, or at Calais, or in the battle off Gravelines, Parma would be sitting in Richmond Palace at this very moment, and you and I would be in the Tower, My Lord of Ravensden. For is that not the truth of it? Out in the open sea, ships will triumph over galleys nine times out of ten, Quinton. You and I know that well enough. But the galleys only need one time. In sheltered, shallow water, like the Thames mouth, they're invincible. If the Spanish ever mass enough galleys in the North Sea, they'll pose a greater threat to England than this Armada ever did. They will rule all, and you and I will have to bow our knees to King Philip.'

'Bow them in that last moment before the Most Catholic King orders our heads cut off, Drake. But come, man! The Dons didn't bring their galleys. Who's to say that they'll ever bring them into these seas? We won, and we command the ocean wave. So in the name of God, Frank Drake, raise your glass for England, Saint George and Good Queen Bess!'

'As you say, My Lord Ravensden. As you say.'

I was still thinking of Drake and his discourse upon galleys when I was relieved at the pumps, and went off to my cabin to confer with my officers.

'We've secured the hull, My Lord,' said Gregory, the carpenter, 'but she won't hold too long. Damage is too bad, both from Spanish hits and from firing our own guns so much. Several of the frames and carlings are near shot through or else shaken nearly to pieces, and that's as well as the ones that are decayed from the ship not having had a refit for so long. Some of the futtocks are in as bad a state as any I've ever seen. The whole hull's in danger of hogging if we hit even a moderate sea. We need weeks in a dry dock to even begin to put her right, My Lord.'

'So what think you to our prospects of making Plymouth, Mister Carver?'

Tom Carver, the sailing master of the *Merhonour*, was a dour, long-faced old Puritan from Dover. I hated his godly cant, he hated my profanity, but we respected each other. Indeed, such was my confidence in Carver that I refused to have aboard my ship an example of that newfangled office which had lately crept into the navy, the 'lieutenant'; a post that seemed to have been created solely to satisfy the ambitions of beardless sprigs of noble families, and whose only purpose aboard a ship was to wait and hope that the captain was killed or else died of drink or gluttony. No, I was perfectly content with the old way, with the captain as God, the sailing master as John the Baptist, none being betwixt them. But I knew I could only justify my stance to the Lord Admiral because of the excellent qualities of Tom Carver, as able and businesslike a man as one might find. Unlike many of his kind, he was open to the new thinking about mathematical navigation espoused by the likes of Doctor Dee; as, indeed, was I. Above all, Tom Carver could sail the ship as well as I could fight it, and in the relations between a captain and a ship-master, nought else matters.

'Wind's been strengthening and coming more nor-easterly with every turn of the glass, My Lord. Even if the ship was sound, we'd have a struggle to tack our way up to Plymouth, or even to Falmouth, with the wind in this quarter. And if Master Gregory's right about the hull, and if this wind brings a storm down from the Pole, only the Lord's mercy will stand between us and the bottom of the sea.'

I nodded and looked down at the charts upon the table.

'Well, good sirs,' I said to my officers, 'the way I see it is this. We have two choices. The first choice, we can sink, for I think the balance of what Mister Carver and Mister Gregory have told us weighs heavily in favour of our sinking. The second choice, we can run for France. Myself, seeing as I can swim, I'd prefer to take my chances with the sea than with the French. But I expect you and the rest of the two hundred and forty-nine men aboard this ship who aren't named Quinton will think differently.'

They looked at me, but remained steadfastly silent. Perhaps they did not know whether I was joking or not? But then, perhaps neither did I.

'Very well, then. Master Carver. We may not have a fair wind for Plymouth, but the charts suggest that with it being in this quarter, we do have one for the mouth of the Loire, and thus for Nantes. Steer us hither, if you please. Then pray that the frogs don't bankrupt the Queen for the cost of our repair, or else she'll have all our necks.'

In the days that followed, as the shattered *Merhonour* was slowly sailed, towed or warped up the Loire to Nantes, I stood upon the quarterdeck, waving my hat at the curious peasants upon the banks. I smiled and laughed and toasted them in wine, for I had a reputation to keep up. But all the time, I was thinking that one same thought.

One Spanish galley, in the chops of the Channel, in November.

Why?

*

Commentary dictated by Louise-Marie, Dowager Countess of Ravensden, September and October 1651

And that was how I met your grandfather.

The court was at Chambord, in the Val-de-Loire, not too far from my family's home near Saumur. You must go to Chambord one day, young Matthew, for it is truly a vision. A great palace of white that rises, shimmering, from the waters: ah, reading Iles' words has quite brought out the poet in me. You see, the Louvre is ruined by the stench of Paris all around it and by all the mean lawyers and merchants that throng its corridors. As for Fontainebleau, it is a rambling warren, full of parasites, nothing more and nothing less. But Chambord is exquisite, full of light, with ceilings adorned with the salamander of *François Premier* and an astonishing double staircase where those ascending and those descending never see each other. Such wonders!

Although it was winter, our king, *Henri Quatre*, had decided there would be balls twice or three times a week. They were halcyon days, you see, in those last weeks of the year 1598. We had peace at last – peace within France, for the religious wars that had torn our land apart for thirty years were finally ended, and peace without, for we had made peace with Spain half a year earlier. And then the great King Philip of Spain, the black-garbed spider whom we all feared, had died. Yes, there was a new King Philip, but he was not half the man his father had been, which meant there was no prospect of the war resuming. So France had cause to rejoice, and if *Henri Quatre* knew anything, my dear grandson, he knew how to throw a party.

It was only my third or fourth ball, although I was already nearly nineteen – shamefully, my father, your great-grandfather, the Vicomte de Beaufay, had kept me shut away on our estate in Touraine until I was long past the age when all of my sisters had married. I still remember the excitement among all of us virgins of the court – what, grandson, you do not know what a virgin is? When you are eleven years old? Ask your uncle Tristram, he is most knowledgeable in such things. What was I saying? Ah yes, the excitement at the news that the famous English pirate, the dread Milord Ravensden, would be present! They said his ship had been forced into Nantes to repair after a great battle with a Spanish galley. Of course, the king invited him to Chambord at once, and from the moment the word got out, we were all agog.

It was my sister who first spotted him through the throng – Anne-Catherine, your great-aunt, the Marquise de Lavelle.

'Look, sis! There he is!'

Excitedly, we pushed our way through the great crowd of French, Spaniards, English and Scots. Our court in those days was a magnet for the world, all the women in the grandest of gowns, all the men in the most exuberant ruffs. And they were all turning to look upon the new arrival. He stood in the doorway of the great hall, tall and proud, accompanied by only one attendant – the poet-actor, Iles, as I later learned. The major-domo beat his cane of office upon the floor and announced *Le comte de Ravensden, amiral de Sa Majesté la reine Elisabeth d'Angleterre*. The Earl advanced toward the throne, and passed no more than a few feet in front of us. I took in the leathery face, the greying, roughly-combed hair and beard, the hand upon the sword hilt even in the presence of the King of France, the way in which his costume of fine purple satin and quite modest white ruff seemed to sit awkwardly upon him. This was the sort of man I usually went out of my way to avoid: an ageing warrior, and God alone knew, after so many years of vicious civil and foreign wars, France had more than enough of those.

But there was something else about this man, something that made me feel strange from that very first moment my eyes settled upon him. Yes, there was the thrill of the exotic. After all, he was English, and Englishmen were both distinctly exotic and very much in vogue in those days. Had they not put the invincible Spanish Armada to flight, and sent an army to help our King gain his throne? Moreover, they were ruled by a woman, a thing unheard of in France. All of us young girls of the court were in awe of the legendary Queen Elizabeth, and secretly wished that we were her. And Lord Ravensden would have met her! He would have kissed her hand and talked with her, just as he was about to do with our king! So if I could but talk with him, I could find out what she was like, from one who knew her in person! And then, of course, the Earl was a pirate, and what woman does not dream of being – Ah, but you are too young, grandson, and I digress. But there was something else about him that I could not name. Something that tightened my stomach and unsettled my heart.

He strode across the great hall and bowed before the throne. The king stepped forward and allowed the Englishman to kiss his hand, then talked to him for some minutes. The ordinary hubbub of idle court chatter resumed all around us.

'He has quite a history,' said Anne-Catherine. 'He and the famous Sir François Drake and Sir Valter Raleigh were forever at each other's throats, it seems, but that is not the half of it, nor the more interesting half. Milady Edmondes, the English ambassador's wife, says that Milord Ravensden has buried three countesses and all his children with them. She says that his mother is mad, and has been locked away in a tower for years. She says that his grandmother is a hundred years old and cannot die. She says that his uncle was a notorious sorcerer, who placed a curse on his brother's line and the entire House of Ravensden before making a pact with the Devil and disappearing into thin air. She says that because of all this, no lady of rank in England is willing to accept him in marriage. So his title will die with him.'

'How sad,' I said, gazing with renewed interest at the distant form of the English Milord. 'A tragic romance, worthy of a poet.'

'You are too sentimental, Louise-Marie, dearest. You always were. And you read far too many romances by bad poets.'

'That is *not true*,' I hissed, although, of course, it was. 'Come, sister. I want to meet this Englishman, curse or no curse.'

'Don't be foolish, Louise-Marie! There is no-one to present us! Our brothers are nowhere to be seen – I expect they are in the kitchens, accosting serving wenches again – and my husband would not forgive us for interrupting his discourse with the Duc de Montmorency.'

'Then we shall just have to present ourselves, shall we not?'

'Present *ourselves*? Who has ever heard of such a thing? And in the king's presence, too? Truly, sister, you must have taken leave of your senses!'

'Very well, then, I shall present myself. Do not look at me like that, Milady la Marquise. I am sure an English Milord will permit it – after all, is he not accustomed to being given orders by a woman?'

The Earl of Ravensden:

She was a damned forward little strumpet, even for the French. But then, she was also a fetching little piece. I saw her approaching, great brown eyes staring up at me. I saw the presentable little bosom heaving away like a bellows, and I thought, 'Half your age, Ravensden. Papist and French, to boot. Quarantined cargo, my lad—'

The Countess of Ravensden:

Quarantined cargo? A damned forward little strumpet? Presentable little –

No, grandson, you should *not* be writing this down.

Why, that strutting old braggart, that arrogant –

Ah.

Matthew, you had better summon Barcock to wipe the wine off the Van Dyck. I did not imagine that at my age, I could aim so well, nor throw so far.

Nicholas Iles:

Was there ever such a beginning to a great love? Anthony and Cleopatra, boast your Nile-blessed romance no more! Tristan and Isolde, look to your laurels. Lancelot and Guinevere, depart the scene, for the glory of your passion is but a flower, crumbling to dust after its season is done. The two of whom Shakespeare wrote, whose names I now forget –

She presented herself before My Lord and the King of France, curtsied, and said, as boldly as a herald proclaiming a war, 'Your Majesty, My Lord, if you will forgive me – I am Louise-Marie de Monconseil-Bragelonne, fourth daughter of the Vicomte de Beaufay. I present myself, great sirs, on behalf of the virgin womanhood of France, to convey to Milord Ravensden our felicitations upon your glorious victories, and to ask you to pass on our respects to your sovereign lady, Queen Elizabeth, the epitome of our kind!'

You will say I am a poet, and that I exaggerate My Lady's words. But I do not. Indeed, even as this mere child-woman spoke and I studied her for the very first time, I cursed her for plucking words out of the air that it would have taken me a week to conjure onto a page.

My Lord looked at the King of France. The King looked at him. Then they both laughed.

'Well, My Lady,' said King Henry, his great grey eyebrows arching merrily, 'I see that a new age is truly come to France, and that it is not merely a figment of the highly paid imaginations of those I employ to write my eulogies. Milord Ravensden, I leave this impetuous harbinger of the future to you. But I advise you to be very careful with her!'

The King moved away, still chuckling. I stood where I was, for it was clearly my duty to record every word of the exchange between My Lord and this remarkable young woman. But I was aware that My Lord was giving me a strange look: indeed, he appeared suddenly to have acquired a tic that made his head jerk violently in the direction of the distant doorway. I prayed that this was not the consequence of some past wound –

He stepped toward me, and whispered, 'For God's sake, Iles, can't you take a hint? Just *fuck off*, there's a good fellow!'

The Earl of Ravensden:
A forward strumpet she may have been, but she was also a witty and disarmingly intelligent one. This was a change from the majority of the women I had ever known, who were mostly dead, mad, or whores. Perhaps that thought was in my mind when I was part way through a prolonged explanation of how I, an Englishman, actually owned an estate much further up the Loire, beyond Nevers in Burgundy, despite such a thing supposedly being prohibited by the laws of France. This, I explained, was by means of a convoluted Scottish inheritance that had passed down through my mother, a Stewart connected by blood to the Aubigny line of that house, who were considered Frenchmen and thus able to own land in –

I must have been boring even myself, for I suddenly blurted out, 'I have buried three wives, a son and three daughters, My Lady. Almost all of my friends have been slaughtered in battle. I have locked up my mother. And my grandmother, if truth be told. So I am done with losing those I love.'

Why did I say that, in the name of Heaven? She was a slip of a girl, I had met her but a few minutes before, yet here I was making her privy to secrets I barely dared admit even to myself. I had already decided to bed her, of course, but as for anything more than that –

The Countess of Ravensden:

Thank you, Matthew, I think there is no need for you to copy any more of this particular piece.

In truth, though, I was as taken aback by this shared confidence as he was. I was aware, too, that many eyes were upon us, and few of them were approving. For a maiden to talk with an unmarried man for so long, unescorted – and he an *Englishman*, in the name of all the saints in Heaven, and so capable of God alone knew what kinds of behaviour – well, that was then still a matter of scandal, even at a court as informal as that of *Henri le Bon*.

'My Lord,' I said, 'I trust that I shall be a friend whom you do not lose.'

His face, so resolutely cheerful until a few moments earlier, was now unspeakably sad.

'Well, then, Milady de Monconseil-Bragelonne, that is a promise to which I shall hold you.'

But alas, I was not the only person in that vast hall who was of interest to Milord Ravensden. I could see his eyes straying from mine, and even from my bosom, and followed his gaze. He was staring at a slight youth in a distant corner: a lad little older than myself, dressed in the sort of plain, Calvinistic garb that was out of fashion in even the most fervent Huguenot congregation. A youth who was standing quietly, and seemingly quite out of place, amidst the loudest and most boisterously drunken group in the entire room: that is to say, the Scots.

'You know that young Scotsman, Milord Ravensden?'

'Know him, My Lady? We're distant cousins, of a sort – as I told you, my mother is a Stewart, and so is his, which makes us even more distantly related to the Scottish King. I haven't seen the boy these two years, since our time as students at Padua.'

'You were a *student*, Milord Ravensden? And so very recently?'

'Went abroad for my health, to recover from the wounds I took at the Cadiz fight. But I was a scholar before I ever became a warrior. Before you stands a graduate in Mathematics from the College of Saint John the Evangelist in the University of Cambridge, My Lady.'

'You are a man of surprises, My Lord.'

'To myself, most of all. But if you will excuse me for a bare half-hour, My Lady – and I assure you, I will then return to your side, and will tell you what Her Majesty Queen Elizabeth is like. Upon that, you have the word of Matthew Quinton, the eighth Earl of Ravensden.'

He stooped, lifted my hand, and kissed it delicately. In that moment, I knew I would marry this man, if he would have me – and I intended to make very certain that he would. He was twenty years older than me, and English, and Protestant. Father would object, and the Abbé Mousnier would object, and my brothers and sisters would object. But the Earl of Ravensden had one thing that would overcome all their objections. The one thing that nearly everyone in France lacked, after thirty years of endless war.

Gold.

Well, he was a pirate, and all pirates have gold, do they not?

So reasoned my young and foolish self. But even if he had not a *sou* to his name, young Matthew, I would probably have set my heart on marrying him anyway. For as his lips touched the flesh of my hand, sending a shiver through my entire frame, he looked up at me. I melted into those eyes, so much younger than the face around them, and my heart was lost. I never found it again.

Then Milord Ravensden stood, turned, and went off to speak with the young Scotsman across the room. That is to say, with John Ruthven, the fateful Earl of Gowrie.

CHAPTER THREE

1599

The neatly tied piles of yellowing, mouldy papers are exactly as I arranged them, all those years before.

No-one had opened them, no-one had read them, since my grandmother and I spent the autumn of 1651 studying their contents. Outside the walls of Ravensden Abbey, our cavalier world was crumbling to heavily sequestrated dust, the one consolation being the slow recovery from his near-mortal wounds of my brother, the tenth Earl of Ravensden. And now the same papers lie before me, in the England of King George the Second and Sir Robert Walpole, as I mend slowly from my fever. They bring back both my own memories of that strange, desperately fraught time when I was eleven years old, and the recollections of those who lived half a century before that. Recollections from the deck of the mighty and ancient warship *Merhonour*, which – rebuilt many, many times – I later commanded in my turn, during the great Battle of Lowestoft in 1665. The recollections, too, contained within the strange, poisonous memoir of the foreigner, Horvath. And the very personal recollections that my dear *grandmaman* dictated to me, and which lie before me now, my childish hand sprawling across the pages. Curiously, the ancient, crabbed hand in which I write these words seems to have reverted very nearly to the same state it was in three-quarters of a century ago. But then, the only Pope I ever met once told me that as we approach the grave, we become more and more the child we once were.

So to the ancient papers once again. I realise that the story told in them will seem too incredible to those brought up on the mountains of dull, worthy 'histories' that have appeared in an endless procession in recent times. Burnet, White Kennett, Echard, Oldmixon…every man sets up as a 'historian', it seems, but not one of them with the slightest awareness of the truth of what actually happened in history. Better, then, to present the truth as fiction, just as fiction is now presented as truth, no man, it seems, being able any longer to tell the difference between the two.

Besides, this business called 'the novel' is not difficult, it seems, but I should have realised that already: the success of that talentless mountebank Defoe proves it beyond question, and he mangles together truth and fiction with breathless impudence.

As for the other sensation of our age, *Gulliver's Travels*: read these words, Dean Swift, and weep.

Laszlo Horvath:

'At least five hundred Janissaries charged our position,' I say, 'and there were no more than a hundred of us defending the wall. True, most of them were good fellows – Wallachians, Moldavians, a few Serbs, a few of us Hungarians. But we were too few to hold the position, My Lord. The Janissaries charged, and charged again. We fought them hand-to-hand in the rubble of the breach, falling back toward the church in the centre of the village. I prayed to the Good Lord, for I thought my last hour had come, especially when a Mahometan scimitar slashed across my side.'

I have no need to exaggerate any of this. I remember it as well as if it were yesterday, a battle in blazing sun and dust in a place whose name none of us knew.

'Show me,' he says, leaning forward.

I lift my shirt and point to the scar. It is easy to differentiate from all of the others, being longer and newer. This fight was barely three years before, and my oldest scars date back more than fifteen years before that. He is impressed by the sight of the wound; he has many of his own, so this is no small compliment.

'We were dead men,' I say, 'and if the village fell, the Ottomans would be able to flank our advance on Giurgiu, down the Danube. Further and further back we went, fighting all the way, right up to the doors of the church—'

'Then how did you survive, man?'

'Thanks be to God, Prince Mihail knew the importance of our position. Just as my foot reached behind me to find the first of the church steps, I heard the trumpets blowing. There was a roaring of men and a thundering of hooves, and then they galloped into the square. Cossacks, My Lord – one of the regiments of the Host that had allied with we Christians. No finer horsemen grace the Earth. They came on like devils on horseback, shrieking and slashing with their blades. The Janissaries fell back, and we went directly into the church to give thanks for our deliverance.'

He leans back, taking a long draught of his wine.

'Fuck me, Horvath,' he says. I now realise, after some weeks of confusion, that 'Fuck Me' is not his nickname for me. 'Fuck me, but you're a lucky bastard to have survived all those years in a war so vicious.'

'You call me a bastard? Why do you do that?'

'Don't be offended, good fellow. In our tongue, "bastard" is not an insult – well, it can be, of course, but it can also be a term of respect, or affection. Depends how you say it. If I say "You bastard" like *this*, I am insulting you. But if I say "You bastard" like *that*, I am calling you my friend.'

'I think I will never master this English, if the meaning of words depends on how they are said.'

'Oh, you will, Master Horvath. A year or two with me, and your English will be as good as the Queen's. But come, I would have you tell me of the great Battle of Keresztes...'

Yes, I will tell you of the battle, My Lord. And I will master this English. I will master it entirely.

Nicholas Iles:

My Lord was much taken with the Hungarian from the moment he first came aboard our ship, at Nantes in April. But I did not like him. I kept asking myself, what sort of man journeys from England to France to volunteer, when we will be sailing back to England in a matter of weeks? What sort of man journeys from Hungary to England, claiming that he seeks nothing more in life than to serve My Lord? What sort of man abandons the war his own people are fighting, against the common foe of Christendom, in favour of a distant conflict, far away from his own land? How can this foreigner, this alien, have obtained a recommendation from the Surveyor of the Navy? So many questions, none of them with an answer.

No, I did not like Laszlo Horvath. I did not like him at all.

But the Earl seemed mightily impressed with the Hungarian's record as a warrior. At first I suspected that he was inventing it all: a storyteller, a creator of pretend worlds, can usually recognise a kindred spirit. But the Hungarian revelled in displaying his battle-scars, and even I had to admit that no man could have suffered so much slicing open of his flesh in mere tavern brawls, the common warfare of we actors and writers. Worse, though, was that My Lord evidently enjoyed the Hungarian's tales of battles with the Ottomans in the far-off borders of Christendom. Indeed, he started to prefer Horvath's stories to the ones I told him of Achilles, Hector and the great heroes of antiquity. Increasingly, too, he practised sword-play with the Hungarian, who seemed to be adept in both the German and Italian methods, and in various less conventional skills learned through long experience on the blood-soaked plains of the east.

I chided myself for the sins of pride and jealousy, but in my heart, I knew I had only to bide my time. After all, Horvath was not the man being paid to write the famous history of My Lord; and if one thing was certain in this world, it was that this Hungarian upstart would not appear in that book at all. Or play. Or epic poem. Whichever form I decided upon in the end. Thus contented, I returned to the task that had occupied me through the long winter months since we arrived in Nantes: getting drunk with the rest of the crew in French taverns making significant progress on my play about My Lord. I had written a prologue, and most of Act One. At My Lord's request, I had included a clown. And a dog. And the words flowed, surely poetry to rank alongside that of Homer and Virgil –

The Sea pays Homage to thee, and roars out
Brave Ravensden's name, who's greater far then Canute.
Neptune to Thee his Trident doth resign,
The Whales cry out with trembling, We are thine!

But then this Horvath came, and the muses deserted me. Still, at least the news from my friends in London was greatly encouraging. Shakespeare, it seemed, could think of nothing better than to churn out yet another version of the life of King Henry the Fifth, a story that had been done to death already.

My star was on the rise, that much was clear.

The Dowager Countess:

We were married in March, in the church adjoining my husband's damp and ruinous hovel in Burgundy.

(No, grandson, upon reflection, strike through 'damp and ruinous hovel' and reinstate 'chateau', for that was what my husband called the pile of decaying stones he owned at Saint-Justin-Le-Boucher. He had great plans for rebuilding it, but then, he had great plans for rebuilding every house he ever owned.)

The speed of our betrothal, and then our nuptials, was considered the scandal of the hour at the French court, and none of my family attended the service. In truth, though, this was but a ruse to save my father's face. Oh, he was furious at first, even though his previous attempts to arrange marriages for me to an ancient, wheezing *comte* and a pox-ridden young *seigneur* ended abruptly with the tragic deaths of both, well before the contracts could be signed. And the more my father thought upon it, the more he concluded that he was delighted to get his markedly precocious and wayward youngest child off his hands so easily, and to have acquired a son-in-law who seemed to be at once rich, famous, and greatly liked by the King of France himself. The Earl of Ravensden might be a heretic, Father said (if only in the fullness of time), but King Henri himself was a heretic until only five years before. And if, as His Majesty famously said, Paris was worth a mass, then surely the financial salvation of the seriously decayed noble house of Monconseil-Bragelonne was worth an Englishman. Especially an Englishman who was rich, who did not insist upon a dowry, and who was willing to allow his new wife to retain the faith of her ancestors, even to the extent of permitting her to attend Mass, albeit in secret, as was the way of things in England.

'Besides, sister,' said Anne-Catherine, as she bade farewell to me, 'he is so much older than you, so he will probably either die of senility or else will soon be killed in a battle with the Spaniards. Then you will inherit his estate, and will be a great woman in England! Why, then you can marry rich husband after rich husband, just as their famous *Bess de Hardvic* has done! Just do not have a son too quickly, though, or else the child will then inherit instead of you.'

Her advice was already redundant: I was with child well before the Earl and I went aboard the repaired *Merhonour* in the road of Saint Nazaire in May. Indeed, I was with child well before the marriage ceremony, too, having ceased to be in the same state as Queen Elizabeth roughly an hour after My Lord returned from his conversation with the Earl of Gowrie at Chambord. My husband's intention was that I would have the child in France, and then come over with him – it could be nothing but a 'him' – in the winter, after the *Merhonour* paid off following the summer's campaign against the Spanish.

'It will be for the best,' he said, as we lay in the bed that his men had rigged in his cabin aboard *Merhonour*. 'We should not risk the heir to Ravensden upon the sea until he is at least a few weeks old. And it will give time – but no, enough. You must rest, my dear, and I must attend to the preparations for sailing. To inspect the cordage, and suchlike.'

'It will give time for what, Matthew?' He was reluctant to answer. For such a bold and fearless man, he could sometimes look like a boy caught in the act of stealing an apple from an orchard. But I thought I had his meaning. 'Time for your people, and for the English court, to accept that there is a new Countess of Ravensden, and she is French, and Catholic, and very young?'

'My people will accept what I tell them to accept. For many of my servants and tenants, the fact that you are French will be seen as an improvement on my mother, who was Scottish. The fact that you are papist – your pardon, my dear, Catholic – will horrify our parish priest and make the Bishop of Lincoln shit himself. And the ignorant will damn you out of hand, as for these last twenty or thirty years, the very name of Catholic has been reviled in England, tarred with the brush of treason and murderous plots against our Queen. But so long as you are discreet, and we pay your recusancy fines promptly, I pray that there will be little difficulty. After all, my Countess, it would difficult for even the most fanatical opponent of Popery to paint you plausibly as a harbinger of the Jesuits and the Inquisition, although I have no doubt that some will attempt to do so.' He smiled, and I nodded my head in gratitude for his tolerance of my perverse decision to remain true to the faith of my fathers. And for his equally perverse decision to marry me in the first place, if truth be told. 'Those of the court will first consider you a great curiosity, and then they will love you as though there is nothing else on earth to love – and then, five minutes later, they will forget you and move on to the next great curiosity of the moment.' He sighed, and shook his head. 'But there is one to whom I will have to answer for marrying you. The same one to whom I will have to answer for the *Merhonour* being in dock in Nantes for six months.'

'The Queen.'

'Indeed. The Queen.'

'But why should she concern herself with your marriage, Matthew? Surely it is of no interest to her?'

'You have not met her, dear heart. When it comes to the lives of those who serve her, the Queen concerns herself with everything. She, who has no children, considers herself a mother to the entire kingdom, with a mother's right to interfere in the lives of every one of us. And she never forgets. Those of the court might lose interest in us after a few days, but not the Queen. My old friend de Vere, the Earl of Oxford, once bowed low before her after a bellyful of bad wine, and let loose the loudest and foulest-smelling fart imaginable. He was so ashamed that he left the court for seven years. When he returned, and had audience of the Queen, she greeted him with "My Lord, I had quite forgot the fart". I was there, and witnessed it. So the Queen will not forget, but perhaps, if we wait before presenting you at court, she might have time to accept our marriage.'

'Or else, perhaps, she will die beforehand.'

I had already seen my husband in many states – happy, amorous, valiant, dead drunk – but I had never seen him afraid. Yet now he looked about like a frightened child, as though he was seeing ghouls and monsters beneath every footstool.

'For sweet Jesu's sake, wife, you must *never* say such things! Never! You could be overheard—'

'Matthew, we are aboard the ship that you command, filled with your men, at anchor in the midst of the sea, off the coast of France! Who can possibly overhear us? Even kings and queens must die – all people know that! Why, France has had five kings since your Elizabeth came to the throne! She is, what, sixty-six years old? A very old woman who cannot live for ever, My Lord. And when she does die – then what will happen?'

The Earl was still mightily uncomfortable, glancing out through the stern windows as though half expecting the vengeful Gloriana herself to start hammering upon them at any moment. Perhaps, too, he was taken aback – as he often was, in those early days – by the discovery that his new young wife had wits, and a keen interest in the ways of the world. At last, my husband settled back down onto the sea-bed. But when he spoke next, it was rather more quietly than before.

'What will happen? There you have it, my Countess. Three words. Three words that form the most important question England has ever known.'

Nicholas Iles:

I was on deck, taking in the last of the French air before we set sail for England. I was full of new ideas for plays and poems. I had been nearly within touching distance of the famous King Henry of France: surely his story would make a fine drama? I could see Burbage playing him, or else perhaps Kemp, who might be better if he had to act alongside a dog. I could even play the part myself, with or without the dog. Or else there was the story of Joan of Arc, which I thought had all the makings of a most excellent tragedy. I could play her, too.

My Lord begged to differ, though.

'A play about a Frog witch that we burned at the stake? With some be-stubbled lad in a skirt pretending to be a peasant girl wearing armour, who talks to God and reckons angels are her personal friends? Oh yes, that'll pack the theatres, Master Iles, if you somehow manage to get the story past the Lord Chamberlain, that is. Roasting virgins on a pyre? How will that play in a land ruled by a Virgin Queen, d'you think?'

But I was not abashed, and was seated upon one of the forecastle guns, noting down ideas in my small commonplace book. It was difficult to concentrate, though. The sight of the sea-birds circling and plunging into the waters in pursuit of fish distracted me. The ships, large and small, that plied in and out of the Loire, were an endless source of fascination. And were those dolphins, over in the far distance? I believed they were –

My graphite writing-stick snapped. Cursing, I went astern, to fetch another from my sea chest.

And then I saw the Hungarian. He was standing in the shadows of the steerage, outside the door to My Lord's cabin, seemingly listening.

I drew my dagger and hissed, 'Spy!'

Of course, this was utter madness on my part. Horvath was a veteran soldier, an expert with every weapon in common use and several that were distinctly uncommon. I was a poet who wore a dagger simply for show, to scare off vagabonds, Abram-men and clapperdudgeons. Never in my life, until that moment, had I drawn my blade with serious intent; like every man connected with the London theatre, I recalled the fate of poor Kit Marlowe, who had drawn his once too often and paid for it with his life, depriving the world of countless unwritten masterpieces.

The Hungarian seemed to sense all of this. He advanced toward me, not even bothering to draw his own blade.

'That is a dangerous word, Master Iles. Dangerous in any language.'

'It is a true word, Master Horvath. I name you a spy, treacherously spying on the Earl and Countess!'

There were relatively few men on deck. Most were below, for My Lord had given both watches a brief period of leave before ordering them to the back-breaking tasks of hauling up the anchors and setting sail. Sounds of singing and laughter drifted up through the hatches. But the men who were about stopped what they were doing and turned their attention to us.

'You are too much taken with plots and fantasies, Master Poet. I am no spy. I am loyal to the Earl of Ravensden.'

He continued to advance. Without really being aware of what I was doing, I started backing away.

'No loyal man stands by a door, prying into the affairs of a husband and wife.'

'That is true. A loyal man seeks to guard the husband and wife.'

'*Guard*? You claim to have been guarding them? What need is there of a guard, here on a galleon of the Queen's Navy Royal? My Lord's own command?'

The Hungarian stopped, no more than a pace in front of me, and stared directly into my eyes.

'There is an old saying in my country, Master Poet. It translates into your English as "Even Christ's coffin was not guarded for nothing". It can be read in many ways, as all great sayings can. For example, it can mean that one should always mount a guard, for one never knows what might happen. Or it could mean that enemies can be everywhere, and you never know who might attempt to approach Our Lord's tomb, or with what intent.'

'I know what I saw,' I said, although I was no longer convinced that I did.

'Ho there, gentlemen!' cried Carver, the old ship-master, who had just come on deck. 'What troubles you, Master Iles, for your blade to be drawn?'

I half-turned to reply. In that moment, Horvath stepped forward, grabbed my wrist tightly with his right hand, and snatched my dagger from my grip with his left.

'There is no trouble here,' said the Hungarian, smiling. 'I was teaching Master Iles a lesson in the art of combat. Is that not so, Master Iles?'

There was nothing I could do. 'That is so, Master Horvath.'

And so we parted. I prayed that My Lord and Lady were unaware of this altercation outside their cabin door; and so they were, as I soon learned. God be praised.

The Countess of Ravensden:

'There are many candidates for the throne of England,' said Earl Matthew, 'in the same sense that every village has many candidates to be its idiot. For one thing, the two sisters of King Henry the Eighth, of blessed memory, managed nearly as many marriages between them as their famous sib, and produced many more children. So now there are Tudor sprigs galore, Douglases and Stanleys and Seymours, each with their own advocates – principally the reflections in their mirrors. But most men of influence, those great men who think they know all, would judge that there are only three candidates for the throne who truly matter. First, and by far the likeliest—'

'James, King of Scots,' I said. 'Son to the Queen Mary who was married first to one of our late kings. Descended from your Henry the Eighth's elder sister.'

Oh, this was familiar ground: how I had devoured histories of the notorious King Henry and the tragic tales of Mary, Queen of Scots, during those long days when it rained in the Val de Loire and I had nothing else to do than read!

'Indeed,' said the Earl, who looked at me in a way that suggested he had never expected to have such a conversation with a woman in his life. 'So, My Lady, the strengths of King James. First, manifestly, he is a man and a king already, so he knows the business of ruling. Second, he has a healthy son and a productive wife who seems set fair to give him more boys. Believe me, dearest, after all these years of being ruled by women, many Englishmen crave nothing more than to be ruled over by a long succession of men.'

'More fool those Englishmen, then. But the weaknesses of King James?'

'He is a Scot, and thus an alien. Englishman fighting Scot is still within living memory – indeed, that was how my English father met my Scottish mother, when he rode into Edinburgh with the Duke of Norfolk's army forty years ago. And James is the son of an executed traitor, your same Queen Mary. And it is said that he prefers boys.'

'So did His Late Majesty *Henri Troisième*,' I said. 'He even liked to dress as a woman. It is no bar to kingship, My Lord.'

'Indeed not, my dear, but that argument holds no weight with many of our bishops. A King who is both a sodomite and a Presbyterian – they cannot decide which is his worse sin. And then… And then. Let us just say, my dear, that there are other matters relating to Jamie Stuart.'

He was staring out of the window of the cabin, and I knew his mind was no longer with me. Young and foolish as I was, I imagined that these 'other matters' were trifling things, mere traits of personality, such as those we would all observe during the years to come: for instance, the unfortunate tendency of much of the food and drink that entered King James's mouth to exit it immediately thereafter, by way of his slobbering lips and thence down into his remarkably malodorous beard. So I changed the subject. As I say, grandson, I was young and foolish. You have no choice but to be the former, but I pray that even now, at your tender age, you will eschew the latter.

'The second plausible candidate, my lord?' I asked.

'The second plausible candidate,' said my husband. 'Well, for many, that would be King James' cousin, the Lady Arbella Stuart. The same bloodline, so as close a relation to the present Queen. But born in England, which many see as an advantage. After all, if an alien cannot own land in the realm, how can an alien possibly be its greatest landowner? Her weaknesses – well, she is yet another woman, and said to be a remarkably stupid one, which of course her present Majesty most certainly is not. So many of those who dislike the succession of King James precisely because he is seen to be a mature and experienced king, and chafe under Queen Elizabeth because she can outwit them at every turn, favour the Lady Arbella because she is seen to be weak and malleable. That is, malleable by those who promote her succession, naturally.'

'And the third candidate, Matthew?'

'The Archduchess Isabella, Infanta of Spain, ruler of Flanders along with her husband. King Philip's sister. Descended from our King Edward the Third.'

'A woman, a Catholic, and a Spaniard, the country with whom you English are at war? Forgive me if I am naïve in this, husband, but those sound to me like quite significant disqualifications.'

'Ah, my dear, that is where we enter the infernal realm of politics. For you see, the two most important men in England, both favourites of our present Queen, are mortal enemies, so whichever candidate the one favours, the other will naturally support his or her arch-rival.'

'Milord Essex and the hunchback, Cecil. Their hatred is notorious even here in France. The one a dashing soldier, the other a spider spinning web after web of schemes and plots.'

'You may say that. Others may say that one is an incompetent mountebank, the other a devious timeserver. I have no time for either of them, Louise. Essex nearly cost me my life in the Cadiz expedition, and has stymied my hopes of commanding every fleet set out these last few years. And I would not trust Cecil beyond using his hump to strike matches on.'

'But whom do they wish to see upon the throne?'

'Essex seeks to act the kingmaker for James of Scotland, Cecil the same for the Infanta Isabella. Do not look so surprised, dearest, she has many advantages. Cecil seeks peace with Spain, and there are many in England who favour that after nearly fifteen years of war. The country is sick of endless taxation, and of the war-cripples, war-widows and war-orphans that burden all our purses. But the Infanta succeeding to our throne would bring us into a union with Flanders. England joined to the Spanish Netherlands – what a prospect that would be, with the two most flourishing economies in Europe joined as one! A more promising united kingdom than one between England and poor, frozen Scotland, that much is certain.'

'Then you favour Cecil, and the Infanta?'

He smiled: that winning, boyish smile which had conquered my heart.

'Oh, I did not say that, Louise. I did not say that at all.'

And with that, he went off to inspect his accursed cordage. An hour later, I was put into the ship's boat, given three huzzahs by the crew, and rowed ashore. From the headland of the Pointe de Chemoulin, I watched the *Merhonour* weigh anchor. I saw her sails fill, and her hull dip to meet the Atlantic breakers, the spray breaking over the part I now knew to call the beakhead. I saw the ensign of England spill out at her stern. And I saw my lord, standing at the very highest point of the poop, waving at me until he was but a speck in the distance, then out of sight altogether. I turned and boarded the coach that would take me back to my father's estate, where my child would be born, using the journey to try (and fail) to deduce exactly which candidate for the English throne my husband favoured.

And in the weeks that followed, while I did little but eat, read, miss my husband terribly, and grow ever larger, My Lord ventured out once again against the might of the Spanish empire.

CHAPTER FOUR

From the Earl of Ravensden's Journal, July 1599

'Fog so thick, you can't see a whore's tit through it,' I said.

I felt the godly Carver, by my side, bridle at that. But he was a dutiful man, and said merely, 'At least it'll keep any Spanish scouts in port, My Lord.'

'And any prizes, too', I said. 'As if the news I'm off their coast isn't enough to keep the Dons skulking in their harbours. Nothing off Bilbao, Santander or Gijon. The men are getting restive, Mister Carver. To keep them in good humour, they need Spanish gold and Spanish throats to slit.'

A bell sounded somewhere across the water. That was *Dreadnought*, our fellow galleon. Somewhere further inshore would be the *Swiftsure*, which I had ordered to look into The Groyne, as we English call it: the port that the Dons call Coruna.

'With respect, My Lord, the men are restive enough about not being paid for a year.'

'They have cause to complain? I haven't had a penny off the Queen in five years, and I have craven arse-crawling courtier *children* promoted over my head. Our illustrious admiral, Sir Richard Fuckwit Leveson, for one. Why, if it wasn't for the need to provide for a new wife and child, I'd – '

A gun fired, very close by. There was a grey, indistinct shape looming out of the fog. Within a moment, it had become the hull, masts and sails of a ship.

'God's death!' I cried, and drew my sword. 'Master Gunner! Make ready to fire larboard guns! Muskets! Pikes! Swords! Man the wales!'

Our men were already at the guns, which had been run out since the fog came down, and Gunner Skipworth set about his business at once. I was determined that we would not be caught napping by a galley or two sneaking out of The Groyne. Our bronze culverins and demi-culverins were loaded and primed, gun captains standing over the touch-holes with lighted linstocks at the ready. I needed only to give my word of command –

'Sir, it's the *Swiftsure*!' cried Carver. Now I could make her out too, as her captain brought her up abeam of us.

What in God's name was Bredgate doing, running in so fast? He could easily have collided with us, or we could have blown him to oblivion in the belief he was a Spaniard, as we very nearly did.

'Ho, the *Merhonour*!' Bredgate bellowed through his speaking-trumpet.

'Ho, Matt Bredgate! What ails you, man?' I replied by means of my own.

'What ails England, rather, My Lord! The fog's lifting inshore, but before it did, I took a fishing boat fresh out of Sada. You'll want to hear what her skipper has to say, and see the proof of it for yourself.'

A half-turn of the glass later, after my discomfiting interview with Bredgate's captured fisherman, the *Merhonour* and *Dreadnought* weighed and began to sail south with the *Swiftsure*, under courses alone until we were clear of the fog. We were a fine sight, three proud galleons of England in company in the Spanish king's own waters. The few fishing boats at sea scattered at our approach. Oh, they knew us well now, from Galicia all the way down the coast of Old Castile and Portugal to Cadiz, for we had been plaguing their coast for weeks. They knew what Englishmen had done, and could do, upon their shores.

The rocky, heavily forested coast of Galicia lay ahead, King Philip's arsenal at Ferrol away to larboard, beyond the horizon. My officers and my gentlemen volunteers, Iles and Horvath, were massing in the forecastle, but I sought a better view. Taking hold of the mainmast shrouds, I hauled myself up into the rigging, finally swinging out to pull myself into the crow's nest. I felt my forty-year-old bones protest. *Too fucking old for this, Ravensden*, I chided myself. *You'll soon be for the lubber's hole, and then in short order for the grave.*

The lookout, a bright Dorset lad named Walbridge, nearly jumped from his perch, such was his shock at seeing his captain, an Earl of England, joining him. But in truth, I loved being in the tops, looking out to the horizon, feeling the rocking of the ship upon the sea and the freshness of the wind upon my face, leaving all the world's cares far below.

'Well, Walbridge, have we sight of The Groyne yet?'

'Coming toward the eastern arm of the bay now, My Lord.' He pointed at the shore, some three or four miles away. 'Yonder, the Tower of Hercules.'

I screwed up my eyes, and could just make out the tall old Roman light-tower upon its headland, on the western side of the bay...

The Dowager Countess

No, Matthew, there were as yet no telescopes, although it can have been barely ten years before they were invented. Your grandfather, being of an inquisitive and mathematical bent, learned of the new device in its very earliest days, and spent a fortune to acquire an example from one of the Dutchmen who first made them. He claimed to be the first man in England to own one, and always said he wished they had existed sooner, for days such as this in the year Ninety-Nine. One day, you will inherit his telescope, although I cannot imagine you will follow him and become a seaman. You lack the devil that drove him, and are much too bright ever to contemplate such a strange life. But it is a fine object, and will impress curious visitors if you place it on display in your house.

The Earl of Ravensden

...and, beyond it, the Saint Anthony Castle. I could see the waves crashing onto the shore of the enemy's kingdom, beneath the castle walls. Now we were coming round, south by west, aided by a westerly breeze that would allow us to run back north for Biscay if the Dons sent anything out after us. Besides, we were race-built, lacking the cumbersome old-fashioned fore- and stern-castles, and could outrun anything they might send to sea. We were the ships that had defeated the Invincible Armada, and we feared nought.

More and more of the bay of The Groyne came into view –

'Jesus, Mary and the fucking saints in Heaven!' I cried, although the Quintons had not been Papist for forty years. 'Tell me what you see, Walbridge. Tell me I am not dreaming.'

'My Lord, I see a great fleet – countless masts—'

'How many ships, Walbridge? How many masts? Come on, man, has not Master Carver spent hours training you for this very task?'

Of course, I was unwilling to admit that my own eyesight was no longer good enough to enable me to make such a count myself. I could see distant blurs, but did their number match the alarming intelligence from the captured fisherman?

'At least forty ships, My Lord. The same of galleys, I think.'

'The fisherman made it seventy ships and a hundred galleys. Could he be right, lad?'

'He – he could be, My Lord – the harbour is so densely packed, it's impossible to count them accurately – and perhaps they have more at Ferrol—'

'Which we couldn't look into, because of the fog. You know what else the fisherman said, Walbridge, so terrified was he that he was going to be tortured and executed by *El Diablo Blanco* – you know that's what the Dons call me, lad, the White Devil, from my days out in the Carib Sea?'

'No, My Lord. Yes, My Lord. The White Devil. As you say.'

'The fisherman said the *Adelantado* himself was in command – the Count of Santa Gadea, their equivalent of our Lord High Admiral. A veteran commander, Santa Gadea is. Captured some of the Turks' galleys at Lepanto, near thirty years ago. So he's a proven fighting admiral. A very different proposition to the addled arse-brain Medina Sidonia who came against us in Eighty Eight, that's for certain. But our fisherman said still more than that, lad. He said the King of Spain himself, the new King Philip, was coming aboard to command his army in person. So tell me what we're looking at, Walbridge, and tell me what I must report to the Queen.'

The boy looked out toward the distant masts, and the vast profusion of gold-and-scarlet banners flying from the walls of The Groyne. He shook his head, still not wanting to believe what he was seeing. But he was a good lad, bright and brave. When he spoke, his voice was clear, with only the slightest hint of trembling.

'We are looking at a new Spanish Armada, My Lord. You must report to the Queen that England is about to be invaded.'

'Too fucking right, lad. And just be thankful you or I won't be in the room when Her Majesty gets that joyous piece of news.'

Nicholas Iles

We saluted the squat round walls of Pendennis Castle, high on its headland to our left – to larboard, as the seamen insist on saying – and the nearly identical Saint Mawes, lower down, off to the right, the Cross of Saint George flying proudly from the ramparts of both. They replied in turn, filling the great bay of Falmouth with gunsmoke. It was a splendid sight, one worthy of an artist's brush or a poet's pen. But the only poet witnessing it had other matters in hand.

We had barely come to an anchor before the ship's longboat was hauled alongside and a boat crew assigned to row me ashore. My Lord handed me the papers that he had just completed, reminded me of the verbal instructions he had given me in his cabin as we entered the bay, and then did something that shook me to the core. He extended his hand, something he had never done before.

'God go with you, Master Iles,' he said. I took the proffered hand, and endeavoured not to cry out as the powerful fingers very nearly crushed my own. 'In the year Eighty-Eight, when the Invincible Armada approached, we lit a chain of beacons to warn that the enemy was approaching. You, and you alone, are England's beacon-chain now, poet.'

'I shall do my utmost, My Lord,' I said.

'Good lad.'

As I stepped ashore onto Penryn wharf, and then mounted the first of the many horses that awaited me, I felt both the burden and the thrill of my responsibility. There was not a moment to be lost, My Lord had said. For all we knew, this second Armada might be but a few days behind us. The favourable winds and benign weather that had brought us home from the north coast of Spain could well be aiding the enemy equally. So there was no time for me to ride to London, deliver the news, wait for the realm's governors to debate, and then for orders to come back down, oh so tardily, to the outlying counties. Hence, acting in the name of the Earl of Ravensden alone and praying that the note he had written to that effect would indemnify me against ill consequences, I, Nicholas Iles, was to warn the kingdom. I was to begin England's defence against invasion.

In practice, this proved not to be as great a mission as it may sound. In the first few towns and villages that I rode through without stopping, I bellowed the sort of noble phrases that I would have wanted one of my characters to declaim upon the stage: 'The Spanish are coming! The Inquisition and Popery are upon the wave! A new Armada sails! Call out the militia! To arms, Englishmen! For God and Queen Elizabeth!'

These words provoked one of two reactions. In the more timorous places, my message was greeted by the terrified screams of women and children, with the men abandoning both as they ran for the hills. In the more sceptical towns and villages, mocking boys and the legions of beggars who infested the land pelted me with stones and shit, crying the likes of 'Fuck off, you lying whoreson!' The consequence was that my canters down high streets turned into gallops, and my shouted warnings became shorter and more abrupt: 'Spaniards! Shift your arses or die!'

It was a similar tale in the towns where I stopped to eat, to change horses or to sleep. In Bodmin, a hundred men sat around me in an inn as I told them my story, then moved off, grim-faced and silent, to open the county armoury and distribute weapons. But in Yeovil, I was thrown into the town gaol as a vagrant and a madman, only securing release thanks to the fortunate intervention of a one-legged old soldier who had served under My Lord in the Cadiz expedition and recognised his signature.

Somehow, though, I got the message across. Indeed, the nearer I got to London, the more I tended to find that my message had outrun me, and was galloping well ahead. Thus when I requested ale, cheese and herring in a tavern at Hounslow while a new horse was prepared for me, a brazen wench took one look at me and said, 'You should be ashamed of yourself, spreading such lies. Every man knows the King of Spain, the Holy Roman Emperor and the Pope have already landed in Ireland in person with two hundred ships and fifty thousand men. Lord Ravensden himself rode through here three days ago, bearing the news. Yellow Sally, yonder, saw him, she did. Eight foot tall he is.'

Thus I was mightily relieved when I rode through Chiswick and saw and smelled ahead of me the familiar cloud of coal-smoke that rose from the city of London.

Laszlo Horvath:

I write for two reasons. First, it is a means of improving my English. I have need of improvement, if I am to become what I seek to become. Second, it may be that I will have need of a written record. I am still unsure of English law, which seems a strange and impenetrable business. For instance, there is this notion that twelve ignorant peasants, plucked from the street or the plough, are qualified to judge whether or not a man should hang. Curious. It will be best, I think, for me to write as much as possible. If the twelve men set to judge me cannot read, and I lay before them an abundance of writing, how then can they condemn me?

Conversely – a word that I have learned today, and of which I am proud – conversely, writing provides me with the evidence I shall require in due course. It is clear to me now that my task will not be accomplished in a matter of days, or even weeks. This will be a business of many months, perhaps years. But I am a patient man. A very patient man. Yet even my patience is dependent on one thing: that there remains a kingdom called England. I saw with my own eyes the multitude of masts in the Spanish harbour. So for the moment, there is no doubt of what I must do. My sword must be drawn, and it must be at the service of Queen Elizabeth and of Matthew Quinton, captain of the *Merhonour*.

So be it.

Nicholas Iles:

'Master Secretary,' said the functionary to the hunchback, 'this is the man sent from My Lord of Ravensden, at anchor in the harbour of Penryn.'

I stepped into the room, deep within the heart of the Palace of Whitehall. A surprisingly small room: bare of tapestries or other forms of decoration to conceal the stone walls of a previous century, and bare of furniture, but for one oak desk and one chair. Upon the latter sat a small, red-bearded man with narrow eyes, a long face and a pronounced lump upon his back. He was intent on some papers, which he was annotating with furious strokes of a quill.

'Well?' he demanded.

I handed over My Lord's despatches. Robert Cecil, Principal Secretary to Her Majesty, son and successor to the late chief minister of the kingdom, William, Lord Burghley – this Robert Cecil broke open the wax seals with some patience, and read rapidly.

As a writer, of course, I had played over his likely reactions many times in my head, during the long ride from Falmouth. At the very least, I expected tears, perhaps even uncontrollable sobbing. I had considered the possibility of him pacing the room, wringing his hands. The true artist in me hoped that he would slit his wrists in despair before me. Instead, he merely laid the papers down upon the desk and rubbed his eyes.

'You saw them yourself?' he said. 'The Spanish ships, in the harbour of Coruna?'

'I saw them, sir.'

He nodded. Slowly, like a priest delivering a benediction, he waved his hand over the papers on the desk.

'You see all these? Letters from Bruges, from Paris, from Brest, from our agents in the Escorial itself. All of them providing me with pieces of the intelligence that you and My Lord of Ravensden have now confirmed in full. Until this moment, I prayed that all of this intelligence was false. But here you stand, before me, and you have seen it with your own eyes. Your master, the noble Earl, says that we face a new Spanish Armada. You concur with his judgement?'

'I am no seaman, sir. But I saw what I saw, and I can read a map. If there is a Spanish fleet on the north coast of their kingdom, they can only be bound for England.'

'Or Ireland,' said the Principal Secretary. 'In which case they are the Earl of Essex's affair. And woe betide if any calamity should befall him, of course.' He smiled; but it was the smile of a serpent. Every man knew of the bitter rivalry between Secretary Cecil and the Earl of Essex. And in every town I had ridden through, the talk was of little else but the manifold calamities that had already befallen the noble Earl during his disastrous campaign in Ireland. 'But yes, in the wider sense you are correct. There is a new Armada, it is bound for these islands, and we are not prepared for it in the slightest.'

He seemed lost in thought, and I was at a loss for something to say. What does one say to England's chief minister, when he might well be contemplating his neck beneath a Spanish headsman's axe, or his flesh burning in an *auto-da-fé*? But, at last, he looked up; and it was as though he were seeing me for the first time.

'Master Iles, is it not?' said Robert Cecil, wearily. 'I believe there is still a warrant out for your arrest.'

How did he know who he was? How could he possibly know –

'It – it was an unfair judgement, Master Secretary. A misunderstanding, that was all. A dispute over a contract.'

'That is the sort of thing you writers tend to say, in my experience. A troublesome crew, all of you – impertinent and scurrilous. And I know the contents of the contract in question. Of the commission you failed to carry out. A commission that was illegal in any case.' I felt myself trembling; the actor could no longer control his limbs, or his expression. 'But it would not do for England to imprison the man who has brought such news as you have this day, Master Iles. It would not do at all. No, not even to a man who serves Lord Ravensden, who is certainly no friend of mine, as I expect you know entirely well. So let me say this as plain Rob Cecil, if you catch my meaning. Her Majesty's Principal Secretary is a very different beast, who ought by rights to have you arrested on the spot. But plain Rob Cecil...well, he might advise a man in your position to make for one of the Liberties, say the Savoy, lie low for a few days, and then to slip over London Bridge in the morning throng before taking the Dover road.'

'Dover, Master Secretary?'

'Indeed. That is where My Lord Ravensden, the *Merhonour*, and the rest of the fleet have been ordered – to the Downs. We have to arm England, Master Iles – arm her against a most dreadful threat to her very survival. Well, man, what are you gawping at? Go, playwright, or I will have you arrested after all. Or, perhaps, I should subject you to an even worse fate than that.'

'Master Secretary?'

'Taking you with me to tell all of this to the Queen, Master Iles. So get out, man. Be on your way!'

I was gone from the Palace before a fifth minute had passed.

The Dowager Countess:

Even on a country estate in the Val-de-Loire, we knew that a new Spanish Armada was on its way to invade England. Anne-Catherine's husband, the Marquis de Lavelle, was one of the deputies to the nominal Governor of Brittany, the Duc de Vendome, a five-year-old bastard of King Henry's. From him, we learned that the Spanish had sought permission to use the anchorage of Brest for the rendezvous of over a hundred great ships and galleys, expected there in the middle of August. I wrote to my husband, and fretted by day and by night, although my term drew ever nearer. One day, though, I was reading de Montreux's *Les Amours de Cleandre et Domiphille* in one of the bower seats within the wooded part of my father's garden. I overheard two of the servants talking nearby, and knew they could not be aware that I was there.

'The old whore Elizabeth's finished this time, mark my words', said Saupin, an ancient soldier who had lost an arm at Ivry, and now served as our wine steward.

'How's that, then, old man?' said a younger voice I recognised as that of Bessat, one of the grooms. 'She and her navy fought off the Spanish before.'

'By luck, lad – luck and a fair wind. And that time, the *rosbifs* had ample warning that the Spanish were coming. Years' worth of warning. Not now. Taken them by surprise, the Dons have. The English will never be able to call together their army and navy in time, and even if they do, the same will hold true as it did in the year Eighty-Eight. All the Spanish have to do is land. I've seen the might of the *tercios* at first hand, Bessat, my lad – where do you think my fucking arm went, eh? The finest army in all the world. Invincible, they are. Put the English militia up against 'em, mere ploughboys who don't know one end of a pike from another, and it'll be a slaughter.'

'Then what of Milady Louise-Marie?' demanded Bessat. Like most of the servants, he ignored my new English title. Unlike most of them, though, young Bessat had always been more than a little in love with me.

'Widow in waiting if ever I saw one, lad. You mark my words. Widow in waiting.'

CHAPTER FIVE

Nicholas Iles:

I rode for Dover through a land making ready for invasion. The streets of London were full of soldiers. It was said that an army of thirty thousand was in position to defend the capital, to save it from the dire fate that had befallen Antwerp not so many years before, sacked and burned by the fury of the Spaniards, women and children slaughtered in the streets. But of course, the army was not there just to defend London: it was also there to defend the Queen, the personification of Protestant England. All across the land, men were taking up arms on behalf of Gloriana. Outside Dartford, I saw the militia exercising with pikes and muskets upon the common. At the outskirts of Strood, I had to dismount for an hour as two regiments marched past, making for Sheppey, which was one of the places where the Spanish were deemed likely to land. Crossing Rochester Bridge, I saw great ships being made ready for sea, carpenters hammering furiously at their timbers. In every town, drums were beating to attract volunteers to the colours. At Canterbury, where I spent a night at an inn, the townspeople lined the road to watch an artillery train pass through. Some shouted for joy, others cried 'God save the Queen!' with the same fervour they would once have expended on *Ave Marias*. But both in the crowd on the road, and among the customers of the inn, other words were being spoken, often in hushed tones and accompanied by sideways glances toward me and the other strangers in the place. Naturally, a writer has an ear for such things.

'The Spanish are coming this time, all right. England's been sold to them by that traitor Cecil. He's a secret Jesuit, the hunchback, mark my words.'

'The Dons have already landed in the Isle of Wight, I tell you. Cecil and all the Parliament-men, they're hiding the truth from us. All the Papists in the north are just waiting for the Dons to come across the Solent and set one foot on the mainland, then they'll rise and slaughter the honest godly folk. But the great men of the kingdom, they don't want you to know that.'

'Where's My Lord of Essex? He's the only man who can save the country, and he's stuck in some Irish bog.'

'They say the Queen will behead him for treason. They say he wants her throne, and she knows it. You know his great-grandmother was descended from King Edward the Third? So she's sent him to Ireland knowing he'd fail, to give her the excuse to be rid of him.'

'No, it's the Jesuits' doing! They know Essex's a good Protestant, and the only man we can trust to stop Popery!'

'It's all a feint, I tell you, this business of the Spanish. Move all our arms to the south coast, then what'll happen? James of Scotland'll be over the border in a trice, with nothing between him and London, and once he's in England, he'll drop all the pretence of being a Protestant and will declare for Rome, just as Henry of France did. Tom Oldry of Chartham, he knows a man whose brother was at the great cattle-fair in Falkirk a month back. Says he saw fifty thousand blood-crazed Highlanders in kilts on the plain below Stirling Castle—'

'Hush, lads! Hush, in the name of God. His spies could be anywhere.'

'Whose spies? The King of Scots'?'

'The King of Spain's?'

'Cecil's?'

'Tom Oldry's?'

I was careful to write down what I saw and heard only when I was in private. This was a lesson I had learned in bitter fashion, having been beaten to a bloody pulp and losing two teeth when a tavern gang in Bristol took exception to my noting their words when we of Lord Sundon's Men were performing there a few years before. But it seemed to me that these rough country-folk's words cried out to be recorded. A kingdom arming for war, and torn with bitter dissension between rival factions. A kingdom brimming with suspicion of the enemy within. Truly, this was ideal material for my *Tragical History of King Stephen*, or else perhaps it could form the basis of Act One of my play about My Lord. Or possibly Act Four. In either event, it would be a prelude to the inevitable last Act, which was surely about to be played out: My Lord's triumph over the second Spanish Armada, making him the saviour of the nation and the recipient of the limitless bounty of a grateful Queen and her people. Some of which bounty he, in turn, would bestow upon his attendant poet.

Yes, indeed. There was no doubt of it.

Laszlo Horvath:

In the great bay called Fal Mouth, we take on fresh stores and pull the ship over onto its side upon the beach. The seamen call this 'careening', and it seems to mean a cleaning of the ship's bottom, to enable it to move faster through the water. Then we sail upon a fair wind, going east up the sea that they call the English Channel, passing headlands, harbours, and a large island that they call White. Eventually we pass the famous castle of Dover, with which we exchange salutes, and come into the broad anchorage called the Downs. Here we find the Queen's great ships that have come about from a place called Medway, where the English keep most of their navy.

I stand with him upon the quarterdeck, and do not need to feign enthusiasm for what I see.

'I have seen the army of the Sultan, My Lord,' I say. 'I have seen the massed horde of the Crimean Khanate, and the siege-trains of the King of Poland and the Holy Roman Emperor. But truly, I have never seen such a sight as this.'

'Oh, I've seen greater, Horvath. The fleet we set out in the year Eighty-Eight was much larger. But England has put this one to sea in a fortnight, and assembled a great army in the same time. No country has ever done the like.'

'As you say, My Lord.'

'Now, see there, Master Horvath. That great ship with the pennants streaming from her mastheads is the *Elizabeth Jonas*, the largest man-of-war in all England. She flies the flag of Lord Thomas Howard, the Lord Admiral's cousin, who commands the fleet. A good man, Tom Howard, capable and loyal. He'd be Duke of Norfolk now, if only his father had been both of those things too and thus avoided having his head chopped off for treason. The title was attainted, although Tom spends every waking hour plotting to get it restored.'

'Attainted, My Lord? That is an interesting word. I have heard it before, I think. Will you explain it to me?'

'An Act of Attainder – ah, that's a fearsome business indeed, my friend. If a peer of the realm commits treason, as Tom Howard's father did, then his title can be stricken from the record, his estates confiscated by the Crown, his children disinherited. Some of England's most famous titles have fallen in that way – Norfolk, Buckingham, and others. But God in Heaven—'

The Earl of Ravensden:

'– but God in Heaven, man, I'm not explaining points of law when the entire navy of England lies in sight! Now, Master Horvath, there is the *Ark Royal*, our flagship against the previous Armada. The Vice-Admiral's ship, this time. Raleigh. Sir Walter Raleigh. Of him, the less said, the better. There, *Nonpareil*. There, *Defiance*. There, *Triumph*—'

'Your memory is formidable, My Lord. I still cannot tell one ship from another.'

'You come from a land very far from the sea, my friend. We English are born to it – the sea is in our blood.'

I saw old Carver look at me askance, and knew what was in his mind: *you are a man of Bedfordshire, My Lord Ravensden, which is as far inland as one can be in England, yet now you set up as a salt-bred tarpaulin*? I returned his stare with interest, and he returned to his duties.

'Those other ships yonder, My Lord?' said Horvath.

'They are the Queen's private ships – the ones she has paid for and armed herself. And behind them, the squadron set out by the City of London. At anchor yonder, Sir Richard Leveson's fleet, which has been cruising to the westward. Let the Don come, Master Horvath, and we will destroy him as we did in Eighty-Eight!'

But even as I uttered the words, I knew they were hollow. I had seen what lay in The Groyne. The combination of royal and private ships that lay before us mustered no more than three dozen hulls. The Spanish ships alone outnumbered us two to one, and that was before one reckoned with their galleys – dozens of them.

An hour or two later, I was rowed over to *Elizabeth Jonas* for a council of war.

'What is an admiral to do?' cried Tom Howard, pacing his great cabin in despair. He held up a piece of paper. 'Here, firm intelligence that the Armada has already rendezvoused at Brest and is sailing into the Channel as we speak.' He put it down, and held up a second piece. 'Here, equally firm intelligence that they have not been at Brest at all, and that their whereabouts are unknown.'

'Wouldn't have happened in old Walsingham's day,' said Raleigh in his lazy Devon drawl. 'This new Cecil—'

The Dowager Countess:

Yes, grandson, this was indeed the famous Sir Walter Raleigh. He of the potato, and the cloak over the puddle. My husband was always hostile to him, and it was easy to see why: they were alike as peas in a pod. For my part, I always found him charming. Quite delightful, in fact – a perfect gentleman, as the English say. And handsome, so very handsome. So I shed more than a few tears when, years later, I saw him beheaded.

Needless to say, your grandfather cheered.

The Earl of Ravensden:

'This new Cecil—'

'Careful, Walter,' said Howard.

'What?' cried Raleigh. 'Are we not all friends here? Are we not all brethren of the sea? Can we not now speak freely to each other?'

He looked at me, for he and I were certainly no friends at all; but I was no friend to Robert Cecil either, and Walter Raleigh knew that. Yes, we were brethren of the sea, and if it came to it, I would rather stand by a vain braggart like Walt than with a devious time-serving pen-pushing arsehole of a hunchback. Raleigh was a few years older than me, but he still made every effort imaginable to look younger, blackening his silly little beard and his long eyebrows in the most ludicrously obvious manner imaginable. Perhaps he still hoped to win back the Queen's heart, but he had disgraced himself by marrying without her approval –

It was a hot August day, but I shivered at the recollection.

'So, gentlemen, your advice,' said Tom Howard.

'I should go west again, My Lord,' said Sir Richard Leveson in his simpering middle shire tones. 'If they are already in the Channel, I can meet them in the west and try to delay their passage, as Drake did in Eighty-Eight.'

'In Eighty-Eight, Sir Richard,' I said, 'we knew exactly where they were, we knew exactly where they were going, we had a strong squadron at Plymouth – and with respect, Sir Richard, you're no Drake.'

Jesus, Judas and all the Apostles, that this day should have dawned – Matthew Quinton siding with Walter Raleigh and speaking up for Francis Drake. Come, lightning bolts, and strike me down.

God forgive me, but that was what I thought at that moment: for just as if I had to choose between Raleigh and Robert Cecil, I would stand by the former every time, so it was in a choice between Sir Richard Leveson and my old adversary. In extremis, true-born warrior shall always side with true-born warrior, no matter how obnoxious he may be, and that's an end of it. Admittedly, Frank Drake had been dead three years, but in a battle, I would still rather fight alongside his fish-eaten bones than with this walking joke of a preening courtier, ten years younger than me. A man who thought it fashionable to square off his great red beard, making it look as though he had a brick hanging from his chin.

The walking joke bridled at my insult, as I hoped he would.

'Damn you, Ravensden, I will have satisfaction for that—'

His hand went to his sword hilt, and I responded in kind.

'Gladly, Leveson! Aye, gladly!'

Tom Howard raised his hands in despair. 'Sir Richard – My Lord – we will have no discord between us! None, do you hear? Do either of you wish to account to the Queen for warring with each other when the enemy might be on our shore at any moment?'

I held my tongue. Tom Howard was a good man, but if it came to it, we both knew that blood would out; Leveson was married to his cousin, the Lord Admiral's daughter. And whatever I thought of Brick-Beard, I respected the Earl of Nottingham, our commander-in-chief against the Invincible Armada in the days when he was plain Howard of Effingham. Besides, he was now the Lord Lieutenant-General of All England, the man in charge of our defence against this new threat, and I did not doubt that his powers would include summarily executing the man who impaled his son-in-law like a suckling pig.

'It cannot harm to send Sir Richard west,' said Raleigh, acting the conciliator. 'After all, it is just as likely that the Spanish intend to land in Ireland, to assist the rebels there. Thus adding quite notably to My Lord Essex's present troubles.'

'Must be difficult for you, Walt,' I said, 'caught between wishing Essex ill and hoping he doesn't fare so ill that it imperils your Irish estates. Your very extensive Irish estates.'

'I wish merely for the success of the Queen's arms, Ravensden, whosoever might command them,' said Walt, uncomfortably. 'But come, My Lord Earl, you are clearly in a mighty peevish mood today. Tell us, then, what you think we, your admirals, should do.'

What you think we, your admirals, should do.

Oh, there was the rub. I had more experience of fighting at sea than any of them, but because I would not bend to every fashion and faction of the court – and because the Queen did not like me – I was doomed to have other men promoted over my head. Yet my rank as an Earl of England meant that they had to give me a place in their councils.

I walked to the stern windows of the great cabin of *Elizabeth Jonas* and looked out over the fleet, the ships swinging at single anchors upon the flooding tide.

'Well, then,' I said, 'Sir Richard to sail west once more – yes, that is for the best.' It also meant the removal of Brick-Beard from my company for at least a few blessed weeks, but I suppose one should not decide the movements of navies in wartime upon such base considerations. 'The rest of the fleet to remain here, in the Downs, to await more certain intelligence of the enemy.'

Tom Howard frowned. 'You would not move the whole fleet west, to Portsmouth or Plymouth? If we remain here, we leave the entire south coast undefended – the Spanish could easily land at Falmouth, or Milford Haven, or else seize the Isle of Wight—'

'True, My Lord, they could. But those places are remote, and easily isolated from the rest of the country. Taking them would gain the Spaniards nothing. No, two destinations, and two only, matter to the Don. The one is Ireland, where there is already a war, a large army ready to ally with their own, and a fine general commanding it, namely the Earl of Tyrone. The other is London, and the Queen. We cannot defend both London and Ireland, so if it comes to a choice, as it always does, then our duty is to protect Her Majesty.'

'Amen,' said Walt Raleigh, ever the consummate courtier.

'Quite so,' said Tom Howard. 'God save the Queen.'

'God save the Queen,' said the other three of us, in unison.

'Very well, My Lord, we shall adopt your advice—'

'One more thing, My Lord Howard,' I said. 'We should send a small squadron to the opposite coast, to co-ordinate matters with our Dutch allies, to watch for signs of the Armada of Flanders moving out of its ports to join the fleet coming up the Channel, and to trap the Dons in a pincer if they try to break through the Straits of Dover.'

'With yourself as the commander of this squadron, Lord Ravensden?'

'If I am thought worthy of such an honour.'

'Raleigh, Leveson – you concur?'

My two rivals nodded their agreement; no doubt they were as enthusiastic to be rid of me as I was of them.

'So be it,' said Howard. 'Take the *Merhonour* and whichever four of the London ships you find fittest.'

London ships, not royal ones. That was the price to be paid for an independent command, then: trying to cajole a bunch of timorous Wapping skippers into taking the slightest risk that might imperil their owners' precious hulls. But it was better than the alternative, and I believe I feigned gratitude effusively enough.

And thus, with our resolutions taken, we waited for the new Armada to come against us.

CHAPTER SIX

Nicholas Iles:
A forest of masts, vengeful in its wrath, sailing up the Channel to –
No. A forest cannot be vengeful.
The ocean carpeted with hulls of Castilian oak, bearing the grim-visaged legions of King Philip –
A carpet of oak? Dreadful, Iles: not even Shakespeare would strike such a jarring note.
Mighty floating fortresses, come upon the west wind to ravage England's sacred seas –
No, no, no.

As I look back over the rough notes I scribbled in those strange days at the end of the summer of Ninety-Nine, I can recall exactly the moods we went through aboard the *Merhonour*, lying principally off Dunkirk with our consorts from London and our allies, the Dutch.

First, there were the days when we expected the Armada at any moment. Prayers were said four, sometimes five, times a day. The men drilled with pikes and cutlasses, grim determination in their eyes. My Lord slept on the deck, the seamen at their guns. And I began to write the great battle scene that would conclude with My Lord's triumph over the enemy. Best to begin it in advance, I reasoned, lest I be wounded during the fight, or else forgot some of the details afterwards.

After perhaps a week of this, the murmuring began. The frequency of prayers decreased. The drills were carried out half-heartedly, if at all. Men crept back into their sea-beds or mattresses upon the decks. I began to write some stanzas about the love of Paris and Helen.

After a few more days, we had daily floggings to suppress mutiny. And one morning, two of the London ships were gone. I expected My Lord to rage against their cowardice, and to issue orders for their arrest to every port in the land. But he did not. He simply shrugged his shoulders.

Throughout this time, My Lord was receiving letters. We knew when he held in his hand a letter from France, because he smiled like a youth smitten by first love. Thus we knew that My Lady was approaching her full term, and all was well. But the letters from England caused his brow to furrow. He refused to discuss the contents with any of us, but their purport was all too obvious.

There was no sign of the great Armada we had all seen with our own eyes. It had simply vanished into thin air.

The Earl of Ravensden:
The worst thing was the smug look on the face of the Bastard Orange.

Bugger all had been stirring out of Dunkirk. I was praying for a chance to fight and kill van der Waecken, the boldest of the Dunkirk privateers, whose depredations in the English Seas had made him feared on every inch of Queen Elizabeth's shores. Only a triumph like that, I reckoned, would provide sufficient redemption for me now. But the devious Flemish knave was said to be on a lengthy cruise, laying up in neutral Scots or Danish harbours, with no likelihood of him returning in the foreseeable future. So I gave orders for us to sail down the coast to Calais, where we could anchor for a few days and take on fresh victuals brought by hoys from Dover. I dared not give leave, not even to the loyal men who would not attempt to desert, but at least the officers could take turns at going ashore. I made sure I took the first turn, too, because the mails that came aboard us in Calais Roads meant that I needed to get mightily drunk, and in as short a time as possible, even though it was only a little after dawn. What I did not need was to walk into the most notorious inn of old Calais, *La Chat Gris*, the one place where I ought to have been certain of encountering no man of rank whatsoever who might witness me drinking myself into oblivion – especially at that time of day – and seeing before me the familiar round face, bald pate and bushy grey beard of the Lieutenant-Admiral of Zeeland, Justinus of Nassau.

'Ho, My Lord of Ravensden!' he cried. His English was atrocious – in truth, his greeting came out as *Whore, Moy Lort off Rahffensdin* – but that was not the reason why my heart sank at the prospect of a morning in his company.

'My Lord of Nassau,' I said, inclining my head slightly.

The man was the son of a prince, after all, albeit from the wrong side of the blanket. Europe's most famous prince, too, in his day: William of Orange, no less, the leader of the Dutch revolt against their erstwhile Spanish overlords. Leader, that is, until some papist Frog blew his chest apart at point-blank range, after which he really did live up to his nickname of William the Silent.

'Ho, then, My Lord,' said Justinus, the Bastard Orange, 'where is your Armada? Your invisible Armada? That is what they are calling it in London, is it not?'

He laughed aloud, although his laugh consisted of a volley of loud croaks somewhat akin to those of a frightened pheasant.

Lieutenant-Admiral he might have been. Half-brother of the ruler of the self-proclaimed United Provinces of the Netherlands he might have been, too. But, there and then, I would happily have pummelled his head, so much like an orange if truth be told, had it not been for the knowledge that we both shared. The knowledge that had come with the mails to both the English and Dutch squadrons that lay off the port of Calais.

'The Armada has gone to the Canary Islands, Lord Justinus.'

'Ho, that is right, Lord Ravensden! To save them from falling into the hands of our Dutch fleet, under my good friend Van der Does. So King Philip considers the little Canary Islands more important than great England!'

The pheasant croaked again, and his companions, Dutch captains to a man, laughed with him. In my mind, I ran him through there and then; but striking dead the admiral of our ally was unlikely to stand me in good stead with the Queen, who already looked askance upon me.

'As you say, Lord Justinus,' I said feebly.

But the Bastard Orange was clearly in no mood to let matters rest there.

'Why, poor Lord Ravensden! Ho, here you are in Calais, that was England's entire empire in the world until you lost it, and it is here you learn that your kingdom is no longer worth a Canary! Truly, how are the mighty fallen!'

Nassau's captains laughed even more uproariously. But I could not argue, for it was only the truth. To prove it, Jacques Liebart, the ancient innkeeper, came over in that moment.

'Good morrow, My Lord of Ravensden,' he said in perfect English. 'Will it be beer, ale or wine today? And some Cheshire cheese, perhaps?'

Liebart spoke with a still noticeable accent, somewhat akin to Kentish. For he was born an Englishman, along with every one of the oldest citizens of Calais. He had lived there through the first twenty years of his life, when it was still as English a town as Windsor, even returning two members to Parliament. Then, forty-one years ago, the French took it. My new wife had discomfited me somewhat by revealing that her grandfather rode alongside its conqueror, the Duke of Guise, as he made his triumphant entry into the town.

'Ale *and* wine, Liebart. And fast, man!'

'Ho,' cried the Bastard Orange, 'the noble Earl has many sorrows to drown!'

I prayed as I had not prayed for many a year, and my prayer was that something, *anything*, would wipe the smiles from the faces of Justinus of Nassau and his Dutchmen.

The door of the inn burst open, and Iles ran into the room. My heart lifted for a moment – perhaps he had news from Louise-Marie of the birth of my son, which had to be due.

But then he screamed, 'The Spanish! The Spanish are in sight!'

No, dear Lord in Heaven.

Upon reflection – anything except that.

Laszlo Horvath:

He comes aboard in a rage, bellowing orders. Men go aloft, the sails are unfurled, ropes are pulled taut. There is much shouting, and the blowing of whistles.

'Cut the cables!' he cries.

Men with axes run to the anchor-ropes and hack at them. Across the water, the Dutchmen do the same. But it avails us little. The severed ropes run out of their holes, our anchors are gone, and I feel the now-familiar creaking and swaying of the hull as it begins to move. Above our heads, though, the sails hang limply in the morning haze. The gales of the last few days are gone, and in their place we have near calm. The English and Dutch ships barely move.

He goes up onto the forecastle and pulls himself up onto the ship's rail, staring out to sea. Now, at last, we can all see what the lookout on our southernmost ship reported.

'Six galleys,' he cries. 'Six fucking Spanish galleys, and they're running the Straits!'

It is my first sight of galleys. They are very different to the high-hulled English and Dutch ships struggling to get clear of the Road of Calais. They have long, low hulls, with pronounced beaks in the bows. They have single masts, which carry the triangular sails that the sailors call 'lateens'. At the sterns, they have curious structures which resemble half-upturned sea-shells. Half way along their decks are squarer upperworks that resemble small castles. From these protrude several large guns, only a little smaller than the great guns mounted in their bows.

They are a glorious sight. Their banks of oars move in unison, propelling them swiftly through the calm waters. Even in Calais, amidst all the noise of our own activity, we can just make out the sound of their drums, beating out the rhythm for the rowers. We can see the morning sun glinting on the armour of the hundreds of soldiers lining their decks. And we can see the red and gold banners of Spain spilling out as the galleys create their own breeze, while our ensigns of Saint George hang limply.

'God's blood,' he cries –

The Earl of Ravensden:

'God's blood, send us a fair wind!' But we had not a whiff of one. Not one fucking whiff. 'Master Carver! Can you not but find us a breath or two of breeze, man?'

Even as I uttered the words, I knew they were hopeless. Carver had men adjusting the top sails every few minutes, the main courses nearly as often, but no matter what he did, there was no wind. We caught no breeze off the land. We found no hint of a westerly even when we were out beyond the shelter of Grease Ness.

My ships, and those of the Bastard Orange, were making a knot or two, if that, as we struggled to make any way at all. Even the Dutch cromsters, trim little war-craft with lateen sails at their mizzens, could make but poor progress. And out at sea, in the very centre of the Strait of Dover, the six great galleys were doing a good twelve knots. I'd served with enough men who'd been slaves in the galleys, and knew from them that to keep up this sort of speed, the rowing masters would be pushing the oarsmen to the very limit. I could imagine the whips cracking on flesh, the blood and sweat of the men as the sweeps cut the water. They could not maintain such a tempo for long. But then, they did not need to. The night and the mist had given them the advantage of surprise, the calm now gave them the advantage of speed, and in truth, the Straits of Dover form but a very small stretch of sea. The galleys' bow waves of white foam were all too visible to we slugs becalmed at Calais, a sure sign that they would soon be past us. But as I clung on to the foremast shrouds, waving my fist at the distant enemy, I knew it was even worse than that. For if we had no wind, then neither did Leveson, Raleigh and Tom Howard over in the Downs. They would be doing the same as us, trying somehow to find a decent breeze and sea-room, but like us, they would be failing. The Spanish admiral, whoever he might be, was both bold and lucky, and in fighting at sea, those are the only qualities an admiral needs.

But as I watched the impressive sight of the galleys, rowing through England's private lake as though they owned it, a suspicion grew upon me that the Spanish admiral had more qualities than those alone. This was not some chance raid, not some hare-brained mission dreamed up on the spur of the moment like so many of the expeditions of, say, Francis Drake and Walter Raleigh. Or Matthew of Ravensden, come to that, if I am honest. A voyage so daring, with such high stakes and high risks, required meticulous planning and preparation. It required careful rehearsal of different options: for instance, the possibility of sending galleys into the English Channel in winter. Suddenly, the fight that had nearly done for my *Merhonour*, and forced us into Nantes to repair, made perfect sense, although the thought was not a pleasant one. God alone knew what a Spanish admiral so efficient and so ruthless – for sending a galley full of several hundred men into northern waters in November, when it would most likely be swamped by the sea, was ruthless beyond measure – yes, God alone knew what such an admiral might achieve.

There was only one consolation. I looked over to the Dutch flagship, and could see Justinus of Nassau clearly, standing there on his quarterdeck. He had buckled on his breastplate, but he wasn't laughing now, by Christ. He was as still as a statue, staring at the huge galleys as they moved away inexorably, out into the North Sea. Oh, they'd be a threat to England, all right – Drake hit that particular nail well and truly on its head – but they were ten times the threat to the Bastard Orange's upstart rebel republic, with its entire economy dependent on sea-trade and all its main ports standing on shallow waterways where galleys were in their element. If the Spanish admiral got safely into Sluys, as he was now nearly bound to do, the Dutch were in more shit than the gong-farmers of Cheapside.

The balance of the war had just changed, there was no doubt of that.

Laszlo Horvath:

I go into the bows to stand beside him.

'My Lord,' I say, 'it is not your fault.'

'Fuck me, Horvath,' he says, looking out all the time at the fast-receding galleys, 'I know it's not my fault. It's the fault of Leveson for going back to the Downs and not staying on station. It's the fault of Secretary Cecil's intelligencers, for not giving us word that the Dons were sending six galleys through the Channel. Above all, it's the fault of God for deciding today should have perfect weather for them and the worst possible weather for us. But you know what, friend Horvath? None of that will matter a damn. Leveson's the darling of the court and can do no fucking wrong. Cecil decides what truth is in England, so you can be certain it's not going to reflect badly on him, either. And the entire country has spent the last eleven years believing the wind is Protestant and on our side, so it's not going to change its mind now. Which means the country needs somebody else to blame, friend Horvath.'

He does not need to name the escaping goat, as I believe the English saying goes. Who was it who saw the Invisible Armada in its harbour? Who was it who commanded at Calais when the galleys passed through the strait that the English regard as their own private lake? Who, indeed, was drunk in a tavern ashore when the Spanish came into sight?

He is not drunk, of course. He was not drunk in the tavern. But I know the English well enough now to understand that the truth is of but slight concern to them. If that is the story which is spread – and it needs only one malicious voice to spread it – then it will be believed.

He knows all of this. He continues to stand there, looking out to sea until the galleys are gone, beyond the horizon. But still he looks, and I realise he is staring at the white cliffs of England's shore. It is almost as though he can hear the very first whispers upon that distant strand.

The Dowager Countess:

Federico Spinola, that was his name, and his galleys' audacious dash through the Straits brought that name before the world. How brightly his fame shone, like a shooting star in the heavens! But, again like a shooting star, he – But I should not jump ahead of myself, young Matthew, and we should see what my husband says of it in these papers of his. Ah yes, you say you have heard the name of Spinola, but it is Federico's brother, Ambrosio, that your uncle will have told you about. They were both commanders for Spain, although they were actually

Genoese. Ambrosio's finest hour came when he took Breda in the year Twenty-Five, for no man believed that mightily fortified city could ever fall. A great painting of the surrender was made by Velazquez, with the Governor of Breda bowing as he handed over the keys of the city to Spinola. Your grandfather got hold of an engraving, and chuckled over it for days on end. For you see, grandson, the Dutch Governor who surrendered Breda to the Spanish was none other than Justinus of Nassau, the Bastard Orange.

But all that was for the future, and at the time, I had other things on my mind. And on my belly, to be precise. I did not know it then, of course, but while the Earl was fretting and raging at Calais as the Spanish galleys sailed imperiously past him, I was in my birthing-bed, enduring a twenty hour labour. I did not know it was possible for a person to bear such pain, but bear it I did, as women have since Eve gave birth to Cain. Still, I consoled myself that it would be worth it, for I was giving birth to the heir to Ravensden, the future Earl.

But God had decided to mock the House of Quinton that day. It mocked my husband, shaking his fist impotently at the galley fleet in the Channel. And it mocked me, as I held in my sweat-soaked arms a tiny but healthy child who was all too evidently a girl.

At Easter, I had somehow managed to persuade my husband to discuss this eventuality. He devoted all of half a minute to the unwelcome thought. A girl, he decreed, would be christened Elizabeth. In those times, of course, virtually every first-born girl in England was named Elizabeth, as a way of displaying one's loyalty to the great Queen. But the Earl had an ulterior motive, as he always did. He reckoned that naming a daughter Elizabeth, and persuading the Queen to act as godmother, might be a way of ingratiating himself back into her good graces.

Alas for My Lord. The fiasco at Calais meant that he would need someone rather more powerful than our little Beth, or something rather more desperate than the birth of a child, to restore him to favour.

CHAPTER SEVEN

1600

The Earl of Ravensden's Journal

Let me be very clear about this, so that there is no misunderstanding: I did not set out to provoke a duel with My Lord of Essex.

Robert Devereux, second Earl of that title, to be precise. The most famous man in all England, the darling of the people, the Queen's great favourite (albeit disgraced), the greatest warrior in all of Christendom (albeit only in his own dreams), etcetera, etcetera.

No.

It was not my fault.

Truly, it was not.

I am still not entirely certain how it happened. It is true that I have a certain recollection of hot words passing between us. It is possible that he called me an idle Frog-loving coward and varlet who had invented an entire Armada whilst waving half-a-dozen Spanish galleys through the Channel. It is not entirely beyond the bounds of possibility that I called him a vain milk-livered ratsbane who had been trounced by the bog-crawling peasants of Ireland and justly humiliated by the Queen.

Whatever the actual words, they were the cause of us circling each other with rapiers drawn, upon the frosty grass of Hampstead Heath during a freezing dawn in February: Matthew Quinton and Robin Devereux, two Earls of England and two of her most famous warriors, each intent on spilling the other's blood.

The Dowager Countess:

Men.

That is what I said at the time, and that is what I say now, grandson.

Oh, my husband was evasive about the entire affair from the very beginning. I asked him why he wished to visit Essex, a man he heartily disliked and who was in even greater disgrace than he was. At least your grandfather was not under virtual house arrest, although he was denied the court and had no immediate prospect of a fresh command at sea. Even so, we lived comfortably enough with our little daughter in

Ravensden House; well, as comfortably as it was possible to live in that crumbling, ugly, timber-framed edifice upon the Strand, surrounded on all sides by the noise and stench of London. It was not yet suitable, he said, for us to go to his principal seat, Ravensden Abbey in Bedfordshire, because it was important for him to stay close to the court and solicit the favour of the great men of the kingdom. I believed him, up to a point. For even though my English was still negligible, I knew the meaning of the word 'repairs', and heard it uttered worryingly often in my husband's discussions with the Abbey's steward, a certain *Barcoq*, whenever the latter came to town.

Although your grandfather cursed and complained about the injustice of his fate, then, he was not in the same dire state as Milord Essex. The noble Earl had not only failed to defeat the Irish rebels, he had actually agreed a shameful truce with the Earl of Tyrone, their leader. Then, against the Queen's express orders, he returned to England and made all haste to the court to explain himself and try to win her over. What happened next was the talk of London for months on end – indeed, the talk of England, if not the whole world. Muddied, booted and spurred, Essex burst into the Queen's bedchamber as she was being dressed. I have it on the authority of two of her ladies in waiting, who were there and with whom I later became close friends, that she was in her nightgown, and that her aged face had not yet been miraculously rendered thirty years younger by the white makeup she always displayed in public. But that was not the worst of it. Why, it seems her hair had not been combed, and was in disarray! Truly, Milord Essex had committed one of the greatest sins imaginable against womankind, let alone against a Queen, by bursting in on her with her hair in such a state. If it had been me, grandson, I would have had him executed upon the spot. As it was, Elizabeth dismissed him from her presence, and he was placed under arrest – although it proved a very loose form of detention, as his rendezvous with your grandfather proved.

So, yes, I asked my husband why in God's name he wished to visit the Earl of Essex, whose disgrace seemed to be as complete as a man's could be. He refused to answer me directly, but gave me that look I had seen upon his face only two or three times before. That look of a small boy caught stealing apples from an orchard. And then I knew at once. Essex and Ravensden, two mighty warriors in disgrace, were going to discuss making common cause. And in those times, even a Frenchwoman new to England and largely ignorant of its ways could divine readily enough what that common cause might be, for it was the only matter that could possibly bring together such inveterate enemies. They were going to plot how to bring down their joint enemy, Robert Cecil, and agree upon their choice of the Queen's successor.

Perhaps they would have done, too, had they not decided first to insult each other beyond endurance.

Men.

Nicholas Iles:

I was My Lord's second, but even so, I could barely believe the sight I was witnessing. Ravensden and Essex in single combat! Truly, here was an epic combat to outdo those of Achilles and Hector, or Guy of Warwick and Colbrand the giant Viking! And yet, as the two noble earls parried and thrust, trading *stoccatas* and *imbroccatas*, I found it more and more difficult to concentrate on the poetry of the occasion, upon the nobility of the battle before me. At best, the encounter was most certainly illegal, and could lead to all of those present – myself included – being thrown into a dungeon and forgotten. At worst, one of them would kill the other, in which case it would certainly be the scaffold for the seconds of victor and vanquished alike. If Essex killed My Lord, then where would I be? Bereft of purpose, bereft of the limited protection from arrest that My Lord's patronage provided, and, more pertinently, bereft of money, even the pitiful allowance, far in arrears, that My Lord deigned to pay me. But if My Lord killed the great Earl of Essex, then might not our case be even more desperate? Killing the darling of the people and the love of the Queen – dear father in heaven, the mob might tear us apart, ripping our limbs from our sockets and feeding them to the dogs of Leadenhall! And so for the first time, I prayed for Horvath, the Hungarian. I prayed that despite my suspicions of him, the many practice fights he had fought with My Lord would bear fruit: that the moves and attacks, learned during the wars in the east, that he had been teaching to Matthew of Ravensden, would both preserve My Lord's life and bring him the victory. But not a victory that entailed the killing of the Earl of Essex. A slash on the arm would be enough. Or maybe a gash in the side. A gash not quite deep enough to kill, but to satisfy honour and to keep My Lord happy. That would be ideal.

One thing was for certain, though. My Lord was more likely to have learned swordplay that would prove useful to him from the warrior Horvath than he had from the mere poet Nicholas Iles, during our mock-fights in the past. Neither the exaggerated thrusts and parries beloved of actors on the Southwark stages, nor the devious little cuts and slashes we writers employed in tavern fights, were likely to be of service now.

The Earl of Ravensden:

Essex's blade whistled past my ear, barely an inch from slicing away the side of my skull.

'That the best you've got, Devereux, you mewling jolthead?'

I thrust my right foot forward, left foot back, lunged and thrust, aiming for his left eye. Essex parried, sparks glinting on our rapiers as they clashed, and stepped neatly to his left and back. Then he danced a little, for he favoured the Spanish fashion of swordplay, all little hops and flourishes.

'Just getting loose, Ravensden, you poxed codpiece. Shall I start to fight now?'

We circled each other. Then he came fast with another attack, this time for my left. But it was a feint. Essex waited for me to commit to the parry and then switched his line by thrusting for my heart. I parried, weaved and countered, swinging and cutting *mandritti* as Horvath and my old fencing-master at Padua had taught, then shifting my weight and pushing forward with a lunge. I hated this new-fangled business of the long-bladed rapier, all lunging, thrusting and offence, so different to the good old English skills I had learned from my cradle. But this was now the fashion, and I prided myself that I was a not inconsiderable master of it. Indeed, this last sudden change of attack of mine surprised Essex, who barely managed to counter it. He took three paces back, caught his breath, and took a fresh guard, the *seconda guardia* as Camillo Agrippa would have it, his extended sword-arm and blade level with his shoulder.

I attacked again, feinting for his belly before bringing my rapier up sharply at the last moment. My blade swung for his neck, but his rapier came up in time, barely an inch from the flesh. We both brought up our free hands to push our blades at each other, for all the world as though we were in a wrestling match with bare steel.

I was so close that I could smell Essex's breath, could see the sweat soaking his beard.

He essayed a smile. 'Jamie Stuart's the lawful heir by blood, Ravensden,' he hissed as we pushed our blades against each other, seeking a hair's breadth of advantage. 'Declare for him, and I'll spare your life.'

'Presumptuous, My Lord Essex,' I said, taking care that my voice did not reach the seconds. 'Presumptuous in so many different ways.'

I pushed him away, and as I did so, the tip of my sword scratched his cheek, drawing blood. Essex wiped the wound with the back of his hand, but as he looked incredulously at his own blood, I attacked again, thrusting for his groin.

'That's for the wounds I took on your behalf at San Fernando, Devereux!'

Essex brought his rapier up, easily parrying my attack.

'Christ, Quinton, you're not still bitter about *that*? It was not my doing, you vain blind-worm – it was your fault, and yours alone! You shouldn't have been there in the first place—'

'My fault? *My* fault, Essex, you arrogant streak of piss? I'll show you what's my fault—'

And with that I charged, intent upon the kill, all science and rules of balance forgotten. I was aware that Essex's second was shouting something, but did not hear it. I feinted high, then thrust low – a hand grabbed hold of my arm –

'Iles! What the fuck are you doing, man—'

'Soldiers, My Lord! Horsemen! Listen!'

The blood-tide ebbed from my eyes. The sound of hooves was unmistakeable, as was the clanking of weapons on saddles and armour. Essex and I looked at each other.

'Another time, Robin,' I said.

'A pleasure as always, Matt,' he said, smiling.

We made our respective exits, well before the Queen's soldiers could arrive. No man would know that Essex and Ravensden had broken Her Majesty's strictest injunctions. So I believed, at any rate.

Laszlo Horvath:

My friend Mister Trevor is showing me the royal dockyard at Deptford, to the east of London. I think he does so to demonstrate his importance, for all the workmen and officers of the yard bow their heads or doff their caps to the Surveyor of the Navy. This puffs him up, and he smiles inordinately often. Perhaps he thinks I will be impressed, but I do not understand why he would need to do this. Since our first meeting at Tyburn, I have serviced him in all the ways he has required, upon many occasions. It has been distasteful, but as the English say, the end justifies the means.

We are standing on the precarious remnants of the deck of an old ship. It lies at the head of a long dock, overshadowed by a large storehouse made of red brick. Only the stump of one mast still stands, and there are great holes in the hull.

'Sad, is it not?' says John Trevor. 'She was supposed to be preserved here for ever, as a tribute to her great commander and his famous voyage, but people will keep chipping away for keepsakes. I cannot understand it. If I have a piece of wood in my house, who can truly tell whether it is a piece of this *Golden Hind*, or a splinter that I have cut from a tree in my garden? It is like the old Papist days, friend Horvath, when relics of the saints were everywhere and there were enough pieces of the True Cross to build a fleet of galleons.'

I look around. The yard is busy, full of the stench of tar, pitch and timber. It is almost impossible to hear John Trevor speak, although he is standing next to me, for the constant noise of sawing and hammering. Flames belch from forges. Out in the river, English warships lie at anchor, taking on stores and great bronze guns. Barges and merchant ships constantly traffic up and down stream. And somewhere far to the north, My Lord of Ravensden will be fighting his duel with My Lord of Essex. I wonder whether he will employ the moves I have taught him. Perhaps he will, if he has the time.

Next to the dock housing the *Golden Hind*, men are at work on the frames of a ship. But even to my ignorant eye, it is clear that this will be longer and narrower than any of the other ships in the dockyard. I ask John Trevor what it is.

'Behold the *Superlativa*, friend Horvath. The first of England's new galley fleet that we are building to counter General Spinola's squadron across the Channel. But it will be much more than that – oh, so very much more.'

'*Superlativa*, Master Trevor? Surely that is not an English word?'

'Italian, friend Horvath. Spinola has made all things Italian the height of fashion in naval war. And it is a new century, a new era. Time for new thinking. The ship has had its day, as have all those dull old names that the seamen cry up – *Dreadnought*, *Warspite* and the rest. No, we owe a great debt to General Spinola, despite the threat he poses to us. He has demonstrated conclusively that galleys are the future for our Navy Royal, the only sure way we can defend England against an invasion by the barbarous Papists. And a means of killing two birds with one stone, come to that.'

'Birds and stones, Master Trevor? I do not follow.'

'Galleys, friend Horvath. They do not need seamen to man them, you see, and seamen are both fractious and damnably expensive, for they will insist on being paid. Whereas rowers... Why, we can now do to the Spanish what they do to us, and make galley slaves of our prisoners.'

'And if you do not have enough Spanish prisoners?'

John Trevor smiles once again. 'Have you not seen the numbers of sturdy beggars, vagrants and vagabonds who plague every inch of this kingdom's roads? Sending them to the new galleys would at once man a great fleet, and provide vast savings in the poor law rates we now impose on parishes. England must end this crushing dependence on alms, my friend. Work transforms men and nations, and what could transform more than a policy which at once entirely removes the poor from the sight of respectable men, and means that we do not have to pay for them?'

'I see now. Perhaps, then, you should be glad that Hungary is landlocked, else we would have the greatest navy in the world.'

'And why is that?'

'We commonly call ourselves a land of a thousand lords and three million beggars, Master Trevor. Imagine the number of galleys we would be able to man.'

'Ah. Yes. I take your point, my friend. I take it entirely.'

We step off the remains of the *Golden Hind*, and begin to make for the dockyard gate.

'Well, friend Horvath,' says John Trevor as we walk, 'have you ever seen such a place as this Deptford?'

'Never, Master Trevor. It is truly a wonder of the world.'

This is a lie. I have seen the Arsenale of Venice, and it is ten times the dockyard that this is. But the English do not take well to being told that they do not have the best of this, or the largest of that.

'Excellent. You are a good man, friend Horvath. A very good man. Now, I have commanded a room to be prepared for us at the Gun Tavern. And then, tomorrow, I have arranged the meeting that you have begged me for since we first met.'

'He will see me privately?'

'Indeed he will. It is a rare honour, you realise? But I think he will be interested in the story that you have to tell, friend Horvath. Very interested indeed.'

At last, my mission prospers. God willing, the end really is justifying the means.

CHAPTER EIGHT

The Dowager Countess:
The spring came, I was with child once more, and my husband was pacing the tiny rooms and narrow corridors of Ravensden House like a caged lion. He was irritable beyond measure, denouncing all and sundry for their perfidy and incompetence. Not the Queen, of course – never, ever the Queen – but the likes of Essex, Cecil, Raleigh, Leveson, and especially the last of these.

'Sweet Mother of Jesus, now he's got command of a fleet going to the Azores! How many arses did he have to lick for that?'

'The Azores, Matthew? That is a good voyage?'

'Perhaps the best voyage of all, my love. With good timing, fair winds, much luck and great skill – skill that Sir-Fucking-Richard-Fuckwit-Leveson certainly does not possess – an English fleet on station at the Azores might capture the entire Spanish treasure fleet from the New World. All the bullion that pays for Spain's vast armies and armadas, Louise, just imagine that. We've all tried in our day – Drake, Hawkins, Essex, myself – and all failed. True, I once captured one galleon, the *Virgen de Guadeloupe*, which had become detached in a storm, and the treasure on her was fabulous enough. But Fate would really kick me in the balls if it decreed that Dick Leveson should be the man to succeed where England's greatest seamen failed.'

I cared nought for Dick Leveson or anyone else. But there was one thing that the Earl had said which certainly made me care.

'Just how much treasure did you capture on the *Virgen de Guadeloupe*, husband?'

He looked at me blankly. Then his eyes went to his feet.

'There were considerable expenses,' he said in a barely audible mumble. 'And naturally, those who invested in the voyage had to be paid their shares. The Queen, above all. Then there were mortgages on outlying estates that had to be redeemed. Debts of various sorts, notably those I inherited from my father. And there was much work to be done at

Ravensden Abbey, and at Alnburgh Castle, our Northumberland property, and here at Ravensden House—'

'I see little evidence of expensive work done here, My Lord.'

'Foundations,' he mumbled. 'And my second wife had extravagant tastes. And my third, if truth be told.'

'Then how much treasure remains?'

Now he bristled. 'A wife should not tax a husband with such things. It is not fitting – it is not the humility and obedience promised in the marriage ceremony—'

Pregnant or not, I was prepared for an argument. If necessary, I was prepared for the sort of argument that entails the throwing of smaller items of furniture. But just then, our pageboy entered – young Barcock, who is now old Barcock, our steward here at Ravensden Abbey. He handed the Earl a note, and my husband tore eagerly at a wax seal bearing a crest that he evidently knew well.

'I'm sorry, my dear,' he said, 'we shall have to return to these matters on another day. I have a summons. A most urgent summons. To Secretary Cecil, at his palace of Theobalds. Perhaps there has been a divine mercy and Leveson has dropped dead, in which case, God willing, I might be offered the Azores command!'

Even in my angry and suspicious state, I had to admit that such an injunction from the most powerful man in England overrode my interest in the financial condition of the House of Quinton. And if my husband was indeed to take a fleet to the Azores, and if he captured the Spanish bullion fleet, then my doubts would be assuaged in any case, and we would live in gilded clover for the rest of our days.

But neither of us knew the truth, nor realised what a deadly course of events was being put in train.

The Earl of Ravensden:

Theobalds was a hellishly remote place, far out of London, even beyond Enfield. But as I rode toward it, I could only be impressed. Cecil's father, the crafty old Lord Burghley, had built it as a palace fit to accommodate a visiting Queen, and that it most certainly was. Behind a large gatehouse and an enclosing wall rose a lofty building, very nearly as grand as Richmond, with two hexagonal corner towers very much like those of Nonsuch, and a square central tower reminiscent of that at Hampton Court. Huge, elaborate gardens stretched out behind it. A cynical man might wonder where the Lord High Treasurer of England had found the prodigious amount of coin necessary to pay for such splendour.

I was very nearly at the gatehouse when I saw a most unexpected sight: Robert Cecil himself, riding out towards me. A hunchback does not sit well upon a horse, and the Principal Secretary was evidently not a natural horseman. But there he was, ensconced upon the saddle of a fine grey palfrey, clad in a red velvet doublet, of all things. I suppressed my astonishment at the sight.

'My Lord of Ravensden,' he said. 'You are welcome. You will ride with me? I like to take the air of an afternoon. A man can be cooped up too long amidst the mountainous papers of state business.'

I cannot quite judge what did more to put me off my guard: the Secretary's revelation that he enjoyed the eminently normal gentlemanly pursuit of riding out of an afternoon, or his air of informality, bordering very nearly upon that infernally suspicious state which men call 'friendliness'.

We rode west, out into the woods and parkland that surrounded Theobalds Palace. Cecil's foresters and warreners touched their caps or foreheads as we passed. Meanwhile, the Secretary talked of the problems of pollarding this tree, or draining that fish pond.

At length, I lost patience with his play-acting the part of the honest yeoman.

'Your pardon, Master Secretary – but may I ask the cause of your summons to me?'

Cecil glanced across at me, seemingly displeased at being interrupted.

'Well, now,' he said, 'it strikes me that I could have many causes for summoning you, My Lord. For example, I could raise the subject of your recent duel with the Earl of Essex. Your entirely illegal duel. We could discuss the length of sentence that would be appropriate for such a flagrant breach of Her Majesty's peace.'

Judas' prick, how did he know –?

'Master Secretary,' I said, 'that was entirely Devereux's fault!'

'Of course it was, My Lord. And, of course, you will know more than enough of how matters stand between myself and the noble Earl to know that I am not displeased to hear you say that. As I'm sure you would upon oath, if I required it.'

Was that it, then? Had I been dragged all the way to Theobalds simply for Cecil to recruit me as a witness in his ongoing war against Robin Devereux, with a threat of arrest for duelling dangled in front of me if I refused?

'Of course,' I said.

'And then there is the matter of your new Countess. I will be blunt with you, My Lord. Many about the court, and in Parliament, think it the height of perversity for an Earl of England to marry a Papist in an age when we pursue and execute Papist priests, and are at war with a Papist power. The simple act of being a Catholic in England today is taken by many as proof of treason. So there are many who would use your marriage against you, My Lord, to question your loyalty to the Queen.'

'Master Secretary, I must protest—'

'No, My Lord,' said the hunchback, cutting me off, 'in truth, the childish quarrels of the nobility, and your choice of a wife, are of little concern to me. And I have even less concern for the ludicrous fears and suspicions of the rude multitude.' He looked away into the distance, then turned back to me. 'But you have been unfortunate, Lord Ravensden,' he said. 'Would you not say so?'

'Unfortunate, Master Cecil?'

'Indeed. I would say you have been unfortunate. As I told your man Iles at the time, we had ample intelligence that the Spanish were about to send a new Armada against us, but it was your report of the fleet you had seen in the Groyne that made the greatest impact on the people. Why, they cried, Lord Ravensden is a great seaman, a true English hero, and he has seen the Armada, *ergo* it must be real. Consequently, and entirely wrongly of course, as soon as the Invisible Armada was exposed as a chimera, much of the blame attached to your name. The blame, that is, for striking fear into the hearts of the people, and causing a great mustering of the army, navy and militia. A very expensive mustering. A mustering that disrupted the harvest. An expense that greatly displeased the Queen.'

'None of that was my doing, Master Cecil!'

'Of course not, My Lord. You know that. I know that. But people will insist on seeing things so very differently to reasonable men like ourselves, and perceptions can be so very difficult to dislodge, don't you find? And then, of course, you were doubly unfortunate to be at Calais when the Spanish galleys ran the Straits. Again, My Lord, you and I know that there was nothing you could do. You had no wind, and your testimony was amply confirmed by our noble ally, the Admiral of Zeeland. But people hereabouts, for example, who have no understanding of winds and tides – nor of ships themselves, come to that – why, such people merely know that the Earl of Ravensden was at Calais when the Spanish went past him. And look at the havoc General Spinola has wreaked, these last months. All the prizes he has taken, and so forth. Why, there are even those who dare to suggest that, because the Earl of Ravensden has a Papist wife, he has turned Papist himself, and deliberately allowed Spinola to slip through the Straits. No doubt after receiving a vast bribe from the Pope, delivered by means of Jesuit agents.' He laughed, but it was a dry, cold laugh. 'Such are the times we live in. But that is the way of it, My Lord. Perception is all, and the perception of you has become unfortunate, shall we say. That is even the case with Her Majesty, alas, despite my best efforts to convince her of your good service and stoutness of heart.'

The lying little shit.

Of course, I did not believe a word of it. Robert Cecil speaking out on my behalf to the Queen was as likely as the Pope dancing a gavotte stark naked in Westminster Abbey. And he could have added himself to the ignorant country folk of Enfield and Cheshunt who had no notion of what a ship was; it was no secret that Secretary Cecil favoured those craven coxcombs who cried up the new galleys that were being built as a jerk of the knee following Spinola's successes. But none of that could detract from the fundamental and unsettling truth of what he had said: both the Queen and the people blamed me for the two dire naval debacles of the last half-year, at least in part because of my marriage to Louise-Marie. And that was why Brick-beard Leveson, not I, would shortly be under sail for the Azores.

'Master Secretary,' I said – and now I was humble, penitent, even imploring – 'Master Secretary, I pray you, get me a command at sea, that I might restore my reputation!'

Cecil shook his head. 'Alas, My Lord, it is very difficult. The Queen has taken against you – yet again, I might add – and all the commands are spoken for. Besides, there are peace talks at Boulogne, and if they prosper, the war could end any day. If it did, of course, the fleet would be paid off, and there would be hardly any commands at all. It is difficult for you – yes, I see that. I see it quite clearly, Lord Ravensden. And I see that what a man in your position needs is a chance to prove yourself to the Queen. For if you can redeem yourself with her, the mood of the fickle multitude toward you will change in the blinking of an eye.'

'Give me such a chance, Master Cecil! In the name of God, sir, I will do my utmost, whatever the chance might be!'

We were riding up onto a little hillock, from which a view of the countryside stretched south, past windmills and church towers, to the smoke of London. For some minutes, Robert Cecil said nothing, seemingly intent only on looking out over the vista before us.

'Tell me, My Lord,' he said at last, 'what do you know of affairs in Scotland?'

Scotland? What in the name of the Virgin's piss did Scotland have to do with anything?

'Only – only the common talk of the streets, Master Secretary. That the King of Scots is so keen to assert his right to—'

I pulled back, suddenly aware of the enormous, even treasonable, error that I had very nearly committed.

'You may speak freely, Lord Ravensden. Look around you. No man can overhear us. But if it reassures you, I shall say it instead. The King of Scots is so keen to assert his right to succeed Her Majesty that he is asking his Parliament for the money to raise a great army, to invade England if necessary.'

'A mad notion, Master Secretary.'

Mad for reasons that surely not even this Cecil could know –

'Quite so, quite so. Perfectly mad. But the King's behaviour is troubling, Lord Ravensden. Erratic, even. Some might wonder whether such a man is fit to be King of England—' Cecil paused and looked at me, and I thought, *Does he know? Can he know?* – 'even if only one day in the very far distant future, of course. God save the Queen.'

'God save the Queen!'

No, he did not know. Or at the very least, he was not certain. Thanks be to God, there was one secret left in the island of Britain that Matthew Quinton knew, and Robert Cecil could only conjecture at.

'Yes, King James has become a problem. There is no doubt of that.'

Aye, a very particular problem to Robert Cecil, who is known to favour the Infanta Isabella – and if Jamie Stuart came to the throne at that moment, nothing could be more certain than that his old ally Essex would be the new chief minister of England, and the hunchback would be the man under arrest. 'A solution to this problem has been put to me, My Lord. It is a daring proposition. Most daring indeed, in truth. It requires bravery and skill. Above all, it requires discretion. There can be no written record of it, and if it were to miscarry, both Her Majesty and I would deny any knowledge of it. Would you be prepared to accept a mission on those terms, Lord Ravensden?'

So that was it. Take all the risk upon yourself, Quinton, my lad, and if at all goes dreadfully wrong, you are on your own, perhaps even to the extent of taking the solitary walk to the scaffold. But what choice did I have? None, by God, and Robert Cecil had known that from the very outset. Which was precisely why he had sent for me, of course.

'With respect, Master Secretary, I am a man presently without honour or employment. Serving the Queen in any way is the summit of my ambition. But if I may ask, Mister Cecil – what would it profit me, if I agreed to undertake this mission?'

'In gold, nothing at all. Indeed, it will cost you a large sum, for you will need to set out one of your own ships. But carrying off such a bold venture as this would put both the Queen and I in your debt, Lord Ravensden. I think you may be confidently assured of further preferment at sea, for instance. Who knows, it is not beyond the bound of possibility that the Queen would look favourably on you for the command of a fleet for, say, the Azores or the Carib Sea – or, if the war really does end, perhaps of a squadron against the Barbary pirates. And, of course, you and your new wife would be welcome at court. Very welcome indeed.'

Perhaps the serpent in Eden had a hunched back, I thought. I could see traps everywhere. But I could see the prizes, too – myself an admiral, and Louise-Marie at court, where she should belong, regardless of her faith. And yet I had to know more before I committed myself. I did not trust this Cecil, any more than I had trusted his father.

'Master Secretary, I must know more of what is entailed.'

'Of course. But it would be best if you had it from the man who instigated the entire business, My Lord. And even if you do not trust me, as I am sure you do not, I believe you will trust him. In fact, I am certain of it, for blood can trust blood, can it not? Come, let us go and talk to him.'

We rode back to the great house, riding through the gatehouse into the outer court, where we dismounted. The Secretary led me inside. The interior was just as splendid as the exterior, with the finest Flemish tapestries vying for space with huge portraits of the Queen and of Cecil's father, the formidably white-bearded Lord Burghley. Servants, of whom there seemed to be an inordinate number, bowed low to the crooked little Secretary, even though he held no noble rank whatsoever.

Cecil took me through into a large library, the walls lined with huge oak bookcases that stretched from floor to ceiling. I did not notice the other man in the room at first, for he was at the far end, close to the window and standing close to the shelves. He was deep in contemplation of a tome that he must have taken down from its place. At first, he was not aware of our approach, but when we were just a few feet from him, he turned and smiled in recognition.

'Master Secretary,' said the tall young man in his gentle Scots lilt, 'and My Lord of Ravensden. It is good to see you again, cousin.'

'And you too, John.'

I stepped forward, and embraced the Earl of Gowrie.

CHAPTER NINE

My blood boils as I read how my grandfather was ensnared by that vile serpent Cecil, and forced to join in one of the most desperate conspiracies in our history. Nowadays, men only cry up the Gunpowder Treason, which happened but a few years after these events in which Earl Matthew was embroiled. This is no mystery: the fifth of November is easy to comprehend, even by the dullest-witted artisan. Blame the Catholics – an unfailing rallying cry in England, God help us – and get blind drunk, nothing more. And, of course, Fawkes and his coterie laid their plot in Westminster, ideal for those sheep-like multitudes who are convinced that nothing important can possibly happen outside the environs of London. So the Gowrie plot, infinitely complex, mysterious, and seemingly Scottish (although in truth, not), is overlooked by posterity, even though it was infinitely more dangerous to the Crown in every respect. But even I, nor, I suspect, my uncle Tristram, who first taught the story to me, had any idea how devilishly complex and dangerous it really was. No man did: no man but my grandfather and Gowrie himself.

The Dowager Countess:

The *Constant Esperance*, that was her name. She was the ship in which my husband had sailed against the Spanish Armada: the real one, not the invisible variety. That June, the Earl took me down to view her during her fitting out. This was in an estuary within the county of Essex, at a place called Pin Mill. Low wooded hills sloped gently down to the water's edge. It was a remote place, reached by the narrowest of lanes. As these were impassable for the state coach of the Earl of Ravensden, all of us were on horseback: myself, the Earl, Iles, Horvath, and a half-dozen others of my husband's retinue. Iles was concerned, protesting that I should not ride in such a condition – that is, in my sixth month – but both the Earl and I dismissed him.

'Christ's teeth, Iles,' he said, 'my grandmother gave birth to the fifth earl when riding into Bedford, got back on the horse straight afterward and rode on to the market cross to berate the mayor for an hour.

Countesses of Ravensden are made of stern stuff, are they not, My Lady?'

I thought that my three prematurely deceased immediate predecessors in that rank did not seem to have been thus, but forbore from saying so. Instead, I reassured the poet, of whom I was increasingly fond: he was a good and eager friend, although, alas, his verses were unutterably execrable.

'My Lord is quite right,' I said. 'You should not worry yourself for my sake, *mon cher* Nicholas. Like all the women of the house of Monconseil-Bragelonne, I could very nearly ride before I could walk. Why, even now the child in my womb will be learning the smell and the feel of a horse.'

But my easy words to Iles were not entirely true. My husband was riding well ahead, eager to catch sight of his precious ship, and I spurred on my horse to catch up with him.

'My Lady?' he said.

'This is a remote place, Matthew,' I said. 'A very remote place, surely, to keep a large man-of-war.'

'It is a convenient harbour. Easy to reach from our London house, and from Bedfordshire. Convenient in so many ways.'

I looked at the fields and woods all around. Apart from the occasional ploughman or charcoal burner, there was hardly a soul to be seen.

'Convenient, too, because of its remoteness from authority, husband? From the Queen's agents, and the customs men?'

The Earl grinned. 'Why, My Lady,' he said, 'whoever might have expected you to start thinking like a privateering venturer?'

The *Constant Esperance* lay upon a mudbank, her bows drawn up onto the shore. Caulkers and occam-boys, as I now knew to call them, were at work on the lower part of her hull, below the water line. Men were pulling on ropes to raise sheerlegs alongside her. Above the high water mark, two dozen or so black, brown or green cannon lay on the shingle, waiting to be put into the ship. Not far away was a pile of muskets, and adjacent to that, a stand of halberds and another of pikes. Whatever voyage the *Constant Esperance* was about to embark upon – and my husband was still suspiciously vague on the matter – it was evident that peaceful trading would not be the principal objective.

Two men approached as we dismounted. Both were dressed in the shabby, careless manner of the English, especially those one encounters outside London. One was a tall, bearded fellow, grey-haired, with an ugly scar running from the top of his head, through the hideous socket where his left eye should have been, to the remains of his nose. My husband approached him at once, and my English was now tolerable enough for me to be able to understand his conversation.

'Well, Avent? We'll have her ready to float on the next spring?'

'Aye, My Lord, God willing. She's still a well found ship, after all these years.'

'That she should be, with the amount of gold I've spent on her. A well found ship. Better than any infernal galley, be it Spanish or English, no matter what the Queen's ministers and the principal officers of the navy say.'

The second man, a shorter and rounder creature than this Avent, said something, but spoke in such a rapid gabble that I found it incomprehensible.

'Who are these men, husband, and what did this one say?' I demanded in French, reckoning that two such unprepossessing individuals would have no understanding of the language of the angels.

'Forgive me, my dear,' the Earl replied, 'this is Elias Avent, master of the *Constant Esperance*, while this—'

The smaller man stepped forward, bowed, and kissed my hand, after the fashion in my country.

'My Lady,' he said in fluent but heavily accented French, 'it is a true honour for a humble subject of the King of Scots to express his respect for the Countess of Ravensden. I am Logan, My Lady. Robert Logan, Laird of Restalrig.'

'Master Logan is a good friend of the Earl of Gowrie, my dear,' said the Earl. 'He is also the new joint owner of the *Constant Esperance*.'

Laszlo Horvath:

The Countess cannot conceal the surprise on her face, and it is evident that her husband has not thought fit to tell her that he has sold a half share in his ship. Nor can she conceal her distaste for this Logan. Neither can Iles, who I can hear talking with the Earl's men. I understand their feelings. Logan is paler, and of course his dress is very different, but in appearance, he reminds me strikingly of a merchant I once knew, far away in the south of the Pannonian Plain. This trader was by far the most duplicitous man I ever encountered, a creature so unscrupulous that he sold his own daughters to the Ottoman governor of Novi Sad. So I wonder if the old legend can be true: which is to say, that somewhere in the world there is an exact twin of each and every one of us. A twin both in appearance and in character.

The Earl of Ravensden:

I laid out my new Dutch waggoner chart upon the table in the captain's cabin of the *Constant Esperance*, afloat at single anchor upon the flood tide.

Avent, Logan, Iles, Horvath and the ship's officers leaned forward and inspected it: Logan with indifference, the rest with suspicion bordering on hostility. My wife sat apart, seemingly intent on watching the flocks of birds flying low over the waters.

'End of the world,' said Groom, the gunner, a testy old Shadwell man.

'Come, Master Gunner,' I said, 'Drake sailed round the world. Why, ships now sail to the Americas nearly every month. This is within our own islands, man!'

Groom looked upon the strange shapes, upon the jumble of islands scattered in apparently random fashion across the chart, and shook his head.

'End of my world all the same, My Lord. Naught but witches and sea-serpents up there.'

Foulis, the lean and pungent Southampton man who served as carpenter, nodded his assent.

'Master Logan,' I said, 'you have been there. Perhaps you can reassure these fainthearts.'

'No witches or sea-serpents, My Lord,' he said in his thick Scots brogue. 'Just no night, this time of the year. And a strange breed of men, that speak Norwegian and still follow Viking law.'

'There you have it,' I said. 'Orkney. Our destination, good sirs.'

'To what end?' said Avent, the only one of Esperance's officers that had anything resembling a decent brain; which was something of a miracle, as that brain had very nearly been hacked out of his head by a Spaniard's blade during the fight off Gravelines.

I stood up and smiled broadly.

'Treasure, my friends. What better end could there be?'

'Treasure?' said Groom, brightening. 'But in *Orkney*, My Lord?'

'I have it upon excellent authority that a great galleon will attempt to run the Pentland Firth, here, between Orkney and the mainland, some time between the tenth and twentieth of next month, August, the Dons not being willing to risk sending it through the Channel. It's carrying enough bullion to settle all the arrears of pay of Spain's Army of Flanders. You know how large that army is, my boys, and its pay is anything up to ten years behind. So imagine just how much gold that will be, eh? And it can all be ours – all of it, that is, but for the share designed for Master Logan, here.' The Scot nodded with appropriate modesty. 'Think on it, my lads. No other investors to rob us of the spoils! And easy pickings, for the Dons won't be expecting a ship as nimble or as heavily armed as the *Esperance* in those parts. The King of Scots has no ships of his own, either, so there's nothing to stop us. We sit here—' I jabbed my finger at the chart – 'behind this island, Hoy, wait for word of the galleon, then fall on it. Exits galore from the great anchorage which lies in the midst of those islands, honest fellows, so whatever the wind, we can sail out and have our fill of Spanish treasure!'

I stood back, grinning broadly. Inwardly, though, I was praying that Avent – and it would only be Avent – did not ask awkward questions, such as where the so-precise intelligence I possessed about the galleon happened to come from, or why the Spanish should take such a great risk while peace talks were taking place at Boulogne, or why the Dons would even consider sailing through the northern seas, where so many of their brethren from the Invincible Armada came to grief. But Avent said nothing, merely staring at the chart in wonderment. I congratulated myself; but then, I have always prided myself on being an excellent liar.

The Dowager Countess:
My husband was a terrible liar.

He could never conceal the truth from me; except, at that time, in one matter, and one alone, of which as yet I had but very little inkling. I might have divined it had there been an opportunity for me to question him about this Logan, as dislikeable a rogue as I ever encountered. What in the name of the dear Virgin was my husband doing consorting with such a man at all, let alone selling him a half share in his pride and joy, the *Constant Esperance*? Did he really need money that badly? And what did Logan have to do with the Earl of Gowrie? My husband had told me of his meeting with his distant kinsman at Theobalds, but was then unconscionably vague about the upshot of their encounter, despite my best efforts to wring the truth from him. Perhaps Gowrie gave My Lord intelligence of this galleon, I thought for the briefest of moments before I looked at my husband again. His expression told me all, for as I have said, he was a terrible liar.

There was no Spanish galleon.

As I looked around the faces of the men in the cabin, though, I knew that the Earl's lies were more than enough to sway his officers, as lumpen a crew as one was likely to find. The prospect of Spanish treasure had them gazing at the chart in admiration, their avarice apparent in every inch of their miserable frames. Truly, the English lust after gold like no other people on earth –

What is that you say under your breath, grandson? That I was attracted to your grandfather partly by the belief that he had a great treasure of gold?

That was not the same thing. Not the same thing at all.

Laszlo Horvath:

The Earl is a terrible liar. Of course, his craven underlings believe every false word that spills from his lips. I put on a show of enthusiasm, of delight at the prospect of the untold riches we are supposedly sailing to seize. For I have two advantages over these others within the cabin.

Firstly, unlike My Lord of Ravensden, I am an excellent liar.

Secondly, I know the true purpose of this voyage.

Nicholas Iles:

My Lord was a terrible liar. But as I watched his performance there in the cabin of the *Constant Esperance*, I realised something more: that he was a terrible actor, too. And that thought brought about the strangest sensation. It was as though a great curtain lifted in my mind, allowing me at last to see clearly what was before me.

This was a stage. My Lord was the principal actor, and a dreadful one. But as I looked around the cabin with my new-found understanding, I realised that he was not the only one in that theatre, truly Shakespeare's 'wooden O' afloat. *Certes*, Avent and the officers were playing their parts from life: they did not realise what was being played out before them. But Logan of Restalrig was acting, of that I was sure. He knew that this story of Orkney was a mere fiction, a tale as tall as those of Robin

Hood. So, too, did the Hungarian; but with him, I had felt from the very first time I met him that everything he did and said was an act. I looked over to the dear Countess, in the corner of the cabin, her hands resting demurely upon her swelling belly.

I felt myself flush, the heat so intense that it threatened to burst through my very skin.

For My Lady was acting too. There was no doubt of it. All of them were acting parts in a play that I had not written, and to which I did not know the ending. Who the playwright was, and who was directing the action, I could not tell. But the heat of my flesh turned at once to cold. I shivered, though it was July. I knew that feeling, knew it too well. It always came upon me at that moment in a play when you know for certain that tragedy and death are about to befall the characters, and there is nothing in the world that you, the spectator, can do about it.

CHAPTER TEN

Laszlo Horvath:

We are sailing north, always within sight of the coast. It is that which the seamen call an easy sail, the wind from the south-west, strong enough to let us make good speed, not strong enough to force us off our course, not an easterly that would push us onto the treacherous rocks and shoals of England's shore. The sea teems with hulls, and I pride myself that I can now tell a fishing boat, bound for the herring shoals, from a collier, taking coals to London. The great fleets of both would be easy pickings for Spinola's galleys, or the ships of Dunkirk, but there is no sign of either, although the Earl has stationed additional lookouts in the ship's tops. He takes pleasure in instructing me in the names of places. Spurn, Humber, Scarborough, Whitby, Tees, Tyne: an endless list, in which I feign interest. This one is famous for its fishery, that for its coal trade, another for its ruinous abbey. And so forth.

It is only when we reach the coast of the territory which the English call Northumberland that he says something of real note.

'Look, Horvath, you see those towers, upon that cliff?' I nod. The towers are plainly visible, outlined against a sky in which dark clouds are gathering. They appear to be ruinous. 'Alnburgh Castle, that. My property. Came into the family through the wife of my uncle, the sixth earl.'

'The sixth? Earl Henry?'

'Ah, so have you been listening after all when I've told you tales of the Quintons! Yes, my uncle Henry. A strange man, Horvath. A cursedly strange man. Or strangely cursed, as many had it. I met him only a few times, but I remember his face vividly. Such a face it was! As though one of old Bosch's monsters had stepped out of the canvas and become flesh. Henry Quinton. Not ever Harry, despite that being the by-name of every Henry since the beginning of time. Named after both the first Earl of Ravensden and the great King Harry the Eighth, of course. He spent all his life searching, although only God or the Devil knew what he was searching for. Travelled here, there and everywhere. Alchemy, necromancy, sorcery – he dabbled in them all, and in the end, one or more of them killed him. Some experiment he was undertaking in a tower of Alnburgh Castle caught fire. They never found a body, but a coroner's jury was convinced of his death all the same. My father, his brother, was even more convinced of the need for him to be dead.'

'Because by that means, your father then became the Earl of Ravensden,' I say. 'The sixth Earl had no sons?'

'No children at all. His poor wife died of a broken heart when he abandoned her and went abroad for years on end. The credulous mob put it out that he'd had her poisoned, and of course when his body never turned up, the same credulous mob were convinced that he'd made a pact with the devil. They say that his evil shade still rides at night, returning from the dead to plague the living. Oh, no need to look like that, my good fellow. The folly of the ignorant, nothing more. If Earl Henry's ghost rides from Ravensden Abbey, I'd have seen it, and if it rides from Alnburgh Castle—'

'My Lord!' Avent's shout interrupts him. 'We should take in sail and put further out to sea. Reckon there's the storm blowing in from the west!'

'Damn,' says the Earl.

He goes back to the poop deck to issue his orders, leaving me looking out toward the distant towers of Alnburgh Castle, and the storm rearing up behind it.

Nicholas Iles:

The storm blew us very nearly to Jutland. I stood upon the deck the whole time, admiring the force of nature in all its majesty, drawing inspiration for a play that I had in mind, a dark story of a mighty tempest —

Not here, Iles. Only the truth, here.

So be it.

I was not upon the deck at all. I was confined to my cabin, if that tiny oblong of canvas partitions and fetid timbers be thought worthy of that name, spewing into a leather bucket. Or, when I missed that target, directly onto the deck. Hence I saw My Lord barely at all. Once, though, he came below decks to see if I still lived. He pulled back the canvas flap and stood there, looking down upon me, swaying easily with each of the insane motions of the ship.

'A summer's breeze, Iles my boy,' he said. 'No more than that. We'll lie up under the lee of Heligoland if we need to.'

I had no more left to spew, and tried to be as cheery as I could. 'Then we will still make Orkney in time to take the galleon, My Lord?'

'Mm? Orkney? Aye, Orkney. Ample time, poet. Be ready to chronicle what you see when we get to – to our destination. But in the meantime, do try and stop puking on the deck, there's a good fellow.'

The Earl of Ravensden:

Damn the gale. It was a bad one, for an English summer at any rate – black skies, ship-killing waves, an evil sea driving us toward the shore of Denmark. I pitied the poet, Iles, retching his guts up, but even some of the hardiest seamen were spewing all over the decks like lubbers. By and by, though, it subsided, and at dawn on an August day, with a watery sun rising astern of us and a gentle southerly breeze very nearly on our beam, Avent and I stood upon the quarterdeck, poring over a rutter and checking our compasses.

'But My Lord,' he said, 'we can still see the cliffs of Heligoland. East-south-east twelve points, by my reckoning four leagues distant. We could not wish a better marker of our position. I can easily set a course direct for Pentland.'

'Indeed you can, Mister Avent. But I would have you set our course for the Firth of Forth, whence we'll sail in sight of the coast.'

'But My Lord, that might add a day or two to the voyage, at the very least – if there was another storm, or if the wind changed, we might miss the galleon altogether!'

Fuck the galleon, there's a much greater game afoot.

'Those are my orders, Mister Avent. The Forth and the shore of Fife, if you please.'

I pulled myself up to my full height and strode to the starboard rail, adopting what I hoped was a pose of unchallengeable authority and warlike purpose. But I could sense Avent's eyes boring into my back, I could see the men within earshot in the waist muttering to themselves, and I exchanged a glance with Horvath, whose expression was strange. It was almost knowing, as though he, and he alone, understood why I had issued my seemingly incomprehensible orders to Avent. That was impossible, of course. There were barely a half-dozen men in the island of Britain who knew the truth of this voyage. And as I gazed out to the northward, across the rolling grey waves of the ocean, it struck me that only two of those men knew the *real* truth, and were playing the others for dupes. It was a reassuring thought, although a false one: for I had yet to learn who the dupes truly were.

The Dowager Countess:

Patience, young Matthew. Perhaps you will learn the truth in due course, unless I change my mind. For it is a truth most dangerous, and I am not certain it is fit for you to know it. Do not be too eager to learn it, then, for it will change your view of everything. *Everything*.

For my part, I knew only a part of the truth at that time: the part which your grandfather had sought fit to entrust to me, after the persistence of my hectoring finally persuaded him to confide in me shortly before the *Constant Esperance* sailed for Scotland. Perhaps it was the enormity of even that amount of knowledge that led me to the next stage of my fate, there at Ravensden House, where I was meant to be resting for the two months or so that remained before the birth of the heir to the earldom.

Such was My Lord's conceit, for rest was the very last thing I had. I could not sleep for worry. My thoughts raced. It was a hot summer, and I was sweating profusely. I prayed endlessly for my husband's life and for the success of the dangerous mission he was about, fingering my rosary and reciting the *Ave Maria*, despite both actions being prohibited by the law of England. In truth, my prayers should have been directed rather closer to home. One sleepless night, in the small hours, the pain began. By dawn, it was unbearable, and four servants had to hold me down as I thrashed about on the bed. Pain beyond description, pain unrelenting, pain that made me scream for hours on end. I knew what the pain meant, and knew at once that I should not have tempted fate and the wrath of God by convincing my husband to confide the purpose of his mission in me. For I had claimed that my ignorance of this purpose was throwing my humours into a furious imbalance, thus threatening the life of our unborn son.

No, ignorance does not upset the balance of our humours. Ignorance is peace. Ignorance is calm. But knowledge, such as the knowledge of a great and terrible deed, overturns the balance, devours it, and spits it out into the flames of hell, which was where my pain now carried me.

The Earl of Ravensden:

'Saint Rule's tower, My Lord,' said Avent.

'And there's the cathedral, and the castle. Saint Andrews, then. A decent enough landfall, Mister Avent, although some way to the north of the one I ordered. But what d'you make of that hull – there, in the estuary, beyond the castle cliff?'

Avent screwed up his eyes. 'On the careen, whoever he is, so difficult to make out his lines. And it's obscured by the sails they've hung out to dry – God knows why they've strung them between those poles, so close to the ship.'

'Your guess, then?'

Avent shrugged. He had been surly and uncommunicative since our dispute off Heligoland. 'Probably a Dutch or Hamburg flyboat, My Lord. Might have been damaged in the late storm, and laid up here to repair.'

'A flyboat. Yes, it would seem to be so. Very good, then, Mister Avent. The rutter says there is a fair anchorage and deep water here, to the north.' I jabbed a finger at the chart. 'We will come to an anchor there, if you please.'

'To an anchor, My Lord? Surely speed is of the essence, if we are to sail north to seize the treasure?'

'We are in good time for the treasure, Mister Avent. Trust me in that. Very good time.'

Doubt was writ large on his damaged face, but loyalty ran deep with Avent. 'Should we not at least hoist our ensign, My Lord, to tell the Scots garrison in the castle who we are?'

'No, Mister Avent, we shall not.'

'As you say, My Lord.'

And so the *Constant Esperance*, flying no ensign, jack or pennants, came to an anchor just outside the mouth of the great river of Tay.

The Dowager Countess:

'She will not live,' said the midwife, thinking that I could not hear.

I glared at her through my tears, but I could say nothing, for a rag was tied over my mouth. The pain racked every inch of my body. It felt as though a torrent was pouring out of me, and I could see the red-stained towels being born away in haste. I screamed and screamed again, although only I could hear each scream. I prayed desperately to every saint I could remember. In my delirium, I thought I could see angels, who transformed into all the previous Countesses of Ravensden, who transformed in turn into demons. I could hear them whispering.

'Failure,' they murmured.

One creature – it might have been an angel, or a demon, or a midwife – said 'Twins, but no hope for them—'

Ah, a kerchief. Thank you, grandson, I had not realised I was crying. But yes, the fact that you are a twin comes down from my family. Two of my brothers were twins, as was our grandfather. And these were boy twins, the elder of whom would have been the Earl of Ravensden. Would have been, had not both of them been born dead. I did not even see them; their bodies were removed at once. And as the pain surged to an even more unbearable peak, my mind began to slip away. I heard the doctor asking if anyone knew of a papist priest who could be persuaded out of hiding to administer the last rites to me. I saw the countesses again, the angels and the demons, and all was dark.

Laszlo Horvath:

Two nights and one day we lie upon the shore of Scotland. The Earl's crew grow more restive with every hour, wondering why we linger when we should be bound for the north, for the Spanish galleon and the promised treasure. He paces the deck, waiting for a message to come to him from the land. A message, or a passenger. A very particular passenger.

It is the morning of the fifth of August. I am on the quarterdeck when I hear the lookout's shout, see the Earl run up from his quarters below and look out to the south.

'Fuck!' he cries.

For there, unfurling her sails as she moves out into open water, is the ship we spied in the bay of Saint Andrews.

'No flyboat, that's for sure,' says Avent.

'Cut for twenty-eight guns,' says the Earl. 'He's our equal.'

'He, My Lord?' I say. 'Are not ships called "she"?'

He smiles, but it is a grim, cold smile. 'That they are, my friend, except when one knows the identity of the captain. Behold, the ensign of Dunkirk, and the man's personal banner, flying from the mizzen. Claims noble descent, does *Meinheer* van der Waecken.'

'Our own ensigns, My Lord?' says Avent. 'Or false flags – those of Denmark, perhaps?'

'If van der Waecken's half the man they say he his, then he'll know us already by our lines – and even if he doesn't, the Scots hereabouts will have told him of us, that's for certain, because they're friends to the Flemings and certainly no friends to the English. So beat to quarters, Mister Avent, unfurl courses, topsails and spritsail, and hoist our own colours if you please, including the arms of Ravensden at the main. Let our friend there know that he fights with true nobility.'

CHAPTER ELEVEN

The Earl of Ravensden:

The Dunkirker held the weather gage, and was coming down upon the breeze. Perhaps the hoisting of our colours and the sight of our guns, the equal of his own, gave him pause for thought; but if so, he gave no sign of it.

'So, Mister Avent,' I said, 'what do you think he will expect us to do?'

The battle-scarred old mariner studied the oncoming ship. She was a fine sight, a trim, well-founded craft with taut sails and a bow that cut the waves purposefully.

'He'll expect us to run for the open sea, My Lord,' the ship-master growled. 'Gain sea room, try to manoeuvre to take the advantage of the wind off him.'

'Indeed. Just like any other captain would do. But I'm not any other captain, am I, Mister Avent?'

The old man had been with me long enough to know the response that was expected of him.

'No, My Lord. You are *el diablo blanco*, the White Devil.'

'As you say, Mister Avent, as you say. So let us be devilish. Helm seven points to larboard, then! Port the helm!'

Avent was dumbstruck. 'To *larboard*, My Lord? But – but that will take us into the Firth of Tay itself! We'll have no sea room, and we have no pilot who knows these waters, with knowledge of the local charts and tides!'

The others upon the quarterdeck, and within earshot down in the waist, were plainly as astonished as the ship-master.

'Oh, but we do, Mister Avent. We have a man aboard who has studied the local charts and tides in far more detail than any illiterate sot of a Dundee pilot will have done.'

'Then where is this man, My Lord? Why have you not brought him to the quarterdeck?'

I smiled. 'Because he's already here, Mister Avent. And I'd thank you to stop quibbling with his orders, else he'll have you flogged for mutiny!'

Avent was open-mouthed, but still remembered his duty sufficiently to knuckle his forehead in salute.

'Aye, aye, My Lord,' he said. 'Seven points to larboard it is.'

Nicholas Iles:

The armourer gave me two pistols, which I tucked into my belt, and a cutlass, which I held with all the confidence of a new-born. Even so, I prided myself that I at least looked the part of a pirate-warrior as I stood by the quarterdeck rail, shouting obscenities and waving my sword threateningly at the oncoming Dunkirker. This was would be a fine fight – Act Three, Scene Two, perhaps, a suitable prologue to the capture of the Spanish galleon off Orkney in Scene Three. My Lord needed a victory, after the calamities that I would have to recount in Act Two; for do not the strict laws of narrative demand that our hero should be brought low, prior to his ultimate triumph?

And yet – and yet, I could not subdue the doubts that beset me, doubts that grew stronger by the day. Why were we there, close to the Scottish coast, when we should already have been in Orkney? Why did My Lord seem to know so much about these waters?

Suddenly, the Hungarian was beside me. I had not been aware that he was even nearby.

'Strange, is it not?' he said –

Laszlo Horvath:

'Strange, is it not?' I said. 'How we come to be here, if we are meant to be in pursuit of a Spanish treasure far to the north.'

Iles looks at me with his customary undisguised loathing. I am not entirely certain whether this represents the common English aversion to foreigners, or whether it is his personal dislike of me. I suspect it might be a large measure of both.

'I trust in My Lord,' he says.

'Of course,' I say, 'he is a great man. But it is remarkable, is it not, how he seems to have such detailed knowledge of this particular place? A man might even think that he has meant us to be here from the very beginning, and that his story of a treasure in the isles of Orkney was but a ruse to persuade the crew to sail with him—'

The bow guns of the Dunkirker fire, and Iles turns away from me. But the look on his face has changed, which is all to the good.

The Earl of Ravensden:

'Hold your course, Mister Avent,' I ordered.

'But My Lord—'

Van der Waecken fired his bowchasers for a second time. Two spouts of water rose, barely two or three cables astern. Twice as close as his first effort.

'Hold your course, I say!'

'Aye, aye, My Lord!'

'Mister Groom! Stern culverins to fire upon my command!' The gunner, down in the ship's waist, saluted and gave his orders. 'As she bears, Mister Groom! Helm amidships, Mister Avent! Steady – steady – *give fire!*'

The quarterdeck of the *Constant Esperance* shuddered as the stern culverins, almost directly beneath our feet, roared out their defiance, sending eighteen-pound roundshot at the Dunkirker. Water spouted up on either side of van der Waecken's beakhead. Another few minutes, another few yards less, and this would be a killing business.

Nicholas Iles:

I swear that the cannon ball can have passed no more than inches from my head. I heard it, I felt the movement of the air. I turned to see it cut through ropes just above me, to my left, and tear a hole through the sail the seamen call the mizzen course.

Our own guns fired once again in reply, and now the air around the two ships was thick with smoke. One of our shots struck the forecastle of the Dunkirker, splintering timber and taking the leg off a man standing close to the rail, who toppled backwards into the sea. The swivel guns mounted on our quarterdeck rail, very close to me, opened fire, although it was still at the limit of their range. But amid all the noise, heat and chaos of battle, I could still hear clearly what passed between My Lord and Avent.

'My Lord,' the master cried, 'if we hold our course, we'll be under the guns of Broughty Castle within a quarter-glass! They're bound to fire on us! On both of us!'

I turned, and saw at once what Avent meant. There, on the north shore of the Tay, was a tall, gaunt tower, with an artillery battery at its base. Through gaps in the smoke, I could just make out the distant, tiny shapes of morrion-helmeted gunners running to man their pieces. From the castle ramparts flew the saltire of the Kingdom of Scots. A kingdom that would not take kindly to having its waters invaded by our private offshoot of the great war between England and Spain.

But then My Lord spoke, and I will remember his words to my dying day.

'Broughty will not fire on us, Mister Avent. Trust me. On this day, of all days, Broughty Castle will not fire on us.'

The Earl of Ravensden:

Avent looked at me as though I were a madman; and perhaps I was. For the truth of it was that I had only the word of one man that Broughty Castle would aid on us on that day, and his word was founded upon that of another, whom he did not trust. But I had committed my eggs to the basket, and prayed to the god of the Quintons that my faith would be justified.

Van der Waecken's bow chasers fired again, but this time, the shots that had found their range at their previous firing fell a few yards astern. The Dunkirker was backing his sails and beginning to fall away slightly to the south, increasing the distance between us. He could not know what the Scottish castle would do, but could surely only assume that it would fire on him if he came within its range. No doubt he hoped that it would fire on me, too, damaging the *Esperance* and forcing us to turn into his path, where we would fall an easy prey.

Every man's eye was on the cannon poking out of their ramparts beneath the lofty tower. We were close enough now to see the lighted linstocks in the hands of the gun-captains. The moment of truth had come. Either the Scottish gunners would avenge their ancestors who fell at Flodden, or –

'Helm hard a-starboard, Mister Avent!' I cried. 'Wear round under the guns of the castle, then bear directly for the Dunkirker, yonder!'

The old man's face was a terrible sight at the best of times, but now he resembled one of the gaping gargoyles lining the parapets of Ravensden church. For he knew, as I did, that wearing ship directly off the castle, presenting our entire side to the Scottish guns, would be fatal if the castle's governor gave the order to open fire. But without a word to me, he transmitted the order to the helmsman on the whipstaff in the steerage. Men scrambled up the shrouds to the yards, and hauled upon the sheets.

Slowly, the bows of the *Constant Esperance* began to turn. To turn directly towards Broughty Castle, and the Scottish guns.

Nicholas Iles:

I swear there was a half-minute when every single man on the ship held his breath at exactly the same time. I could see men with their eyes shut, perhaps in prayer, perhaps in fear. It was a hot day, but many were sweating even more profusely than from the heat alone. I saw one of the ship's boys piss himself, a dark stain spreading across the front of his breeches. I felt only regrets: regrets that I had not had more women, that I had no sons, that perhaps Horvath the Hungarian was right, that no play of mine would ever be performed, that my name would never be remembered.

Slowly, so slowly, the ship came through her turn. With a start, I realised I was standing on the larboard side, but did not remember crossing the deck. We were side-on to the gun-battery in the castle now, but still the gunners did not fire. Away to starboard, to the south-east, the Dunkirker was lying nearly motionless, close to the shore, clearly not sure what would happen next, or of what he should do. I could see the faces of individual gunners, saw them poised at their weapons, ready to take up the recoil if they fired. For a moment, our great English ensign flapped directly in front of me, obscuring my view –

The Earl of Ravensden:

And then we were past the castle, and fully onto the starboard tack. The lead-line confirmed we had ample water beneath our keel. So the time for feints and dainty sailing was over. Time, instead, to attack.

'Fighting sails, Mister Avent!'

'Aye, aye, My Lord!'

The men at the yards furled all the sails except the foresail, main topsail and mizzen. The *Constant Esperance* was rigged as she was when she attacked the Invincible Armada off Gravelines. It was almost as though the old ship was alive, and recalling exactly what she was expected to do.

Van der Waecken was in dire trouble now, and he knew it. True, he still held the weather gage, but it was of precious little use to him. He could not manoeuvre to the south lest he ran onto the shore of Fife. He dare not run to the west and turn under the guns of Broughty Castle, as we had done, for he did not have even an unreliable assurance that those guns would not open fire on him. So, apart from fleeing ignobly to the east, the only thing he could do was what he now did. He began to move north, directly for us. But he had backed his sails, and had nothing like our momentum. Although we were attacking from leeward, the *Constant Esperance* was like a mighty war horse at full gallop, charging a nearly stationary target.

Laszlo Horvath:
It is my first experience of a proper sea-fight.

As we come up toward the Dunkirker, the Earl orders our forward guns to open fire, causing the entire hull to shake and blowing a cloud of thick smoke back across the deck. Then our ship changes course a little so that the guns along the side can fire too. The noise and smell are beyond description. Of course, I have heard and smelled artillery fire before, in battles on the Hungarian Plain or the Danube; but I have never been this close to it, nor do armies ever concentrate so many great guns into such a small space. The hull shudders with every firing, and smoke blinds us for minutes on end. It is how the Calvinist ministers of Carpathia describe Hell.

Now the dying starts. A man standing two paces from me is spun round by a shot, and when he falls to the deck, I see that half his skull is blown away, the brains and blood spilling onto the planks. We are at pistol range, and I fire at the Dunkirker. All around me, the English are screaming oaths at the enemy, and the Flemings are replying in kind.

'God save the Queen! For England and Ravensden!'

'*Lang leve de aartshertogen! Voor God en Sint Eloi!*'

The ships are no more than a dozen yards apart. The Dunkirker has a much larger crew, and they man the sides, brandishing swords and billhooks, waiting for a chance to grapple and board –

The Earl of Ravensden:
Not in this life nor the next, Meinheer van der Waecken, I thought. *You'll have no opportunity to board this day, my friend!*

'Keep firing high, lads! Shatter his rigging! Bring down his masts!'

We had to keep our distance from the Dunkirker. To allow him to close and board would be fatal, but I trusted in my gun crews: reliable, experienced men, some of whom had sailed with me for the best part of twenty years. Now, at last, we were fighting in the English way, the way that had done for the so-called Invincible Armada: attack on a curving course, fire bow, broadside and stern guns in turn, take the ship through a full figure of eight and repeat the attack. Groom barked his orders, each gun firing as it bore, the smoke rolling back over the deck upon the south-westerly breeze. Chain-, bar- and langrel-shot whistled through the air, slicing through the rigging and decapitating any man in its way. Our rate of fire was better than the Dunkirkers, and now we would see if our seamanship was better, too –

'On my command, Mister Avent – wait – wait – now! Helm hard a'starboard!'

'Aye, aye, My Lord!'

Our beakhead was clear of the stern of the Dunkirker, and if we turned smartly enough, we would be able to rake him, sending a murderous broadside through his fragile deck to slaughter those on his main gun deck, or at the very least, use our stern guns to shatter his quarterdeck –

But van der Waecken was too good a seaman for that, although he had just ceded the weather gage. He put his helm over at once, and men scuttled up to the yards to adjust his sails, seemingly oblivious to our murderous cannonade. The Dunkirker began to fall away toward the west, thus keeping his stern well clear of our main battery.

'Damnation,' I cried. 'Fucking damnation! Very well, Mister Avent, bring her round, we'll charge him again, and again after that if we need to!'

But all the while, I had another thought in my mind. We were well into the afternoon now, and the tide was upon the ebb. If this truly was the day, and if all had gone to plan, then our cargo would be on its way. Our very unusual and very precious cargo. I had to finish the Dunkirker as quickly as possible, to be ready to receive it.

Laszlo Horvath:

The enemy is moving away from us, and we are turning to pursue him. Suddenly there is a great cheer from the Earl and his men. The sound of a loud crack carries over from the Dunkirker, and as I watch, the rearmost of his three masts, the one called the mizzen, falls down over his stern. The ropes securing it to the mainmast pull taut, and many snap. But not all do.

'The main's hanging by a thread, my boys!' he shouts. 'We have him now, by God!'

But Mars is a fickle god, as I had learned many times in the wars in the east. The Dunkirker is still firing, and almost at once, we feel the impact of a cannonball right at our stern. At once, the ship slows and begins to turn, the head swinging round toward the open sea, away from the enemy.

The Earl of Ravensden:

'Rowle and rudderstock both shot through, My Lord!'

I stared blankly at the boy who brought me the report. A splinter protruded from his shoulder, blood drenching his chest and the few tattered rags of what had been his shirt.

'Then get forward, lad! Find the carpenter, tell him and his crew to make haste and repair it! Then get the barber to pull out that oak and stitch you up.'

'Aye, My Lord!'

I stamped upon the deck. Van der Waecken was finished, if we could only get up to him. But with the wind now directly astern of him, he still had enough wind in his sails to make headway. Whereas the *Constant Esperance*, unable to steer, was being pushed away from him by the tide, our sails unable to counter the effects of the strong ebb. I cursed our luck, and prayed that it was not an omen.

Nicholas Iles:

Guns, drums, and trumpets stop the soldiers' ears,
From hearing cries and groans; and fury rears
This fatal combat to so strange a height,
That higher powers express the effects of fright.
Great Neptune quaked and roared, clouds ran and pissed,
The winds fell down, and Titan lurked in mist.
Then belch huge bullets forth, smoke, fire, and thunder:
Their fury strikes the gods with fear and wonder!

True, there was no rain, and no mist either. But what did that matter? The rhyme was all, and as I was fast learning, nothing on earth inspires a poet's muse more than the thrill and dread of battle.

The Earl of Ravensden:

The Dunkirker fell further away to the north-east upon the wind and the ebb flowing out of the Tay. I could see van der Waecken's men, working feverishly to erect jury rigs and to repair the other critical damage to his ship. But they would not be in time. My carpenter's crew had already repaired our damage astern, and our rudder was answering the helm. Within a half turn of the glass, we would be able to wear and make sail toward the enemy. The notorious van der Waecken, the most brilliant of all the Dunkirk privateers, would fall an easy prize to Matthew of Ravensden: a fine omen ahead of the main business of the day, which would change the fates of two kingdoms. For this was the day, without a doubt. I was certain of it.

'Herring boats coming out of the Tay, My Lord,' said Avent. 'Strange. Never seen fishermen so happy when putting to sea.'

It was true. As the tiny craft approached, I could hear singing, could see the fishermen raising flasks to their lips. I sent Cameron, the one Scot in the crew, up into the bows to hail his fellows. His words had their effect: one of the boats scudded up toward our quarter, a rarity in itself for a Scottish craft to place itself voluntarily under the guns of an English man-of-war.

'Whence the rejoicing, boys?' I cried, affecting what I hoped was a passable imitation of the seafaring folk from Alnburgh, whom these Scots might perchance look on more favourably as being very nearly their own kind.

I wished for one answer, but received quite another.

'A great day, *Sassenachs*!' shouted a mean fellow in the stern of the fishing boat. 'Lord Gowrie and his brother dead at Perth! Tried to kill the King, God sooth, but the royal green coats did for them! Slaughtered on their own stair in Gowrie House!'

'So you cheer the life of King James?' cried Avent.

The fisherman spat over the side. 'A pox for Jamie Stuart, who'll soon rule over you Sassenachs too, God help you. But we're Dundee men good and true, and the Gowries ruled Perth.' The man lifted his tankard. 'We hate fucking Perth!'

I barely heard the fisherman's words. A red film, akin to a torrent of blood, was clouding my eyes. *John – young, poor, brilliant, dead John Ruthven –*

And poor Matthew Quinton, too. For if my kinsman's plan had miscarried so fatally at Gowrie House, then it was a fair wager that I was set upon an inexorable path to the gallows.

We were through our turn, the men setting the sails as Avent and the helmsman put us onto a course to bear down on the crippled Dunkirker.

My men were lining the wales, eager to finish her and take the fair prize that they had fought and bled for.

'Master Avent, there!' I cried. There was, perhaps, one hope left. One thing, and one alone, that could save me from a traitor's death. 'Bear away, if you please! A new course, south by east!'

'South by east, My Lord? *South*...by east?' said Avent, his tone turning swiftly from protest to anger. 'Away from the Dunkirker? Away from the galleon in Orkney?'

'Those are my orders, Mister Avent. Away from the Dunkirker, and Orkney.'

CHAPTER TWELVE

The Dowager Countess:
The dead countesses were gone, the angels and the demons with them. Instead, there was light. At first, before I opened my eyes, I believed it to be the light of heaven, and rejoiced that I would soon look upon the saints, and the Virgin, and the face of God. But then I realised I could still feel pain. Not the terrible, unbearable pain of before, but pain nonetheless; and surely there was no pain in heaven, for that was what every priest at every Mass I had ever attended proclaimed? But I had not been able to attend Mass for so very long. Perhaps eternal pain in purgatory was the price of such a grievous sin?

I blinked, and looked upon the familiar, cracked ceiling of my room in Ravensden House. Widow Jones, my husband's vast Welsh housekeeper, leaned over me, assailing my senses with her foul breath, unable to conceal her disappointment that this unsuitable slip of a papist countess still lived. By some miracle, then, I had survived, although my children, twin boys, the heirs to Ravensden, had not.

I had ample time to mourn them, during the long August days that I lay there, slowly recovering my strength. But soon there were others to mourn, too. A few days later, word reached London of the strange events that had taken place on the fifth day of the month at Gowrie House in Perth. The official story, the one told by the King of Scots and his hired scribblers, had it that the King was out hunting when he was accosted by Alexander, Master of Ruthven, brother of the Earl of Gowrie, and thus another distant kinsman of my husband. Sandy, as he was by-named, told James Stuart that he should come to Perth at once to interrogate a mysterious stranger who had been found in a field, carrying a pot of gold. So the King and his party rode there, but found both brothers behaving very strangely. After dinner, Sandy took him to a tower chamber, where – Well, according to the story that came down from Edinburgh, Sandy began to wrestle with the King, threatening to kill him. His courtiers, standing outside the house, saw his head protruding from a window, screaming 'Murder!' Some of them, led by a fellow named

Ramsay, rushed up a stair, slew Sandy, and then slew Lord Gowrie in turn, when he came to his brother's aid. Within hours, it seems, the King and his men had decided upon the one acceptable truth: namely, that the Ruthven brothers, secret dabblers in the dark arts of necromancy and devil-worship, had sought to kill the King of Scots, there in their own house in Perth.

What, grandson, you think it a tall story? You think the tale of a mystery man with a pot of gold incredible? You disbelieve, then, the words of the Prayer Book service to celebrate the King's deliverance that you once took part in, every fifth of August, in the heretical – that is, the Anglican parish church of Ravensden, before such fripperies were abolished by our enlightened Lord General Cromwell and his lickspittles in the Rump Parliament?

So did I, from the first moment I heard it.

So did all of London, if not the world. Soon there were very different versions of the story, put about by the enemies of James Stuart: versions in which the King and his men were the murderers, who had set out deliberately to destroy the young brothers. Since that day, all sorts of other strange tales have sprung forth to explain what happened.

But you see, I had an advantage over almost everyone in the world who heard the tale of the affair at Gowrie House.

I knew that the Ruthven brothers had not plotted to kill King James. Instead, thanks to the confession I had finally managed to extract from the Earl before he sailed, I knew precisely what they intended to do.

And because of that, I feared desperately for the fate of my husband.

Laszlo Horvath:

There is much murmuring among the men. I go down to the main deck and move forward through that dark, low space, making for the cook's galley forward, where I will take a bowl of the tepid, foul-tasting mess that he calls lamb stew. All around me, men are talking in low voices. They do not seem to care that I can hear them. They know I am a foreigner, so to a man, they believe either that I cannot speak English or that I am an imbecile. Or both.

'Earl's gone mad. Possessed by that new Papist witch of a wife. Did you see her, when we were fitting out? A Jezebel, a whore of Babylon. She'll be cuckolding him with Jesuit priests, mark my words.'

'Gone mad? Turned coward, more like. We had the Dunkirker. All that plunder we could have had from her.'

'Fuck plunder. What of the treasure we were meant to have? What of the galleon?'

'All the fault of his Papist whore of a witch-countess, I tell you. And she's got no tits, neither.'

I listen, but say nothing. I recall a mutiny I once took part in, among the Wallachian regiments during the campaign of Nicopolis. This is how it began. Once men lose confidence in their officers, it is but an easy step to the taking of those officers' heads.

Nicholas Iles:

Even from a distance, from the sea, it was a remarkable sight. The land fell steeply to the water's edge, purple heather-carpeted slopes giving way to precipitous cliffs. And there, in the midst of them, was the most astonishing castle I had ever seen. Admittedly, it was not large. Indeed, it was a very small place, its low buildings and walls crowded into an impossibly minute space. But those same buildings and walls seemed to be carved directly from the sea-stack on which they stood. On all four sides, the walls sat atop cliffs that fell straight to the sea, a hundred or more feet below. Waves lapped against the rocks, and seabirds swooped all around the sea-girt towers. Fast Castle did not need the vast curtain walls of, say, a Dover or a Tantallon, the enormous red fortress that we had sailed past earlier that day, a few miles to the north. Its location, and the security which that afforded, made its unusual name entirely appropriate. For this was fast indeed, an impregnable fastness that could withstand vast armies far better than many much grander fortresses.

It would be a glorious setting for a drama, but as I stood upon the deck of the *Constant Esperance* as we sailed south along the Scottish coast, I had no thoughts at all of plays or poetry. Instead, I fretted, and bit my lip. For two years, I had set My Lord upon a pedestal. I had venerated him. Here was the perfect hero, whose story would be my road to fame and riches. Yet I could not explain or excuse whatever he was now about. The galleon at Orkney was a lie. I did not need to listen to the mutinous whispers of the men, nor to the persuasive insinuations of Laszlo Horvath, to know that. God in Heaven knew what he had been doing, waiting at the mouth of the Tay. Only that self-same God in Heaven knew what we were now about, sailing directly for this strange castle upon a cliff. I continued to hope against hope that My Lord had some secret, higher purpose in all of this, but I could see no sign of it.

With a heavy heart, I realised that for me, Matthew Quinton was now a hero with feet of clay.

Laszlo Horvath:

He attempts the direct approach. The ship anchors to the north-east of the castle, and we go ashore in a longboat, the Earl leading a party consisting of Iles, myself, and a dozen chosen men. Iles is unusually quiet, and looks away when the Earl speaks to him. This interests me, but I have no opportunity to explore the possibilities that this might present. Instead, we land upon a small gravel beach and begin a scrambled ascent of the cliffs. At length, we come to the landward side of the castle, but the drawbridge is raised. Without it, there is no way of crossing the deep chasm that falls away to the churning waters below.

The Earl of Ravensden:

'Ho, Fast Castle!' I cried. 'I am Ravensden. You know of me. I am the lord of Alnburgh, a friend to your master Logan of Restalrig, and kin to My Lord of Gowrie.'

I prayed that word of the calamity which had taken place in Perth had yet to reach this remote place. I also prayed that the said Logan of Restalrig had not got here before me, because if he had –

'Ravensden? The Earl? The one who fought the Armada, and at Cadiz?'

It was a woman, her head just visible above the rampart of the gatehouse. She spoke in a strong Scottish accent, but it was of the lowland variety, not too different to the speech of my tenants around Alnburgh.

'The same, goodwife. We are here upon a matter that relates to the Earl of Gowrie.'

'Is it so, now? Well, then, My Lord, you'll know the watchword.'

Watchword. There was a watchword. And John of Gowrie, utterly convinced that God was with him, that his scheme would succeed, and that the course of action I was now about would never be necessary, had omitted to tell me what it was.

'Watchword? Damnation, woman, I need no watchword! I am Ravensden, kin to Lord Gowrie, I tell you! The Laird of Restalrig will be most displeased with you if you do not admit me!'

'You can tell him that yourself, My Lord,' said the impudent wench. 'He's expected here, that he is.'

I was silent, digesting this intelligence. If Logan was expected at any time, I had to take action immediately. But the strumpet in the castle seemed most unlikely to be shifted. I could have offered her gold, of course, but to obtain it, she would have had to lower the drawbridge – and even I had to confess to myself that not even the most stupid sentinel ever to stand guard was likely to be so foolish.

On the other hand, the hussy at the rampart appeared to be the one and only sentinel of Fast Castle. There was no sign of another living soul; a dog yapped in the courtyard, but that was all. One woman and one dog. Even if there chanced to be a stray groom or scullion, about their business in the kitchens, it was hardly a garrison to strike fear into the heart of a besieging army. If I elevated a saker or two and peppered the castle walls, I could doubtless frighten her into submission –

But that would take time, and time was a luxury I did not possess.

'Very well, goodwife,' I said, 'I shall return to my ship and await your master's return. But he will be most displeased with you. Most displeased indeed.'

Nicholas Iles:

We returned to the *Constant Esperance*, and I digested what I had just seen. Matthew Quinton, the mighty Earl of Ravensden, repulsed from a castle gate by a mere goodwife? It seemed beyond all belief. Would Caesar have turned back from the Rubicon if just one old hag bade him defiance from the other side of the stream? Would Joshua have commanded his trumpets not to sound at Jericho if one harlot on the ramparts was mildly insolent?

No. For they were true heroes, not men of straw.

Horvath sidled up to me. 'What are we doing here, friend Iles?' he whispered. 'What in the name of God is *he* doing here?'

I stepped away from him, but my thoughts were in turmoil. I went below, to my tiny canvas-shrouded space, and wept.

I took out the sheet on which I had written the title *The Glorious History and Famous Deeds of Matthew Quinton, Earl of Ravensden*, and the prologue spoken by the Chorus:

I sing thy arms (Bellona), and the Man's
Whose mighty deeds outdid Great Tamberlane's.

Thy Trump (dire goddess) send, that I may thunder,
Some wondrous strain, to speak this man of wonder –
This man of wonder.
I tore the paper into tiny pieces.
Laszlo Horvath:
Night falls, the sun setting behind the cliffs to the west. We can see one light burning in the windows of Fast Castle, a thin wisp of smoke coming from its chimney. This confirms him in his impression that the place is very nearly empty.

Once again, we descend the ship's side and get into the longboat. But we are no longer bound for the shore. One man with a lantern sits in the bows, the Earl, Iles and myself in the stern with the helmsman. The poet seems more sullen than usual. Perhaps this is simply a passing mood, one of those fits of melancholy to which his kind appear to be addicted. Or perhaps it is the effect of my words.

The remaining men row. They, too, are sullen, as well they may be. The Earl has deprived them of not one prize but two, and now he has them out on the water at night, with little moonlight, pulling directly for the base of the cliffs on which Fast Castle stands. They can hear, as we at the stern can see, the waves breaking on the rocks. If he gets our course wrong, every man in the boat is liable to drown, and they know this. But the Earl's name and reputation still have a power to them, and more than enough men in the ship's crew are convinced of their potency to volunteer for the longboat.

For there is a new rumour sweeping through the lower deck. The cynics say that this rumour has been planted there by the Earl himself, to delude gullible men, to distract them from seeking reparation for the riches denied to them thus far in our voyage. But others say that they should trust the Earl, that he has done right by them in the past, that he will give them their just deserts now.

He has been here before, these men say. He has been to this castle. He knows exactly what he is looking for.

And what he is looking for is the most valuable treasure in the island of Britain.

Nicholas Iles:
I sat in the stern of the boat, cursing at myself for allowing him to persuade me to come.

'It's a sight you'll not want to miss, poet. A wonder of nature. And within it, a treasure beyond – Well, a treasure, at any rate. You'll want to write this scene.'

I had not been able to pluck up the courage to tell him I was leaving him. I would take my chances in London again, attempt to remove the charges standing against me, make a new life. Find a woman, perhaps. Act again, if my name were cleared. Write for the stage, even, if necessary only in the lowest capacity of all: scribbling the additional lines and minor speeches that the likes of Shakespeare did not have the time to write before they moved on to their next commissions.

No, I had not told him. For one thing, I feared his reaction, especially aboard his own ship, so very far away from the safety of London. He might throw me over the side – old men in the crew told me of when he did exactly that, to a man who crossed him while sailing in the waters off Hispaniola. Or, nearly as bad, he might put me ashore, in these wild northern parts with their strange, violent people, who spent centuries on end feuding with each other and raiding across the border. Poetry had no place in the north, that much was clear.

So I went along. But as we got ever closer to the rocks, I cursed myself for staying silent. In the darkness, the towering black cliffs seemed even taller than they did in the day. The waves broke over the rocks, the water forming fantastical shapes as it spat up into the air. It was possible to see the screaming faces of dead men, there in the foam. Closer and closer –

The Earl of Ravensden:

'Steady the helm,' I ordered. 'Keep the bow aiming just to the left of that window, up in the west tower -'

'I see no window, My Lord!' cried Bentley, up in the bow with the lantern.

Neither could I, but I was not going to tell the men that. I had come this way only once, in daylight, some six years earlier. Logan had given the orders, and Napier, the mathematician, sitting at the stern as I was now, had shat himself in fright. I cursed the fact that only the argumentative goodwife was in residence; for if the castle had anything like a full garrison, there would have been a light in the window I sought.

The boat was rearing up now, riding the swell as we came ever nearer to the rocks. Iles and even Horvath clung onto the wales with grim determination. For my part, I silently mouthed the words of the Forty-Sixth Psalm.

God is our refuge and strength, a very present help in trouble. Therefore will not we fear, though the earth be removed, and though the mountains be carried into the midst of the sea; though the waters thereof roar and be troubled, though the mountains shake with the swelling thereof. Selah.

For the thousandth time, I wondered where or what the fuck 'Selah' was.

'Rock – dead ahead—'

Bentley turned, the lantern lighting up his terrified face and giving him the look of a phantom.

'Port the helm! Hard a'larboard!' I cried.

I grabbed the tiller myself. There was a loud crack, then another. I thought the bow must have struck, and that our end had come. But the two bow oarsmen on the starboard side raised their hands, and I knew in that instant that it was only their oars shearing off. A surge of the tide pushed us past the rock, into the channel that I knew. We were in.

Nicholas Iles:

Despite the heaviness of my heart, I marvelled at the sight before me. We were in a large sea cave, illuminated both by our boat's lantern and, strangely, blazing torches, set in holders fastened to the rock face. At the far end, what appeared to be a tunnel, again lined by torches, seemed to lead upwards, presumably to the cellars of the castle above. On either side of the cave were relatively level rock ledges, high above the point reached by the breaking waves; although in any case, these had very little force within the confines of the cave. And the ledges were stacked high with barrels, boxes, chests of all sorts.

'Behold, Logan's treasure,' said My Lord. 'Or to be exact, the treasures of half the men of rank on both sides of the border, who would rather that the Queen's exchequer or the King of Scots' treasury were unaware of their existence. This place has another purpose, too. After all, if an English lord and a Scottish lord both know exactly where their principal riches are kept, what is the point in raiding each other? Nothing has kept the peace on the border more effectively these last twenty years than Fast Castle's cave.'

'But if every great man of the border knows this is here,' I demanded, 'why have none of them attempted to seize it all? And why has Logan himself not absconded with it?'

'Logan is a good man of business, my friend, which means he knows he'll live rather longer by charging extortionate commission for storing men's property here than by robbing the lords of the Border Reivers, men who head families that have been fighting constantly for five hundred years. Lords who know more ways to kill a man as painfully as possible than the Spanish Inquisition. There wouldn't be a hermit's cell in the mountains of China remote enough to hide Robert Logan if he betrayed any of us – of them, that is – and he knows it. As for why no-one has ever attempted to seize it all – how would any man get it all out, when the only ways in and out are one narrow passageway to and from the castle and a perilous sea channel, so narrow that only one small boat can go through it?'

The man in the bows secured us to a mooring ring, and we stepped up onto the more southerly of the rock ledges.

'What is it we seek, My Lord?' asked Horvath.

'A casket,' said the Earl. 'One small, bejewelled casket. It should be one of the smallest things in here, and it should be on its own. A gold sovereign to the man who finds it.'

The boat's crew set about the task with vigour, possession of a gold sovereign being well beyond the wildest dreams of most of them. Even I, who had held sovereigns in my hand before (and lost them, soon after), set to with a will.

Laszlo Horvath:

It takes perhaps a half hour of searching behind barrels, moving crates, and shining flaming torches into dark corners. At last, a shout comes from one of the men, a hard drinking Londoner named Starkey.

'My Lord!' he cries. 'Is this it, My Lord?'

We go over, he inspects it, and casually hands the gold coin to Starkey, whose eyes widen at the prospect of the amount of ale this will buy him.

'Well done, Starkey,' he says. 'Well done indeed.'

I stand by it as he opens it. I expect to see jewels, at the very least; perhaps a lost treasure of the Caesars, or the Grail itself.

Instead, the casket contains an old cup, some papers, and a dead snake.

The men look at each other. Their eyes betray their disappointment, but there is more, with some of them: there is anger.

But the Earl is beside himself. He smiles, and nods vigorously. He takes hold of the cup and the snake, looks at them for a moment, then throws them into the sea. He snatches the papers, checks them, and thrusts them inside his buff jacket. Clearly, they are the treasure. These few scraps of paper are what we came to Fast Castle for.

The Earl of Ravensden:

The papers were not many, and they were light, but it seemed to me as though the bundle weighed a hundredweight. As my father used to say, 'Words can be the heaviest burden of all', and he was never more right. For words can change the destiny of kingdoms, too, and that was certainly the case with the ones I now carried.

There was a commotion at the far end of the cave – a shout – a clash of steel on steel.

I swung round, and my men thrust torches and our lantern toward the noise. Men were coming into the cave by way of the passage from the castle. Armed men, who were already crossing swords with Jackson, whom I had ordered to stand guard. And at their head was Robert Logan, sword drawn, clad in a breastplate, looking every inch the Reiver warlord that he was.

'Ye're a fucking duplicitous shit, Ravensden!' he bellowed.

'Simply retrieving my kin's own property, Logan. John of Gowrie asked me to fetch it, in the event—'

'A duplicitous shit and a bad liar! Gowrie's dead at Perth, but you knew that full well before you came here! I'll have back whatever ye've ta'en, and I'll see your head on a spike!'

With that, Robert Logan lifted his sword and charged.

CHAPTER THIRTEEN

Nicholas Iles:
The ledge allowed precious little space for standing, let alone fighting. But Logan and his men were between us and our boat, so we would have to fight our way through them. My Lord led the way, crossing swords with Logan himself and forcing the Scot back. I edged around to his side, keeping my back against the boxes and barrels, hoping to avoid an encounter with one of the ferociously armed men at Logan's back. But one of them came for me, screaming some obscenity in the Scots tongue. I weaved away from his blade, executed a perfect ..., and pierced the varlet to the heart, between his ribs –

No.

I slipped. The surface of the rock ledge was wet, and my feet went from under me. The Scotsman's blade flashed above my head; if I had still been upright, it would have sliced through my neck. But my feet flew forward, striking the Scot in the knees and knocking him backwards. The man waved his arms frantically, then fell into the water below. I was about to join him –

A hand gripped my arm, and pulled me back to safety.

'One day, we shall discuss repayment,' said the Hungarian, in the moment before he turned and traded blows with the next of Logan's men.

The Earl of Ravensden:
I fought Logan nearly back to the boat. He was a hard fighter, but like most of the Reivers I had ever fought, his swordplay was of the cruder variety – ugly great cuts and slashes intended to intimidate farmers and slice open English horse-thieves. This was a stage below even the brutal blade-work we seamen employed upon each other, and a very long way below the elegant Italianate duelling skills practised by the Queen's courtiers. The sort that, say, two Earls of England might conceivably have employed against each other on Hampstead Heath.

'I'm toying with you, Logan,' I cried as I forced him back against the rock face, aiming a thrust at his side which deliberately missed by inches.

'You know I'm the better swordsman. Better by far. Withdraw now, man, with your honour intact.'

He cut at my shoulders, but I brought up my sword and deftly parried the attack.

'Not until I get back what you've taken, Quinton!'

He sliced downward, aiming for my waist, but it was a clumsy move. I had ample time to parry, and could have pierced him to the heart there and then, had I wished.

'In fuck's name, Logan, look at me! Look at my men! What have we taken? What can we have possibly concealed about us?'

He held his blade out in front of him, but did not attack.

'Don't take me for a fool, My Lord. I know what you've got. The only thing that would make you dare to come here, with Gowrie dead and half of Scotland believing he tried to kill the king. You've taken the letters, Quinton.'

I kept my sword level with his. I fixed my eyes on Logan's, looking for the first sign of a movement of the eyeballs, the slightest forewarning of his next attack.

'And what do you know of the letters, Logan?'

'What Gowrie told me. What every man of rank in these islands knows. He never showed me the contents.'

'And you never thought to look?'

'He made me swear so many oaths, I dared not. And he protected the casket with some of his magical charms. An undead snake, the conduit for Satan into this mortal realm, for one. My soul would have gone straight to hell if I had even touched those papers,' said Logan. 'Strange that yours has not, My Lord.'

'Perhaps my soul is already there. *El diablo blanco*, remember.'

Silently, I gave thanks to God that Robert Logan, the cynical, devious man of business, was, at bottom, as superstitious and as frightened of witchcraft and eternal damnation as any simpering virgin. But then, it seemed to be a peculiar trait of the Scots, this abiding obsession with witchcraft.

I could afford a glance to either side, and saw that the battle was going the way of my men. This was due in no small part to Horvath, whose fighting skills, honed in the great war in the east, were of the most formidable sort. So, too, was his tactical sense. Taking his cue from me, he was being careful only to wound, and then not seriously. The rest of my men, in turn, were following Horvath's lead. We were beating back Logan's men, but taking care not to kill.

'I'll make you an offer, Logan,' I said. 'The remaining part of the *Constant Esperance*, in return for the letters. The ship will be yours. What d'you say?'

'A ship, My Lord Ravensden? If the letters are half of what men say they are, they're worth an entire Armada's worth of ships.'

'True. But I think you have need of only one ship, Logan of Restalrig.'

'How so?'

'Unless the border's moved in the night, perhaps due to some of our dead friend's incantations, then we're still in Scotland. I'm a lord of England, an alien in this kingdom. I can't be guilty of treason here, Logan. But you're still a subject of the King of Scots. And I imagine that at this very moment, that self-same King is intent on tracking down all the known friends and likely accomplices of the Earl of Gowrie. Your dealings with the Earl are common knowledge, my friend, and thus some clerk is probably scratching your name at the very top of the list of wanted men the King's ministers are compiling, or have already compiled. Just how long do you think it'll be before Jamie Stuart's men come for you, Robert Logan?'

I could see the indecision in the man's eyes.

'Ye're saying I should leave Scotland? Leave Fast and Restalrig behind?'

'Fast and Restalrig are already gone, Logan. You know that, deep in your heart. They'll be the property of an attainted traitor, and thus forfeit to the crown. But if you have the ship, you can be on your way to a new life within hours.' I waved my sword point toward the other contents of the cave. 'A very comfortable new life. I can't see many of John of Gowrie's old friends coming after you to demand their property back, can you? They'll be burning the incriminating letters as we speak, then keeping their heads down for years. So I'd reckon you could appropriate a fair portion of the contents of this cave and not face any consequences. Should you wish so to do, of course.'

Logan stared at me, long and hard, but I knew his decision was already made.

'*Pax*, lads!' he called out to his men.

'Hold, men!' I cried.

The fighting ceased at once. Wounded men on both sides sank to their knees, groaning and tearing their shirts to make bandages.

'You'll give me the ship now? This very hour?' said Logan.

'She's yours as soon as I've cleared her of my own possessions,' I said. 'Horvath! Iles! Here, if you please. You need to witness a document, gentlemen. A bill of sale.'

Nicholas Iles:

At dawn, we rode out over the drawbridge of Fast Castle, on horses supplied by Logan of Restalrig. When we reached the summit of the cliff, My Lord reined in. Horvath and I, the only men accompanying him, did likewise, and followed his gaze out to sea, to the longboat putting out toward the anchored *Constant Esperance*. If the Earl felt any regret at parting with the ship in which he had fought the Spanish Armada, he did not show it. Instead, he seemed to be in a markedly cheerful temper.

'Poor Logan,' he said. 'How do you think my crew will receive him?'

I thought back, to all the discontent and incipient mutiny aboard the ship during our voyages upon the coast of Scotland. I thought of the bitterness upon the lower deck when the longboat returned from the cave, and word spread among the men that the only treasure the Earl had brought aboard, out of all the riches piled up in Logan's store, was a small bundle of old letters.

'They will be discontented,' I said. 'They've been deprived of the prize money they were promised—' he glared at me – 'that they believed they were promised, and now they find that an unknown Scotsman owns the ship outright.'

I did not add that they were my thoughts, too. Matthew Quinton had betrayed his men, and he had betrayed me.

'Yes, I rather think that's how they'll think,' said the Earl, merrily, and seemingly oblivious to my discontent. 'In fact, I wouldn't be surprised if Master Logan, there, doesn't face an out-and-out mutiny as soon as he tries to order the ship to sea. I wouldn't be shocked to learn, say, that Avent and the men take control of the ship at the first opportunity, put Logan ashore, seize his treasure, and sail her to a safe port in England. I wouldn't be surprised at all.'

With that, he turned and began to ride south, toward the English border. I exchanged a glance with Horvath, whose face was as inscrutable as ever; but his slight nod indicated that we had the same thought. The Earl's message to Avent, despatched from Fast Castle and ordering both that his sea-chest be sent ashore and to expect the imminent arrival of a new commander, evidently contained an additional set of instructions, of which Robert Logan of Restalrig knew nothing at all.

The Earl of Ravensden:

I took them south, toward the English border, by way of the back roads further away from the sea; roads I knew well from my days in hot pursuit of Reivers who stole cattle from Alnburgh lands. My reasoning was that, by now, the Scots were bound to have soldiers on the main road and at the border – partly to prevent Gowrie's younger brothers from fleeing to England, partly to demonstrate to the people that the shocking event at Perth had been an aberration, that King James still remained in full control of his kingdom.

We dismounted at a ruined hovel in a forest glade, a mile or so north of where I knew the border to be, with another two miles from there to Berwick, the first town in England. Once there, we would be safe.

After I had explained all this, Horvath said 'I should scout ahead, My Lord, to see if any Scottish troops lie in our way.'

'No need for that, Horvath. We can move forward together, and if there's any sight of patrols, we can wait under cover until nightfall, then ride hard for Berwick. Besides, I doubt if Scottish border guards would even deign to stop us. They're not looking for us, and they know damn well that arresting an English lord within sight of Berwick would bring down the wrath of Queen Elizabeth in the blink of an eye.'

'Forgive me, My Lord, but what if Logan has escaped from the ship, and raised the alarm?'

'Robert Logan, of all men, raising an alarm over this? Robert Logan escaping from a ship at sea? One manned by a hundred prime English rogues? Come, man!'

'But surely the Scots will be hunting the captain of the man-of-war seen off the Tay at the time Lord Gowrie was killed? And surely you should not endanger that which you have taken from Fast Castle? I am adept at scouting, My Lord – it was my task for years on end during the war in the east. Let me ride ahead.'

I thought upon all of this. I thought upon it very hard.

'Very well, Horvath,' I said, 'ride ahead, and scout out the border. Take no more than an hour, though. I want to sit down with a plate of good English stew and a tankard of ale in Berwick before nightfall.'

Nicholas Iles:

We waited. My Lord and I spoke of many things, and I undertook some tasks. Still we waited. Finally, the tolling of a distant church bell told us that five hours had elapsed since Horvath rode for the border.

'Well, poet,' said Matthew Quinton, 'it seems we ride on alone.'

'But what if there truly are Scottish patrols on the border, My Lord, and Horvath has been taken or killed?'

He looked at me seriously, and shrugged.

'Then we shall avoid those patrols, my boy.'

In the event, we spotted only one group of armed horsemen under the saltire banner, well off to the west and riding away from us. Horvath's whereabouts remained a mystery. But now, there ahead of us was Berwick upon Tweed, a colossal fortress town ringed by vast new ramparts, bristling with cannon, from which flew the banners of Saint George.

'Christ alone knows how much the Queen has expended on those walls,' said the Earl. 'No doubt that's where she spent all the money she should have paid to those of us who fought the Armada, and in all her other campaigns for these fifteen years last past.'

'Then why lavish so much money on it, My Lord, if England and Scotland are now meant to be friends, and the King of Scots—'

I held my peace in time; or not quite in time enough.

'The King of Scots set fair to be the King of England, and in short order, too? Well, now, that's a good question, young Iles, and here's the answer. If you seek proof that Her Majesty and her ministers don't trust King James one jot, and think he's mad enough to bring a great army over the border at any moment, then there it is, directly ahead of you. And myself, I'd call the great ramparts of Berwick a fucking convincing proof.'

We rode boldly toward the gate that faced Scotland. At the northern end of the bridge over the dry moat, a party of musketeers and a sergeant were interrogating each traveller seeking admittance: Scots hawkers, carters and farmers galore, seeking markets among the better-heeled English.

When it came to our turn, My Lord rode forward boldly.

'I am Ravensden,' he said. 'The Earl.'

The sergeant looked him up and down. My Lord's face was well known, albeit from bad woodcuts, but he also wore silk jerkin and hose, clothing reserved by the sumptuary laws for men of his rank, and the sword-hilt at his side was evidently that of a warrior and a man of quality. The sergeant despatched a musketeer across the bridge, into the gatehouse, and then brought up his sword in salute. The remaining musketeers snapped to attention.

'Pass, My Lord of Ravensden,' he said.

I breathed a sigh of relief –

But ahead of us, in the gatehouse passage, a file of troops was forming to block the way. Stepping out ahead of it was an officer – a captain, by the looks of him – with his sword drawn. He raised his free hand to halt us.

'Matthew Quinton, Earl of Ravensden,' said the captain in a loud and confident voice, 'in the name of Her Majesty Queen Elizabeth, I arrest you upon suspicion of conspiracy.'

'Conspiracy?' cried My Lord. 'Conspiracy to do what? Conspiracy against whom? Conspiracy in itself has never been a charge in English law, sirrah.'

'Suspicion of conspiracy,' the captain repeated, albeit with rather less uncertainty, 'upon charges that have been laid against you.'

'Charges? Laid by whom?'

A man stepped out of the guardroom door.

'By me, My Lord,' said Laszlo Horvath.

CHAPTER FOURTEEN

Nicholas Iles:

'Why?' I demanded. 'Why have you done this, Horvath?'

We stood in a tower chamber within the citadel of Berwick. My Lord had been taken to a room across the courtyard; comfortable, well furnished, but still all too obviously a cell. His sword had been taken from him, as were the papers he took from the sea-cave beneath Fast Castle.

The Hungarian looked at me with contempt.

'I have reason enough,' he said, and there was a coldness about him that made me fear for my very life. 'Ample reason enough. And you, Iles. You have a choice to make. You can either stand by Matthew Quinton, and suffer the same fate, or you can throw in your lot with me. I have powerful friends, poet. Above all, I have a very powerful master.'

'Why should I join with you against My Lord? And who is this mysterious "master" of yours, Horvath? What could he do for me?'

He smiled. 'You have witnessed things, Iles. You were in the cave at Fast Castle. You saw and heard what Quinton did and said there, and when the ship was off the Tay. You were his second in his duel with the Earl of Essex. And you know that I was outside his cabin door, when the *Merhonour* was in France. You can testify that I would have heard what was said within.'

'Then you truly were spying on them,' I said.

'I really convinced you otherwise? You are meant to be the actor, not I.'

'So you want me to lie, in order to condemn My Lord.'

'Not at all. I want you to tell the truth – simply the truth of what you saw and heard. No more than that.'

'To bring what charge against him? Not this "conspiracy" that he has been arrested for. That's meaningless under the law. But…' The truth rose up in front of me, like some dreadful beast of legend, and just as terrifying. 'Treason. You need two witnesses to bring a charge of High Treason.'

'An oddity of your English law,' said Horvath, 'and an inconvenience that has weighed on my mind.'

'My Lord is no traitor, Horvath!' I said angrily. 'No man has been braver in the Queen's service! No man more loyal!'

'Really? Others think differently. My master, for example. He thinks very differently. And he is a man who could do much for you, Iles.'

'You think you can bribe me into denouncing My Lord? Into condemning him to a traitor's death? You think me so cheap, so base?'

'Come, Iles, don't pretend you still think Quinton is a perfect hero. I have seen your face, and heard your words. I have read your scribblings—'

'My diurnal? You've read my diurnal?'

'An easy matter, when you were on deck and your sea-chest was unattended. You really should get a lock for it that is less easy to pick, my friend.'

'I'm not your friend, Horvath, damn you!'

'No. But you're no longer a friend of the Earl of Ravensden, either, as is very clear from your writing. A man of straw, you called him? And when did he last pay you, Iles? What has he ever done to obtain a pardon for you? My master could do all of that for you with a mere stroke of a pen. An unconditional pardon. You would be free to return to the playhouses, and to find rather more generous patrons than Matthew Quinton, too. And my master rewards good service to him. Amply rewards it. All you have to do is dictate and sign a deposition, when the time comes.'

My head swam at the enormity of it all.

'You ask too much—'

'Oh, I do not demand an immediate decision. I know you will find this difficult, Iles, but believe me, the Earl of Ravensden is finished. As soon as an escort can be assembled, we ride for London, to lodge him in the Tower.'

'I – I would ride for London now—'

'No, friend Iles, that will not be possible. You will ride with me, and with the prisoner. So much more companionable if we all ride together.'

And then I knew: I might not be locked into a cell, but I was just as much a prisoner as My Lord.

The Dowager Countess:

The news was relayed to me by Widow Jones, who seemed to take a perverse delight in it. At first, I refused to believe her. My husband a traitor, being brought south from Berwick to meet his fate? It was impossible. I raged. I wept. I raged again, and threw wine glasses. Then I set about the throwing of bottles. Finally, I determined upon action. I had to go to court, to solicit all the great ministers of the kingdom, to seek audience of the Queen itself –

But it proved impossible. The court was closed to me, the ministers ignored me, and my pleas for an audience fell on deaf ears. In the streets, too, I sensed the change. Formerly, I had been the wife of an Earl of England, a hero of the realm, and was treated with due deference, despite my faith and my nationality. Now, men turned their backs, women made lewd gestures, and market stalls mysteriously closed as I approached. I saw the murmuring, heard some of the whispers about Jesuits and popery and false un-English superstitions, but I carried on, determined to rise above the ignorance and hysteria all around me.

I was walking in the Strand near Ravensden House, accompanied by my maid Alice and perusing the wares of the street hawkers, when a common whore spat on the ground in front of me.

'Papist French bitch,' she hissed. 'Traitor's strumpet.'

The jostling mob separated me from Alice, who screamed. I rushed into the nearest church for sanctuary, jeers and catcalls ringing in my ears, tears flooding my eyes. Of course, the church was heret– Protestant, but as I wiped away my tears and murmured the proscribed *Ave Maria* under my breath, I looked about and realised that I was in a strange edifice, most unlike the common run of English churches. True, it possessed the tedious whitewashed walls that disfigured all of them, obliterating the colourful paintings of Dooms, of saintly majesty and the true doctrines of purgatory and transubstantiation. But this particular church was round, and more like some of the basilicas in my native country. What was more, tomb effigies of ancient knights in armour were littered all around. Then I realised my husband had once spoken of this place, and promised to show it to me some day. This could only be the Temple Church, once home to the crusading Knights Templar.

So, then.

I settled myself upon a stone bench set against the wall, breathed deeply, and took stock. French and Papist: that I could not deny. Bitch:

indeed, if the mood took me. Strumpet: possibly. But a traitor's strumpet? That I most certainly was not.

I was the Countess of Ravensden, and I would crusade with all my strength for my knight in armour.

The Earl of Ravensden:

We skirted the City and approached London from the east. This, the captain of the guard explained, was to avoid the prospect of being pelted with rotten fruit, dung, and other such delicacies hurled by the mob, who commonly treated suspected traitors thus. I knew this; on several similar occasions in the past, I had been one of those throwing the dung. The captain was a young fellow, barely older than Iles, and an apologetic one. He had evidently grown up with the stories of Drake, Ravensden and the rest, and was mortified to find himself leading one of that doughty band into captivity. He longed for action, and was evidently delighted with the news he imparted to me of the failure of the peace talks at Boulogne. So the endless war with Spain would continue: a fair prospect for both a young captain and an old one, if only the one could be freed from the tedium of garrison duty and the other from the prospect of the scaffold. Encouraged by such exchanges, I dared to suggest to him that his sympathy towards me might extend to permitting us to escape: accidentally, of course, or so it would be reported to the authorities. But although he evidently detested Horvath, his sense of duty would not permit such a thing. I silently cursed my luck in finding myself under the charge of one of the few honourable soldiers left in England.

And then there was Horvath, or whatever his name really was. A man whom I had taken into my entire confidence, only for him to betray me so utterly. I detested being any man's dupe, but especially so when the man had no conceivable grievance against me. He said almost nothing to me during the entire journey, speaking only to Iles. The poet, in turn, was distant toward me throughout: but then, it was only fitting that the second prosecution witness in a case of High Treason should be distant towards the man he would be accusing. So I had ample time to think as we rode south, and by the time we reached London, I believed I knew the gist of matters.

Horvath alone could not have been responsible for my arrest, that much was clear. The word of an alien as justification for arresting an English nobleman? The notion was inconceivable. No, there was one man, and one alone, who had both the power and the cause to act against me in this way. The man who was always bound to turn on me if the scheme that he, the Earl of Gowrie and I discussed in the palace of Theobalds, those months ago, should miscarry, as it had done in such a tragic fashion. Gowrie was dead, and could not tell what he knew; but Ravensden lived, and at all costs, Robert Cecil had to ensure that Ravensden's mouth remained closed.

It was dusk as we rode into the Tower by way of the Lion, Middle and Byward towers. The horses' hooves echoed on the cobbles as we passed through those gloomy walls, into the precincts where so many English traitors had ended their days. I was determined that I would not be one of them; and I still had one advantage, one card to play, that none of the other prisoners of the Tower possessed.

Or at least, I prayed that I did.

Laszlo Horvath"

I attend my master within the Palace of Whitehall.

'You are sure that these are all of them?' he says. 'All the papers that the Earl of Ravensden took from Fast Castle?'

'As certain as I can be, Master Secretary.'

Robert Cecil stares at me intently. Then he says, 'So be it. You have done well, Horvath.'

'I would prefer to be called by my true name, Master Secretary—'

'All in good time. For now, I think, it is best if you remain plain Laszlo Horvath, a Hungarian, a stranger in this realm.'

'But sir, will I not need to appear under my own name at the treason trial?'

'Indeed you will. But there is no prospect of such a trial in the immediate future.'

'But – Master Secretary, I have a second witness, and surely our testimony to what happened in Scotland—'

'No English court will convict a man, least of all such a very famous man as Lord Ravensden, on the basis of what happens in Scotland. It is a foreign land, Master Horvath, so his actions there cannot be construed as treason in England.'

No, Master Secretary, I think, *especially as you ordered him to go there.*

'Then when will he be charged? When will I receive the reward you promised me?'

'Do not grow impatient, my friend – surely you have already waited long enough, so that another year or two will matter? Much may happen in England in a year or two.' *In other words, the Queen might die.* The one great unspoken hope and fear of every Englishman. 'In the meantime, Lord Ravensden has offended the Queen sufficiently for her to keep him in the Tower indefinitely, without charge – although Her Majesty being a woman, she still seems more animated by his marriage without permission to a slip of a French papist than by any real crimes he might have committed. And I need to be sure that these papers are the originals, and all of them at that, before we can proceed further. I need to know that they really do contain what they are said to contain. To be certain of this, I must have the papers studied by one who saw the original letters, and that person cannot be in England before the spring. So be content, good Horvath. Live well in London this winter, upon the generous bounty I have paid you. Yes, I know you seek a greater prize, and God willing, that will come your way soon enough. But for now, be content. Call on Master Trevor, if you wish – he seems most discontented that you have deserted him for my service. And, of course, ensure that the poet Iles is closely watched. We do not want our second witness to slip away from us, do we?'

'No, Master Cecil,' I say.

Nicholas Iles will not slip away. He is entirely mine now, seemingly at one with me in a determination to bring down Matthew Quinton. And if he is not, then I will end his life as quickly and simply as I would snap a twig upon a woodland path.

CHAPTER FIFTEEN

1601
The Dowager Countess:
That autumn and winter, after I recovered from the initial shock of my husband's arrest and imprisonment in the Tower, I thought often upon the words that my sister spoke to me at Chambord, when we both looked upon the distant form of Matthew Quinton, eighth Earl of Ravensden.

'*...his uncle was a notorious sorcerer, who placed a curse on his brother's line and the entire House of Ravensden before making a pact with the Devil and disappearing into thin air.*'

I thought of all of the misfortunes that had befallen my husband – the Invisible Armada, Spinola's galleys, the Gowrie House affair, his arrest following betrayal by Laszlo Horvath, our failure to have a son who would be the heir to Ravensden. Surely such a litany of disasters could only be the consequence of a terrible curse? And surely that curse could only have come from Henry Quinton, sixth Earl of Ravensden? Thus I reassured myself, for it was better to blame a strange, long-dead necromancer than to contemplate the only reasonable alternative: namely, that all the disasters which had befallen my husband had occurred since he married me. In other words, that I was the cause.

For I also recalled the awful words of the Abbé Mousnier, our family's chaplain and my childhood tutor, when I told him that I was to marry this English Milord.

'*Marriage to a heretic damns you for all eternity, Lady. It damns you, and your seed – you, a scion of this noble house, which has been so stalwart for Holy Church, time out of mind! Yes, you will be doubly damned, for how will you celebrate the Mass in a land where it is proscribed? As for your so-called husband – he is already bound for Hell, as all Protestants are. But you are condemning him to spend all eternity in a very special part of Hell, where those who persuade good Catholics into apostasy suffer even more terribly than all the other benighted souls who burn in the fires below. I have failed, in that I did not teach you well enough to keep you from such temptation. Your carnal lust has damned you, Lady Louise-Marie. It has cursed you. Mark my words, girl. You are damned and cursed.'*

Many times I thought upon those words, and shivered. I had attended Mass so very few times since coming to England: always in secret, in the private chapels of the ambassadors of the likes of Savoy or Florence. I had confessed but once in two years, to an English Jesuit who was hanged, drawn and quartered barely a month later. Was the Abbé Mousnier right after all, and I was already damned? And had I damned my husband too, both in this world and the next, by acquiescing in his perverse decision to take me for his wife?

Always, I put such thoughts to one side. The salvation of my immortal soul would have to await another day, for there were more pressing matters to attend to. Then I would return to the writing desk below one of the few windows fitted with glass in Ravensden House, looking out over the Strand, lift the quill from the ink, and apply it to paper.

For it was a winter of writing letters.

I wrote regularly to the Queen, and as often to Secretary Cecil. I wrote at least once to each of the great men of the kingdom –Dorset the Lord Treasurer, Egerton the Lord Keeper of the Great Seal, Whitgift the Archbishop of Canterbury, all of them. I wrote twice to the King of Scots, requesting his intercession; twice to the King of France, with the same intent. But to no avail. I did not receive even one reply.

Most of all, I wrote daily, sometimes twice daily, to my husband. He received them, for he replied; once a week if I was fortunate, every two or three weeks if I was not. He was as comfortable as a man in his position could be, he said. He had a warming fire and acceptable wine. But I knew these were lies, designed entirely to reassure me. For he was in the Tower of London, a fortress as dreadful and feared as the Bastille. I imagined him in rags, chained to a wall in a dank cell, wasting away on thin gruel and foul water.

No, grandson, I know that *now*, but I did not know it *then*. I know *now* that My Lord was telling the truth, or even something less than the truth, and was actually living rather more comfortably than I was in the permanently damp and cold environs of Ravensden House, surrounded by mouldy tapestries and suspiciously cracked walls. So comfortably, in fact – what with the excellent victuals and the lack of exercise – that the noble Earl was actually growing fatter by the day.

But, imagining the worst, I redoubled my efforts to bribe the Constable of the fortress, for I had heard that it was often possible for wives to gain access to their husbands in the Tower if they placed enough gold in the right hands. Nothing availed. It was as though the Queen herself had given specific orders that the Countess of Ravensden should be treated with particular harshness; as though Gloriana herself were somehow a part of the curse.

And then the world changed.

It changed one February day, when I heard a commotion in the Strand, beyond the front door of Ravensden House.

'Treason, My Lady!' cried Widow Jones, clearly terrified beyond measure. 'Rebellion!'

She made to run for the back of the house, but I gripped her by the shoulders.

'Whose rebellion?'

'Lord Essex! He and his men marched into the City, to raise it against the hunchback! But the Lord Mayor closed the gates against them, and they've returned to Essex House, to hold it against all comers!'

I ran to the uppermost floor of the house and flung open the window of the garret that overlooked the Strand. From there, I could see Essex House, not too far away on the other side of the road, near the Temple Church: a veritable palace that I envied greatly. And I could see troops advancing toward it from both directions, from Ludgate and the Fleet River and thence through Temple Bar to the east, from Whitehall by way of Charing Cross to the west. There was a strange sound, a deep growl like thunder. Then I saw them: two cannon, presumably from the Tower, were being hauled across the cobbles, and were turned noisily into position directly opposite the gates of the Devereux palace.

I looked back toward Essex House. I could see directly into its courtyard, and saw barely a few dozen men, running hither and thither. They were a pathetic force to set against the great army now assembling in the Strand. So the mighty Earl of Essex, erstwhile favourite of the Queen, was doomed: that much was clear. But if he was doomed, what fate would befall my husband?

I prayed for a miracle. I prayed for a sign. I was on my knees, imploring the Virgin with every breath in my body.

And then, when I opened my eyes, I had my miracle, and saw my sign.

He was there in the Strand, riding purposefully through the Temple Bar, mounted on a huge black stallion. He wore full armour but no helmet, so his great white beard spilled down onto his breastplate. The soldiers cheered as he rode past them. The few onlookers brave enough to remain on the street waved. But unlike them, I knew this man. My husband and I had dined with him, just a few months before. He was My Lord's friend.

I ran downstairs and unbolted the door, despite Widow Jones' efforts to stop me.

'My Lady! Please! It's madness to go out there – they're going to bombard Essex House—'

But I was through, and out, running past the soldiers advancing from Charing Cross, running toward the armoured man on the great black horse.

'My Lord!' I called. 'My Lord!'

He looked down on me from his great height.

'My Lady Ravensden,' he said. 'Sweet mercy, My Lady, go indoors, in the name of Heaven! Essex and his rebels might open fire at any moment!'

'My Lord, I come to offer you Ravensden House as a headquarters! It has a view into Essex House!'

He stroked his beard.

'A view, you say? That would be useful. Aye, very useful indeed. My thanks, then, My Lady. I accept your generous offer, in the name of the Queen!'

It was a joy to behold the shock on the face of Widow Jones as she opened the door of Ravensden House to admit Charles, Lord Howard of Effingham, Earl of Nottingham, Lord High Admiral of England, the conqueror of the Spanish Armada.

Nicholas Iles:

'Essex or Cecil?' demanded the drunk with the knife.

Behind him, a table was overset, scattering pewter tankards onto the rush-strewn floor. An Essex men stabbed a Cecil man in the neck before two Cecil men fell on him with their daggers.

'Essex or Cecil?' repeated the drunk.

I, who was very nearly as drunk as he was, squinted at him uncertainly.

'Neither,' I said. 'I am for My Lord of Ravensden.'

'Ravensden?' It was obviously not the answer the drunk was expecting. 'Ravensden? Fucking dead man walking. You're either for Essex, or you're for Cecil. And this here tavern, this tavern is for My Lord the Earl.'

Of course it was. After all, the tavern was adjacent to the Globe Theatre. I was drinking there only the previous afternoon, when it was full of Essex's men, both before and after they visited the theatre to view the special performance they had paid for.

A performance of Shakespeare's *Richard the Second*.

A play about a vigorous young nobleman who rebels and overthrows a weak, erratic monarch before taking the throne himself. As I thought to myself at the time: no contemporary resonance at all, then.

'Well then, I said, if it's one or the other—'

I retched, as though fear and drink had turned my stomach and made me want to vomit. As I doubled up, I reached down to my ankle, snatched out the small dagger I kept concealed there, and thrust it upward, directly into the man's guts and then up again, toward the heart. He looked at me in astonishment as he died, having failed to learn the two lessons that every man who drinks in the stews of Southwark should know: first, never trust an actor; and second, never drop your guard if you think someone's about to spew all over you.

I withdrew my blade. As I did so, I looked over to the far corner of the room. A man sat there, his hands cradling a pot of ale. He was a small, greasy fellow with an eyepatch and no teeth; too quiet and too nondescript to attract the attention of those warring for Essex and Cecil.

I nodded to him, and he nodded to me in return.

That was the most dialogue I ever had with any of them: Horvath's spies, the men appointed to watch me at all times. The men who ensured I did not try to run before I could appear as the second witness in My Lord's trial for High Treason, whenever that might take place. The men who ensured I made no contact whatsoever with the Earl, incarcerated in the Tower, or with his lady at the house in the Strand.

The Dowager Countess:

It was a strange experience, standing in the garret room of Ravensden House alongside the victor over the Invincible Armada and his companion, the second Lord Burghley, brother to Secretary Cecil. They and a half dozen of their officers watched Essex House intently for hours, alert for any sign of resistance, prepared to give order to the two cannon lined up directly opposite the entrance of the great palace, at point blank rage to the gates. Night fell shortly after their arrival, but only a few candles lit the windows of the Earl's residence.

'They'll be arguing the toss,' said Nottingham, a little before nine. 'Come out fighting and die with honour, or surrender and throw themselves on the Queen's mercy. They have no other courses available to them.'

'There is no way of escape?' I asked.

'Their only chance would be the river,' said Burghley, 'and we have boats full of armed men thronging it.'

'Then might they not take their own lives?'

'Good God!' cried Burghley, 'With respect, My Lady, this is England. Noblemen of England do not do such things.'

This Cecil was taller and straighter than his brother, as most men were, sporting elaborately combed red hair and a beard that was tinged with large amounts of grey, the latter sitting atop an unexpectedly greasy ruff. I once asked my husband why the hunchbacked younger son, rather than this, the eldest, had succeeded their father as chief minister of England.

'Old Burghley had no illusions about his sons,' said the Earl. 'He knew only Rob had inherited his political skills. He said of the eldest, who's now Lord Burghley, that he wasn't fit to govern a tennis court. A tennis court!'

My husband always laughed loudly at his own jokes, but he seemed to have a particular liking for that one.

'Wait,' said the man deemed incapable of gathering lost balls, 'there is activity at the gate! Look, My Lord Admiral!'

It was a dark, cold February night, but there was more than enough light from the flaming torches of the soldiers and the braziers on the street to see that the gate of Essex House was opening.

'And behold, a white flag!' said Nottingham. 'Essex has seen sense. Thanks be to God. I did not fancy spilling the blood of Englishmen this day.' He turned to me. 'My Lady, if you will forgive us, we must go down to accept the surrender of the Earl. We owe you our deep gratitude for permitting us to use your house in this way.'

I bowed my head in acknowledgement of the compliment.

'A Quinton, even if one only by marriage, is always ready to assist the Queen's cause in any way, My Lord Nottingham. But I trust you will not consider me presumptuous if I make a request of both you and the noble Lord Burghley, here. Perhaps we may call it a way of demonstrating your gratitude, My Lords?'

The Earl of Ravensden:

The good thing about prison is that it gives a man ample time to read. When they brought My Lord of Essex into the Tower, I was reading Digges' *Errors in the Art of Navigation*. When they took him away to stand trial for High Treason, I was re-reading Foxe's *Book of Martyrs* for the third time. When they cut off his head, just out of sight of my window, I was reading my old friend Philip Sidney's *Apology for Poetry*. Indeed, the sound of the axe striking the block momentarily distracted me from my page. I put down my book for a moment, and offered up a prayer. Not for the soul of Robin Devereux, a man who deserved to burn in the flaming seas of Hell alongside Francis Drake, whose eternally irritating shade would probably spend entire millennia working out how to circumnavigate them; no, I prayed for the soul of Matthew Quinton, whose neck might well be the next to nestle into that groove upon the block.

A few days after Essex went to meet his maker, the turnkey came into my room.

'A visitor, My Lord,' he said. He was a surly, bent brute who looked a hundred years old, but insisted he was the same age as me.

'A visitor? Not another fawning priest, sent to save my soul?'

'No, husband,' said my wife, entering the room, 'your Countess, come to save your body.'

I kissed her heartily, and as soon as the turnkey was gone, I began to lift her skirts -

The Dowager Countess:

Thank you, grandson, I think it is best if I retain that particular fragment.

A little later, as I was rearranging my clothing, I explained how I had managed to obtain access to the prison, after so many months of failing to do so.

'Howard?' the Earl said, admiringly. 'And Burghley, too? Both in one fell swoop?'

'The one to intercede with the Queen, the other with his brother. And after helping them to force the surrender of Essex, not even Her Majesty nor Robert Cecil could deny my suit with justice or honour.'

He smiled.

'What an amazon I married! What a – what was the name of that warrior queen who slaughtered Romans? Begins with B. No matter. You are her reborn, My Lady!'

'I fear not, Matthew. Getting myself into the Tower was one matter. Getting you out of it will be quite another.'

'Ah. Upon that, my dearest, you may be wrong. I have had ample time to think, all these months. I dared not commit anything to writing, as all the mail is read by the Constable of the Tower, and, if it contains anything of interest, duly copied and forwarded to Master Secretary. But I have a plan. You, my love, must see the Queen.'

'The Queen? I have written, pleading for an audience, almost daily. The Queen hates you, and she hates me even more. The Queen will not see me.'

'Oh, she will. Trust me on that, Louise-Marie. At bottom, the Queen is a woman, and like all women, she cannot resist having a dainty trinket dangled in front of her.' I drew in breath, ready to protest, but My Lord was unstoppable. 'And I – we – can dangle before her a trinket she has always wanted. One of the most precious trinkets in all these islands.'

'Then what is this trinket, Matthew? Where do I obtain it?'

'Ah, there's the rub. The one slight difficulty. But as I say, I have had ample time to think upon such things, these last few months, and have conceived a way to do it. So are you with me in this, My Lady Countess?'

'With you unto death, My Lord!' I said, running to him, flinging my arms about his neck, and kissing him.

With that, he began to disarrange my skirts and silk stockings once again.

CHAPTER SIXTEEN

Nicholas Iles:
This time, no dagger at the ankle would save me.

It was a larger inn, not far from Lambeth Palace; and it was a larger brawl, by far. Twenty or so lusty, drunken lads were set against the same number, and for a far greater cause. With Essex dead, and it being treason to take sides in the names of the King of Scots, the Lady Arbella, or the Infanta, there was only one great bone of contention worth fighting over in the taverns along the Thames.

'Shakespeare!' cried the lads toward the door.

'Marlowe!' bawled those nearer me.

'Kit Marlowe's never going to write another word, you fuck-spittles!'

'Aye, but he's still a better writer dead than old Shakeshaft is alive!'

'*Once more unto the breach, dear friends*!'

'*Our swords shall play the orators for us*!'

A Marlowe man struck a Shakespearean full upon the jaw. The rogue fell back, tripping over a stool and falling against a table, which collapsed under him. Knives were drawn. I saw the latest of Horvath's spies edge toward the door, while still keeping his eyes on me.

'Nick Iles, you arse-beetle!' cried an ugly brute whom I knew to be Stoddart, one of the Globe company. 'Come here and fight for your precious atheistical Kit Marlowe, then!'

I raised my hands and shouted across the room.

'Friends, surely we should not be fighting over art? Surely we should all be thankful that England has such great writers, and not taking sides between them? A false division indeed, this between dear Kit Marlowe and fair Will Shakespeare, who have both given us verse and prose to make the angels weep with joy! Come, my dear friends, let us be of good cheer, for we lovers of the theatre should be as one, bound together in fellowship and respect!'

Stoddart looked nonplussed. Then he frowned, thrust out a dagger in front of him, and ran straight for me.

'Damn you to hell, Iles,' he cried, 'what purpose is there in an Englishman being alive if he doesn't take sides? I'll show you fellowship and respect, you droning death-token!'

He lunged forward, and I felt the dagger strike my chest. I saw the blood pour down my shirt. The tavern fell silent. I saw Horvath's man look on in horror, then move swiftly toward the door.

'I die,' I said, falling forward.

Laszlo Horvath:

I am summoned to Whitehall again. My master is unhappy, and paces the room, his hands clasped tightly behind his back.

'Dead. Nicholas Iles is dead. Your second witness, Horvath. Without him, there can be no treason trial.'

'I – I know that, Master Secretary—'

'You have failed me. And you do not even have an inkling of how badly you have failed me.'

'But, good sir—'

'No, I am not your good sir, for none of this is good. You assured me you had all the papers that Ravensden took from Fast Castle. You gave me that guarantee, Master Horvath. But I find it is not so. The person who studied the papers, the one who had seen the originals before, long ago – that person is willing to swear that, beyond doubt, almost all of them are the same. All of them, except one.'

He walks to his desk, and lifts a sheet of paper. It appears identical to the others: to the letters that Matthew Quinton took from Fast Castle, and that I took from him at Berwick.

'This one – the most important letter by far – has ten lines missing. The vital ten lines, without which it is worthless, if its contents truly are what they are said to be. It is also a forgery, Horvath. A recent forgery, and a good one. It would be difficult to tell, were it not for the person who saw the letter years ago knowing that those lines were missing. So I had my clerks examine it again, and they identified it for what it is. A very recent, very good forgery. You were duped, Horvath. And you, in turn, have failed me.'

'Sir, it is impossible – it cannot have been so – the only time Quinton and Iles were out of my sight was when I rode ahead into Berwick, to show your orders to the Governor and to prepare for the Earl's arrest—'

But even as I say the words, a terrible thought occurs to me. A terrible, impossible thought.

Robert Cecil must see this upon my face, for he says 'How long would that time have been, Horvath?'

'Four – perhaps five hours—'

'More than enough time to make a copy of the letter, leaving out the critical lines.'

'But Master Secretary, that could only have been so if – if—'

The terrible, impossible thought.

'If the Earl of Ravensden already suspected that you were false to him. And if he had someone to hand who could both make a convincing copy of the letter, and also take custody of the original in case anything should befall the Earl. You do know, perchance, that the criminal charge laid against Nicholas Iles was that of forgery? No, I thought you did not. He was reputed to be a remarkably skilled practitioner of the art. So I think there is one other question you should consider, Horvath.' He looks at me from the side of the window, with half his face in shadow, the sunlight striking his deformed back and making him appear, just for one fleeting moment, as a sort of demon. 'Are you really certain that Nicholas Iles is dead?'

*

Resurrection is a messy business.

So writes Nicholas Iles; and even as an eleven-year-old, I realised that dead men do not generally write such things. Nor do they generally write accounts of their own deaths, and of the plunging of daggers into their own breasts. Even so, and despite all the bravado I displayed in an attempt to convince *grandmaman* that I was not frightened out of my wits, I breathed a deep sigh of relief as I read the next paper in the poet's unmistakeable hand.

Nicholas Iles:

Stoddart's stage-blade retracted into the hilt on impact, as it was meant to do. But he had wielded it with rather too much enthusiasm: typical, I thought, of Shakespeare's crew, who were notorious for over-acting. Thus the pig's bladder full of blood, concealed beneath my shirt, burst open as if I had been hit in the chest by a three-pound cannonball, rather than stabbed through the heart by a stiletto. Fortunately, though, Horvath's man was too terrified of the apparent war going on before his eyes – the finest mock-war that some of London's best actors, bought by the Earl of Ravensden's gold, could contrive between them – to examine the supposed corpse, or to stay and check that the cadaver being carried off in a cart for inspection by the Southwark coroner was the same as that of Nicholas Iles, the man he was meant to be watching.

But Stoddart's unduly vigorous play-murder had drenched my shirt and breeches with pig's blood, so I had to spend the best part of a half-hour scrubbing myself clean and dressing in fresh clothes before I could present himself in the oak-panelled principal room of Ravensden House, my crimson-stained shirt in his hand.

'Bravo, Iles!' cried the Countess, applauding me as I entered. 'You look most healthy, for a corpse.'

'As you say, My Lady. I hope this proved to be one of my more convincing death scenes.'

'We should have a little time before Horvath and Cecil discover that you are very much alive. Time to do what my husband wishes to be done.'

I held the bloodied shirt in my hand, went to the left sleeve, and ripped at the fabric. Sewn within was a small purse of leather, undetectable within the generous folds of the cloth. I took it out and handed it to the Countess. She, in turn, opened it, and took out the paper that it contained.

'The original, My Lady,' I said, 'as given to me by My Lord, in an alehouse north of Berwick. Where he told me of his suspicions of Horvath, and assuaged all my foolish doubts. Where he got me to make a copy of that letter – omitting the critical lines – and gave me the original.'

'My husband is a very shrewd man,' said the Countess, 'although he often gives the impression of being quite otherwise. As you know better than I, methinks, Iles.'

'As you say, My Lady. The Earl told me he had been suspicious of Horvath for some time, and feared he had gone into Berwick to betray us. But he reasoned that Horvath could only know there were a certain number of letters, and that he would not know the contents. So if he believed he was taking all of them off My Lord, he would have no reason to search me.'

'And he did think he had them all, thanks to the forgery you placed within them.'

'One of the more difficult pieces of that sort of work I ever undertook, My Lady – and all of that was a long time ago, of course, before I put it behind me for the stage—'

'You do not need to justify yourself to me, Nicholas Iles. It is as well that you had that skill.'

'Indeed so, My Lady. For some reason known to God alone, it was an ability I had from my earliest days – I made many friends at school by being able to forge the hands of all the masters. But it was still a difficult task. The inn offered little by way of inks and papers, and my ageing of the paper had to be more rushed than I am accustomed to—'

'You did well,' she said, 'very well. And my husband will reward you generously. I shall see to it that he does.'

She opened the letter in her hand, and read.

Moi, Marie, par la grâce de Dieu, reine d'Ecosse, jure solennellement...

'Your French is good enough for you to understand this, Iles?' I blushed, tried to say something, and blushed some more. 'I see that it is. So, then, you know what this letter is, and why it is so important. Why Cecil wants it, and the King of Scots wants it. And Queen Elizabeth, too.'

'Yes, My Lady. It is one of the Casket Letters. One of the ten missing Casket Letters – the papers that My Lord took from the cave in Fast Castle.'

'The most important of them, Nicholas. You have read it. You have copied it. You know what it says. And you know that it can remake the history of two kingdoms.'

'As you say, My Lady. But what I do not understand is how My Lord came to know of it, and of where it could be found. That day we spent outside Berwick, and he got me to copy the letter – well, he told me something of why we sailed to the Firth of Tay on the very day that the Earl of Gowrie's plot, whatever it was, misfired at Perth. But not all.'

'No, he would not. My husband believes that you and I are innocents who should be protected from the consequences of his actions. The less we know, the less we will be able to confess to if he faces a trial for High Treason. But I think we are well past that stage now, Nicholas. And you have risked so much on our behalf that I think you deserve to know the full truth. So sit, *mon ami*, and let me tell you.'

The Dowager Countess:

So, grandson, you wish to know the contents of the mysterious letter? The one that your grandfather nearly gave his life for, that the Earl of Gowrie died for, and that both Queen Elizabeth and King James were so keen to obtain? You want to know what I said to Iles, all those long years ago?

Not even your uncle Tristram has that knowledge, although I am sure he would very much like to have it. His Lord General Cromwell certainly would, I am quite certain of that. Your father did not possess this knowledge – who knows, perhaps if he had, he would not have ridden to his death on Naseby field. Your brother does not know. And although I have debated the matter these last weeks, since Captain Fensom and his rude troop came to Ravensden, I have come to believe that you should not know either, else the secret will weigh upon you for the rest of your life, as it has weighed upon me these last fifty years. I know you will be disappointed, and will chide me for the old and capricious woman that I am, but –

What is that you say?

Ah. Well, then. That alters the case.

You are a clever lad, Matthew Quinton. Too clever, perhaps. But yes, you are truly worthy to bear your grandfather's name. I wondered if you would deduce the truth, and it seems you have.

So be it.

But first, young Matthew, I would have you swear upon my Vulgate, here, that you will never reveal what I am about to tell you to any living being. Not to your brother, nor your uncle, nor your wife and children, when you eventually acquire those trying commodities.

Good.

Well, then. As far as I can recall, this is the substance of what I said to Nicholas Iles.

*

As you know, the Casket Letters were copies of papers by Mary, Queen of Scots, that implicated her in the murder of her second husband and the father of her son, namely the drunken peacock that was Henry, Lord Darnley. But the letters that were made public in England after Queen Mary fled here were copies, and ten were known to be missing. The Queen, King James and Robert Cecil all had an idea of the contents of the missing letters from persons who had seen the originals, and they all knew the identity of the man who last possessed those originals – the first Earl of Gowrie, father to the Earl who perished at Gowrie House.

Before his downfall and execution, the first Earl hid the papers at Fast Castle, entrusting the secret to his wife, to pass it on to his son when the time came. So Earl John, when he came into his inheritance, learned of the Casket Letters, and the hold they might give him over King James. But by then, it was obvious that they were even more important, for King James seemed set fair to succeed to the throne of England. Earl John was very young, and badly needed advice. Above all, he needed it from someone who was knowledgeable in the affairs of England, and from someone he could trust. So it must have seemed like divine providence when both he and my husband, a kinsman, found themselves studying together at the University of Padua, where My Lord went to recover from the wounds he received in the Battle of Cadiz. At Padua, as he told me in the Tower, Gowrie related to him the history of the Casket Letters, and they began to consider what they might do. Gowrie stayed abroad for several more years, but on his return, and unknown at first to my husband, he approached Robert Cecil, reckoning that a scheme as bold as the one he was contemplating needed the support of the most powerful man in England. Remember that Cecil has long been known to be no friend of King James – indeed, some say he is convinced that the King is unstable, a near-madman obsessed with witches, who was likely to invade England at any moment and install Lord Essex as his chief minister. Besides, Cecil wanted the succession of the Infanta, as a union with Flanders would bring greater benefit to the men of money within the exchanges of London. So for all of those reasons, Cecil was more than ready to give his support to a scheme to bring down King James.

In essence, the scheme was this. Gowrie and his brother were to lure King James to their house in Perth, separate him from his entourage – yes, the story of the pot of gold which only the King should view, a tale perfectly designed to appeal to James Stuart's avarice – and then bundle him onto a boat upon the River Tay, at the foot of the gardens of Gowrie House. Gardens which were full of apple trees in full flower, so the abduction would be hidden from view. My husband examined the tides of the River Tay in great detail, and assured both Gowrie and Cecil that it could be done on certain days, and certain days only. The boat would then sail downstream to meet an English man-of-war in the estuary, and that man-of-war would be his own ship, the *Constant Esperance*. In her, the King would be taken to Fast Castle, hence that foul villain Logan's part in the business. The castle was ideal, My Lord told me. Even if forces loyal to the King besieged it, they would never take it; Fast could only be invested from the sea, and the Scots had no men-of-war. And it was ideal in Cecil's eyes, for it meant that the deed would not be done upon English soil, thus avoiding the mistake his father made with the disposal of James's mother, Mary, Queen of Scots.

What deed, you ask, friend Nicholas?

(*It is still I, Matt Quinton, and these are the words* grandmaman *dictated to me when I was eleven years old. But I think she had forgotten to whom she spoke, and when she was speaking; her voice was clearer, almost younger, and I think she was back in the great Queen's time once more. Even at that tender age, I knew better than to disillusion her.*)

No, not to murder the king. Why, if murder was the objective, do you not think Gowrie could have had him killed easily enough at Perth, without all the dangers involved in smuggling him to the *Constant Esperance*?

No. At Fast Castle, James Stuart would be compelled to abdicate – compelled by the threat of the publication of the missing originals of the Casket Letters. Of this letter, above all. Cecil calculated, and perhaps he was not wrong in this, that James would be willing to abdicate in favour of his son if he received assurances that the said son would succeed the Virgin Queen, and the Casket Letters would be suppressed so as not to tarnish the reputation of England's new King Henry the Ninth. After all, James had given the lad that name, a sure sign that he intended him to sit upon the English throne; and if it was made clear to James that he could not have England, then would he not at least want to ensure that his son did?

But as you know, it all went tragically wrong.

Gowrie's brother bungled matters so badly that King James was able to shout out to his courtiers, who stormed the house and slaughtered the young men upon their own stair. James had his men put out a tale of attempted regicide, the tale most of the world believes to this day; most of the world being full of the credulous and gullible. And, of course, Cecil needed urgently to suppress any hint that he might have played a part in the disaster, in case he incurred the wrath of his royal mistress. Hence his vindictiveness toward my husband, fuelled by the hostility of Horvath. Cecil must have already recruited him both to spy upon My Lord and to ensure that he did not attempt to betray Master Secretary – but why he hates my husband so, God only knows. And God only knows how it might have ended, too, had not my husband possessed the quick wits to conceal the critical Casket Letter from Horvath and Cecil. For as he told me, the moment he heard that John of Gowrie was dead, he knew he would have to throw in his lot with James Stuart –

Ah yes, Nicholas, you are quite right.

God knows how it might have ended, too, had not the Earl of Essex destroyed himself when he did, for that removed the possibility of my husband colluding once again with that fateful Lord. And, of course, the part I played, or rather the garret of Ravensden House played, in Essex's surrender, has given me the opportunity to obtain audience with the Queen, to persuade her, God willing, that the missing Casket Letter is worth my husband's release –

*

Grandmaman suddenly stared at me, her eyes wide, unrecognising, and I realised that her mind had returned to 1651. She no longer saw Nicholas Iles before her, but instead, the confused, concerned face of a lanky eleven year old boy. She pleaded a headache and retired to her chamber. I did not see her again for two days, giving me ample time to think upon the full import of what she had told me, and upon the enormity of the oath I had sworn. For now I possessed the greatest secret in all of Britain: the secret made plain in the next fragment written by Iles, which I pored over line by line, and now do so again.

Nicholas Iles:

The Countess held the paper in her hand, almost reverentially.

'Queen Mary's own hand, Nicholas,' she said. 'What utter folly, to commit such words to paper.'

'Why do you think she did so, My Lady?' I asked.

'It was a kind of written confession, I think – perhaps to be produced when she had a child by her lover and later husband, the Earl of Bothwell, to ensure that their child would take precedence in the succession to the Scottish throne; or perhaps simply as a way for her to expiate her guilt. We papists are greatly fond of confession, as you heretics constantly remind us.' She smiled. 'Utter folly, as I say. An admission that her then husband, Lord Darnley, was not the father of her son James. Instead, the father was her secretary and musician, David Rizzio.'

'Surely, My Lady, the entire world has whispered that from the very beginning?'

'Of course it has. Just look at the portraits of King James – have you ever seen a less Scottish-looking face? A face more at home in Siena than Stirling? So, yes, the world suspects. The world suspects that the King is secretly a bastard, and that he and his children thus have no right to the thrones of England or Scotland, but the world has no proof. Except we do, Nicholas, and here it is.'

I have acted the emotion of stunned horror many times, but I did not need to act it now. Even as I shuddered at the enormity of what I now knew, though, I ached for a quill and for vellum. Oh, here was a play to end all plays, a poem to cap all poetry! But in the same blinking of the eye, I knew this story could never be written – not in a form that could ever be made public, at any rate. This was the kind of secret for which entire cities and empires perished, not just a lone poet.

And yet, amidst the incoherence of my thoughts, coherent words still formed in my mouth.

'Then what did My Lord hope to achieve my joining with Lord Gowrie?'

'Ah, Nicholas, he has not told me all. But I know him well enough now to have deduced it, I think. Cecil held out the prospect of restoration to command, of course, but it is much more than that. It outrages My Lord's sense of honour that the bastard spawn of an Italian lutenist should sit on the throne of England. But the bastard spawn's young son is a very different matter, especially when the alternatives are Arbella Stuart, a woman so stupid that she apologises to doors which close before her, and the Infanta, a proxy of the kingdom that my husband has spent twenty years fighting. And if I know my husband, he will have calculated that a long regency might create countless opportunities for such a bold and brilliant man as Matthew Quinton, Earl of Ravensden.'

I nodded. 'Then what do we do next, My Lady?'

The Countess turned, and placed the Queen of Scots' letter on the table behind her, next to her own quills and ink.

'What we do next, friend Nicholas, is to follow my husband's instructions for your safekeeping, and get you out of London before our enemies start to hunt for you. They will most certainly come here, so we need to act quickly.'

'And you, My Lady? Will they not come for you?'

'Not before I go to them, I think. Before I go into their lion's den. Or rather, that of the lioness.'

CHAPTER SEVENTEEN

The Dowager Countess:
A brisk breeze from the west chopped the surface of the Thames, making it heavy going for the two watermen rowing me upstream. The tide was on the ebb, too, they complained, and I had no doubt that they were going to overcharge me outrageously. But then, it was a very long passage from the Savoy wharf, and watermen prepared to undertake the voyage knew well enough that passengers bound for this particular destination could afford to pay handsomely for the privilege. Soon we had left Westminster behind us and were rowing through open country, the river banks heavily wooded and interrupted only occasionally by a village or two, such as Putney, by the grandeur of Fulham Palace, or by the various horse ferries that plied between the banks.

And all the while, it was as though a phantom hand was slowly tightening its grip on my heart, threatening to crush the worthless life out of my frame. Such was the strength of the fear I felt; a fear that grew with every sweep of the oars, with every contemptuous stare from a passing swan. I was dressed in my very finest, a farthingale beneath my taffeta petticoats, kirtle and gown. I wore the largest ruff of my life, a starched monstrosity of cambric, the glorious gold-and-ruby pendant jewel of the second Countess of Ravensden at my breast. And yet, despite all of my finery, I felt entirely naked.

We came to a great bend in the river, and one of the watermen nodded over his shoulder.

'Just round 'ere it is, My Lady. Nearly there, now.'

Above the tops of the trees, I could see smoke rising from dozens of chimneys, and the topmost pinnacles of turrets. Then we cleared the bend, and the full spectacle lay before me.

Richmond Palace was not large by the standards of, say, the Louvre or Fontainebleau, but it was magnificent nonetheless. A tall rectangular block rose directly from the river, the spring sunshine glinting from its many windows and off the gold leaf that adorned the cupolas and pepper-pot turrets. The gold and azure weathervanes sang in the breeze. Red brick walls and galleries surrounded the substantial gardens that lay to either side of the principal block; two large buildings that appeared to be halls or chapels stood a little way inland. Several boats jostled for position at the palace wharf, waiting to come alongside to discharge the distinguished personages they carried. For the royal arms of England flew from the turrets, and that symbol was all it took to attract the bees to the honeypot.

My wherry eventually took its turn at the wharf, I paid the watermen (an exorbitant sum, as expected) and found a young pageboy willing to show me the way. The great building fronting the Thames, he explained, formed the royal apartments, but he then led me through the courtyard in the middle, over the bridge across the moat, into the much larger courtyard beyond, and so past a large fountain and into the great hall, a vast space decorated with martial paintings of England's kings in golden robes, and thronged with hundreds of people. The audience was about to begin, my pageboy informed me; and if I gave him a second coin, he would ensure I advanced a few places up the Lord Chamberlain's list. I complied, he scurried off, and I never saw him again. I wondered if he had cheated me, and was about to seek out a liveried attendant myself, when trumpets sounded an elaborate fanfare. The entire hall fell silent. My stomach turned.

By the time we at the back of the great hall bowed or curtsied, those at the front had already risen. Thus I had no sight at all of the great Queen's entry, for the throng was too great.

The audience commenced. Each of the solicitants was called forward in turn, but at first they, too, were from the front of the crowd. I was alone, at the back, among strangers. No-one spoke to me. The English were at their most English, laughing uproariously at the private jokes of those they knew intimately while shunning those whom they knew not, particularly if they were foreign and Catholic. And the audiences went on endlessly. The Chamberlain announced the Earl of This, or Milady That. If the Queen found the suit tedious, she would despatch it in a minute or less: as I could not see or hear her, I could judge only by the interval between the Chamberlain's introductions. But if she found a suit interesting, an entire quarter-hour might elapse, with those at the back of the hall – in other words, all those around me – falling back into their own loud conversations. Thus it was, in the midst of a hubbub, that I very nearly missed the Chamberlain's cry: 'The Countess of Ravensden!'

The Red Sea parted. A great highway opened up through the throng, and the eyes of all, on either side, were fixed avidly upon me; for, of course, they had known who I was from the very beginning, and were murmuring words like 'papist', 'French' and 'traitor'. And there, at the end of the highway, was my destination.

My fate.

My Queen.

From a distance, she seemed so very small, there upon the dais. The throne itself was dwarfed by an enormous scarlet canopy, emblazoned with the royal arms of England and its supporters, a roaring lion and a red dragon. A vast red oyster revealing the tiniest but finest pearl in all the world. She shimmered in the spring sunlight that streamed through the great windows of the palace. It was as though she was the queen of light itself, its beams streaming forth from her luminous frame. I walked forward as though in a dream, dimly aware of the murmuring all around, terrified that the warmth of the rays emanating from England's royal majesty would melt me long before I reached the dais.

But as I came closer, I realised – yes, realised through my fear and awe – that the light was but an illusion. Scores, perhaps hundreds, of jewels were sown into the Queen's dress, reflecting the beams shining through the windows.

And that was why I trembled no more.

For this was theatre. The royal audience had been timed for precisely the moment when the rays of the Sun in March would shine through the windows of the Presence Chamber, so as to reflect from the astonishing number of precious stones adorning the frame of Gloriana.

The very old frame. For now, as I came closer, I could see that the stunning red hair was a wig. The eternally youthful face that stared out from portraits hanging in great houses the length and breadth of England was an illusion, too: for no matter how much white paste was applied to the royal face, not even an ocean of it could conceal the wrinkles and folds upon her neck and bosom, the eternal tell-tales of a woman's true age. As I now know too well, grandson –

But, of course, my growing confidence was yet another illusion. For as I came within three or four steps of the throne, I realised that I was committing the worst sin imaginable in the entire realm of England. My eyes were not cast demurely upon the ground, as the age-old rules of the court dictated. Instead, I was staring directly at the face of the Virgin Queen herself, Elizabeth, by the Grace of God, sovereign lady of England, Supreme Governess of its heretical church, defender of its unlawful faith. And she was staring back at me, the white mask singularly failing to conceal the hatred in her expression. Her true expression, the one that she took such great pains to conceal from the world. The one that no-one, but no-one, was permitted to look upon.

I curtsied as deeply as I could, lowering my eyes to the royal shoes as protocol dictated, and cursed my pride and arrogance. Whatever I said now, my husband was already damned.

'My Lady Ravensden,' said Queen Elizabeth. She spoke slowly, in an imperious tone that I had expected, but with a quivering, bordering on a croak, at the end of each phrase; the voice of an old woman trying, and failing, to conceal the fact that she is old. 'Well, well. How surprising that *you* should have snared Matthew Quinton. You are too small. Too flat in the bosom. Too French. Too Papist. Nothing like the Earl's first three wives. I liked the second one. The others were worthless.'

'Your Majesty,' I said, 'I crave pardon, both for my presumption and on behalf of my husband, asking that your most gracious Majesty might show your renowned mercy towards him—'

'Matthew Quinton has displeased me time upon time. Marrying *you*, of all womankind, without my permission, is but one of his more recent offences.'

I was drowning, dragged down by the whirlpool of royal contempt. Although part of me wanted to scream defiance at this crabbed, petulant old woman, another part could only admire the authority that exuded from every inch of her frame. Here was a woman who had ruled an entire kingdom for over forty years, a woman who had ridden out in armour to lead her own armies against a mighty invader, and despite myself, I could not be anything but awestruck in her formidable presence.

'Your Majesty, I humbly beg you to consider that my husband may be many things – impetuous, often intemperate, no doubt foolish in electing to marry one so feeble and so French as I – but he is no traitor. There is no man in England more loyal to you, Your Majesty.'

'That is not what Secretary Cecil tells me. He tells me there is a very good chance that the second witness to your husband's treason is alive after all. And even if he is not, My Lady Ravensden, I think the Tower is the best place for the Earl to be. By far the best place. For no Englishman who is truly loyal to me would ever besmirch that loyalty by marrying a Papist.'

She raised her hand to conclude the audience. The courtiers nearest to the throne clapped at her disdainful dismissal of both me and the faith I followed. Several sneered at me. The chamberlain stepped forward. There was one chance, just one chance, and I had to take it. I reached into my petticoats, between my breasts, and produced the paper. Those immediately around the throne gasped in shock – to make such a sudden movement in the Queen's presence was unheard of – the guards stepped forward, their halberds levelled, fearing I was a Jesuitical assassin –

For half a moment, no more, I saw raw fear in the eyes of Elizabeth Tudor. Then I thrust out the paper toward her.

'Your Majesty, I beg you to read this – the paper of which I notified you in my last letter –'

The chamberlain stepped forward to snatch the paper from me, but I kept a tight hold of it.

'Subjects do not thrust papers under the nose of their Sovereign!' cried the Queen, in a shriek loud enough to silence several of the rows nearest her. 'You have offended us, Lady Ravensden. Deeply offended us! Guards, arrest this impertinent harpy.'

A halberdier came up to each of my shoulders. The chamberlain held out his hand, and I placed the paper within it.

'Trust me, Your Majesty,' I said, before they could lead me away, 'you will want to read this paper yourself. It concerns one close to you in blood, and comes from a certain casket in which you have long taken an interest.'

The white mask was impassive. She waved a hand, and the guards turned, gesturing for me to accompany them. But before I left the hall, I saw the Queen take the paper from the chamberlain, unfold it, and read.

Nicholas Iles:

It had rained for days. The roads were at best quagmires, at worst entirely impassable, forcing long detours onto rocky upland tracks that were full of drovers and their herds, heading in the opposite direction.

Great mountains rose up all around, water flooding down their sides in torrents. The inns were damp and vile, not fit even for the meanest English beggar. The people were shifty and incomprehensible. Yet I felt a lightness in the heart that I had not known in months. I was free of the spectre of Laszlo Horvath, and the even more menacing wrath of Robert Cecil. I had been true in my duty to the Earl and the Countess. I had acted the part of a man of honour, and played it well: so well that the part had become the man I really was.

But now I was playing another part, and at last, my destination opened up before me. An extraordinary vast harbour, many miles long, yet very nearly devoid of shipping. But in a bay near its mouth, a small man-of-war lay at anchor. She was taking on water, the barrels being rowed out to her from a beach that lay beneath a decayed old fort of King Henry's time. If I were King Philip of Spain, I thought, I could surely devise no better place to invade the Queen of England's realms than here at Milford Haven.

A large, aged, white bearded fellow, clad in scarlet satin finery distinctly at odds with his circumstances, watched my approach with interest.

'You'll be the man Lord Ravensden recommended, I'll wager,' he said as I reined in before him, his accent the broadest Devonian.

'I am. My name is—'

'I know what your name is. Or at least, the name that you and Matt Quinton have conjured up between you. Don't matter a jot to me. Only matters that he's paying good gold for me to enter you on my ship's books as a gentleman volunteer. Not that you look much like a gentleman, nor like a fighter, come to that. But that don't matter a jot neither. The noble Earl and I, we have an understanding that goes back twenty years, since he went out with me on his first voyage as a young gentleman volunteer, as I expect he told you. We owe each other more debts than the Fuggers and the Habsburgs, My Lord and I. Besides, you're not likely to see much fighting on the Irish station – Lord Tyrone and his rebellious papist hordes don't like getting their feet wet, that they don't.' The old man held out his right arm. 'So welcome aboard Her Majesty's ship the *Halcyon*, my friend, and accept the hand of Captain Griffin Rugg.'

The Dowager Countess:

It was only after the key turned in the latch that I realised the enormity of it all. I had offended Queen Elizabeth herself, to her face, before her entire court. I had been arrested, and placed in a cold, barely furnished tower room, with a view of the Thames far below. Perhaps I would shortly join my husband in the Tower. Perhaps we were both destined for the block, and then what would become of little Beth? Alone with nothing but my fears, I began to sob.

I must have been there for two or three hours. I sobbed. I prayed. I sobbed again. Then the key turned once more, and the chamberlain who had been present in the Great Hall stood in the doorway, gesturing for me to follow him. Without a word, he led me down a stairway, through a tapestried gallery, down another stairway, along a bare stone corridor, courtiers and servants becoming fewer and fewer with every step we took. Finally, we came to a great oak door, guarded by two halberdiers. The chamberlain knocked and entered.

I followed him into the splendidly decorated room, and fell at once into a curtsy even deeper than the one I had executed in the great hall.

Alone in one of her most private apartments, the Queen seemed infinitely taller than she had in the vastness of the hall. Indeed, she seemed like a giant, a blazing scarlet sky framing the setting sun through the great window behind her.

She held the paper I had given her, and raised it slowly, as though contemplating it for the first time.

'This is a copy, My Lady Ravensden. Thus it might well be a forgery, for all I know,' she said. The Queen now spoke in flawless French, rather than the English she had employed in public. 'You have the original?'

'No, Your Majesty,' I lied. 'But my husband can obtain it readily enough, if he were free to do so, that is.'

'You seek to bargain with me, Lady Ravensden? With the Lord's Anointed? The Queen of England does not haggle like a fishwife in Billingsgate, *madame*.'

'No, Your Majesty. I crave your pardon for my presumption. But you must know my husband is no traitor – he has been unjustly maligned by an alien named Horvath—'

'Rich words, coming from a fellow alien!'

'By birth, perhaps, but by marriage a Countess of England, Majesty, despite my clinging to a faith that you and your people find hateful beyond measure—'

She raised a silk-gloved hand.

'Your faith is of no concern to me, Lady Ravensden, in spite of what it might be needful for the Queen to say in public. I have said before, and often, that I will not make windows into men's souls, although there are many in this land who would have the windows broken with hoe-staves and the souls sent directly to hell.'

'Your Majesty is most gracious. But whatever cause the man Horvath has for his malice towards my husband, he cannot prove a charge of treason. The second witness he procured proved true to My Lord, and is now dead in any case.'

'Dead, is he? Secretary Cecil doubts that, Lady Ravensden, and I have learned to take the Secretary's doubts very seriously. But no matter. Whether he lives or feeds the worms is of no real concern to me. What is of concern is your claim that your husband can obtain the original of this letter. If he were truly loyal, he would offer it up to his Queen freely, and then depend upon divine mercy. That is to say, my mercy.'

'My husband is...constrained...in that, Your Majesty.'

Her eyes narrowed. I sensed the fury coursing through her. I expected the full force of royal wrath to strike me at any moment. She would order her guards to take me away again, to rot, forgotten, in a cell.

Instead, the Queen's next question was unexpected, and mildly worded, almost whispered.

'You know the contents of this letter?'

'I do, Your Majesty.'

I decided it was best not to tell her that I was the one who had copied it from the original, which nestled at that very moment in a secret hiding place within Ravensden House.

'Then you and your husband will know its importance to me. Its importance to England, perchance.' The Queen turned away, walked to the window – a slow, slightly unsteady walk – and looked out over the Thames to the bank beyond. To her England. 'I would have the original. So I have a proposition for you, Lady Ravensden. Your husband's release – but for appearance's sake, it will not be a full and immediate release. House arrest, I think, at Ravensden Abbey, if he has finally put it into enough of a state of repair to be habitable. Bedfordshire should place him sufficiently far from the court, and above all from the attentions of Secretary Cecil, who will disapprove of my acting thus, beyond doubt. In return, the original of this letter to be delivered to me by Lady Day.'

I could not resist a thought: *is this not haggling like a Billingsgate fishwife after all, Your Majesty?* Instead, of course, I merely curtsied deeply and offered up a silent prayer to the heavenly Virgin Queen, in grateful acknowledgement of the royal mercy displayed by England's great Elizabeth.

CHAPTER EIGHTEEN

Laszlo Horvath

Iles has disappeared. Matthew Quinton has been freed from the Tower. My condition is not what I would wish it to be.

Indeed, I fear my condition will soon become worse. Secretary Cecil refuses to see me. It is clear that he regards me as a broken reed, and has no further use for me. Even Master Trevor, no doubt following the lead of the hunchback, will have nothing to do with me. And it is as certain as night follows day that some time, very soon, the Earl of Ravensden will seek me out, to be avenged upon me.

I consider returning to Hungary, to the life I once had and the war I know so well. But I chide myself that these are the thoughts of a coward. I have come this far, and I have sworn an oath upon my mother's grave.

No. I must look to the future. And that future rides into Whitehall, one March day, preceded by the foulest noise imaginable, made by men in skirts who appear to be blowing into sacks.

I still have enough coin to be able to buy information from a knowing fellow selling knives by the Charing Cross. The dignitaries, it seems, are Lords Mar and Kinloss: ambassadors of James, King of Scots. For a second coin, my informant tells me the tale that is sweeping the kitchens of Whitehall Palace, that place where the truest information in the kingdom is to be found. With the Earl of Essex dead, my informant says, there is nothing to stop Secretary Cecil supporting King James as the successor to England's throne – nothing but the hunchback's previous support for the Infanta, and the King's consequent suspicion of him. So this embassy will repair the breech between James Stuart and Robert Cecil, and make it even more likely that the former will be the next monarch of England.

Yes, I must look to the future, and as I watch the ambassadors ride into the heart of the palace, I know that my future lies in Scotland. It lies there until one old woman's overlong life finally comes to its end.

The next morning, I set out to ride north.

Nicholas Iles:

'This is what you meant by very little fighting on the Irish station, Captain Rugg?' I shouted, above the roar of the firing of our forward chase guns.

'A lesson I learned alongside Drake and Hawkins back at San Juan de Ulua in Sixty-Eight,' said the old man, gruffly, 'and that I taught to Matthew of Ravensden in his turn. A simple rule of life, my friend. Whenever you see a fucking Spaniard, open fire.'

We had stumbled across the small galleon an hour earlier, when we rounded a headland to the west of the town called Sligo. She was at anchor, as large as life, as though she had every right to be there. Every right to take her ease within the Queen's own waters, off Her Majesty's own coast. She cut her cables briskly and sailed directly eastward upon the breeze. But surely there was no escape to the east –

'He's running for Sligo,' said Rugg. 'Red Hugh's territory. He knows he'll be safe there, under the rebel guns.'

'Red Hugh, Captain?'

'Hugh O'Donnell, the Earl of Tyrconnell. Leader of the rebellion in these parts, just as O'Neill of Tyrone is over in Ulster. Cunning bastard, the O'Donnell, but brave with it. And he's got a Spanish ship visiting him. Now why would that be, I wonder?'

Our bow guns fired again, but the splashes fell well short of the Spaniard, who now had all sail set. Rugg pressed the *Halcyon* forward, bellowing orders to the men in the tops, berating the helmsman for his tardiness.

'Too foul,' he said, 'too fucking foul by far. I wanted to careen at Milford, but would My Lord Deputy Mountjoy allow it? No, My Lord Deputy Mountjoy would not, despite him being an old friend of Matt Quinton and knowing my connection to him. "You must be on station, Rugg, to burn cottages on the shores of Munster and kill a few flocks of papist sheep." Words to that effect, at any rate. We're a sixteen-gun pinnace and should be the fastest ship between here and Cadiz, but can we even outrun a Spanish slug? Damnation if we can, friend Nick, damnation I say.'

We were only a mile or two off shore, a featureless level landscape broken only by occasional tower-castles flying the Irish colours from their ramparts. It was meant to be part of Queen Elizabeth's empire, but it looked very much like an enemy nation. That impression was heightened as the Spaniard passed into the estuary that led up to the walls of Sligo, and the batteries at the mouth of Sligo Bay fired a mighty bombardment to warn us off. Griffin Rugg judged the limits of the Irish gunners' range as revealed by the fall of shot, listened to the leadsman's shouts as he reported the depth of water, and finally gave order to drop anchor.

'Well, then,' said the captain of the *Halcyon*, 'our Spanish friend isn't going to stay there for ever, you can be certain of that. King Philip's accounts will need balancing, so he'll need to be back in Lisbon or the Groyne by a certain date, whatever that might be. Which means the Don's going to have to come out some day, and when she does, we'll be waiting for him.'

The Dowager Countess:

We left Ravensden House at dawn and went north in the Earl's coach, an extravagant contraption similar to that used by my King Henri; our fellow road users must have cursed us for the depth of the ruts we created. The road to Bedfordshire was busy, full of carts, wagons, horsemen and above all beggars, their hands extended toward each and every passer-by in the hope of alms, most of them shuffling slowly south toward the promised land of London.

Finally, we crossed into the demesne lands of the Earls of Ravensden, and my husband breathed a great sigh of relief. If he was not yet entirely a free man, returning to his own estate was a form of liberty beyond measure.

'I remember when all this land was wooded,' he said, 'and that land over there was all ridge-and-furrow. Now look at it. My father had all the trees cut down, and enclosed the old open fields. Progress, he called it. Following the fashion, he said. More profit, he promised. And perhaps, one day, he will be proved right. But sometimes, I regret the passing of the old England that I knew. The England of bountiful harvests and good cheer, before the people turned fearful and began to see Jesuit murderers and Spanish plots everywhere. The days when we had a great Queen, and great ministers serving her.'

He fell silent, lost in thought, and I knew better than to disturb him.

Finally, Ravensden Abbey itself came into view from the window of our coach, and my husband brightened. The Earl pointed out this glory and that wonder, this historical curiosity and that architectural novelty, but all I saw were ruins.

'My grandfather planned to demolish the chancel,' he said, 'especially after the roof collapsed, but my grandmother, the Countess Katherine, was determined that it should stand, and out of respect to her, I have kept it standing too. I think she secretly prays that the monasteries will be restored one day, and Cistercians will perform their holy offices within its walls once again. So the fourth Earl converted the nave into a great hall, the transepts and crossing into the principal rooms, the monastic refectory and chapter house into—'

'Your grandmother,' I said. *His grandmother is a hundred years old, and cannot die.* 'She is here? At Ravensden?'

'She is,' said my husband, with evident discomfort. 'In a room high up in the south transept. We shall have to pay our respects to her, of course, but she will not know we are there. She does nothing but sit in her window, looking down at the graves in the chancel. It is a miracle that she has lived so very long, and a tragedy that she has buried all her children. And their wives. Her grandchildren, too, but for me.'

'And your mother?'

'Her wits gone beyond all hope, these last five years.' *His mother is mad, and has been locked away in a tower for years.* 'We keep her in the dower house across the valley, Quinton Hall.'

I fell silent, thinking of the terrible nightmare that had afflicted me during the loss of my twins. And now I was living it, for in all truth, I was surrounded by nothing but dead countesses on the one hand, and mad countesses on the other. Was I destined shortly to be one or the other? Or, perchance, each in turn?

For the first time, I doubted the wisdom of marrying Matthew Quinton.

Nicholas Iles:

We lay at anchor off Sligo for seventeen days.

In the past, I would have used such an opportunity to write a sonnet or two, or to work on some scenes of a play. But somehow, I no longer had the appetite for words. More and more, though, I had the appetite for action. Thus when Griffin Rugg proposed a cutting-out expedition, I volunteered eagerly.

'You're certain, young Nick? Cutting out can be a furious business. An uncertain business, too. If you fall into the hands of the Dons, well, that's one thing, if you fancy the rest of your life as a galley slave. But if you fall into the hands of the Irish…then God help you, my friend.'

I was undeterred, and that was how I found myself upon a moonless night in the lead boat of four, being rowed into the bay of Sligo.

'Coney Island to starboard, Rosses Point to larboard, Oyster Island ahead,' murmured Larkin, the square-shouldered boatswain of the *Halcyon*, pointing to each low, dark mass in turn. 'The Spaniard'll be dead ahead, behind Oyster, close to the north shore where the deep channel is, close to Sligo town.'

The oars cut the water quietly and slowly, so as not to make splashes that might be seen from the shore. The Halcyon's crew were greatly experienced in such expeditions, it seemed. And at last, there ahead of us, was the Spaniard, as Larkin predicted. The hull was black, the masts and yards only dimly visible. There was no sign of light at all. The Dons were asleep, and we would bring this off exactly as Rugg had explained it. Two boats to the bow, two to the stern, board silently, kill silently, cut the anchor cables, tow her out before the Irish batteries flanking Rosses Point and Coney Island knew what was happening –

'*Madre de Dios*! *El Inglés*!'

I saw a sudden flurry of movement on the beakhead, and knew at once what it meant. The ship's head was there.

'Christ's fuck,' said Larkin, 'that one of them needed a shit at this time of the night!'

The Spaniard had been there long enough to get his night sight, for we were still a good thirty yards short of the bow. But there was now no chance of reaching it. I saw the flash from the forecastle of the first musket's match, then heard the report. A moment later there was a second gun alongside it, then a third. A bell was being rung with the ferocity of an alarm against the horsemen of the Apocalypse.

Larkin picked up a primed musket and handed it to me.

'You know how to fire one of these?'

'I have mock-fired one upon the stage—'

'The *stage*? Jesus!'

With that, Larkin fired his own weapon, then bawled the order to the helmsman to bring the boat about. I lifted the musket to my shoulder. Surely there was something about checking the match? But the cord was glowing red, and that was surely right – And should I not check the pan?

A Spanish ball splintered the boat's wale at my left side, and the fright made me squeeze the trigger.

The musket slammed into my shoulder, knocking me backwards. Only Larkin grabbing my arm saved me from falling out of the boat, and to my death in Sligo Bay. My eyes and nose streamed from the acrid cloud of smoke given off by the shot. I was deaf, the sound of my shot blasting out again and again in my head. But I could just hear a distant screaming, too, and knew it was not my own, nor that of any of the men behind me.

'If you're that lucky in war every time, my friend,' Larkin was saying, 'then I want to fight all the rest of my battles alongside you, by Christ!'

We were through our turn, and my senses returned as we made headway away from the Spaniard. There was no need to hide our oar splashes now, and the men were straining their backs with the effort. But our progress was slow, and even such a lubber as myself knew why. Rugg had timed the attack so we would go into Sligo Bay at the height of the flood tide. By the time we secured the ship, according to his reckoning, the ebb would have begun, and we would have an easier task of towing her out. But we were coming out of the bay much sooner than he had intended, which meant we were rowing against the tide. And it meant we were in a race against the horsemen we could see and hear ashore, carrying blazing torches as they galloped along the foreshore towards Rosses Point. A losing race, for even by night, a horseman will easily outstrip a row-boat.

'The next quarter hour will be hot work,' said Larkin.

So it proved. We were in the very middle of the channel between the Point and Coney Island when the first cannon fired from the shore. I saw the spout of water, perhaps ten yards off to our larboard.

'Elevated to hit a ship's hull,' said the boatswain. 'They'll adjust the range downward—'

A second shot –

This time the waterspout erupted barely five yards directly astern. The boat pitched and rolled. Water soaked every one of us. Now the cannon were joined by musket fire, and although the Irish were firing blind, and at the limit of their range, they were still a deadly proposition. There was a cry from the middle of the boat, and I saw one of the men slump against his oar. The man by him felt for a pulse, shook his head, and at once slung the corpse over the side.

I felt no shock. I felt no fear. I knew what I had to do: without Larkin saying a word to me, I immediately stepped over and took the vacant place at the oar. It was on my second or third pull that the boat immediately astern of us suddenly tore apart, wood, limbs and water blown to the heavens, as a cannon shot struck it square on. No more than a dozen strokes later, the fourth boat in our little fleet was struck. In one sense, she had luck; she was only holed, and turned for the shore, where her crew could beach her. But that shore was full of Irish rebels. *If you fall into the hands of the Irish, then God help you.*

When we got back to the ship, Rugg said not a word to me, but placed in my hand a bottle of the favoured drink of those parts. Whiskey, they call it. And I drank it as though it were the very nectar of the gods.

The Earl of Ravensden:

I could not sleep. This was a rare state of affairs, as I had been known to sleep through entire broadsides. But being back at Ravensden Abbey had a strange effect on me. It was a homecoming, and freedom of a sort. I should have relished the joys of my own home, my own hearth, and my own bed. But all the thoughts I had suppressed during my time in the Tower, or else channelled into the efforts to secure my release, now came pouring out.

I longed to be at sea, to have the command I believed myself entitled to, to be avenged on the Spanish and especially General Spinola and his cursed galleys. I envied Iles, who was at sea at that very moment, in the rough but steady hands of old Griff Rugg. I wanted nothing more than to fight Spaniards, but there seemed but a very distant prospect of that.

I longed for a son. As I dressed, I looked down at the sleeping form of Louise-Marie, and wondered if she would give me that. If she *could* give me that, after one girl and dead twins; and none of my wives had ever given me more than three children. Or would she go the way of –

Then there was England's great matter. The Queen wanted the letter by Lady Day; yet if I surrendered the letter, what guarantees did I have for my future, and that of my unborn heir?

Above all: Laszlo Horvath. Where was he? Who was he? How could I have been so foolish as to be gulled by him for so long? Why had he sought to bring me to a traitor's death?

I went down, and out into the ruins of the chancel. It was a cold, moonlit night, past two in the morning. I walked among the graves, standing in turn before those of my father, that most guarded and enigmatic of men; of his eldest brother Matthew, the fifth Earl, the prodigiously gifted friend and playmate of King Edward the Sixth, but dead at twenty-two; and of their father Henry, the builder of Ravensden Abbey in its present form. Then the graves of my wives: dear Letitia, whose death in childbirth drove me to seek solace at sea; bold Anne, so much older than me, lying alongside our two daughters; and sly, treacherous Mary, next to the graves of our girls and the son she bore me, poor Harry, dead at but four years of age. Three dead wives, all of them devoted daughters of the Church of England by law established. Perhaps marriage to a Papist would succeed where theirs failed, just as it had done for my grandfather, another old warrior Earl who married a very much younger woman. Or was my marriage a terrible mistake, which served only to cast me further into the outer darkness of the Queen's disfavour?

No inspiration came from the dead, only the recollection of unbearable sorrows and fear of a childless future, of the extinction of the House of Quinton. No answers, only the sense that I was alone, and would go to my own tomb in this place remembered solely as one of the very many whose star briefly shone brightly during the reign of Elizabeth the Great, only to be extinguished just as quickly as it had risen.

I turned to go in, and noticed candlelight in a high window: my grandmother's window. But that was impossible. Her nurse would have put her to bed at nine, and the ancient Countess never stirred until four, when she woke unfailingly with the stroke of the clock; as she always had for the office of Lauds, in her days as a Gilbertine nun. Perhaps this was the moment, at last, when my grandmother went to meet her maker, to explain to Him why she had forsaken her vows for the bed of Harry Quinton –

I ran up the stairs, and into my grandmother's room.

'My Lady! Grandmother!'

She was alive, sitting where she always sat. She must have been watching me, down in the chancel, and now she turned her head, very slightly, to acknowledge my presence.

Then some force, some strange instinct, made me do what I had always done as a child, when the family was riven by the increasingly strange behaviour and prolonged absences of Henry, the sixth Earl. I sat down upon a stool and began to pour out all my troubles to my grandmother, this frail, impossibly ancient creature who had been born when the first Tudor, Harry the Seventh, still sat upon the throne of England. In my youth, of course, she responded to my words, and her particular marrying of blunt good sense with a nearly tangible spirituality always seemed to make things better almost at once. As I grew older, I wondered if this stemmed from her early life in the convent; although the Quintons were Protestant and had, like England as a whole, abandoned confession as a false construct of Rome, there was always a powerful sense of release in opening one's heart to one who had done nothing else for fifteen years but speak directly to God on high, and whose confession was once heard by Cardinal Wolsey himself.

I told her everything; or very nearly everything, for I judged it inopportune to tell a woman who had buried all her children and all but one of her grandchildren that I feared I would never have a son, and would die the last Earl of Ravensden. But I told her of the fate of Gowrie, of my reasons for going to Fast Castle, and of what I had obtained there. I told her of the Queen's hostility to me, and how all of England blamed me for the calamities of the Invisible Armada and the Spinola galleys. God knows, I even told her how ignorant men in power were convinced that the day of the true-hulled English ship was over, and were determined to replace it with the infernal monstrosities called galleys, as being at once more fashionable and cheaper, as they falsely believed, for even the greenest swabber could have told the greatest minister of state that galleons carry fewer men and more guns, and are thus cheaper by far.

In response to all of this, she made not one sound. The ancient eyes were fixed upon me, but they were blank, merely blinking from time to time to signify that their owner still lived.

Dawn was breaking beyond the ruinous east window of the abbey church.

'But there is one matter that strikes me in the heart more than any of these, grandmother. I placed my trust in one who betrayed me – who sought, indeed, to destroy me, by bringing a charge of treason against me. If he had succeeded, this very house and the title itself might have been lost to us by attainder.' I hoped the notion of the House of Quinton losing everything might provoke some reaction, but the ancient face remained entirely impassive. It was like speaking to a statue. 'This man is a stranger in the realm, an alien, who can have no possible grievance against me. So before we both attempt to find our second sleep, let me tell you how I took him in, and how he proved false – this Hungarian, this man who calls himself Laszlo Horvath—'

I continued, my eyes fixed upon the floor rather than looking into the fixed expression of the gargoyle that my grandmother had become. But then a strange, rasping sound made me look up. Katherine, Dowager Countess of Ravensden, who had not spoken in over ten years, was clearing her throat. The ancient face was contorted with effort. I moved toward her, convinced that this was her long delayed death-apoplexy.

Instead, another sound emerged from her mouth. A word.

'Horvath,' she said, her voice a barely audible rasp.

I was astonished; I had thought never to hear her speak again. But this was no cause for rejoicing. After all, many a dumb avian can simply repeat the words of its owner.

'My Lady?' I said, cautiously. 'Grandmother? You are well?'

'Horvath,' she said again. The mouth opened and closed without a sound. Then, unbelievably, it formed an entire sentence, as her ancient eyes bored into the very depths of my soul. 'What a fool you have been, grandson, to nurture that viper in your bosom.'

CHAPTER NINETEEN

1601-2

The Earl of Ravensden:

A swaying deck beneath my feet. Spray spilling from the cutwater. A cold sea breeze ruffling my hair and straining the medrinacks and poldavy canvas of the sails overhead. The shrill call of the boatswain's whistle. The shouts of the men in the tops. The *Merhonour*, sailing west with a squadron of our fellow race-built galleons, the crosses of Saint George streaming proudly from our staffs. A squadron with Matthew Quinton, Earl of Ravensden, as its vice-admiral. A squadron sailing to do battle with the Spanish. The only thing that could have made life better was for a mighty sea-monster to rise from the vasty deep and devour all of those upon the quarterdeck of the flagship, the *Warspite*, especially our illustrious admiral, Brick-Beard Leveson, the finest seaman ever to come out of Wolverhampton.

There was a rare urgency about our voyage, despite the fogs and then easterly winds that had delayed our passage from the Medway. In addition to our two flagships, we had the *Defiance, Garland, Swiftsure, Crane, Nonpareil,* and six victualling ships, all upon a mission of the utmost importance. For the Spanish had landed an army at Kinsale in the south of Ireland, fortifying the town and threatening to use it as a base to drive the English out of the entire country. My friend Lord Mountjoy, the Lord Deputy of Ireland, was moving to besiege it, but his forces were overstretched. Worse, the two rebel armies in the north of the country, those of O'Neill, Earl of Tyrone, and O'Donnell, Earl of Tyrconnell, were marching south to join the Spanish and to trap Mountjoy between them, as though in a great pincer. The fate of English rule in Ireland hung in the balance; and if Ireland fell, there could be little doubt that the Spanish would use it as a platform for an invasion of England itself. There would be no Invisible Armada this time, and no Invincible one either, for no Armada would be needed. If need be, on a calm and clear day, the Spanish could simply row themselves across the Irish Sea.

So we were sailing to besiege Kinsale from seaward, to attack the other forts the Spanish were garrisoning along the Irish coast, and to fight the squadron the Dons had stationed in those waters to support their army. It was a most glorious prospect, despite my being under the command of a coxcomb -

But it was no time to be churlish, I chided myself as the cold Irish rain stung my face. The Queen had been at once merciful and generous, in restoring me not only to my freedom but to a high command at sea. All this, despite the considerable awkwardness of my private meeting with Her Majesty at Greenwich Palace on the day appointed for the transfer of the Casket Letter to her.

'This is the original?' she demanded.

'You have my word of honour upon it, Your Majesty.'

'Matthew Quinton's word of honour. Well, then. Remember, My Lord, that I have encountered your "word of honour" before. For instance, your word of honour about the scale of the profit that would accrue to me from your various voyages. Your word of honour is not worth a fig, Lord Ravensden.'

If she had been a man, and not the Lord's Anointed, I would have issued my challenge there and then. Indeed, I felt my fingers twitch, instinctively seeking my sword hilt. But the perversity of Elizabeth Tudor being at once a woman and England's divinely ordained sovereign gave her a licence in what she said that would have been intolerable in any man, even in a king. I believe that Edward the Second had a red-hot poker stuck up his arse for insulting his nobility rather less often and less violently than the Virgin Queen insulted hers.

'Your Majesty, what possible reason could I have for keeping the original from you?' I said, as mildly as I could manage, all the while endeavouring to suppress the regicidal twitching in my fingers.

She looked at me – through that ghastly, fixed white-paste mask, which visibly cracked if she showed too much real emotion – and for a moment, just one moment, I wondered if she knew. If the legend of Gloriana's omniscience was, in fact, true.

'No,' she said at last, 'no man who desires a return to court and to a command at sea would be so foolish as to deceive his Queen.'

I bowed. 'Indeed not, Majesty. Then the return to court and to a command—'

'We shall think upon it, Lord Ravensden.'

With that, she waved her imperious hand, and ended the audience.

It took several months for the Queen to think upon it; a markedly rapid decision, by Her Majesty's standards. In the meantime, I lived with my wife at Ravensden Abbey, trying and failing to conceive the heir to Ravensden, while also brooding upon the astonishing revelation that had fallen from the ancient lips of my grandmother. Thanks to her, I now knew exactly who the man calling himself Laszlo Horvath really was, and why he wished to bring me down. He was beyond my reach, but only for the time being. I would have my reckoning with him – I had sworn it in the ruined chancel of Ravensden Abbey, before the graves of countless dead Quintons – but in the meantime there were Spaniards to fight, and a kingdom to save.

Nicholas Iles:

'Did you ever think you'd see the day, friend Nick?' said Griffin Rugg. 'The red and gold of Spain, flying over the soil of the Queen's own dominions. At least now we know why that fucking galleon was up at Sligo, those months ago. To tell the traitor Earls that their Castilian friends were coming.'

I remembered. A few days after the failure of our cutting-out expedition, Rugg ordered the *Halcyon* to abandon its anchorage close to the mouth of Sligo Bay, and to move several miles out to sea. We were upon a hostile shore and running desperately short of victuals, so he hoped that, by offering the Spaniard searoom, he would tempt her to come out. Which she duly did.

And outsailed us with an easy, mocking grace and speed which caused Griffin Rugg to remark, 'I'll tell you one thing, young Nick. The Dons won't have sent a ship that good to these parts just to deliver King Philip's respects to Red Hugh, or to send him a few bottles of Jerez. Mark old Rugg's word on it – something's afoot.'

The *Halcyon* now lay in the mouth of Kinsale harbour. Despite the relentless, bitterly cold rain, we could clearly see the Spanish colours streaming out from the towers of Ringcurran Castle. This fortress guarded the eastern approach to the town itself, out of sight beyond a great turn in the river. It had been the same story as we sailed along the south coast of Ireland: Berehaven, Baltimore and Castlehaven, together with Donneshead and Dunboy Castles, were all garrisoned by the Dons.

But their main strength was here, at Kinsale, where General Don Juan del Aguila and some 3,500 men awaited the arrival of the armies of the Irish earls, said to be marching down from the north of the country.

There was a puff of smoke on the hillside above Ringcurran, then another, followed by the distant booms.

'Lord Mountjoy's guns are active today,' I said.

'Much good it'll do them,' said Rugg. 'Even if the castle falls, Mountjoy hasn't got the strength to take the town itself. And once the rebels get here, God alone knows what the issue of it will be.'

I looked out at the gloomy prospect: one of the Queen's own castles, and one of her own towns, under the heel of the murderous papist Spanish invaders. It was the stuff of a play, if I had but the inclination to write it.

'Sails, ho!' cried the lookout.

'Where away?' demanded Rugg. He knew, as did we all, that sails from the west could only be Spanish reinforcements, but sails from the east meant the promised relief from England.

'Eastward, Captain!'

'Thanks be unto God,' said Rugg, a man whose religion usually consisted chiefly of charms and suspiciously pagan oaths.

During the next hours, the hulls became clearer through the rain.

'The *Merhonour*!' I cried.

'Aye, and flying a vice-admiral's flag at the fore, too,' said Rugg. 'It seems My Lord Ravensden has prospered. And I expect he'll want you back, to chronicle his mighty deeds.'

'I shall base a character upon you, Captain Rugg,' I said, smiling.

In truth, I had no intention of returning to the *Merhonour*, at any rate in the immediate term; too many aboard her knew me by my true name, and several of them were bound to know that a fat reward could be obtained by reporting my presence to Secretary Cecil. But my light-hearted aside had a strange effect upon Griffin Rugg.

'Sakes, no, lad!' he cried, his face ashen. It was the first time I had ever seen the old warrior seem genuinely afraid. 'There's a wise woman outside Barnstaple who swears that if you have your portrait painted, or your name appears in a book or a play, then the devil steals your soul.'

'My Lord has had his portrait painted,' I said through my shock. 'His name has appeared in many books, and I am writing a play about him. Does that mean the devil has stolen his soul, Captain?'

The old man did not answer. Instead, he looked away, toward the approaching fleet.

The Earl of Ravensden:

Trumpets blew, pikes, halberds and muskets were brought smartly to attention, and the crew of the *Warspite* gave three huzzahs as her distinguished visitor stepped aboard. He was a little younger than me: a tall, extravagantly dressed fellow, clad in dark satin and cloth of gold, with an open face, a grave expression and arched eyebrows. But the two features that distinguished him most were the astonishing bush of curling black hair adorning his head and the thick cloud of smoke that always surrounded him, pouring forth from the clay pipe that hardly ever left his mouth.

He acknowledged my admiral perfunctorily.

'Sir Richard,' he said. 'Your fleet's arrival is timely.'

'Thank you, My Lord. We will do our utmost to support—'

'My Lord of Ravensden! Damn me, Matt Quinton in the very flesh.' He grasped me by the shoulders. 'You won me a fair purse, Matt – I'd wagered you'd leave the Tower a free man, rather than having your head cut off! And so you have, man. So you have.'

Although his intent was light-hearted, he spoke the words as gravely as an Archbishop delivering a sermon.

I bowed my head, smiling as I did so.

'I am always content if I can improve your lordship's condition,' I said merrily, as sycophantic as a Cecil.

I looked up, and caught the look of utter discomfiture on the face of Sir Richard Leveson. Admiral he might have been, but he knew full well that in the council of war we were about to embark upon, he would have to defer to this new arrival, Charles Blount, eighth Baron Mountjoy, the Lord Deputy of Ireland: to all intents and purposes, Her Majesty's viceroy upon that benighted isle.

A little later, as we pored over the maps and charts in the great cabin of the *Warspite*, the shift in power became ever more apparent.

'I have sent Sir George Carew west to try and intercept Lord Tyrconnell's army,' said Mountjoy, still drawing vigorously upon his pipe, 'but I cannot depend upon the success of his venture. I must base my calculations on the assumption that both of the Irish armies will be here before Christmas, after their march from the north. So time is of the essence, gentlemen. Now, Ringcurran Castle, here—' Mountjoy stabbed at the map before us – 'will fall within a day or two. It is too isolated from the main Spanish garrison. Del Aguila knows that, and has only been putting up a show of resistance there for appearance' sake. But Castlenipark fort, here, on the other side of the estuary, is a different matter. If we reduce that, we have free passage up to Kinsale town itself, and del Aguila knows that too. So I would have you assault Castlenipark, gentlemen. And then I would have you attack the Spanish fleet, which sits within the harbour of Castlehaven, here, to the west.'

'A sound strategy, My Lord,' said Leveson, trying hard to sound as though he knew what he was talking about. 'If the general knows that he will not be relieved by sea, and has no means of escape, then he may be more inclined to treat for terms.'

'Unless, of course, the Spanish are preparing to send another, larger fleet to relieve or reinforce the garrison in Kinsale,' I said.

'Quite so, My Lord,' said Mountjoy, approvingly. Another noxious cloud billowed from the bowl of his pipe. 'Thus as I say, time is of the essence. We have to capture Kinsale before the Spanish can reinforce it, and to do that, we must do everything in our power to convince General del Aguila that his position is hopeless. Hence the attacks on Castlenipark and Castlehaven. God willing, the Spanish will surrender before the rebel armies get here.'

Neither Leveson nor I needed to utter the obvious caveat to Mountjoy's assessment: that if the Spanish did not surrender by the time the Irish arrived, Mountjoy would have to face their three conjoined armies in the field, and there would be precious little our fleet could do to help him.

'Very well, My Lords,' said Leveson, stroking the brick. 'I shall lead the ships up to Castlenipark, and then take them west into Castlehaven, while Lord Ravensden, as vice-admiral, blockades the mouth of Kinsale harbour in the meantime—'

'Sir Richard,' said Mountjoy, suddenly and unexpectedly abrupt in his tone, 'you are Admiral here, and of course, the question of your dispositions at sea is for you, and for you alone. With one exception, naturally.' Leveson frowned; and, I must confess, so did I. An admiral at sea was, in almost all senses, a god afloat, his authority unchallengeable, even if the admiral in question was Sir Richard Shit-for-Brains Leveson. 'I have here a letter,' said Mountjoy, handing the item in question to Leveson, 'from the palace of Greenwich, which came by way of Milford Haven and the Cove of Cork, arriving in my camp only yesterday. Both of you will recognise the seal, and the signature.'

Leveson studied the document, his mouth opening and closing, but no words came. He handed it to me. Oh yes, I recognised the seal. And the signature. And the intent behind the peroration.

Thus we have determined that any close and direct action against the enemy should be commanded in person by our most loyal and trusty servant Matthew, Earl of Ravensden, this being in no way a diminution of our trust in, nor a derogation of the honour of, our most worthy admiral, Sir Richard Leveson.

Elizabeth R.

I looked once again at the letter, then at Mountjoy, then at Leveson. In the former's face, I found sympathy; in the latter's, something that manifested itself as an unsubtle blend of shock, disgust, hatred, and hurt pride. Both reactions were entirely understandable. For all three of us in that cabin were thinking that the Queen's message could have only one meaning. For reasons of her own, Elizabeth Tudor wished me to go into harm's way. And if her reasons were what I suspected them to be, Her Majesty would not be displeased if the Earl of Ravensden returned from harm's way clad in a shroud.

Nicholas Iles:

When I went to him, in a private room he had secured in an alehouse of Rathmore, around the headland from Kinsale, he was already third-bottle morose.

'My Lord,' I said, when the flow of self-pity ebbed briefly and I was able finally to say my piece, 'it cannot be as you imagine it.'

'No, fuck and damnation, Iles—' he had forgotten my false name, the one he chose for me – 'it's every bit as I imagine it. She wants me dead, but not in any way that reflects on her. No trial, no execution, but Matthew Quinton dead, all the same. So why would she want me dead so soon after seeming to forgive me?'

'Because she is a woman, My Lord?'

His eyes narrowed as he attempted to focus on me with a little more steadiness than the third bottle provided.

'For one so young, Iles, you have a fucking jaundiced view of womankind. I don't think I had such thoughts until at least my second wife.' He waved a hand, in the vague way that sots favour. 'No, something, or someone, has turned the Queen against me – even more against me – since I last had audience of her. You're the poet, man. You invent motives for your characters with every stroke of your pen. So tell me what her motive is in this, if you say it is not what I think it is?'

'My Lord, even if the Queen put Secretary Cecil's finest onto the task of examining the letter, they would never have discovered it was a forgery. Monsieur Dehaene is a legend among our frat – that is, among those with whom I formerly consorted. That is why you paid him so much, upon my recommendation. If Dehaene had forged the Donation of Constantine, it would still be accepted by all of Christendom, and Martin Luther would have died in obscurity, just some disgruntled former monk that no man had ever heard of.'

'And if Dehaene himself betrayed us?' The Earl was eyeing a fourth bottle. 'We took the mightiest of risks, my friend, to deceive a crowned monarch so. I might not have been guilty of treason before, but I am certainly guilty of it now.'

'But My Lord, if the Queen suspected you of treason – of giving her a forgery – why would she not order your immediate arrest? Why would she insist that you, and not Sir Richard, should lead attacks that are so important to her realm's very existence?'

He seemed not to hear me. 'Of course,' he said, 'it might be Horvath – you know, Iles, I still cannot bring myself to call him by his true name? Perhaps he has wheedled his way back into Cecil's good graces. Perhaps...' He reached for the fourth bottle, and uncorked it. 'Ah, fuck and damnation, it's no longer worth the candle, my friend. If Gloriana herself wants me dead, then dead I shall be, soon enough. So come, let us drink, and you can tell me a cheery story. No, not a tale of classical heroes. I am done with heroism, I think. Tell me one of your stories of the stage, of a time when something went amiss. That one you told of scenery falling on top of Shakespeare made me laugh for weeks. And the story of the stage in Lincoln going up in flames and setting fire to the inn where you were performing – fuck me, I nearly wet myself over that one.'

So I told him the story of the performance of the second half of Marlowe's *Tamburlaine* in Chester, where one of the actors had slipped, fallen to the stage, somehow lashed out with the very real dagger he was carrying – the company's manager was a tyrant for authenticity – and managed to slice off the right foot of Tamburlaine at the ankle.

'Thanks be to God,' I said, 'I was playing Bajazeth that afternoon. If it had been the next day, when I was meant to be Tamburlaine again, I would now be upon a crutch in the gutter, begging for alms like so many thousands.'

My Lord laughed, and took another long draught of wine. Quite suddenly, though, he frowned, as though trying and failing to remember something very important. Then he looked at me. It was as though he was seeing me for the first time. His eyes widened, and he said, slurring his words, 'What did you say? Just now, about the attacks, and the Queen?'

By now, I, too, had drunk enough wine to be not entirely certain what he meant. But then I remembered, and essayed to look as serious as I could.

'The Queen insists on you leading them, My Lord, not Sir Richard. Nothing is more important to England at this moment than expelling the Spanish and defeating the Irish armies. So why would Her Majesty order you to lead the attacks, if she truly had no faith in you? If she suspected you had deceived her, and were guilty of treason? Surely, My Lord, it is more likely that this is a mark of the Queen's confidence in you?'

He thought upon it as hard as a three-bottle mind would permit, then poured himself a large measure from the fourth. Just before he raised the glass to his lips, he smiled.

'The Queen having confidence in me? Truly, that is a strange notion. A very strange notion. Perhaps, though – aye, just perhaps – you might be right, my friend. But when the last trump sounds, it really does not matter, does it? Whether she wants me alive or dead, tomorrow I lead the fleet upriver to attack Castlenipark Fort, and *that* is all that matters. So tonight, before they row me back to the *Merhonour*, let us drink, and you can tell me the old tales of Achilles and Hector again, friend Iles – ah, no, that is not your name now, is it? Remind me what I decided to call you, so I do not betray you in public.'

'Musk, My Lord. Nicholas Musk.'

'So be it, Nicholas Musk. Raise a glass with me, for tomorrow, with God's providence to help us, we'll remind the Spanish why they should never venture into the Queen of England's lands and seas. Just as we reminded them in 1588, by Christ.'

CHAPTER TWENTY

Nicholas Musk.

Musk.

Now, of course, Musk is a name that has loomed large in the history of the house of Quinton – in *my* history. Phineas Musk was nominally steward of Ravensden House in my brother's time, but somehow arranged to be in almost constant attendance upon me during my campaigns at sea. Phineas Musk: the most impertinent rascal who ever lived, and yet a man who would have given his life for the Quintons a hundred times over, and who saved my own more than once.

So when I read that name in Iles' papers, on a storm-lashed October day in the year 1651, I ran at once to *grandmaman*, who was reading a collection of Lovelace's poems, and demanded to know if Nicholas Iles – Nicholas *Musk* – was related to our Phineas. Was the poet the father of the steward, or had my grandfather chosen the false name by taking it from another Musk he already knew?

And this is what *grandmaman* said.

'What is that you say, grandson? Musk? The same name as that impudent rogue at Ravensden House? The impudent rogue who brought your brother back to us from the Worcester fight? That Musk? Related, you ask? Coincidence, you ask? Believe me, grandson, there is more to this world than relationships and coincidences. But not a great deal more, if truth be told.'

And with that, she returned to her reading and never uttered another word upon the subject, no matter how much I pressed her. The same was true of Phineas Musk, the three or four times that I posed the same question to him before abandoning the effort as a forlorn hope.

'Asking a man who his father is,' he said, the last time I raised it with him. 'Always dangerous, that. Always problematic. As members of your family should know better than most, Sir Matthew.'

The Earl of Ravensden:

'A shore battery of eight guns,' I said, 'and large ones, at that. Admiral Zubiaur has been busy.'

The distant Spanish guns, on the shore right at the entrance to Castlehaven harbour, fired occasional warning shots, but we were anchored too far off for them to come anywhere near us. The masts of the Spanish ships were clearly visible, further up the harbour: five big galleons, several lesser ships.

Brick-Beard and I stood upon the quarterdeck of the *Warspite*, surrounded by the captains of our little fleet. Our illustrious admiral was still in a rage at the Queen's orders, but was doing his utmost to conceal the fact. Regrettably, though, concealment of his true feelings was not Sir Richard Leveson's strong suit.

'Your proposal, then, My Lord?' said Brick-Beard in a sullen, peevish tone.

'There are only two things we can do,' I said. 'We can sit here at anchor and blockade the Dons all winter, but that will never serve – storms are bound to blow us off station, and we will have to send ships off to Cork harbour or Milford to revictual, weakening our strength. Zubiaur will choose his moment, then come out, and at all costs we must prevent him joining the defenders of Kinsale.'

Several heads nodded. All captains knew this: close blockade, especially in winter, was a fool's game.

'That leaves attack,' I said. 'We force the harbour. We send in a smaller ship to clear a channel for the *Merhonour* and whatever ships you choose to allot to my wake, Sir Richard. Fortunately, I have much experience of forcing harbours, although this Castlehaven seems to me no Cadiz or Lisbon.'

Leveson scowled at my boast of greater experience, but he knew that it was simply the truth. In that regard, at least, the Queen's orders made perfect sense: Matthew Quinton was the ideal man for this task. As was another.

'Begging pardon, My Lord, Sir Richard,' said Griffin Rugg, stepping forward, 'I volunteer to lead the Earl's flagship into the harbour. My *Halcyon* is the ideal size, and I know the haven, having taken her in there many times. And like My Lord, I have forced a few Spanish harbours in my day.'

Leveson waved a hand.

'So be it,' he said. 'Make your dispositions, Lord Ravensden.'

Nicholas Iles:

In one sense, the campaign seemed to be prospering. Ringcurran Castle fell before our attack on Castlenipark Fort began, and the latter proved an unqualified success. The Earl angled our guns high, so that they could reach the ramparts upon their hilltop, and then kept up a ferocious bombardment, joined by Lord Mountjoy's great culverins in their batteries ashore. The Dons held out, though – held out, that is, until a mighty explosion signified the blowing up of their magazine. We learned later that our assault brought an even greater disaster the way of the Spanish General del Aguila: the explosion of the magazine destroyed his personal stock of fine wines.

With the outlying forts taken, Lord Mountjoy could concentrate on the siege of the town itself. But that was the end of the promising news, for in every other sense, disaster seemed about to befall the Queen's forces. Lord Tyrconnell and the western Irish army had given Sir George Carew the slip and were coming through the mountains. Tyrone's eastern army could not be far away. There was nothing to stop the Irish joining forces with the troops from the outlying Spanish garrisons, and advancing to combine with their friends in Kinsale itself. And all the while, the relentless rain and cold formed a fourth army, perhaps the deadliest of all. Sentries were being brought in dead from their outposts. Trenches were filling with water as soon as they were dug. There was too little food, the horses were dying, and disease was ravaging the army. So we needed a victory, and it fell to My Lord to provide it. At Castlehaven.

The Earl of Ravensden:

'If the Queen had a hundred Griff Ruggs, England would rule the entire world,' I said to Tom Carver as I watched the *Halcyon* sail into the narrow channel of Castlehaven harbour.

The Spanish batteries ashore, and those on their outermost ships, were blazing away, but my old teacher was undaunted. His own guns fired from both sides at an astonishing rate, transforming his pinnace into a veritable *Ark Royal*.

And now it was our turn. The *Merhonour* moved forward, followed in line by Matt Bredgate in the *Swiftsure*, then the *Crane* and *Defiance*. The crosses of Saint George streamed from our mastheads. Streamed rather too vigorously, and rather too much toward the north –

'Wind's strengthening, My Lord,' said Carver, 'and coming round more southerly with each turn of the glass. We're going to be on a lee shore.'

'So I observe, Master Carver. Let us deal with that after we've killed Spaniards, shall we?'

We came to the Spanish battery on the west bank of the harbour mouth. The eight guns fired at a formidable rate, or at least, formidable for the Dons. At such close range, they could not fail to hit. Shot tore through our sails, cut up the standing rigging on the mizzen near me, lacerating halliards and shrouds, and I felt the impact of at least three balls striking our hull. By now we were even within musket range, and the Spanish must have had five or six hundred musketeers massed on the bank. They volley fired in the grimly efficient way of the *tercios*, in three ranks, the first firing and retiring to the rear to reload, and so on.

'Very well,' I said as the musket balls flew about us like gnats, 'time for the Don to taste a little of England's mere honour! Master gunner! Upon my command – *give fire*!'

Our larboard demi-culverins, minions and sakers roared defiance as the *Merhonour* found her voice. Truly, there is nothing as pleasant as the feel of a ship's battery firing upon the Spanish. The hull shudders, the flames erupt from gun barrels, the smoke swirls over the deck, the smell of powder fills the nostrils, and if you are very fortunate, as I was that day, you will see Castilian heads and limbs being torn from their bodies as your shot hits home.

Ahead of us, the *Halcyon* was taking an almighty pounding, her maintop now hanging at a crazy angle, but she was still giving as good as she got. I prayed that Griffin Rugg and young Iles – that is to say, young Musk – still lived. Then I returned to bawling encouragement at my gun crews.

Nicholas Iles:

There was still a part of me that thought, now I can write a play about Hell, for I have been there.

The deck of the *Halcyon* was red with blood. Pieces of men were scattered among the guns, the broken wood, and the fallen rigging. The sails were in shreds. Yet still Griffin Rugg stood there, roaring like a lion, firing his pistols at the Spaniards. For we were at small arms range now, with musket fire pouring down from the high-hulled ships on either side of us, as well as from the shore.

'See, boy,' the old man cried, 'our fire's too hot for them, by God! They're moving aside, and that's making a channel for the fleet! Keep it up, my brave lads! Keep—'

A ball struck him in the neck, and spun him round. Rugg fell to the deck. I ran over and lifted him. I tore a piece of clothing from the corpse of the ship's carpenter, which lay next to him, and used it as a bandage to stop the spurt of blood. But it did little good, and Griffin Rugg knew it.

'Fight the ship, lad,' he said. 'Officers all dead. Only you can take command. Only you—'

The lifeblood of Griffin Rugg flooded out, over the bandage, over my hands. The good old man had gone to meet whichever gods would receive him.

I looked up, and saw half-a-dozen men staring down at me. I was an actor, a forger, a poet and a coward. But the Spanish guns were still firing upon us, and now I could be none of those things. Or, perhaps, just one: the actor, playing the role of his life. After all, had I not played Hector, Tamburlaine and Hotspur upon the boards of Southwark, to popular acclaim?

I stood and raised my sword.

'To your stations, men!' I declaimed, as a Babbage or an Alleyn might have done. 'For God and the Queen, this day we avenge Griffin Rugg!'

Several nodded, two echoed my cry, and one said, 'Aye, aye, Captain Musk'.

The Earl of Ravensden:

'Four of them running ashore, My Lord!' cried Tom Carver.

It was a most glorious spectacle. Four Spanish galleons, two on either side of the haven, were putting themselves beyond the reach of our murderous gunfire and the likelihood of being boarded in the only way they could, by using a combination of their sails, towing longboats, and warping cables slung around great trees ashore, to run themselves into shallow water and thence onto the shore itself. But there was still one great Spanish ship in the middle of the haven, and we were closing it rapidly.

'I fancy it's a fair day for boarding a Spanish flagship, men!' I cried.

The crew in the ship's waist cheered. Carver steered the *Merhonour* directly for the great galleon, Admiral Zubiaur's *Maria Francesca*.

'He's cutting his cables,' said Carver. 'Seeking room to manoeuvre.'

'Let him try,' I replied. 'Hold your course for her beakhead, Master Carver!'

'Aye, aye, My Lord!'

I ran down from the quarterdeck, through the ship's waist, up to the forecastle, grabbed hold of a shroud, and hauled myself onto the rail. Behind me massed five score Merhonours, armed with swords, daggers, half-pikes and halberds. The Spanish admiral greeted us with a volley from his lower battery, and although I felt shot strike our hull, low down, I did not fear serious damage. The Dons' shot was lighter than ours, and unlikely to cause much hurt. But if Zubiaur managed to take the advantage of the wind from us, that would be a very different matter –

The Spaniard's bows were edging further to the east, to try and avoid our grappling hooks as we came in to board. But that brought him dangerously close to the wind, now a stiff onshore gale – Zubiaur had to try and come round onto the other tack – but the chart of Castlehaven harbour was clear in my head –

I ran back to the quarterdeck, shouting as I did so.

'Master Carver! Helm hard a-larboard!'

But Carver knew the chart as well as I, and had already given the order. The bow of the *Merhonour* came round. But the *Maria Francesca* was not so fortunate. The sheet of the foresail was flying, but despite the best efforts of the men at the mizzen and the helmsman, the great ship was missing stays. And given where she was, according to my chart, that could have only one outcome. There was a great noise, like the roaring of some submerged sea-monster. The bow of the Spanish flagship rose into the air, and for a moment, the keelson itself was exposed. There were several great cracking sounds.

'She's broken her back', said Carver. 'They'll never get her off the rocks. She's finished, My Lord.'

Nicholas Iles:

From the quarterdeck of the *Halcyon*, I watched the death throes of the Spanish flagship. The men cheered, but only feebly: exhausted from their efforts, they were slumped against gun carriages or tackle. We had come to an anchor past the last of the Spanish ships, and Captain Nicholas Musk finally had the leisure to take a long draught of Pembroke ale.

Captain Nicholas Musk. What a part to play that had been! Waving a sword, admonishing shirkers, screaming defiance at King Philip, the Inquisition and all things Spanish. Finally I understood why, all those years ago, the young nobleman Matthew Quinton, born and bred so very far from the sea, took to that strange element under the tutelage of Griffin Rugg, whose corpse lay under a tarpaulin a few feet from where I stood. I thanked God that I had not been called upon to play the more difficult elements of the role – say, setting a course, or deciding which guns should fire upon which target, or boarding and testing my inadequate actors' swordplay against a Castilian veteran – but in the circumstances, my performance seemed to have been adequate enough.

Moreover, I had spent enough time at sea to realise what every real ship's captain, and every seaman in our fleet, now knew. True, we had beaten the Spanish. Their flagship was wrecked, and four of their ships were ashore. But the wind was onshore, and strengthening all the time. The Spanish still had guns in batteries ashore, and could still bring to bear those on the grounded ships. They still had scores of those same Castilian veterans. And while the wind stayed as it was, we could not get out of the harbour.

We were trapped.

The Earl of Ravensden:

By the third day, the fleet was no longer worthy of the name. The *Merhonour* was peppered with the marks and holes of over three hundred great shot, had lost her bowsprit and foremast, and had a score of dead. The *Swiftsure*, directly astern of us, had lost her mainmast. *Defiance* was holed below the waterline, and listing to starboard. The *Crane*, the sternmost of our ships, had taken damage, too, but was too far away for me to judge how badly. The *Halcyon*, at the head of the harbour, was taking relatively little new punishment, but had taken so much during the initial forcing of the haven that she was little better than a wreck.

The wind remained stubbornly brisk and from the south, bringing in frequent squalls of driving, freezing rain, so there was simply no prospect of us being able to get out of Castlehaven. It was equally impossible to summon a council of war, because rowing between the ships was out of the question. The Spanish kept up a relentless bombardment, by day and night, from both their batteries and musketeers ashore and from their grounded ships. None of us had slept for three nights. Our own fire was becoming ragged, the damage to our hull and tackle increasing by the hour. And one thought was growing upon me with the speed and force of a death-fever.

So much for your restoration to the Queen's favour, Matt Quinton, if you lose her four galleons and a pinnace. So much for the integrity of your neck, My Lord of Ravensden.

The one saving grace was the thought that there would be ample time to repair the ships before the summer's campaign; ample time, that is, if we could get them out of this infernal haven at all. And in the afternoon of the third day, that proposition seemed a very long way away.

'The Dons have reinforcements, it seems,' I said. 'Get me an Irishman!'

A round shot passed close to my head and severed a shroud behind me, but I gave it no thought. Instead, I focused on the sight of a column of fresh troops coming along the road from the west, cheered by the Spanish manning the battery.

Dunne, a Dubliner who served as caulker's mate, came onto the poop deck and knuckled his forehead.

'My Lord.'

'Those fellows yonder, Dunne. The impudent ones, laughing and cheering upon the shore as though they had not a care in the world. Who might they be, do you reckon?'

The Irishman screwed up his eyes, looked at the oncoming host, then nodded knowingly.

'O'Sullivans, My Lord, and O'Driscolls. The traitorous rebel scum of these parts. Villains to a man.'

'Well-armed villains, by the looks of them.'

'That they would be, My Lord. King Philip is most generous to his friends, so they say.'

I looked at the pitifully depleted piles of shot next to each gun on our upper deck, and thought *would that Queen Elizabeth were as generous to hers.*

'Very well, then. I think we should give a special greeting to King Philip's friends! Master Gunner, there! Master Skipworth! It strikes me that these O'Sullivans and O'Driscolls have but a very poor idea of demi-culverin range. Would you not say so, Master Gunner?'

Skipworth frowned. 'Even so, they're a fair way beyond point blank, My Lord.'

'True. But with a fair volley of case and langrel, we don't need to be at point blank. Two guns of your choosing, Master Gunner, to fire upon my command!'

'Aye, aye, My Lord.'

The O'Sullivans and O'Driscolls continued to strut merrily upon the shore, gesturing obscenely toward the Queen's ships and waving to their Spanish friends.

Skipworth gave me the signal.

'Give fire!'

For what seemed like the thousandth time there in the harbour of Castlehaven, the *Merhonour* roared defiance against Spain and Popish superstition. The smoke cleared, and Skipworth and I beheld the scene.

'Satisfactory, Master Gunner. My commendations to your gun captains and their crews. I'd reckon, what, two dozen slaughtered?'

'So I'd say, My Lord. And that fellow staggering around with his right arm shot off won't be long for the world.'

'The rest of them scattered and cowering. Most satisfactory indeed. Perhaps now the O'Driscolls and O'Sullivans will give a little more respect to the Queen's ships.'

But it was the kind of victory the ancients called Pyrrhic. In truth, we were still trapped; and within the hour, the surviving Irishmen were joining their fire to those of the Dons. As darkness fell, I offered up the fifty-ninth psalm. *O my God, deliver me from mine enemies; defend me from them that rise up against me...* A Spanish shot struck the mizzen, tearing a great splinter from the truck that missed me by inches. *But I will sing of thy power, and will praise thy mercy in the morning: for thou hast been my defence and refuge in the day of my trouble.*

Thy mercy in the morning.

The torn strips of cloth that had once been flags had been hanging limp overnight, but now, as yet another grey, damp dawn came up over that infernal dungheap named Ireland, I thought I observed a change.

'What think you, Master Carver?' I demanded.

'Nor'-westerly, My Lord. Freshening. With God's grace, we may be able to warp out of this place by noon.'

And so we did, exhausted men hauling upon hawsers attached to the kedge anchors of each ship of the squadron. All the while, the Dons kept up their fire from the shore, and we replied with our ever-diminishing stock of powder and shot; but, little by little, the Queen's ships edged out of Castlehaven harbour and back into the open sea, where we were able to make sail.

Despite all the carnage that had befallen us, it was clear that we had won a great victory. The Spanish squadron was broken. All the stores that squadron had brought for the army ashore were reduced to cinders. Above all, General del Aguila's only line of retreat was cut off, unless more ships came from Spain – and that they were hardly likely to do in December. So now the issue of the entire campaign hinged upon Kinsale, and the battle that had to be fought there.

Nicholas Iles:

The *Halcyon*, the first ship into Castlehaven, was the last out. The men in the tops, and the helmsman at the whipstaff, seemed to know their business, and worked in that strange way which, I believe, the old Greeks termed a 'democracy'. This was as well, for their nominal captain had not the first idea of what orders to give. The men seemed perfectly content with this. Thus as I stood there upon the quarterdeck, watching the crippled *Merhonour* make her way slowly out to sea under the makeshift masts and sails that the seamen term jury rig, I pondered whether ships really needed captains at all.

I chided myself, for in that heretical way of thinking lay the felling of the entire chain of being. If ships had no need of captains, then perhaps nations had no need of kings –

The Spanish battery at the mouth of the harbour fired. I saw the flash from the muzzle and the cloud of powder smoke, then heard the blast, then witnessed the fall of shot, a small waterspout off the starboard bow. A perfunctory effort, I thought, no more. The Spanish gun crews would be as exhausted as we were, and with all of the Queen's galleons now safely out of the harbour, they had little cause to assail us.

I reckoned without the damnably heightened sense of honour of the Dons. A second gun fired – again I saw the flash, and the smoke, and heard the blast – and heard the whistle of a shot flying through the air, nearer and nearer –

I felt myself thrown through the air, and had a glimpse of our mizzen mast upside-down. There was a moment of searing pain. Then all was dark.

CHAPTER TWENTY-ONE

The Earl of Ravensden:
The fleet lay in Oysterhaven, the broad inlet to the south-east of Kinsale. Fuckwit Leveson was furious that I had returned him only the *Crane* in a state fit to return to sea at once, and on this one occasion, I have to confess that I took his point. True, the *Swiftsure* would be ready to sail as soon as a new mainmast was stepped, but that had to come from Milford Haven. As for the *Defiance* and *Merhonour*, they were both hauled ashore for repairs beneath the waterline. I was a captain without a ship, a vice-admiral without a squadron. Which was why Charles Mountjoy's offer, made over a flask of ale in his headquarters tent within our army's camp, north-east of Kinsale town, proved irresistible.

'The Irish will attack, as soon as they finish their New Year feasting,' said the Lord Deputy.

'New Year, Charles? The morrow's but Christmas Eve, man!'

'For good English Protestants, perhaps. But the Irish keep the same papist calendar as the Spanish.'

'Great God, what barbarians!'

'As you say, Matt. But our scouts report advance guards are already on the march from their camp in Coolcarron Wood. The Irish are going to attack tomorrow, mark my words. And in that event, My Lord Ravensden, I'll need every good man I can get.' He took a long draw on his pipe, and exhaled a great cloud of noxious smoke. 'You've led cavalry before, as I recall.'

'Christ, yes, but not for many years – I rode with Philip Sidney at Zutphen—'

'Which more than amply qualifies you, I think. If you're willing, Matt, you can ride alongside Wingfield and Clanricarde, leading the van. Besides, having the famous Earl of Ravensden, the White Devil himself, riding at their head will inspire the men beyond measure.'

'Sir Richard might object,' I said.

'Oh, I doubt it. After all, am I not merely obeying the Queen's injunction to place you as much in harm's way as possible?'

The Dowager Countess:

He did indeed ride with Sir Philip Sidney at Zutphen. What was more, he never tired of telling the story of how he had ridden with Sir Philip Sidney at Zutphen; I probably heard it, oh, four or five hundred times during the course of our life together. He was not at sea in that summer of 1586 because of yet another falling out with Sir Francis Drake, so being of an impatient and warlike nature, he went off to join the army fighting in the Netherlands instead. There, he became fast friends with Sidney, England's romantic warrior-poet. He was alongside Sidney when Sir Philip was fatally wounded in the thigh, and was at his bedside for much of the month that he lingered, dying slowly of gangrene. The Earl was one of the principal mourners during the great funeral at Saint Paul's, as yet the only state funeral England has ever bestowed upon a commoner; although I have no doubt that General Cromwell will order one for himself when the time comes for him to make his deserved descent to hell.

Of course, that was all before my time. But one of the few consolations of having to learn that unspeakable barbarity called the English language is that I have been able to read Sir Philip Sidney's poetry in the original. *Arcadia…Astrophel and Stella…*they still bring tears to my eyes. Be a poet, grandson, and make women weep for centuries to come. Better that by far than becoming a warrior like your grandfather, or being a warrior-poet fated to die young in battle, as both Sidney and your own father were.

The Earl of Ravensden:

I made my way to the hovel where Nicholas Iles lay – or rather, Captain Musk, whose praises the crew of the *Halcyon* could not sing loudly enough.

'How does he fare?' I asked the dolt of an army surgeon attending to him.

The fellow, a bald, sweating creature, wiped his bloodied hands on his breeches.

'Should be dead, with such a wound. But it's not infected, My Lord, and that's the miracle. He must be the only man in the army not infected with something.'

'Then why does he not wake? He's been dead to the world for two weeks, man.'

'That I can't say. Struck his head when the shot blew him to the deck, perhaps? That's what some of his men said.'

I looked down upon the still face of the young poet, and felt – I do not know, but for one fleeting moment, I wondered if it could be that which fathers are said to feel for their sons. As it was, I knelt down by the side of his pallet and began to recite the forty-first psalm. But as I spoke the words, I vowed to Our Lord that if Nicholas Iles lived, then to repay all his good service to me, I would send him back to Ravensden Abbey to recover his strength.

The Dowager Countess:

And that, grandson, was how, one day in January of the year Two, a horse-drawn litter came through the gate passage. I was but recently returned from a visit to the Treshams, not far away in Northamptonshire, who were loyal sons of Holy Church and always seemed able to secure the services of a priest to celebrate Mass and hear confessions. Thus I was in the library of Ravensden Abbey, feeling spiritually uplifted and reading, if I recall correctly, Moderata Fonte's *The Worth of Women: Wherein is Clearly Revealed Their Nobility and Their Superiority to Men*, when I heard an altercation involving Old Barcock – no, the Old Barcock that was *then*, not the one that is now. So I went down, donned boots, trudged through the snow in the courtyard, and found two rough fellows who, nevertheless, knuckled their foreheads at my approach.

'What is the meaning of this?' I demanded, as imperiously as I imagined a Countess of Ravensden should demand.

'Begging pardon, My Lady,' said the rightmost fellow, 'we are Halcyons, here by My Lord's command—'

'Halcyons?' I said. 'What, pray, are Halcyons?'

'I'm afraid, My Lady,' said a weak but familiar voice from within the litter, 'that they are part of my crew.'

Ah, but it is as though I can hear my husband chiding me for interrupting him. Look at him, grandson, there in the Van Dyck. Do you not detect a frown upon that imperious face which was not there a moment ago? Let us return to his journal, then, a few weeks before Nicholas Iles came to Ravensden Abbey; and so to the Battle of Kinsale, where the fate of one of Queen Elizabeth's kingdoms was decided.

The Earl of Ravensden:

Nothing can trump the blood, glory and thrill of a sea fight.

That said, I had nearly forgotten the very particular feelings of exhilaration that a warrior only experiences in a cavalry battle. True, there is the thrill of the charge, but one can feel something akin to that any day of the year, when in chase of some decayed stag or scabby fox across one's own fields. But there is something about being upon a fine steed, riding straight at an enemy. Man and horse become one, a kind of martial centaur, and all other senses are blotted out. It is as though the horse's blood runs through you and yours through the horse. Mountjoy had given me Menelaus, a fine black steed from his own stables, and I sensed at once that this horse and I would greatly enjoy killing Irishmen and Spaniards together. I wished I had my best full armour, rather than merely the battered breastplate which I wore about ship; but then, blue-and-gold Milanese armour was likely to be wasted on the bog-Irish, and would probably rust in their endless, infernal rain.

The Irish armies lay before us now, advancing across the ridge to the south of the forest, north west of Kinsale itself, aiming to fight their way through us to their Spanish allies in the town.

'Six, maybe seven thousand men,' said Dick Wingfield on my left, surveying the host before us. 'Your countrymen have turned out in force, My Lord Clanricarde.'

'The Irish will never fail to rush headlong to their deaths in a hopeless cause,' said the young Burke, Earl of Clanricarde, who in his manners and speech was as English as Wingfield or I. 'That is Ireland's tragedy, time upon time.'

We three sat upon our mounts at the front of the royal army's cavalry, studying the advancing lines. Harp standards, the red hand of Ulster and the personal banners of the treacherous earls of Tyrone and Tyrconnel flew before them. Pipers and drummers sounded their defiance. I turned to look at our own men, a motley collection of English and loyal Irish, fighting under the flags of Saint George and the golden crowns of Munster – the province ever firmest in its allegiance to the English crown, unlike the notorious traitors of Ulster.

'Mountjoy's taking time with his orders,' said Wingfield. 'And that's an almighty risk. If the Spanish come out of Kinsale town before we've dealt with the rebels over there—'

I had fought with Dick Wingfield before, in Holland, Portugal and Brittany. Now Marshal of the loyal Irish army, he was an old soldier who did not suffer fools gladly; a man after my own heart.

'I think your wish is granted, Dick,' I said, pointing to an impossibly young despatch rider galloping directly for us, Mountjoy's standard in his hand.

'My Lords! Marshal Wingfield!' Clanricarde and I exchanged a glance: the lad was so young, his voice was only just breaking. 'The Lord Deputy's orders! Your cavalry to advance across yonder stream and charge the enemy forthwith!'

'Surely the enemy will expect that?' said Clanricarde.

'I think not,' I said. 'They're northerners, My Lord. They don't know the land, so they certainly don't know the depth of that stream.'

'From the way they're forming up,' said Wingfield, 'they're going to try to mire us in the bogs. And their columns are too far apart – a five year old child could set out a toy army in a better disposition than that. The Lord Deputy has the right of it, I reckon.'

Wingfield raised his hand, and our trumpets sounded. The royal cavalry advanced, at first at a walking gait, then a trot, then a canter as we approached the stream. The Irish were frantically redeploying their own cavalry to meet the threat, but as we reached the water's edge, Wingfield gave the signal to our trumpeters, and we broke into a gallop, the demi-lances lowering their points and directing them toward the enemy. Menelaus seemed to revel in the shallow water splashing up over his haunches. For my part, I drew my sword – a good old plain English sword, not a fancified rapier – extended my arm, and prayed that my blade would shortly bury itself in the heart or brain of a traitor.

A moment later, the killing business began.

The Irish, as was their wont, were on much smaller steeds, their hobbies: nimble in their wild bogs and mountain passes, but no match for proper war-horses on open ground. No matter how brave the soldier, or skilled the horseman, a fighter is at an almighty disadvantage if his opponent towers over him. Menelaus was like a great beast in the ancient tales, rampaging through ordinary mortals as though they were chaff. He seemed positively to revel in the soft, marshy ground that the Irish clearly hoped would prove our undoing. And as for his rider –

I hacked and stabbed with abandon, always with the advantage of height, slashing downward into skulls and shoulders. The Irish, for their part, persisted with their age-old tactic of throwing their spears, a fatal strategy against armoured men on proper war horses – men armed with lances and swords, or else the muskets and pistols of our shot-on-horseback. One fellow, more valiant than the rest, tried to keep me at a distance and to work around Menelaus' flanks to my blind side. He was a remarkably able rider, but then, the Irish had to be: their horses were too small for war saddles, and they rode without stirrups, ideal for skirmishing and ambushes, but a fatal combination in combat such as this. My adversary was also a capable swordsman, parrying and weaving dexterously to avoid my thrusts and cuts, trying to make me lose my advantage by over-extending. Curling red hair and a thin beard that curled outward at its end: a face I shall never forget. Finally he stabbed at Menelaus, no doubt hoping to unhorse me, but the fine beast only neighed furiously, not rearing up out of control. Reining in with my left hand and shifting my balance, I swung round and slashed hard, severing Thin-Beard's head clean from the neck. The great gush of blood drenched both Menelaus and me –

'My Lord!' cried Wingfield. 'You're not hurt?'

'A fine bath on a bracing day, Marshal! What could be better?'

But as I answered Wingfield, I looked behind him. Although we were slaughtering Irishmen by the dozen, our advantage in size would swiftly be offset by the sheer numbers the enemy were bringing against us –

'Great God, Dick, look at Clanricarde! Did you ever see the like?'

For the moment, the Irish were ignoring us and concentrating all their attention on the young Earl. But Clanricarde seemed to have a veritable legion of invisible guardian angels around him. Every one of his thrusts struck home. Every one of his parries deflected oncoming steel. Every pistol aimed in his direction missed. It was very nearly a sight to make a man turn Papist: for Richard Burke, Earl of Clanricarde, was as loyal to the Church of Rome as the traitors Tyrone and Tyrconnel, but he saw as clearly as they did not that Ireland could only prosper under English peace and law, with the incomprehensible superstitions of the Gaels banished to the outer darkness.

Inspired by Clanricarde's astonishing example, our cavalrymen rallied and began to press the rebel Irish once again. The matter might have been very different if del Aguila had brought his veteran troops out of Kinsale town; but apart from a token force, far off on the other side of the engagement, the Dons did not stir.

'Time to second the noble Earl, Marshal!' I cried.

'Aye! And look there, My Lord! Tyrone won't have expected that, by Christ!'

A little way downstream, the main body of Mountjoy's cavalry was advancing across a ford which the rebel army simply could not have known about, else they would surely have guarded it. It was the last I saw of this part of the battle: a moment later, Wingfield and I charged back into the melee, and once again my entire world consisted only of Menelaus beneath me and the man I was about to kill in front of me. But from the accounts of others, notably that of Charles Mountjoy himself, I know that the charge of the Lord Deputy's cavalry proved the last straw for the mounted Irish. The rebel cavalry broke, and even I, my eyes and mind clouded by the red mist of battle, became aware that fewer and fewer opponents were before me.

Then there was Mountjoy's young officer again, galloping over the prone bodies of dead and dying Irishmen.

'My Lords and Marshal! Lord Deputy's orders! Regroup, and fall upon the enemy infantry—'

He was barely ten feet from me when one of the wounded traitors raised himself upon one arm and fired a pistol with the other. It was as though the lad's chest exploded, the blood and bone and organs spattering his shocked young face.

I rode over to the killer, made Menelaus rear, and brought the great horse's forelimbs down upon him. I repeated the move again. And again.

The Dowager Countess:

Cornet John Taylor. That was his name, it seems. The solitary Englishman of birth to die in the entire Battle of Kinsale, such was the scale of the victory.

The news reached Ravensden Abbey in a letter from my husband. It must have been one of those kept in the main part of the library, amid the muniments that the rats ate twenty years ago, and thus is lost to history. But in essence, Kinsale was the great victory in Ireland that had eluded the English for years. The Irish rebels, forced to fight the battle on the kind of open ground they had always avoided, were slaughtered in their hundreds. When the Spanish finally deigned to sally forth from the town, they were easily beaten back. General del Aguila surrendered soon afterwards, and the Dons evacuated Kinsale and all their other garrisons. Admiral Zubiaur's fleet, refloated in Castlehaven harbour, carried them back to Spain, chastened just as they had been in the Armada year. The rebel Irish Earls fought on for a few more years, but their cause was hopeless. They and their retinues finally left Ireland for perpetual exile in Spain, and an entire world perished. Ulster, the stronghold of the fallen Earl of Tyrone, was settled by good Scots Protestants. How successful that stratagem proved, grandson, you may gauge from the terrible massacres of those same Protestants that took place in the year after you were born, and from the equal horrors that General Cromwell has committed upon the Catholics in Ireland, these last few years.

As a Countess of England, I have one opinion upon it all. As a true daughter of the Holy Mother Church, though, I have quite another.

But it is probably best if you do not write that.

CHAPTER TWENTY-TWO

Laszlo Horvath:

Even as I stand alongside the Macrae, looking over the corpses of the men we have slaughtered, I know that he intends to betray me, and I know that I will kill him before the next rising of the sun.

For now, of course, he smiles, and slaps my back, and calls me his 'good Horvath'. As indeed I am. It was I who chose the ground, so that the much larger force of Lundins were hemmed in by the great bog where their bodies now lie. It was I who trained the Macraes in musketry, a brutal but effective art barely known by these wild Scots. It was I who led the flanking attack, leading part of the Macrae's force through the trees on the side of the glen to emerge behind the Lundins and cut off their retreat. It was I who cut down a dozen Lundins with my own sword, they being no match for a man who has fought with Janissaries and still lives.

But despite all this, the Macrae will betray me. When I mention the gold he owes me, he mumbles something about the Edinburgh banker who holds it. And when I mention the more important matter, his eyes shift from mine.

'So, My Lord?' I say, though he has no more right to such an honour than – than many another. But the Macrae, as he is termed, is susceptible to flattery, and is considered a great man by the few hundred herdsmen and cutthroats who form his so-called 'clan'. 'So, My Lord, will you now secure the audience you promised me? The introduction to the King?'

'Aye, of course, good Horvath. But in good time, eh? It'll take a wee while for my friends at court to smooth things over with His Grace, for killing so many of the Lundins, there. A great man for peace, His Grace is, or at least that's what he tells us, his lords and chieftains. But enough gold in the right purses – gold we'll now get from Lundin lands, and Lundin ransoms – and Jamie Stuart will look kindly on the Macrae again. And then, my friend, you shall have your audience. But for now, Horvath man, there's feasting and drinking to be done, and ballads to be sung of the day the Macraes slaughtered the Lundins!'

It is dawn when he is finally carried to his bed, and I lie beside him, seemingly responsive to his attentions. To the men who have carried him to his chamber at the top of this remote tower-house, I will seem as drunk as he is. But the ability to hold drink is given to every Hungarian as a birthright, and not even a Scot can better one of us. So as the Macrae passes out in the midst of his fumbling, I remain very much awake. I look down upon his nakedness, running now to fat, and wonder how I ever allowed myself to believe that this empty, boastful brute could ever help me to my goal. But he wanted a man to train an army – or the tiny, pathetic apology for an army that I later discovered it to be – and was prepared not to ask too many questions about why I left England.

I curse myself for my folly. There is now nearly no time to remedy it: the reports from London say that Elizabeth is weakening. I have one course open to me, the course I now see I should have embarked upon in the very beginning. The direct course. The course of revenge. But before I can embark upon that course, I have to deal with the inconveniences that are the Macrae and the men he will have assigned to kill me.

I cross the floor to the small chest that contains the things precious to me, take out my finest rondel dagger, and draw the point slowly across the Macrae's throat, giving him a new, scarlet, smile, watching the tide of blood darken the furs upon his bed.

And then I wait. An hour or so, I reckon: having seen me fight at the head of them, Macrae's men will want to leave me long enough to be entirely certain I am fast asleep.

At last, I hear steps upon the spiral staircase. Three men, making the unmistakeable cacophony of drunkards trying to be very, very quiet.

The door opens. It will be bright daylight outside, but the room is shuttered, and their eyes will take a moment to adjust to the dark. But they do not have a moment. I have a rapier in each hand, and pierce the first man through the heart with that in my right, the second through the throat with that in my left. The third turns to run, and begins to shout, but I am upon him, and thrust hard through his back, so that the point of my weapon strikes the wall of the staircase ahead of him.

I return to the room, pack my weapons carefully in my chest, and carry it down the staircase. I glance into the hall, where dozens of Macraes lie upon tables or the floor. The stench of spilled drink, piss, vomit and sweat is overwhelming. No man stirs. I reach the door, and unbolt it.

There is no guard. But then, there is no enemy, for the enemies of the Macraes lie dead in a bog several glens and lochs away.

A thought occurs to me. I go down into the cellars, and make several journeys between there and the entrance floor, immediately beneath the hall. At last, all is prepared. I take a burning torch from the wall, throw it onto the pyre that I have built, and slam the door behind me, propping a beam against it.

As I ride away from the castle of the Clan Macrae, I turn and watch the flames begin to lick the roof. The smell of roasting meat upon the summer breeze puts me in mind of breakfast.

The Earl of Ravensden:

The fleet sailed out of Plymouth Sound upon a fine, blustery day, the wind south by a little easterly. In one sense, we were a splendid sight, half a dozen great galleons and perhaps a dozen smaller vessels. But only in one sense.

'Gladdens the heart, My Lord,' said Carver, at my side upon the quarterdeck of the *Merhonour*, 'to be once again about God's righteous business of attacking the Spaniards on their own coast.'

'Amen to that, Master Carver. But I would that we had rather more ships, and many more men.'

'Men serve for coin, My Lord. For too many years, they've been paid only with empty promises. In a word, with fresh air. Is it any wonder they flee inland rather than join the Queen's ships?'

'And is it any wonder we have too few ships, either, when England's ministers see fit to spend what coin they do have upon fucking galleys instead?' I looked out towards Devon's fair shore. 'When they think to make up our numbers with a Dutch fleet, of which there is as yet no sign? When they victual us with beer and stockfish that's already foul? Ah, listen to us, Tom Carver. We've turned rebels, you and I.'

I could not tell him my true thoughts, which were not merely rebellious: they were positively treacherous. But for all that, I held out hopes that despite too few ships, too few men, and Sir Richard Leveson as our admiral, this expedition might succeed. God willing, it might even win the war outright, at this eleventh hour. Failing that, it might yet enrich the Earl of Ravensden.

Brick-Beard surprised me beyond measure with the strength of his opinion upon these matters. Whether it was out of a determination to win a name for himself, or to equal my achievements, or simply to build bridges to me, the older, wiser warrior and better seaman, he persuaded Cecil and the rest of the Queen's timorous ministers to adopt a plan that I could not have bettered myself. He even invited me to a noontime dinner aboard the *Warspite*, at anchor in the Plymouth Cattewater, to explain it.

'The only way to defend Ireland, and thus England, is to attack Spain,' he said, in between gnawing a leg of lamb.

'I won't demur from that, Sir Richard,' I said, gnawing in my turn. 'Indeed, if Essex or Drake were here now, they wouldn't demur from that either.'

'So I have proposed to Secretary Cecil that we sail to the enemy's coast, and if we find a fleet in Lisbon or the Groyne, we blockade it there.'

'Blockade is a tedious affair. An unprofitable affair, too. As I know from bitter experience.'

'But so it is for the Spaniards, My Lord. And if we arrive at the right place at the right time, we prevent either the sailing of their outgoing East India ships, or the arrival of their incoming bullion fleet from Havana. Or, God willing, both. In either event, the Dons have to either lose all the profits of those trades, or they have to send out their fleets to protect them. In which case, we fight and defeat them.'

I stared at Leveson. I recalled a young man of very nearly the same age once making a very nearly identical speech before his elders and betters at a council of war, many years before. Did this vain, peculiarly-bearded jackanapes have something about him after all?

'A sound strategy,' I said. 'If it can be accomplished, that is. Many of us have attempted it before, and failed. And Charles Mountjoy will be mightily discontented if we take away the only ships that could defend Ireland from another Spanish invasion. Above all, the Queen will be mightily discontented if the Spanish slip past us and put yet another army ashore in County Cork. Or County Kent, for that matter.'

'Ireland, and England too, can only be defended on the shore of Galicia or at the mouth of the Tagus. Doubly so, in this case.'

'Doubly so, Sir Richard?'

He put down the leg of lamb.

'Your friend General Spinola has been very quiet these last months. Have you not wondered where he was, My Lord?'

Was it that obvious, even to this prating varlet of a courtier? Was it so obvious to all of England that Matthew of Ravensden craved revenge against the galleys that had humiliated him, and especially against their commander?

'It is a matter of some interest to me,' I conceded.

Wordlessly, Leveson went over to his sea-chest and produced a paper, which he handed to me. I recognised it at once as a copy, and a translation: I was now something of an authority upon such matters. But I also recognised it as the sort of intelligence report that crossed the desks of the Queen's intelligencers a dozen times a day, sometimes even a hundred. At least, that was the sort of frequency with which they had appeared on my father's desk.

I read it.

Spinola was in Spain. Not in disgrace, not in retirement: he had returned in triumph, and was feted at the Escorial by the young King Philip and his entire court. The young general's strategy of taking galleys to Flanders and deploying them in the North Sea seemed to have succeeded beyond even his wildest expectations, beginning with his success in slipping past my squadron at Calais. And now Spinola was proposing something much more ambitious. *Give me more galleys*, he was telling the King of Spain, *and I will give you England*. The Catholic King acceded readily, eager to see his sister upon England's throne as its new Queen Elizabeth the Second, a monarch set fair to preside over a dark age of persecution, corruption and arbitrary government. So Spinola was massing a new and greater galley fleet, which he would take to Flanders to embark an army. Then he would cross the Channel, take a port, and use it as a base from which his army could trigger a rising of English Catholics: the same strategy the Dons had employed at Kinsale, writ large and writ upon the shore of England instead of Ireland. Why, there was even a proposal to attack and burn the Queen's ships lying in the Medway, off Chatham. Preposterous as this notion was, I felt a chill as I re-read the document. If Spinola succeeded –

But Spinola would not succeed.

The truly important thing was the news that Spinola was coming, and this time, the Earl of Ravensden would be ready for him.

This time, Matthew Quinton would have his revenge.

The Dowager Countess:

With the Earl at sea and probably unlikely to be home before the winter, the Abbey's forty-three servants well managed by Old Barcock, and young Beth prospering in the care of a wet nurse who loved her, I turned to those activities that have occupied womankind since Eve: or at least, to the activities that do not involve any aspect of the production of babies, namely, the reordering of kitchens and the improvement of gardens. In truth, Ravensden Abbey had much need of both. For fifteen years, it had suffered from the absence of a woman's touch. One of its chatelaines sat, senile, in her tower room, another had been locked away as a madwoman for years, the others barely had time to choose the plots for their own graves. Thus I was walking along one of the newly cleared pathways, planning a parterre in my mind's eye while Iles limped alongside me, reading aloud the poetry of Thomas Wyatt, when old Barcock appeared to say there was an unexpected visitor.

'Bell, My Lady,' said the gaunt old man who awaited me in the hall, 'Christian Bell. Steward of Alnburgh Castle to the Earls of Ravensden for near forty years.'

'You are a long way from Alnburgh Castle and your charge, Steward.'

'Begging pardon, My Lady. But it could not wait, with it not being known how long the Earl will be at sea… And that's why I've come all this way, to explain it in person, for it's too complicated a business to put on paper. By rights, it's a matter only My Lord could resolve, he being both the owner of the lands and lord of the manor, but the lawyer in Alnwick, he says that the verdict of Your Ladyship would serve, if the parties will accept it, which all say they will, and thus avoid the necessity of convening a court leet, or even referring it to—'

'Stop, Master Bell!' I looked toward Iles, who nodded his support. 'What is this matter? What verdict?'

We sat, and for the next hour, Bell expounded an intricate and tedious tale of disputes over fishery and grazing rights, of rival claims under obscure kinds of tenure peculiar to that neighbourhood, of encroachments upon common land, of the violence, actual and threatened, that the disputes were inspiring among the tenants on the Alnburgh estate. Only the direct judgement of the Earl in person would quell all discontents and satisfy the populace; but in his absence, it seemed that the provisional verdict of the Countess would suffice.

'It has to be resolved before Michaelmas, the next quarter day, My Lady,' said Bell, 'else the Charltons of those parts will take matters into their own hands, as they are threatening to do. And they're a violent crew, honed on years of reiving. There'll be fire and devastation all across Alnburgh land, My Lady.'

I thought hard upon Bell's words, and exchanged a glance with Nicholas Iles.

'It is no easy matter, to travel so very far,' I said. 'I would need several days, at the very least, to make ready. The state coach requires repair, as my husband informed me, and that, too, will take time. Then the journey itself – a matter of, what, a week at least? It could be a month or more before I can reach Alnburgh, Master Bell.'

Bell frowned, but said nothing. He knew the distances better than I did, even if he had no grasp of how long it would take for a lady of rank to prepare for such an expedition; and, of course, he had to take my word for the state of the Earl of Ravensden's coach.

'I will accompany you, My Lady,' said Iles.

'No, good friend, you are still too weak.' The poet made to protest, but I raised a hand. 'Remember that you are meant to go to Cambridge on the very morrow, to be examined by an eminent professor of physic.' Iles frowned, and was silent. 'Very well, then, Master Bell. If only the presence of the Countess of Ravensden will prevent a war, then the Countess of Ravensden shall go to Alnburgh.'

CHAPTER TWENTY-THREE

The Earl of Ravensden:
The orlop stank of shit and corrupted flesh.

'Sixteen sick, My Lord,' said Sinkgraven, the ugly Dutch saw-bones who served as the *Merhonour*'s surgeon. 'Three set fair to die before the day is out. And there will be more.'

I looked around at the pungent, sweating men upon their pallets. We were already badly undermanned: an epidemic would soon force the ship back to Plymouth, unable to fight, nearly unable even to sail. And if the state of the crew did not do for us, the state of the ship would. The moans of the sick were drowned out by the hammering of the carpenter's crew, up forward, as they attempted to staunch yet another leak. The repairs made to the *Merhonour* after the Battle of Castlehaven had been rushed in order to get her back to sea as quickly as possible. She was an old ship, rebuilt and refitted many times. She was showing her age, but as usual, the Queen's parsimonious Principal Officers of the Navy had expended too little coin. A man might weep, to see the state to which the Navy Royal of England was reduced.

But it could be worse –

'My Lord!'

I heard the boy's shouts when he was on the deck above. He tumbled down the ladder into the orlop, very nearly breathless with excitement. Ielden, this, a sturdy Bedfordshire lad whose father was one of my tenants on Ravensden land and who had joined the ship at Plymouth. The boy preferred the notion of the sea to that of the plough, and at once became a favourite on the lower deck on this, his first voyage, because of his talents for playing the fiddle and improvising songs upon the names of his messmates.

'My Lord! Master Carver's compliments, for there is a sighting! Many ships!'

'Where away? How many sail?'

'I – I don't know, My Lord – just a sighting, far off to the right—'

'To starboard. If you venture to be a seaman, lad, you'd best learn how to report to your captain! Numbers, Master Ielden! Bearings! Distances!'

I went up to the poop deck. I could feel the excitement among the crew: the murmurs, the pointing toward the sails just visible on the horizon.

'My Lord,' said Carver. 'Perhaps God in Heaven looks kindly upon us after all.'

'You think it's them?'

Carver shrugged. 'It might be the Dutch. We are too far away to tell.'

'The Dutch fleet? Our noble allies? I'll take wing and fly to the maintop before I believe any longer in that fiction. No, it's the Dons. Can you not smell the bullion, Master Carver? After all these years, after all these failed attempts, there it is. The Spanish plate fleet. The greatest treasure in the world. And this time, Tom Carver, it will be mine.'

The Dowager Countess:

Alnburgh was a wild and blasted place, a half ruined castle upon a sea-cliff. Bare moors stretched away inland. Vast flocks of sheep roamed free. A few sails were visible upon the sea, and three other ships were anchored in the bay to the south, riding out the storm. Otherwise, there was no sign of life. Black clouds swept across the sky upon the strong gale, disgorging hail and freezing rain in what was meant to be England's summer. It was as though the state coach of the Earls of Ravensden was making its way through the land of the dead.

I could tell that my attendants were fearful. Young Barcock, up alongside Higson the driver, had never been out of Bedfordshire before; and thus had never seen the sea, until this very hour. My maid, Alice, was a simpering creature, afraid of her own shadow. But even I was surreptitiously fingering my rosary as the coach made its way through the barbican and into the courtyard of Alnburgh.

Bell, who had ridden ahead, awaited us. His face was even more gaunt and unreadable than it had been at Ravensden.

'My Lady,' he said, as I stepped from the coach.

But he spoke the words without respect. If anything, he spoke them with a sneer. And behind him stood a half-dozen grim faced men. Three of them stepped forward, and seized hold of Barcock, Higson and Alice, who screamed pitifully.

'Bell! What is the meaning of this affront – the Earl shall hear of this—'

'Your Earl shall hear of nothing, Papist bitch. That a man bearing his name should have stooped so low as to marry you, a sprig of the Whore of Babylon, that has made the people of the earth drunk with the wine of her fornication! For you are a fornicator, woman, your sham marriage to Matthew Quinton invalidated by the sin and corruption of the false faith you espouse!'

His eyes were glazing over and cast towards the heavens: that expression I had seen countless times on the faces of the street preachers, or those who declaimed at Saint Paul's Cross. The expression of those who would gladly see me, and all who shared my faith, burn upon a pyre.

'Bell,' I said. His eyes returned from the hallucination of his notion of heaven, and focused once again upon me. 'Bell, it is not too late – my husband is a forgiving man—'

'I do not need the forgiveness of the son of Edward Quinton, that foul betrayer and murderer!'

Edward Quinton? My husband's father, the seventh Earl? What madness was this?

Bell gestured with his hand, and his men led my servants away to a door on the far side of the courtyard, poor Alice screaming all the while. Then the remaining three men stepped behind me, and I feared for a moment that they would strike me dead there and then. But Bell nodded and turned to climb the steps into the principal tower, and his men stepped forward, forcing me to follow him.

The Earl of Ravensden:

More than a dozen great carracks. *More than a dozen.* Each one full to the brim with silver. Each one on its own rich enough to pay off all of the Queen's debts. Each one on its own with enough silver in just one sea-chest to make the Earl of Ravensden the richest nobleman in all England. Oh, it was a sight to behold as we closed, that day in the year of grace, 1602.

There was just one minor difficulty.

'I make it sixteen galleons, My Lord,' said Carver.

'Then we concur,' I said, although I could see but blurs in the very far distance, and thus had to depend upon the ship-master's estimate. 'Heavy odds.'

I looked around, toward the fleet sailing in her wake, and wished I was looking once again at the mighty floating arsenal England sent out against the Invincible Armada. But I was not. I was looking at three ships. Four, counting the *Merhonour*.

'But not insuperable odds,' I said, as convincingly as I could. 'It looks to me as though the Dons are scattered. Many of their galleons are downwind, and will have the devil of a job to beat back up to defend the carracks. Is that not so, Master Carver?'

The old Puritan looked at me doubtfully.

'It might be so, My Lord. But it is still a mighty risk—'

'Is not the Lord Almighty with us, Master Carver? Is He not with England?'

'Let us pray that He is this day, My Lord.'

'Very well then. Give me a course for the rearmost carrack, yonder, and signal to the squadron to fall into our wake.'

The Dowager Countess:

Up a narrow spiral staircase, to the topmost floor of the tower; to what must once have been the personal chamber of the Lords of Alnburgh. Bell walked into the room, and I followed him.

Another man was already in the room. A man dressed finely, in puffed breeches and a satin shirt. A man I knew well enough.

'Welcome to Alnburgh, My Lady,' said Laszlo Horvath.

The Earl of Ravensden:

Upon my command, our starboard demi-culverins opened fire at point blank rage, some three hundred paces from the carrack. As the smoke rolled away from the hull of the tall, lumbering vessel, I could see several shot holes in her sides. Only one gun returned fire, and she forlornly. The plate ships carried only a small armament, they being designed to carry as much bullion as possible, and the men in the Escorial assumed there would always be galleons to escort them and frighten off any potential assailants. But not in this case. Dons ran about her decks, screaming and pointing; but she still seemed under command and answering her helm, for still she fell away down wind, trying to draw us toward the escorting galleons that were beating up toward us. Meanwhile, the three ships astern of us – the *Repulse*, *Defiance* and *Dreadnought* – were coming up on our larboard quarter, bound for the next carrack of the plate fleet.

'Merhonours!' I cried. 'To the forecastle!'

A pitifully small band, probably no more than two dozen, responded to my exhortation. We were so short of numbers that only these could be spared from the yards and the guns; only these were healthy enough to avoid Sinkgraven's attentions down on the orlop. But they would have to do. After all, they were English, and that alone ought to be sufficient.

Now our beakhead was nearly at touching distance from that of the Spaniard, although the latter was much higher out of the water. The men in our bows – I could see young Ielden among them – stood poised, grappling hooks and ropes in their hands. I waited. I judged the distance. I thought of bullion, and chided myself. *Nothing like avarice to make a man lower his guard, Ravensden.*

Closer – closer –

There was a crash as our bowsprit struck that of the carrack. Our shrouds and hers seemed as one, an impenetrable forest of rope.

'Now!' I cried.

Men threw the grappling hooks, and pulled tight the ropes. In that moment I jumped from the forecastle onto the beakhead, sword in hand, and hauled myself over onto the bow of the Spaniard. My men followed suit –

The cheek of the man at my left shoulder blew apart, spattering me with flesh and blood. He fell back into the sea, but was dead long before he entered the water. I looked up, and saw half a dozen Don musketeers at the forecastle rail of the carrack. Brave fellows. Foolish fellows. For they had no time to reload before we were upon them. I carried an English short sword of the old fashion, but the first Don I stuck through the guts swiftly learned the lesson that being unfashionable does not make a blade any less adept for killing.

'Merhonours! To the quarterdeck!'

They did not need that order; every man knew what was necessary, for every man could see silver coins before his eyes. The roughly equal number of Dons facing us on the forecastle fell back. These were not true fighting men, after all. King Philip had as much difficulty manning his ships as Queen Elizabeth did hers, and Spain's best men would be aboard the galleons –

The galleons.

As I reached the quarterdeck of the carrack, and saw her captain's sword extended toward me, hilt first, I could see the escorting galleons coming up from the south. Coming up too fast for my liking.

I took the proffered Toledo blade, but turned down the captain's invitation – issued in truly execrable Latin – to take wine with him in his cabin.

Instead, I went below. Only Ielden stood alongside me, for he was the only man in the boarding party I could trust not to plunder remorselessly among what lay before us in the vast hold of the carrack.

Chests. Countless chests, filling the space between the decks. I went to the nearest one, and forced the lock with the point of my sword.

I lifted one silver piece from the very top of the countless quantity within, studied it, and handed it to Ielden.

'See that, young Jack? That's what it's all for. What it's always been for. This is what Drake and Hawkins and I strived for – aye, and all the rest of them, too. A bullion cargo. Remember it, lad. Keep that piece as a namesake, but hide it from your messmates, for every man aboard the *Merhonour* will kill you to lay their hands on such a coin. Then go back above and pass on my order to abandon the prize and return to the ship.'

His eyes opened wide.

'Abandon the prize, My Lord?'

'Nothing else for it, Jack Ielden. If I had eight or nine galleons with me, I'd fight sixteen Dons in the blinking of an eye. But I have three. We can't get the prize away, and if we don't make shift, we won't get away ourselves, either. And I don't care for the prospect of going the way of Dick Grenville.'

'Aye, aye, My Lord.'

Ielden went above, and for a moment, just one moment, I was alone with the treasure of the Americas, with riches beyond the imagination of mortal man. Riches that I was about to forsake.

The moment passed. I sighed. Then I hastily scooped up as much silver coin as I could and filled my pockets with it.

No, I trusted no man of the *Merhonour* not to plunder remorselessly: and that included her captain.

The Dowager Countess:

Yes, my husband sometimes had nightmares about suffering the same fate as Sir Richard Grenville.

You will know the story, of course: what English schoolboy does not?

Grenville's *Revenge*, alone and surrounded by fifty-three great Spanish men-of-war, which slowly blasted her to pieces. Grenville's crew dying around him in their droves, until at last, the officers surrendered the ship, contrary to the wishes of the dying captain. Oh yes, he died with honour: but then, my husband always said that he also died an idiot, to have got himself into that position in the first place. So on the day when he briefly took the great bullion carrack, he was mindful above all of not being surrounded as Grenville had been. True, my husband loved riches, and he never had more within his grasp than he did that day. But he loved being alive more; and in those days, grandson, he was determined to remain alive until he could father upon me the heir to Ravensden, the son yet unborn who would one day be the ninth Earl.

Perhaps it is as well that, at much the same time when he was making his decision to abandon the Spanish prize, he did not know that I was in immediate danger of death: or, perhaps, worse than death. For I was standing but a few feet before the most inveterate enemy that my husband and I had in the whole world.

CHAPTER TWENTY-FOUR

Laszlo Horvath:

She is not as shocked as I had hoped. She is not as scared. She is not on her knees, pleading for her life.

She stands there, very small, very still, but I do not doubt that she is shaking with fear. She will be imagining all the things I might do to her, now that she is entirely in my power. She will be having thoughts of chains, of racks, and of whips. But I doubt if she can even to begin to imagine what I will actually do to her.

I have dismissed Bell, so that I may be alone with her. I want no other soul to share even one small part of her fear.

I circle her. I move close to her, and touch her hair. I breathe in her ear. She does not flinch. This is good: it is better when they do not cower and scream.

I go to the table, and write these words. For I wish to have a record of exactly what I do, and exactly what I feel. But –

But there is something unsettling about her stillness. She stares at me. She even begins to smile. This is not what I expect. This is not what I want.

'This amuses you, *madame*?' I say in Latin, which we both speak better than English.

'I know you,' she says.

'Of course you know me. I am Horvath.'

'No. You are not.'

'No, I am not. But you do not know my name. My true name. The name that damns you, and your husband above all.'

She looks at me. There is a silence, and she maintains that cursed stillness.

I shall lay down the quill now. This is not as I wished it to be.

For I can see it now. I can see it in her eyes.

Her unafraid eyes.

She knows who I am.

The Dowager Countess:

I kept staring at him, though my heart was racing. Surely the fear I felt would betray itself at any moment? But the words had to be spoken, even if they proved to be my death warrant.

'But I do know your name. Thanks to the memory of a very old woman, I know your name as well as I know my own, and my husband's. For it is the same, is it not? Your name, your real name, is Quinton.'

The Hungarian stood stock still. I can still see his face, just as if a portrait of him, drawn from life, stands before my eyes. A face drained of colour. A face in shock.

'How could you know? How could you know *that*? Which old woman?'

'Your grandmother. My husband's grandmother. The Countess Katherine.'

'She lives? The old nun still lives? *Isten*, she must be nearly a hundred years old!'

'She lives. Or refuses to die, whichever you prefer. But she remembers your story well enough. The story of Balthasar Quinton, her grandson.'

He swayed upon his feet.

'And what is that story, as you have it from her?'

This was no time to dissemble. Saying it plain, the story my husband had from the ancient Countess, bought me time. Horvath – that is, cousin Balthasar – could strike me dead at any moment. But he would want to know what his own grandmother said about him. He had to want to know. For at bottom, what man or woman does not wish to learn the innermost thoughts of those closest to them in blood?

'She told me – that is, she told my husband – she said this of your history. Henry, sixth Earl of Ravensden – her son, your father – was a troubled soul, forever seeking answers to the mysteries of life and death. He spent years travelling to far countries, abandoning his wife and mother, searching for the Philosopher's Stone, or the Holy Grail, or other secrets of the ancients. And then, in Hungary, he met a woman who bore him a son – a son who would be Earl of Ravensden, if Henry was legally married to the mother. But his wife in England still lived, and thus any marriage to this Mistress Horvath would be bigamous—'

Horvath stepped forward suddenly, raising his hand, and I feared he was about to strike me. But for a reason I have never understood, this man, this creature, who was capable of the most terrible violence, halted himself.

'My parents' marriage was legal,' he said, very quietly. 'The wife in England was already dead. Thus in the eyes of God I, Balthasar Quinton, am the rightful Earl of Ravensden.'

'As your mother claimed, years later, when she wrote to the Dowager Countess and the seventh Earl, my husband's father. But there was no proof, was there? The abbey where she claimed the papers were held was destroyed in an Ottoman attack, and the sixth Earl left no record of a second wife or a son when he died here, in this castle.'

'The proof was my mother's word, sworn in the name of God! And I swore upon her grave, in the name of that selfsame God, that one day, I would lay claim to my rightful inheritance!'

He was angry now, but there was also a sadness about him that touched a part of my heart. Oh, I was still in mortal fear of him, but Balthasar Quinton was a real person now, standing there before me instead of the illusion that was Laszlo Horvath, the murderous man of war. And whether rightly or wrongly, Balthasar Quinton believed that he was putting to rights an injustice, and fulfilling a vow made to a dead mother.

'One thing perplexes me,' I said, 'and perplexes my husband, too. You have known who you are since you were very young. Why, then, did it take you so many long years to come to England and stake your claim?'

He could still kill me. He *should* kill me. If I was in his position, I would have killed me. All of the men of the house of Monconseil-Bragelonne, my father, my brothers, my ancestors, would have struck me dead by now and not given it a moment's thought. But in a strange paradox, this man, who was more brutal than any of them, seemed to need to talk, to let his story spill out at last. And I needed to keep him talking.

'My mother was firm on that, and in time, I came to learn the wisdom of her judgement. I had to be prepared.' He paused, perhaps thinking back to moments with a dead mother. 'I had to know something of the law of England, and it was in the library of an abbey in Carpathia that I read of the laws of treason and attainder—'

'Of course,' I said. 'Only the conviction of my husband on a charge of High Treason, and the nullifying of his title by an Act of Attainder, would mean that the same title could then be created anew for you. If you found allies at court influential enough to secure such an outcome, that is.'

He looked at me curiously.

'A woman who knows English law,' he said. 'And as the English would say, too, a fucking Frog who knows English law. Unheard of, in both cases. You are a curious creature, Lady Louise-Marie. Curious, and intelligent. But yes, I had to know how I could become Earl of Ravensden when no man in England believed my father had a son who could succeed him. Also, I had to be able to speak enough of the language to make my way in this realm, and there was a monk in that same Carpathian abbey who was once a seminarian at Douai, amidst all the English priests. Above all, I had to be a warrior, able to hold my own against all comers – certainly against the mighty Matthew Quinton, whose exploits in the Spanish Main were legend even in our distant hills.' The Hungarian turned away and went to look through the window that faced north, over the cliff. 'When I was twenty-one, the Ottomans began their great war against the princes of the east, the war that still continues. In one sense, I had to fight in any case, to defend our villages and people from the heathens. But I knew that every tactic I learned, every *azap* I fought, every Janissary I killed, taught me lessons that would be useful to me when the day came for me to claim my birthright. And when my mother died, three years ago, I was released from the vow I had made to her, the vow not to pursue the claim to the earldom while she lived. For she feared that if I went to England, I would be killed out of hand through the malevolence of your husband. She could not see how strong I had become, how not even the vaunted Matthew Quinton could withstand me.'

'You could still be my husband's friend,' I said. 'His ally in war. He could bestow lands upon you, honour you as his cousin—'

I saw it in his eyes at once. *The wrong words, Louise-Marie.* That is what would happen in the sort of books I read. But I recalled my sister's words, spoken to me at Chambord: *you read far too many romances by bad poets.* And now, my taste in reading would kill me.

'Lands that are not his to give,' he snarled. 'Lands that are mine. A title that is mine. And if I can have none of it, then he shall not have you.'

He drew his sword. I offered up a silent prayer to the Virgin, took a deep breath, and said the one thing left to me to say.

'No, Balthasar Quinton, you will not kill me. You will not, for there is one question you should have asked yourself much sooner, is there not?'

'A question? You have no questions left to ask. You are a dead woman, and your husband's title will die with him, even if I do not succeed to it. My father will be avenged at last.'

'Think on it. I knew who you were before I came here. And if I knew that—'

I saw the change in his expression.

'Bell!' he cried. 'Bell!'

'Look to the bay,' I said. 'The bay to the south.' I saw his eyes go to the window, to the scene beyond. 'Look at the ships at anchor. Does not one of them look very familiar, even to a man from a distant and land-locked country?'

'Bell!' he cried again, more urgently.

The door opened, but it was not the treacherous steward of Alnburgh Castle who entered.

'He is detained,' said the newcomer. 'As are you, Horvath, for I will not deign to name you Quinton.'

Nicholas Iles stood there, a pistol in each hand, two of the men of the *Constant Esperance* at his back.

Nicholas Iles:

It was a desperate, frantic effort, after that day at Ravensden Abbey when Bell told his lies to My Lady. As soon as he was gone, she told me her suspicions regarding this mysterious and sudden summons to Alnburgh, which she believed could only have come from the man once known as Laszlo Horvath. Old Barcock confirmed it: Bell, he said, was always known for his loyalty to the sixth Earl, but had been kept on by the seventh and eighth simply because of his efficiency and unrivalled knowledge of the estate and its people. The Countess said she would delay going north for as long as possible, to give me time to alert the crew of My Lord's ship. For it truly was his ship again; as soon as Robert Logan realised King James had not identified him as a suspect in Gowrie's conspiracy, he was more than willing to sell the *Constant Esperance* back to the Earl. What became of the treasure of Fast Castle was another matter; but the crew seemed mightily fat, drunken and well content when I went aboard her at Lynn, having ridden hell-for-leather from Ravensden (or as hell-for-leather as my wounds from the

Castlehaven fight permitted). They were rather less fat after working double watches to get her ready for sea in a week, and then sailing her for Alnburgh Bay under Avent's command. I did not adopt with them my strange and violent new persona as Captain Musk; but it was he, and not the craven actor-poet Nicholas Iles, who ordered the men of the *Constant Esperance* through the many breaches in the crumbling walls of Alnburgh Castle, it was he who held a pistol to the treacherous Bell's temple, it was he who released My Lady's servants from the dungeons.

And it was now he, Captain Nicholas Musk, who confronted the man who believed himself the rightful Earl of Ravensden.

The Dowager Countess:

Balthasar Quinton said something to himself in his own tongue, then smiled.

'That it should be you, Iles. A poet. A very bad poet. How God mocks me!'

He brought up his sword, and Iles levelled the primed pistol in his right hand. But then the Hungarian reversed the blade, and presented the hilt to me.

'My Lady Ravensden,' he said, inclining his head slightly.

I took the sword. Curiously, it was the first time I ever held such a weapon in my hand. It was heavier than I expected it to be.

Iles ordered two of the crew forward, and they bound the Hungarian's hands in front of him.

'Your orders, My Lady?'

'As we discussed, Nicholas. Put him aboard the ship, take him south to await My Lord's return from sea, then see if you can get passage in a pinnace or victualler going out to our fleet. Take the news to my husband in person, for none of this can be committed to letters.'

It was a somewhat fraught conversation, that day in Ravensden Abbey when Iles and I agreed upon what we would do if Horvath, as we still called him, was taken alive. Iles was all for striking him dead upon the spot and burying him without a trace. But I knew my husband would want the final reckoning with this man. We could not keep him at Alnburgh, a place so very remote, where – as Bell's treachery proved – the loyalties of the people were uncertain. Taking him south held risks. It was possible that Secretary Cecil might learn of it, and seek to free the Hungarian for his own purposes; or else, he might insist on the case going to law, with all the tedium and uncertainty of that business. In any case, what capital crime had the man formerly known as Laszlo Horvath committed? The prospect of him walking free from an English court, that most unpredictable of entities, free to resume his campaign against my husband, a threat to the life of our daughter and any children yet unborn –

No. The Hungarian would be kept aboard the *Constant Esperance* in the remote haven of Pin Mill, there to await the Earl's return from sea. And I was certain my husband would know what to do with him.

Nicholas Iles:

It was my fault. I was not then accustomed to pistols, and should have checked my match. I should have had another armed man covering us: a man rather more experienced in the use of such weapons. But as we marched the Hungarian out into the courtyard of Alnburgh Castle, my pistols were at my belt, and there was no other man with a gun anywhere in sight. All of the other Esperances were engaged in searching the buildings for any concealed followers of Steward Bell and the man I still called Laszlo Horvath.

We were half way across the courtyard when I heard a sound behind me, followed a moment later by My Lady's cry of 'Iles!' from the steps of the Keep.

I turned to see one of the Esperances doubled up, seemingly struck in the stomach. Horvath was behind the other, pulling the rope which bound him ever tighter around the man's neck. I drew the pistol on my right side, but the match was cold. I reached for that at my left –

Horvath discarded his victim and ran for one of the many breaches in the curtain wall. I levelled my pistol and fired, but my aim was false. I could see him scrambling over the rubble and fallen masonry.

My Lady screamed again.

'Bastard!' she cried. '*Bâtard*!'

I ran towards Horvath. Out of the corner of my eye I saw Avent appear at the doorway of the south tower, levelling a musket at the Hungarian. But Horvath was already over the crest of the fallen wall –

With nothing before him but air. For here, on the north side of the castle, the ground fell away immediately beneath the castle wall, a sheer cliff standing precipitate above the sea.

Avent fired. I did not know if Horvath was hit, or if he jumped. But in the blink of an eye, he was gone.

I ran to the cliff edge, but there was no sign of him in the churning waters beneath.

Could he swim? I did not know. But then I realised the other mistake I had made: I should have ordered the Hungarian's hands tied behind his back, not before his front. If I had done the latter, the matter would be beyond all doubt.

The Countess came and stood beside me.

'He might live, My Lady,' I said.

'So he might.' She looked down at the sea, then at the ruinous walls of Alnburgh Castle. 'This place has a curious effect upon Quintons, Iles – he and his father, both disappearing into thin air in the same spot. But I have a sense that, unlike his father, cousin Balthasar will return to haunt us yet.'

CHAPTER TWENTY-FIVE

The Earl of Ravensden:
Sesimbra was a shallow south-facing bay, framed by the foothills of a mountain range. These, in turn, formed a peninsula separating the sea which Sesimbra village fronted from the great estuary of the Tagus and the city of Lisbon. An old Moorish castle stood upon a hill overlooking the village and the bay. Upon the beach was a modern fort flying the green and red colours of the King of Portugal; but the King of Portugal also happened to be Philip the Third, King of Spain, the Dons having obtained the entire kingdom and its great empire over twenty years earlier, when the last King of Portugal rode to his death in a needless battle without having had the good sense to father an heir first. So Portugal was England's enemy, and Sesimbra was where our particular enemy lay this day.

A very particular enemy.

Leveson and I had come together off the Rock of Lisbon, with little but failure to report to each other after weeks of fruitless cruising. Indeed, it was the unspoken sense of what the Queen might do to such abject and irredeemable failures that caused us to take a glass of wine together in the great cabin of the *Warspite*. And then another glass. And then another: say what you may about Brick-Beard, he had the best taste in wine of any English admiral I ever knew. We were almost at the very moment of sharing confidences – of telling each other what we really thought of Her Majesty, of the matter of the succession, of the unfathomable nature of womankind in general, and so forth – when the lookout's cry took us to the flagship's quarterdeck, there to see a caravel wearing toward us to the south. A caravel bearing the tidings that the *Nonpareil* and *Dreadnought*, which were detached to cruise, had discovered a great carrack lying in the bay of Sesimbra. A great carrack from the Indies, with barely thirty men said to be alive from her crew of six hundred after a terrible two-year voyage and the ravages of disease. A great carrack said to be carrying a cargo worth two million pounds. A great carrack protected by eleven galleys.

'Spinola,' I said, the fog of wine evaporating from my mind like a morning mist.

'Undoubtedly,' said Leveson. 'Last heard of sailing from Cadiz for Flanders, but not yet come past Lisbon. So the Dons must have ordered him to defend the Indiaman.'

'We have few ships,' I said, looking Brick-Beard straight in the eyes, 'and they undermanned, leaky, and long overdue for repairs.'

'That is true,' he said. 'But we have one thing the Dons do not have.'

'Sir Richard?'

'Why, we have the Earl of Ravensden, do we not?'

And that was how we came to be at Sesimbra Bay.

'A pretty proposition, My Lord,' said Tom Carver, as he surveyed the scene.

'Indeed it is, Master Carver. It is difficult to tell which is the prettiest part. The carrack, there, three times our size. The great guns in the fort, there to starboard, directly covering it. The other guns up in the castle, there. The veritable army the Dons appear to have lining the shore, there. Ten thousand men at least, I reckon. And the small matter of the line of eleven galleys, there, sealing the western end of the bay between the carrack and the headland. Each one with a sixty-pounder cannon in its bows. Aye, most pretty, for sure.'

I surveyed the scene once again. And as I did so, I felt a strange emotion. I looked once more, screwing up my eyes, calculating distances in my head. The strange emotion became a growing certainty. Oh, it was a pretty scene all right, but not in the way I had imagined.

'Master Carver,' I said, 'you would favour me by bringing forth a rutter. I intend to study the chart for this bay, and then I would have the boat made ready to take me over to the *Warspite* for a conference with the admiral.'

Nicholas Iles:

While My Lord was aboard the flagship, I stood upon the poop of the *Merhonour*, surveying the scene and contemplating the prospect of battle. Once, not many months earlier, I would have cowered and run. Now I felt only anticipation: an eagerness to be at the Dons, the very same eagerness that had made me persuade a sometime shipmate of the Earl, now commanding a fast pinnace bound for the fleet with despatches, to carry me with him from Portsmouth, following my return from Alnburgh. And, of course, there was eagerness for the riches in the carrack, and the prospect of what my share of them might be. But even without such a tempting prize in sight, I would have relished the imminence of battle in any case. Some men, like My Lord, are born warriors, but others become warriors accidentally, without any intent or expectation to become so. Such was the case with me. One day, perhaps quite soon, the war would end, and if I could find no other vocation, I might have to return to the stage. Not, I prayed, to forgery, but if needs must –

No, it would have to be the stage. But I knew that if I did so, I would have one inestimable advantage over every other poet and actor in London. Who else, acting out a mock-fight between two Greek or Roman heroes, would actually have fought such duels to the death, against real enemies in real fights? And who else, writing plays of war and scenes of battle, could do so from experience? Certainly not Shakespeare, that overrated mountebank. How could he, who had never killed a man or fought in a battle, possibly conjure up convincing portrayals of Agincourt or Bosworth? It beggared belief. But in truth, Shakeshaft's fantasy battles were just as convincing as the ones I had penned in my earlier works, which I now realised were but false confections, unreal beyond measure.

No, if ever I returned to my previous vocation, it would be as England's war poet.

I looked over to the *Warspite*, and saw My Lord climbing down into the longboat. Now, truly, we would see a battle worthy of the stage.

The Earl of Ravensden:

'What in God's name is Leveson doing?'

'His sailing master more like. This is a true seaman's fault – begging pardon, My Lord.'

Tom Carver and I stood together on the quarterdeck of the *Merhonour*, watching incredulously as the Warspite's sails flapped helplessly in the freshening north-easterly breeze. For whatever reason, the flagship had failed spectacularly to execute a simple turn into the wind. She had missed stays entirely and was being carried out of the bay by the twin forces of wind and tide.

'There's Leveson now, going down into the longboat,' I said. 'Shifting his flag to the *Dreadnought*, no doubt. But whatever his intent, there's no doubt of ours, Master Carver. Hold our course, if you please!'

The *Merhonour* alone was sailing directly into the bay. The *Dreadnought*, *Nonpareil* and *Adventure* were sailing across its mouth, engaging the galleys and the fort at long range. The captains of the three ships had been adamant upon the matter at a rancorous council-of-war, the previous day. Attempting to take the carrack was folly, they said, for the position was too well defended. Besides, the Spanish were bound to have taken off her cargo. And thus we came to the strangest of passes: Matthew of Ravensden and Brick-Beard Leveson supporting each other's arguments like true brothers-in-arms, both of us determined to take the carrack and defeat General Spinola in the process, finally conceding that the two flagships alone would make the attack. Except now, by misjudgement or craven cowardice, Leveson's ship-master had let him down. Which left only the *Merhonour*, her crosses of Saint George streaming in the breeze as she entered Sesimbra Bay.

'Helm amidships and steady!' I commanded, as we steered directly for the position I sought. 'And steady, boy.'

Young Ielden was at my side, ready to carry my orders wherever they were needed. His face was as white as a clean bedsheet.

The first Spanish gun fired: the sixty pounder in the bow of the headmost anchored galley, Spinola's vice-admiral. A vast spout of water, far greater than any cannon of ours could make, erupted a fair way ahead of our larboard bow.

I felt myself grin. 'Thank God for the Dons, young Ielden. One day they'll learn not to fire before they're in range, and one day they'll use guns that don't take an eternity to reload, rather than monsters like that, which are designed solely to frighten the timid. And when that day comes, England should tremble indeed. But thanks be to God, that day is yet a very long way off, as they have just amply demonstrated. Ho, Master Carver, there! Boatswain Fellowes, there!'

'My Lord!' the two men chorused as one.

'At my order, if you please!'

I looked starboard, to the carrack and the fort. I looked larboard, to the line of galleys. Any moment now. A few more yards – just a few more –

'Now!' I bellowed.

Carver and Fellowes both blew on their whistles, the former's a reedy tenor, the latter's more of a bass. The men in the tops took in sail. And up forward, there was the unmistakeable sight and sound of anchor cables playing out.

'Master gunner!'

'My Lord!' cried Skipworth, from the ship's waist.

'At my command, master gunner!'

'Aye, aye, My Lord!'

The headway came off the ship. Again I looked starboard to the carrack and the fort, then larboard to the galleys. Very nearly perfect. Today God smiled upon England and Matthew Quinton.

I raised my sword.

'Merhonours! For God, England, and Queen Bess! *Give fire!*'

I dropped my sword, and the gates of Hell opened. Culverins and demi-culverins, minions and sakers, spat forth a veritable hailstorm of death. Ielden gripped his ears. Even I was taken aback by the noise, the smoke and the shaking of the hull. But then, it was only the fourth or fifth time I had ever ordered a double broadside, both sides of the ship firing at once. And never in my life had I ordered an immediate repeat. And another. And another. And so on, my gun crews keeping up an exemplary rate of eight shots an hour of thereabouts, for hour upon hour.

Carver came back to the poop deck and smiled at me.

'A pretty spectacle indeed, My Lord. As you planned.'

I nodded. There can have been no more than a few dozen yards of sea-room in the bay of Sesimbra that served the purpose, and between us, Tom Carver and I had taken the *Merhonour* there as unerringly as a gerfalcon returning to the glove. To larboard, the Spanish galleys were moored in such a way that they masked each other's fire. Thus none of them could bring their guns to bear on us while we pounded the vice-admiral, at the head of the line – or at least, could not bring their guns to bear without breaking their formation, which in turn put them directly in the teeth of the broadsides of our other three galleons, or else left them rowing hopelessly from side to side, trying somehow to avoid the English fire coming at them from both sides. And the vice-admiral, barely able to fire one shot in reply to every five or six of ours, was soon a shattered and immobile hulk.

That was but the half of it. For as I had reckoned, from this particular position in the bay we could also fire to starboard upon the carrack, the fort and the town at one and the same time; but although we cared not which of those three targets we hit, the gunners in the town and the fort had to take care not to hit the impossibly high sides of the carrack, which largely masked the *Merhonour* from their fire.

'Keep it up, my brave lads! Let's make General Spinola dance, by Heaven!'

Truly, I cannot think of three or four hours in my life that were happier than those where the *Merhonour* lay at anchor in Sesimbra Bay, and I strode back and forth along our decks, sword in hand, encouraging the gun crews to ever greater efforts. Every ball we fired, every ball that struck home, erased one more part of the humiliation I had suffered at Calais, at Spinola's hands.

'See, Merhonours, the vice-admiral surrenders! See the galley slaves, swimming to their freedom! Today we do God's work! Truly, we do!'

'My Lord!'

'Aye, Master Carver?'

'Astern, My Lord! The *Dreadnought*, with the admiral!'

Silently, I cursed. Brick-Beard would somehow interfere with my triumph, would find a way of claiming all the credit for himself. Even before the *Dreadnought* anchored directly astern of us, in very nearly as propitious a position for wreaking havoc upon the Dons, Leveson's long boat was casting off, bearing him toward the *Merhonour*.

I went up to the quarterdeck to await him, although I was aware that I was barely fit to beg in the streets, let alone to greet the admiral of one of Her Majesty's fleets. I was begrimed with gunsmoke and sweat, bare footed and bare chested, hardly the image of an Earl of England. Indeed, Richard Leveson looked at me from head to toe, his face impassive. For a moment, I thought he was about to reprimand me for endangering the *Merhonour*, or for not having visited sufficient devastation upon the Dons. But then he flung open his arms and embraced me with an enthusiasm so effusive that it bordered on the French.

'My Lord! My brother! May I call you my brother? Oh, you have won my heart today, Matthew of Ravensden! What a sight! What a triumph!'

'Not yet won, Sir Richard,' not a little disconcerted by this unexpected effusiveness. 'General Spinola still resists. And we have still to take the carrack.'

Finally, he released me from his grip.

'Fear not, My Lord. The *Dreadnought* is smaller, with a shallower draught. I'll take her further into the bay, and then once her fire is joined to *Merhonour*'s, we shall have a perfect crossfire that the galleys cannot avoid. Spinola will be finished. And you will not be deprived of your prize this time. You have my word of honour upon the matter.'

Brick-Beard was right in one sense, but very wrong in another. He was right about the smaller *Dreadnought* creating a perfect crossfire once she had moved a little way ahead of us. But he was wrong, very wrong, about Spinola being finished. All through the afternoon, the Genoese general and his galleys kept up the fight, constantly weaving hither and thither, trying to avoid our blazing broadsides and to find the range for their sixty-pounders. A second galley surrendered. Three more, which I later learned came under a separate local command and were not part of Spinola's fleet, bolted for Lisbon. But still the obdurate general and his six remaining galleys fought on.

'He is finished, My Lord,' said Tom Carver, echoing Leveson's words at about four of the clock.

'When he has only one galley left, Master Carver, or preferably none, then I will consider him finished. Then I will be avenged. Then we will have proven that galleys are no match for ships. Only then.'

Our shot continued to rain down on Spinola's galleys. By now, the half dozen that remained were little better than wrecks. I dreamed of boarding, but we had too few boats. We had too few men. Instead, all I could do was to watch helplessly as, a little after five, Spinola finally gave up the fight. The six shattered galleys slipped out of the bay to the south and west, then turned along the coast for the safety of Lisbon and the Tagus. The great general, the invincible Spinola, was running from the guns of Matthew of Ravensden. But still the triumph felt hollow.

'Wind's too light to overtake them, My Lord,' said Tom Carver.

'I see that, damn you!'

I stormed below, poured myself a jug of ale, and downed it in one. As I refilled the jug, I looked out of the stern window toward the carrack.

Then I remembered Admiral Sir Richard Leveson's promise upon his word of honour. And I smiled.

Two boat crossings under white flags followed. The third bore me toward the carrack, my boat's crew taking care to keep us under her lee, away from the fire of the guns ashore. As we drew nearer, I marvelled at the extraordinary size of the ship, her many decks carrying her far higher out of the water than any ship England possessed. She had taken many balls in the hull, but none seemed to have breached her timbers. She was a floating fortress, and as such, she deserved the treatment that any warrior of honour would afford to a fortress under siege.

As I stepped onto the deck, her captain came forward to greet me and bowed low in the florid Spanish fashion. He was taller than the average Don, and fairer. I had a speech ready in my mind, fashioned in both fluent Latin and passable Spanish, but this fellow surprised me by greeting me in perfect English.

'I am Don Antonio de Guzman, captain of His Catholic Majesty's carrack the *Saint Valentine*. Whom do I have the honour of addressing?'

Taken aback by being addressed so fluently in my own tongue, I neglected the niceties of honour.

'Your English is notable, Captain. The best of any man of your nation I've ever encountered, in truth.'

'I was born in Kent, sir, whence my mother's family hailed for generations untold. My father was in the retinue of our late King Philip, when he was your King Philip too, married to the late Queen Mary. But your name, sir?'

'I am Quinton,' I said, 'the Earl of Ravensden.'

It was as though Antonio de Guzman had been struck in the face. I heard murmuring among his men, all around us on the deck, and saw not a few cross themselves.

The captain of the *Saint Valentine* recovered himself, and bowed again.

'It is a great honour, My Lord of Ravensden. A very great honour. Shall we go below and take a glass of Jerez?'

'I would gladly take a glass with a Kentish man, Captain de Guzman, as long as we discuss terms over it.'

De Guzman lived in some state. His great cabin was hung with tapestries and adorned with silks. The deck above our heads was painted with a rustic scene that I took to be the Adoration of the Shepherds. A weighty golden crucifix formed the centrepiece of his personal altar, set against the starboard side. It was a floating throne room, hardly the great cabin of a ship that had endured a two-year voyage from hell.

'Now, My Lord,' said the captain, 'my mother taught me plain speaking, after the English fashion, and thus I will not demean you with prevarication.'

'I am glad to hear it, Captain de Guzman. I have encountered too much of Spanish prevarication in my time.'

He blanched a little at that, but continued nonetheless.

'My officers and I have considered our situation and find it, shall we say, disadvantageous, especially now that General Spinola has seen fit to withdraw himself. But, of course, it will be difficult for you to take this ship out from under the guns of Sesimbra. Therefore, we have a number of terms that we would offer you, My Lord.'

'*You* have terms that you would offer *me*? I shall be interested to learn of them, Captain. Most intrigued, in fact.'

'First, my men and I, with all our arms, to be allowed to go ashore this very night. Second, that although you may have the cargo, the ship will remain here, at anchor, in the possession of King Philip. Third, the *Saint Valentine* will continue to fly the flag of Spain, and we shall not be compelled to lower it.'

I set down my glass of Jerez and looked directly at de Guzman. Yes, by God, he really was being serious.

'Well now, Captain, those are terms indeed. You may have learned your English from your mother, but you learned everything else from your father, it seems.' I drew breath. 'Your pride. Your arrogance. Your high-flown detachment from the real world. So as to your so-called terms, Captain de Guzman – the first I accept, because I am merciful, just as my Queen is merciful. You have fought well and you have suffered much, both in your voyage and upon this day. You deserve the respect of leaving this place with your arms, with your honour intact. As for your second term…it is the finest joke I have heard since the last time I attended the playhouse, and saw a clown perform an amusing trick with a dog.' De Guzman made to protest, but I raised a hand. And recollection of the theatre put me in mind of that fine fellow, young Iles. I knew what he would whisper to me now, were he here: *lay it on, My Lord, lay it on.* 'And thus to your third term, Captain. You are in the presence of the ensigns and banners of the Queen of England. The only way in which the colours of Spain will continue to fly is trailing in the water, beneath the cross of Saint George.'

'Lord Ravensden, this is intolerable—'

'Intolerable, is it? Very well, Captain de Guzman. If my terms are refused, I shall return to my longboat this very minute. And you know what that means, Captain. We will come in our boats, and we will burn your ship, whether or not you and your men are in it.' *Lay it on.* 'I am Matthew Quinton, Earl of Ravensden, Baron Caldecote, Privy Councillor of England, *el diablo blanco*. Cross me, and I will summon forth the ghosts of Drake, Hawkins and Essex. The four of us, I alive and they dead, will plague the length and breadth of Spain like the veritable horsemen of the apocalypse. Your children will not sleep for fear. Your women will run screaming into the night. Your grandparents will turn over in their coffins and try to dig themselves deeper into the soil.' I turned to leave. 'Think upon it, Captain. Think upon it well. A most excellent Jerez, though. My compliments upon your excellent taste, sir.'

'W-wait, My Lord! I beg you, be not so precipitate!'

I smiled and turned back to face Captain Antonio de Guzman, who suddenly seemed so very much more English.

And that was how the fleet came to sail for home in company with the carrack *Saint Valentine* and its fabulous cargo from the Indies.

The Dowager Countess:

'Then how great will your share be, husband?' I demanded.

'Ah, now, that is a matter difficult to measure,' he said.

Of course it was. It always was.

We stood in the principal room of Ravensden House, the Earl having no time to travel into Bedfordshire. The cause of his summons to London was still a mystery; he had an appointment with Secretary Cecil at Greenwich that very afternoon.

'Creditors, I suppose?' I demanded. 'The Queen, I expect?'

'Many creditors. And, yes, the Queen. This is only the third great carrack we have taken during the entire war – there are many determined to claim a share in her, Her Majesty above all. A veritable legion of commissioners has been sent down to Plymouth to assess the *Saint Valentine*. There will be books and inventories galore. A shame that they will not find her as rich as she is said to be.'

He smiled, and I knew him well enough to know what that meant.

'Not as rich, My Lord? And how would you know that, pray?'

'Ah now, Louise-Marie my love, there are countless things that may happen to a prize ship during a voyage. The portable goods – the gold and jewels, and such like – have a habit of vanishing. Even heavy bundles of spices may strangely disappear from a ship's hold before she comes to an anchor, and before she suffers the scrutiny of prize commissioners. It is truly remarkable how such things happen. One could swear that the spirits of the sea simply conjure away such riches into thin air.'

'But would such disappearances not be theft from Her Majesty's treasury, My Lord?'

'That would be the same treasury which can find no money to pay Her Majesty's loyal officers and seamen, who risk their lives on her behalf each day while treasury clerks sleep comfortably in their beds? Theft is a relative term, my Countess. As, it seems, is death.'

He lifted a paper from the large pile upon the table: the papers which had awaited his attention upon his return from sea.

'My mother's kinsman, Stewart of Whitekirk, relates a curious tale in his latest letter. It seems a Scots ship, bound from Yarmouth for Leith, discovered a man stranded upon one of the Farne islands. This man was foreign, and fought like a colossus to avoid capture, killing four of the ship's men. When the ship finally docked, the man was taken off by Sir George Home, Lord High Treasurer of Scotland, in person, and escorted under guard to Edinburgh Castle under a warrant from the King himself. Now why should that be, do you think? Why should one foreign castaway so excite the interest of James Stuart?'

'You think it is your cousin, Balthasar? That he cheated death when he leapt into the sea at Alnburgh?'

'I am certain of it, but Whitekirk is making enquiries for me, and promises to confirm the matter.'

'Then what will you do if it is, husband? If he is in Edinburgh Castle, you cannot reach him. And King James is hardly likely to deliver him to you *gratis*.'

The Earl smiled.

'No, not *gratis*. He is a Scot, after all. But I think I know what price James Stuart will demand.'

'You only think you know? You, husband, who are usually so certain in all you do?'

'There you have it, my love – if I am wrong, the price he will demand instead is my head. No doubt of it. But the letter must be written, and the horse dealing commenced. So I shall write it now, before I go to see what the hunchback wants of me.'

'And in the interval between the letter writing and the interview, My Lord?'

I could see the look in his eye, and knew what it presaged.

'In the interval between the two, My Lady, it would convenience me greatly if you discarded your clothing, yonder.'

The Earl of Ravensden:
'Superlative folly,' said Sir Walter Raleigh.

'Superlative arrogance,' I replied, a little more loudly.

'Superlative extravagance!' cried Raleigh, louder still. More than a few of the courtiers upon the shore of Greenwich Palace turned to look at us. I could swear that even the Queen's red wig twitched in our direction, but that might have been wishful thinking upon my part.

'Superlative error!' I yelled.

'Superlative madness!' bawled Raleigh, who was out of favour (yet again). I must have been unspeakably bored, or else angry beyond measure, to have taken part with him in such a foolish schoolboy game.

In the midst of the river, the Queen's galley *Superlativa* swept past, her oars cutting the water somewhat shabbily, the drum giving the beat for her mixed crew of Spanish prisoners and English beggars. There was no wind, and she was rowing against the tide, going where no man-of-war could possibly go. A fine spectacle, which proved precisely nothing. Yet Her Majesty's ladies, surrounding their mistress like bees in the hive, applauded politely. I shook my head, but not merely at the ignorance of the simpering ladies in waiting, who would have applauded a man with a mildly unusual wart. Even after the lesson of Sesimbra, some about the Queen were still convinced that galleys were the future of England's Navy Royal. I knew better. Raleigh knew better, hence our rare good humour with each other. And then there was the Queen herself, a frail figure a little ahead of everyone else, upon the bank of Greenwich's shore. But less ahead than once she would have been: two ladies stood discreetly close behind her. Every single soul present that day knew they were there to catch her in case she fell. Great Elizabeth would still betray no sign of age or weakness in public: for instance, by viewing such a demonstration seated. But that, in itself, merely demonstrated how old and weak she was.

'A fine sight, is it not?' said Robert Cecil, appearing suddenly by my side.

'By no means as fine a sight as a galleon under full sail, Master Secretary,' I said.

'Ah, you seamen...' He nodded a greeting to Raleigh. 'My compliments, Sir Walter, but I trust you will forgive me if I have a word in private with Lord Ravensden.'

'There is still no prospect of my having private audience of Her Majesty, Master Secretary?'

'Be thankful that you have your liberty and are still permitted to be about the court, Sir Walter.'

Cecil led me away, back into the gardens of Greenwich Palace. A dozen or so solicitants endeavoured to approach the Secretary, waving their petitions in front of them, but Cecil ordered two guards to block their way, and we proceeded unmolested.

'Your fortune has turned, My Lord, these last months and years.'

'As you say, Master Secretary. I owe all to God and to the Queen's mercy. And to yourself, of course.'

He smiled graciously, and bowed his head. He knew it was a lie, of course, and an outrageous one at that: after all, this was the man who had taken the side of my cousin Balthasar and ordered my imprisonment in the Tower. The man who might still bring me low again, if he chose to betray my part in Gowrie's plot; but there again, in that we were bound in a mutual bond of silence, for Cecil knew full well that I, and only I, could reveal upon oath what was said at the meeting in Theobalds Palace, so long before. And if that did not matter one jot to Elizabeth Tudor, it mattered very much to another, who would soon sit upon her throne. So yes, we were bound to each other in silence, Robert Cecil and I.

'I brought you here to give you good news, My Lord. Two pieces of good news, in truth. First, Her Majesty has seen fit to bestow upon you a generous bounty for your part in the capture of the carrack at Sesimbra. A most generous bounty. Three thousand pounds, to be exact.'

Three thousand! Generous indeed, by Queen Elizabeth's standards. Whether she actually had that much money in her treasury, and whether I would ever see it, were other matters.

'I am most grateful for Her Majesty's bounty, Master Secretary.'

'As indeed you should be, My Lord. It is as well that Her Majesty appreciates that her captains, especially an Earl and thus a man of the most unimpeachable honour, would never seek to enrich themselves by plunder, so that the just profits of prize are concealed from Her Majesty's treasury.'

'As you say, Master Secretary.'

'But in one sense, the Queen's bounty may be seen as a down payment in anticipation of services yet to come. General Spinola has been refitting his ships at Lisbon.' I winced: only the most profound of lubbers could possibly call a galley a 'ship'. 'He is sure to attempt the Channel again. For we have it upon sound intelligence that his brother has brought an army of five thousand from Milan to Flanders. Once, England would have laughed in the face of an army so small. But now...'

I could not say what was in my mind: namely, that if England was under threat, and lacked the force to oppose it, then such a perilous state of affairs could be due only to the parsimony and ignorance of this man, and of the person he served.

'Surely, Master Secretary, the Queen's new galleys can be set forth to counter General Spinola?'

I had my tongue firmly in my cheek, but thankfully, Cecil took me seriously.

'Sadly, My Lord, the galley crews and their captains are as yet too raw, especially when set against the veterans under Spinola.' *And so they always will be, Master Secretary, for the Dons know what they are doing with galleys, and we do not.* 'No, the likes of My Lord of Nottingham have convinced Her Majesty that only the old-fashioned galleons can do the business in this instance. So, then, My Lord, we come to the heart of the matter. Her Majesty, her Privy Council and the Lord High Admiral have decreed that Sir Richard Leveson shall remain at Plymouth to cover the western Channel, and to prevent any new Spanish landing in Ireland. The eastern Channel will be covered by a new commander.'

He raised his hand and snapped his fingers. A page boy ran over, bearing a leather pouch. He reached within and handed Cecil a folded vellum parchment, secured by two wax seals bearing the unmistakeable imprints of the Lord High Admiral of England upon the one, and the royal arms of England upon the other. The Secretary contemplated it, as though wondering whether it was some dreadful mistake, and then handed it to me.

'I give you joy of your command, My Lord Admiral,' he said.

CHAPTER TWENTY-SIX

The Earl of Ravensden:
Admiral of the Narrow Seas. The Saint George Cross flying at the main.

Oh, it sounded splendid.

But the reality of it, in those straitened days in the autumn of 1602, was that my 'fleet' consisted of one galleon, and one alone: my flagship, the *Merhonour*, leaky and crank after being out for so long. I had two small crompsters, the *Advantage* and *Answer*, and four Dutch ships, these but recently joined and under the command of a Vice-Admiral Cant, a somewhat inauspicious name in all respects.

And Spinola was coming.

Four days we waited. I had placed a first line of ships off Dungeness, the *Merhonour* inshore, then the *Advantage*, then two Dutchmen, large and clumsy fly-boats both. Cant was in the Downs with his other two ships and the *Answer*.

'My Lord,' Tom Carver said, after I told him of the dispositions, 'surely it is a risk to divide so small a fleet—'

'And equally great to keep both halves on England's shore, running the risk that Spinola slips past us on the French side, as he did the last time. But this time, the Dutch have squadrons off Dunkirk and Sluys. He knows that. He will come this way, Master Carver.'

Even as I spoke the words, I prayed that God would repay my confidence. And at dawn on the fourth day, it seemed instead as though God was laughing in my face. There was a thick mist, as there was the last time. It was barely possible to make out the shape of the *Advantage*. But the mist was accompanied by a stiff south-westerly breeze, perfect for any vessels attempting to run the Channel.

I stood upon the quarterdeck, Iles at my side, and cursed my ill fortune. Spinola would make a fool of me yet again.

The Earl of Ravensden was finished.

Nicholas Iles:

A gun fired, somewhere off to the south-east. Then a second, in short order.

'The signal!' the Earl cried. 'Spinola! The fucking galleys! Set the courses, Master Carver! South by east, as close to the wind as we can manage, if you please! Signal the *Advantage* to fall into our wake! Master gunner, you know your duty, so go to it, man! Master boatswain, put aloft every fucking pennant and ensign we carry – aye, my personal banner at the mizzen! We are the flagship of the Narrow Seas, and General Spinola shall know it!'

The main course was barely set, and the ship slowly beginning to gain speed, when dark shapes began to emerge from the mist. Dark, low shapes. Six of them, in line abreast.

'Come on, you Don spew-sacks!' shouted the Earl, hauling himself up onto the ship's rail while clinging to a shroud. 'Come on, Federico Spinola, and taste more of the fire that did for you at Sesimbra!'

'They're taking in sail, My Lord!' cried Tom Carver.

'Oh, you won't avoid me that easily, General! I know your game!'

Even I could see what their game was. Oars were being deployed all along the sides of the six galleys, and their bows were already swinging round, back toward the south-west. The Spanish were going to go where we could not, directly into the wind. And if they could win the race that was about to begin, they would get to the south of us, toward the French shore, and then turn and run up the Channel to safety.

Just as they did before.

The Earl of Ravensden:

It was not a day to be a man of action.

A man of action craves nothing more than to have his sword in his hand and enemies within reach that can be impaled upon the end of it. A man of action who commands a man-of-war craves the shuddering of the deck beneath his feet as an entire broadside of demi-culverins tear apart a hostile ship at point blank range. A man of action with a score to settle against a certain Genoese general craves to be in the midst of his galleys

But no, it was not that sort of day.

Instead, it was the sort of day where General Spinola's six galleys tried to edge south-west, then a little south, then a little south-easterly, then a little more to the south-west, all the while trying to work round to the south of us as we struggled to sail as close to the wind as we possibly could. At her cleanest, straight out of dock or the careen, the *Merhonour* could sail perhaps seven points from the wind. But as she was then, foul-hulled and slow, she could barely make nine. Carver had men aloft and at the ropes constantly, adjusting this or that halliard or topsail every few minutes. But despite all his efforts, we fell further and further away from the galleys and from the two Dutchmen on the other tack. The *Merhonour* was stranded in the middle of the English Channel.

Or so it would have seemed to General Spinola.

Nicholas Iles:

'My Lord! The galleys are hoisting their sails again!'

The lookout's shout came late in the afternoon. My Lord exchanged glances with Tom Carver, but his face was unreadable. I looked out and saw the six galleys swinging round onto their new course: north-east, into the great gap between the *Merhonour* and the two Dutch ships, mere specks on the horizon far off to the north-west. The galleys were running back onto their original course, to hug the English coast.

'Enough of this tiresome nudging of the wind, Master Carver,' said the Earl. 'Time to sail large, in pursuit of the galleys, yonder!'

'Aye, aye, My Lord!'

He turned to me.

'Well, poet – damn me, do I still call you a poet? Do I call you Iles, or do I call you Musk? At any rate, did you ever see so fine a spectacle?'

He was unconscionably merry. There, in plain sight, history was repeating itself. Yet again, Federico Spinola was taking six galleys directly through the Straits of Dover to wreak havoc upon the coast of Flanders, and perhaps to threaten an invasion of England itself. Yet again, My Lord was being outrun and humiliated. Yet the Earl of Ravensden was grinning like a youth who had just taken his first maidenhead.

'This is a fine spectacle, My Lord?' I asked.

'Oh yes, the very finest. Come, now, Captain Musk, you who have commanded a Queen's man-of-war! Look upon the scene, man, and think. Spinola thinks he has outwitted me, but it is I who have outwitted him. Look out yonder, Nicholas Musk, and tell me why that is so.'

I studied the positions of the galleys, and of the Dutch ships, and of the *Merhonour*, and of the distant coasts of England to the north and France to the south. I thought of the maps and charts I had seen—

All became clear, like the opening of a door from a darkened room into a beauteous garden.

'You have forced him into a trap,' I said. 'You wished him to think that you were determined to keep him off the English coast. So when he made for that of France, you made as though you would block him from that course, too – trying and failing to follow him, making it look as though you were making every effort to bring the *Merhonour* as close to the wind as possible. Whereas what you were really doing—'

'Was creating a gap that Spinola would find irresistible. A gap that he had to make for, as our apparent attempts to sail close to the wind actually took us further and further into the middle of the Channel, blocking him from the French coast. So now the great general is going exactly where I want him to go, but he does not know that yet. Ah, my friend, I tell you this – being an admiral is a truly wonderful thing.'

And with that, he slapped my back; slapped it just as the *Merhonour* pitched as she gained speed sailing large in pursuit of Spinola's galleys.

The Earl of Ravensden:

What a spectacle we must have been from Dover in the dying light of evening!

The six galleys close inshore – so close that it was said some of the slaves were able to jump clear and swim ashore to freedom – pursued by the *Merhonour*, her bow chasers blazing away! And all the while, I kept us far enough out to sea to herd General Spinola where I wished him to go, like a sheepdog guiding a flock into a pen. There he was, clear against the chalk face of the White Cliffs, making inexorably for the Downs.

'Do you see Walmer Castle?' I demanded.

'There, My Lord,' said Carver, pointing toward a blur upon the shore. 'His flag-galley is level with the castle now.'

'Very good, Master Carver. Then we shall fall away, as we discussed. Let us see what General Spinola makes of the surprise that awaits him.'

As the *Merhonour* took in sail and came round as westerly as she could manage, a succession of flashes blazed out in the north-west, followed by a roaring like thunder.

'They have fallen into the trap,' said Iles.

'Let us pray so,' I said, watching the fire from Vice-Admiral Cant's ships.

But at first, it seemed as though papist prayers were proving more efficacious, and that General Spinola had an entire legion of saints interceding for him within the celestial realm. As entire darkness fell, the wind died away. And then, when the breeze got up again, it was north-westerly. The calm would allow the galleys to row away from Cant's squadron and get clear of the Goodwin Sands. The new wind would allow them to sail directly for the French coast, and thence, perhaps, inshore of the blockading Dutch squadrons. Spinola would escape again, and he, King Philip and the Inquisition would proclaim it a holy miracle.

'Damn him! Damn him to fucking hell!' I bellowed.

'Galley! Closing the starboard bow!'

'Sweet Christ in Heaven – God's blood—'

I could see it, a low, black shape, its lateen sail just visible in the darkness.

'Master Gunner! Starboard battery to—'

I saw the flash, heard the roar, and knew at once it was a sixty-pounder at very nearly point blank range. The great shot struck the starboard quarter, causing the entire hull to shake. The quarterdeck rail shattered, shrouds tore apart and sprang from their cleets, a saker was blown into the air like a leaf upon an autumn breeze –

A great splinter of oak planking broke from the *Merhonour*'s desk and struck Tom Carver in the groin, a little above his privates. Had he not been standing where he was, that same fateful piece of wood would have struck me, and the noble house of Quinton would have become extinct there and then.

Carver did not cry out; did not even stumble. Instead, he gripped the shard as though making to pull it out. But he could not see, as I could, that an oaken point was protruding from his back, around the base of his spine. Great stains of blood were soaking down his breeches, front and back. I went to him and gripped his shoulders. He looked at me, and his mouth formed words. But he was no longer speaking to me. He was speaking to another lord, the Lord he was about to meet: the words of the one hundred and eighteenth psalm.

'I shall not die, but live, and declare the works of the Lord...'

'Tom! Tom Carver! Do not die on me yet, Master Carver!'

'Open to me the gates of righteousness: I will go into them, and I will praise the Lord—'

He fell forward, into my arms. I trust that his spirit went at once to the Saviour to whom he had prayed so often and so long. For my part, I only had time to offer up the most perfunctory prayer for his soul, for his newly-minted widow at Wapping, and for his eight newly-orphaned children. Then I let the body fall to the deck, and returned to the fight.

Gunner Skipworth had not awaited any order from the quarterdeck. His duty was obvious, and our starboard battery was blazing away, jets of flame from our gun barrels casting a momentary light upon the scene. And now there were other lights, too: the light from fires aboard the galley, which was at so close a range that not even the feeblest gun crew could miss. There were other sounds, and they were unmistakeably the screams of men. Many of them, God help me, were English screams, the death agonies of my own countrymen, slaves chained to the galley's oars. I still hear their cries, over and over, in my dreams. My only consolation is the knowledge that, in one sense, I delivered those poor souls from the torment of slavery.

Nicholas Iles:

Our victory was brief indeed. Another low, black shape appeared to starboard, then another. One to larboard, and another, and another. We were in the midst of General Spinola's galleys.

'Bear away!' the Earl cried. 'Bear away *now*! Master Skipworth, make ready both sides! On my command, Master Gunner! Steady, my lads, steady! *Give fire!*'

A sea-fight is terrible enough by day, but by night it is as though one has fallen through the portals of hell into the very heart of the satanic furnace. The glow of linstocks in the darkness – the matches taking light – the great spit of flame from the cannon's mouth – its recoil, the wheels of its carriage screaming – the sound of the blast – the dozens of lesser firings from muskets, like infernal imps emulating the Lucifers of the great guns – the smoke and flame from the black, nearly invisible forms of the galleys – the death-screams of stricken men –

'Mister Iles – Musk, rather!'

'My Lord!'

'It strikes me that this is one instance where a lieutenant might be of some use, especially now that Master Carver has fallen. And you, my friend, who have commanded a Queen's ship in battle, are amply qualified for the part, I think.'

'But what does the lieutenant of a man-of-war actually do, My Lord?'

'The very question I ask every time the Lord Admiral has attempted to saddle me with one. But here, in such darkness that I can barely see beyond the mainmast, the duty is clear. To the forecastle, sir, and do there what you did aboard the *Halcyon*. Preferably without being shot this time. God be with you, Lieutenant Musk!'

'And with you, My Lord!'

I ran forward, past the sweating, grunting men heaving upon the tackle of the guns.

'Keep up your fire, men!' I cried as I reached the forecastle, waving my sword above my head. 'The Earl's orders! For God, England and Ravensden!'

'God, England and Ravensden!'

One of our sakers fired, and for one fleeting moment, the light of her fire illuminated a galley, barely a hundred yards to larboard. But the same light showed us to them, too, and a volley of musket fire rained down upon the forecastle. A ball struck the man upon one of the swivel guns, who was about to fire. He fell to the deck, clutching his chest as his life-blood drained away. Without a thought, I ran to the gun. I had seen these fired, the shot-canister and powder were already in the breech. I picked up the fallen man's lighted linstock from the deck, aimed at where I judged the quarterdeck of the galley would be, applied fire to the fuse, and, as the gun fired, I felt as though a giant was shaking every bone in my body, such was the force of the blast. And then there was the thrill, the surging of the blood, and a prayer offered up for my shot to have taken Spinola's head off his shoulders.

We kept up our fire, but I could also feel the movement of the ship as the *Merhonour* swung round onto her new course, east by south. Slowly, we moved away from the encircling galleys and the risk of being surrounded and boarded. All the while our batteries kept up a ferocious fire, and I bellowed at the men on the forecastle guns. But after a little while, it was obvious even to me that we were well out of range, and that the galleys were not pursuing us. I returned to the poop deck.

'My Lord,' I said, 'surely our broadsides are firing into empty sea?'
He was calmer now.
'There are more ways than one for a broadside to sink a fleet,' he said.
And so there were.

All night, we saw the flashes of gunfire to the north and east, and heard what sounded like collisions amid the cannon fire. For the *Merhonour*'s furious broadsides had alerted the Dutch squadrons blockading Sluys and Dunkirk, and given the bearing to Cant's ships coming out of the Downs. In the morning, we encountered the Dutch vice-admiral's flagship, searching the sea for survivors of the night battle. Cant came aboard, and reported that five of the galleys had been rammed, sunk by gunfire, or run aground by their crews. Only one had escaped, getting into Dunkirk by the skin of its teeth: the *San Luis*, the flag-galley of Federico Spinola himself.

'It is a great victory, My Lord,' said Cant, 'and much of it your doing. You sprang the trap that forced Spinola into the Downs. You blocked his course to the French coast. You alerted our ships to his whereabouts.'

'We should have had them all!' cried the Earl. 'Spinola has one galley still! I have not killed enough Spaniards. We have not sunk enough galleys! Perhaps there are still fools and cravens in Whitehall who believe that galleys are the future -'

'No, My Lord,' I said, as firmly as I dared, 'no man will cry up the galley in England again. Here, and at Sesimbra, you have blasted their reputation forever. England will yet be a nation of ships, and of ships alone. A nation wedded to the sea. And you have played your part in that, Matthew Quinton of Ravensden. A very great part.'

He looked at me, a hint of disbelief still apparent in his eyes. Perhaps he might have been more accepting of my words if he could only have seen a very few months into the future, when General Federico Spinola was killed leading one last, desperate attack against the Dutch blockaders: his arm blown off, his stomach full of musket balls, the potential to become a new Hannibal cut off abruptly at the age of thirty one.

'We should still have had them all,' My Lord said, in the end.

All around, the crew of the *Merhonour* were cheering like madmen. All around, the sea was strewn with the corpses of dead Spaniards and the timbers of sunken galleys. The Dutch ships were firing guns in joyous celebration.

Time after time in the previous few months, I had told myself I was done with the quill. I tried to convince myself that I had put the stage behind me. Yet there was something in the scene before me that was irresistible: the contrast between the greatness of the victory and the unbounded celebration of it on the one hand, and a single man's regret upon the other. Joy. Regret. Range of emotions. Dramatic tension. Yes, this was a poem that had to be written. The words were beginning to form, the stanzas and pentameters beginning to fit together in my mind.

Why, it even had a musical feel to it. Perhaps I would see if young Ielden could turn it into a song.

And I knew its title, too.

I would call it 'Lord Ravensden's Lament'.

CHAPTER TWENTY-SEVEN

Nicholas Iles:

My Lord and I were on horseback upon a crest in the hills, looking out over a landscape of vast, empty, high moors. The first light snowfall of the winter lay upon the ground. It had been a ride of several long hours from Alnburgh Castle. The border between England and Scotland ran somewhere across this land, but it was impossible to tell where that border might be, or on which side of it we stood. There was not another soul in sight.

'He's not coming, My Lord,' I said; for it was well past the time appointed for the meeting.

'Oh, he's coming. If one thing on God's earth is certain at this moment, my friend, it's that he's coming.'

Sure enough, a small banner appeared above the ridge across the valley, followed in short order by a dozen or so horsemen, riding directly for us. They rode together as a group, but for the flag bearer and the man who rode before him. As their horses splashed through the stream below, it was possible at last to make out the emblem on the flag: a red lion rampant upon a golden field.

Only one man on earth was entitled to ride ahead of that emblem.

He reined in before us. He was a strange spectacle altogether: clad from head to toe in green hunting garb, his shoulders covered by a fur stole, he possessed great, staring, sad eyes that seemed too big for his head, a beard flecked with grey even though he was years younger than My Lord, and a swarthy foreign appearance, very different to the pale features adorning the faces of the men who rode behind him. The heavily armed men, who could easily kill us in a trice if ordered so to do.

The Earl bowed deeply in the saddle, and I followed suit.

'Your Grace,' said My Lord.

'So ye're the famous Earl of Ravensden, then. Son to a Stewart mother, though, if I read my genealogies rightly. One of the offshoots of the Aubigny line, eh, My Lord, and thus close kin to my cousin Lennox?

Means there's good blood in ye somewhere, laddie. Aye, good Stewart blood, cousin Matthew.'

James the Sixth, King of Scots, spoke in an accent so strange and rapid that it was difficult to get the gist of what he said. Indeed, it was difficult to accept that this peculiar, shambolic figure could actually be a King at all. Here was no Alexander, no Charlemagne, no Harry the Fifth, that was certain.

The King looked me up and down. There was something unsettling about his gaze.

'And who's this braw laddie, My Lord?'

'Nicholas Musk, Your Grace. He distinguished himself greatly in the Queen's service at the Battle of Castlehaven.'

'Is that so? Musk. Nicholas Musk. An unusual name. As rare as your namesake, forsooth, Master Musk. *Rosa moschata*, eh? A sweet smelling rose. Fragrant, even. What's yon Sassenach poet say? Some'at about a bank wi' wild thyme and oxlips, o'er-canopied with musk roses? Shakespeare, that's the laddie. But you wouldna ken him, I suppose, Master Musk.'

The King's expression was as innocent as his words were loaded. I bowed my head to acknowledge His Grace's learning, and as I did so, I chided myself for suspecting that this most unlikely example of divinity upon earth could possibly know who I truly was.

'I have seen some of Master Shakespeare's works played upon the stage, Your Grace,' I said.

'Mayhap,' said the King. 'But tell me, cousin Matthew – ye've brought it?'

'As I promised, Your Grace.'

The Earl reached into his saddlebag and drew out a small pouch. He urged his horse forward a couple of paces, and handed it to the King. James Stuart undid the ties and reached eagerly inside the bag. He took out the paper within, opened it, and read.

'Aye, weel,' he said. 'So this is what you think will save your head, Matthew Quinton. And this is the original?'

'It is, sire.'

'Of course it is. Although I ofttimes hear strange blethering to the effect that there might be several originals. But that could not possibly be the case, could it, My Lord, if an Earl of England gives me his word of honour upon it?'

The Earl inclined his head.

'As you say, Your Grace.'

'And this Musk, here – he knows the content of this?'

'He does, sire.'

Once again, the King looked at me rather too intently for my liking.

'I could have ye both killed, here and now,' he said. 'Men who are privy to this secret are dangerous to me. Men who took the cause of the Earl of Gowrie are doubly dangerous to me. Traitors. Would-be regicides. Such men deserve to die.'

I felt myself go rigid in the saddle. Had My Lord miscalculated? I stole a glance at him. His face was pale, paler than I had ever seen it, and I knew then that he was having the same thought. James's wrath toward all those who had been even slightly involved in the Gowrie plot was a byword, the King's vengeance utterly implacable. And yet the Earl of Ravensden, who was more involved in that plot than any, had just handed James Stuart the only thing that could possibly save his life.

But the King simply sighed, and nodded toward the paper in his hand.

'The eternal folly of womankind, eh?' he said. 'Not only the sin, but feeling compelled to record the sin. Like an adulteress bawling news of her fornication to all and sundry at the Mercat cross.' The King shook his head. 'And it was for this that you and Gowrie thought to overthrow me and place my son upon the throne, reckoning that one generation's remove from a taint in the bloodline was sufficient to cleanse the Augean stable. Ah, don't bother with false protestations and denials, Lord Ravensden – there were witnesses enough to the mysterious English ship at the mouth of the Tay, and her fight with the Dunkirker off Broughty. For some reason, though, Master Secretary Cecil seems determined to convince me that you could not possibly have been the captain of this ship. He is even more determined to convince me that any action against Gowrie's English confederates would go down most ill among the English nobility, and with him, too. Assuming Gowrie had English confederates, of course, for the late Earl made sure that all the evidence he left behind claimed he and his brother had acted entirely alone. As Master Secretary Cecil reminds me. And everyone falls over themselves to tell me how indispensable Master Secretary Cecil is, how entirely essential he will be to me when I become England's King. This being the same Master Secretary Cecil who now beds Gowrie's sister, who saw this same letter twenty years ago. 'Tis strange how the world turns, is it not? Mighty strange.'

I could see that My Lord was greatly discomfited by the King's speech. But it was not only his words that were unsettling: for James Stuart's broad, almost incomprehensible, Scots accent had ebbed away in the blink of an eye, replaced by merely the gentlest lilt. Now he spoke like a King, and a King of England, too.

'Your Grace knows the law and history of England, I think, as well as that of your own Scotland,' said the Earl. 'So if you will permit it, I shall put to you a legal hypothesis, founded upon historical precedent.'

'We're on horses in the midst of a wilderness, and you choose this place and this time to quibble on points of law with the King of Scots? We, James, who have out-foxed archbishops, the finest professors at St Andrews, and countless of Edinburgh's sharpest attorneys? We, James, who could have you condemned for treason for your dealings with Gowrie, the moment we ascend the throne of England, regardless of what yon hunchback says? We, James, who could order the bonnie lads behind us to stick you with blades here and now and spare the expense of a trial? And you want to put to us a legal hypothesis, founded upon historical precedent? Now there's a pass. You're not what I had in my mind as the model of a famous English warrior, My Lord of Ravensden.'

Was My Lord thinking, as I was, *And you're not what I had in my mind as the model of a King*? If he was, his expression gave not the slightest hint of it.

'As you say, Your Grace. But the history of England tells us that many men have come to the throne despite having no blood claim to it – William the Norman, Harry the Fourth, your own ancestor Harry the Seventh, and others besides. Now, many might have disputed their claim before they succeeded, and questioned their right to the throne. Questioned their very bloodline, perhaps. But the moment the crown was placed upon their heads in Westminster, these kings became the undoubted, divinely ordained monarchs of England, entitled to the unswerving loyalty of every man in the land.'

'As I will be, once I am crowned in Westminster, you mean?'

'Undoubtedly, Your Grace.'

'The coronation ceremony overrules all? Even this?'

The King held up the letter.

'Even that, sire.'

'And at that moment, I will have your unswerving loyalty, My Lord Ravensden? Even though you know what this letter says?'

'You will be my lawful, anointed King, and I will fight for you with every breath left in my body, Your Grace. Even though I know what that letter says. Especially because I know what it says.'

The large eyes narrowed slightly, but otherwise, King James was impassive.

'And you, Master Musk? What of you?'

Careful, Nicholas – the future location of your head depends upon how you answer now. Time for the best speech you have ever written, and the best you will ever deliver.

'Your Grace, I know nothing of law, but it seems to me that your crowning at Westminster will surely be proof of God's will that you are the rightful, divinely ordained sovereign of all England. And in that sacred moment, I will throw my hat in the air and proclaim you with gladness in my heart and tears in my eyes, in the English style – Your Majesty.'

James Stuart smiled.

'Majesty. Aye, I have a liking for the English notion of Majesty. A very great liking. You speak well, Master Musk. Almost like a poet, in fact. Almost like an actor.'

The King of Scots smiled again, and I was dumbfounded.

The Earl of Ravensden:

'Sire,' I said, knowing this might be the best opportunity to raise the matter, 'you have thought upon my request?'

The King's face changed in a trice. From the jovial fellow flattering Nicholas Iles, James Stuart turned in an instant into a suspicious, petulant cynic.

'Your payment, you mean? The payment for returning to me what was always rightfully mine? The payment for my not ordering your death, either now or when I come to England's throne? Is your life not payment enough, My Lord Ravensden?'

'The other matter was but a humble request, Your Grace, nothing more.'

The King nodded.

'Aye, humble indeed. As is right and proper, when mere men seek to approach God's divinely appointed. But, perchance, it suits me to accede to your request, My Lord of Ravensden. Suits me for my own purposes. For I am told that England's monarch needs good admirals, and I have it upon good authority that the victor of Castlehaven, Sesimbra Bay and the fight in the Narrow Seas is not only a man worth keeping alive, whatever treasons he might have committed, but a man worth accommodating. I have that upon the very highest authority, if you catch my meaning.'

Oh, I caught his meaning well enough, although I struggled to believe it. Elizabeth, Queen of England, who had spent the last fifteen years denying me command after command – now, at the very end of her life, the dying old crone was recommending me to the man who was bound to be her successor.

The King raised a hand. Moments later, two riders appeared on the crest of the ridge to the north; but the rearmost of them was facing backwards upon his horse, and had his hands tied behind his back. Even so, I recognised him in short order.

'A strange fellow,' said the King. 'Throughout the time he's been kept in the Edinburgh tolbooth, he's done nothing but petition and petition again for an audience. I ask you, an audience! Despite his having killed the Macrae, who was a loyal friend to me. It seems he can think and talk of nothing but his ambition, so much so that it has become a kind of madness, I think. His ambition to be you, My Lord. To be the Earl of Ravensden.'

The prisoner and his guard were close now, and Horvath even turned his head to sneer at Iles. But he would not look me in the face.

'I could say that it is good to see you again, cousin Balthasar,' I said, 'but we both know that would be a lie. And I am one Quinton who does not lie before Kings.'

CHAPTER TWENTY-EIGHT

The Dowager Countess:
I pummelled my husband's chest. I screamed. I wept. I pummelled again.

'It is *madness*!' I cried. 'Kill him! Go down to the dungeon now, this very minute, and slit his throat! You are the Earl of Ravensden, and no man will gainsay you!'

He grasped my shoulders and held me far enough away that I was pummelling only air.

'No,' he said. 'If I killed him in such a way, I would answer before the law. That is our English way, and no man stands above it.'

'But single combat, husband? With all the risks in that?'

'You have seen him fight, My Lord,' said Iles, coming to my aid. 'You know – that is, you must be aware—'

'Of what, poet? That on dry land, he's a better fighter than I? Do you think I do this without knowing that?'

We three were in the principal room of Alnburgh Castle: a cold, bare space warmed by an inadequate fire and hung with mouldy tapestries. Rain lashed the window shutters, and I could hear mighty storm-waves breaking upon the rocks below. Three floors beneath us, the son of Earl Henry festered in chains.

I went limp, and he enfolded me with his arms.

'Then why, Matthew? In the name of God and all the saints, why?'

He stroked my hair, and Iles looked away.

'It is so that I can answer to God – and to the saints and the Virgin, too, if your church is right and mine is wrong. But God alone should judge which Quinton, Matthew or Balthasar, has the right to be the Earl of Ravensden.'

'But you are the rightful Earl – your uncle's marriage to Horvath's – to Balthasar's mother was bigamous!'

'A marriage of which there is no record, my love. A marriage of which the date is uncertain.'

'Then you think he might have a true case, My Lord?' said Iles. 'That Earl Henry's first wife died before he married in Hungary?'

'That, my friend, is what God must decide. In the old way – the way that our common ancestors, all the way back to the Quinton who came over with the Conqueror, would approve of. Single combat.'

'And what of your common grandmother?' I demanded. 'What would the Countess Katherine say, if she knew that one of her grandsons was set fair to kill the other?'

'Oh, she has already said it, my love. She said it the night she told me who Laszlo Horvath really was. *Destroy him, Matthew*, she said. *Destroy him, as I destroyed his father.*'

I looked up at my husband in astonishment. Iles was open-mouthed.

'She killed her own son?'

'She arranged his destruction. So yes, she killed him.'

'What sort of a mother can do such a thing?'

'Do not judge her too harshly, wife. It was a different time. A different age altogether. Remember, Henry was never meant to be Earl – that was the destiny of his elder brother Matthew, my namesake. Brilliant beyond measure, loved beyond reason, as my mother said many times in the days before her madness. But when Matthew died in his youth, Henry inherited. A strange, unsettled creature, from his very beginning, as my father told me. My grandmother feared that he would sell all the Quinton lands to fund his quests for the Holy Grail, the Philosopher's Stone, and all the other secrets of the ancients, leaving nothing for my father and I. She will not say who carried out the deed, or how it was done, somewhere here within the walls of Alnburgh. But as I say, it was a different age.'

For a moment, my fear of what my husband was about to do was driven out by another emotion, just as powerful, namely the kindred spirit of motherhood. And I wondered what I would do if I were ever in the Countess Katherine's position: if, say, little Beth turned out to be a monstrous she-wolf, a new Lucrezia Borgia, or if the son we would surely have one day proved to be a second Balthasar Quinton.

As I thought those thoughts, a new understanding came to me. I saw it now, as clear as day. Yes, my husband had to fight the Hungarian in single combat. He had to kill him, or be killed. It was the only way to expiate the guilt of the ages and the sins of the Quintons.

Nicholas Iles:

A cold dawn upon a Northumberland beach, beneath the walls of Alnburgh Castle. The two men were similarly attired, in long white smock-shirts and buff breeches, and for the first time, I noticed the faint family resemblance between them: between the cousins, Balthasar and Matthew Quinton, one of whom was about to kill the other. I looked away, to the castle ramparts, and saw a very small figure standing there, so still she seemed like a part of the stonework. The Countess was determined to watch, even to the very end.

There were other witnesses, too, so that no man could say this deed, regardless of its outcome, was done in a dark corner. Two of the Earl's Northumbrian neighbours, a knight and a gentleman of good acreage, were in attendance, as was an Archdeacon. Avent of the *Constant Esperance* was there, as was the boy Ielden, who, if necessary, would carry to Ravensden Abbey the news that it had a new lord. Sinkgraven, the Dutch surgeon of the *Merhonour* (newly paid off and dry docked at Chatham, every man believing that the war with Spain was as good as over), was present, to attend to any wounds short of the fatal kind. Christian Bell stood upon the sands in chains, guarded by men of the *Constant Esperance*. If his Earl triumphed, he would be a free man that day; but if mine was victorious, Bell was bound for the gallows. So there was quite an audience upon the sands of Alnburgh.

My Lord's sense of honour extended to affording the Hungarian the choice of weapons, for he was essentially the challenger.

'I take it you have no scimitars hereabouts,' said Horvath. 'In which case I choose the rapier.'

'The rapier alone? Not with a dagger? Very well, then,' said the Earl, 'but he who suffers the first blooding may change weapon if he wishes.'

'A curious rule. But you are judge and jury here, cousin Matthew, so you may make whatever rules you wish.'

The two men walked a few yards away from each other, and fell to their knees in prayer: Horvath in the language of his own country, My Lord offering up the thirty-fifth psalm.

Finally, they both took guard.

The Earl of Ravensden:

He came at me with anger, but also with control. Such control. Always favouring *terza* and *quarto* guards, the rapier held low. He had the fastest sword arm of any man I ever fought, and the best balance, even when lunging. I knew this from our mock-fights, in the first weeks and months that I knew the man who called then himself Laszlo Horvath. But it was clear that he had concealed or held back many of his skills during those bouts. Anticipation is the key to swordplay, and he must have anticipated that one day he and I would fight each other for real, and to the death. He anticipated the need not to reveal all of his techniques to me; and I knew now that if he had a *botta segreta*, an unstoppable secret thrust not taught by the masters or the manuals, he must have kept it back from me.

For my part, it proved just as impossible to anticipate what he would do in fight as it had when he was conspiring against me.

I tried all I knew. Feints at his left, forcing him to parry – lunges for his heart and his head – counter-attack, always trying to work round to his left – *stoccata* thrusts at the belly – taking a high guard, using my height, angling down for his head – but he was always ready for me.

I watched his eyes. I watched his wrist. I watched the blade. I watched how he stood, the angle of his body. But as we fought along the sand of Alnburgh, the waves lapping the shore at our side as steel struck steel over and over again, I found no weakness in my cousin, not even a hint of a mistake.

I could barely anticipate his moves, but he seemed always to be able to anticipate mine. His blade always seemed to be in the right place, a second before I even thought of placing my own there. He was always on the offensive, always advancing on the right foot, forcing me further and further up the beach. I do not know how long we fought thus, but one thing I knew: I was losing.

I thrust again for his head, but he brought up his rapier from beneath, at once deflecting my blade, pressing it back toward my body, and threatening my face with his own. We stood there for a moment, face to face, barely inches apart, and I saw the all-consuming hatred in his eyes. Then he suddenly brought up his left foot, thus shifting his entire balance forward, and gripped my sword-hand with his own, trying to prise my fingers away from the quillions.

Fuck and damnation – no need for him to have a botta segreta, *for he's undone you with a schoolboy trick, Ravensden – disarmed and pierced with your own blade would be a fine way to die.*

I swung at him with my left arm, hoping to use my reach to land a punch. He ducked away from the blow, but in doing so lost balance slightly on the wet sand and let go of my sword arm. But as he parted, he somehow flicked his wrist to manage a little *mandritta* cut. I felt the point of his rapier slice my cheek, felt the familiar sensation of blood flowing over flesh, and knew he had drawn first blood.

I half-expected him to charge me instantly, to follow up his advantage by attacking furiously and finally. But instead, he stepped away.

'You have suffered the first blooding,' he said. 'By your rules, you may change weapon, if you wish.'

'I never expected you to permit that, if you had the upper hand.'

'Is it not the honourable thing? The thing that an Earl of Ravensden would do?'

His answer dumbfounded me. After all, then, and in spite of all, some of the honour of the Quintons had found its way into the Hungarian's blood.

'It is. It is indeed. I am grateful to you, cousin Balthasar.'

I called for Iles, and he brought me a new weapon. Or rather, an old weapon: a very old weapon, and its attendant. An English sword of the old fashion, with a cross hilt and a shorter, broader blade than the rapier, together with the buckler that nestled on my left forearm. It is difficult to explain the sense of relief and familiarity I felt as I gripped the sword. For this was the weapon I had learned and mastered as a boy, when it was still the universal blade of choice in England, before the damnable rapier, its complicated grips, and all its Italian and Frenchified tricks, became the rage of the hour.

I nodded to the Hungarian, we took up our guards, and resumed.

Oh, this was better. No more of the incessant offence, the constant lunging and thrusting. The English sword was made for cutting and defending, complimented by the indispensable buckler. Now I could parry the Hungarian's thrusts with the latter while cutting with the blade; and, as even the simplest grasp of anatomy reveals, a cut to the head, the shoulders or the body with such a sword is made with far more force than a rapier thrust, where the body is lunging forward unnaturally far.

It was my turn to attack, and for perhaps a minute, cousin Balthasar seemed confused by this new-old weapon, by the different lines of attack. But then he adjusted, countering my cuts by using the rapier in the same fashion that I was using my sword – eschewing quite so many thrusts as before, relying more on the quarters of his weapon nearest the hilt for blocking my attacks, parrying and cutting double-bladed.

Now I was on the back foot again, parrying his relentless attacks with my buckler, and the truth came to me. His weapon of choice was a scimitar; another cutting weapon. This method of fighting favoured him just as much as it did me, if not more.

I was tiring now. For just as each attack with a cutting sword carries more force, so it expends more, too. My left arm, now bearing the brunt of defence as endless cuts rained in upon the buckler, felt like it was carrying a pail of coal. Yet still Balthasar came on, seemingly as fresh as when we began, seemingly inexhaustible.

I failed to bring up the buckler in time – his blade sliced across my left shoulder, and as I brought up my own sword to clash with his, I tripped over a hummock of sea-grass, falling heavily onto the wounded shoulder.

I saw the shadow of cousin Balthasar upon the sand, his rapier raised and levelled in a high guard, poised to thrust for the kill.

I heard Iles' cry – 'My Lord! Remember Tamburlaine at Chester!'

I saw Horvath's right foot step forward toward me, then come forward again as he steadied himself for the final, fatal lunge –

I swung my sword low and hard, barely three inches above the sand. I felt the impact of steel through flesh and bone. I saw the blood spurt as the leg came very nearly entirely away from the foot. Fatally off balance, Balthasar Quinton, or Laszlo Horvath, fell forward.

I brought my sword up, hard and fast, directly between his legs.

He fell beside me, his face no more than inches from mine, his eyes staring at me. I lifted myself on my right elbow, and saw the terrible flow of blood spilling onto the sand. I was aware of Iles running toward me.

The Hungarian's lips moved, and he formed a word. His name.

'Balthasar,' he said. 'Balthasar, Earl of Ravensden.'

Then the eyes ceased to blink.

The Dowager Countess:

I ran faster than I had ever run, even when I was a girl chasing her brother in the groves around our chateau. Down the spiral stairs, through the courtyard, out of the postern, down to the beach. I stumbled more than once – skirts are not well suited to running on sand – and felt a pain in my arm which I immediately dismissed, only to learn a little later that it was a broken wrist.

By the time I reached him, the Dutch surgeon was already stitching the fierce wound in his shoulder, and Iles was pouring a flask of some fiery liquid down his throat in between his roars of pain. I flung myself to his good side, and wept copiously.

He kissed me on the top of the head.

'It is done,' he said. 'God's righteous judgement has prevailed. And tonight, my countess, we can return to the business of begetting a son who will be the undoubted, unchallenged Earl of Ravensden.'

'And you will go no more to the wars,' I said, 'and put your life in peril as you have here, today?'

'As to the latter, my love, I certainly intend to fight no more duels. It is a young man's game, and I do not think at my age that I can learn to love the rapier. Besides, who is there left for me to fight? But as for the former... Soon there will be a new age in England. A new King. And whether he maintains the great war with Spain or not, he will still have enemies at sea, and he will still need an admiral.'

I sobbed, but he held me tightly, and it all seemed better.

Nicholas Iles:

Once again we three were in the principal room of Alnburgh Castle, where the man once named Laszlo Horvath had sought to do hurt to my countess. The Earl, his shoulder heavily bandaged, was eating a leg of mutton and swilling a tankard of ale. The countess fussed over him protectively, telling him to be careful not to jar the wound. He humoured her, although I knew what he was thinking: which was, that a man who has been wounded a score of times really has no need of such advice.

We were attending to the consequences of the death of Balthasar Quinton. A chest which must have been his, abandoned when he fled the castle those months before, had been brought up, and I was endeavouring to break the lock. Meanwhile, the Earl was dictating orders to the lad Ielden.

'The body will be buried at Ravensden Abbey,' he said, 'in an unmarked plot.' The Countess made to protest, but My Lord raised a hand. 'It is what I want. I, the Earl of Ravensden. And it is what my grandmother wants. Whatever else he was, Balthasar Quinton was the son of Henry, sixth Earl, my uncle and her son. He is entitled to that mark of respect.'

Finally, the point of my knife prised open the lock, and I lifted the lid of the Hungarian's private chest. I drew out a dagger: a long, fearsome blade, still with dark stains of blood upon it. There were clothes, and two pistols, and –

'Look here, My Lord,' I said. 'Papers. Notes in his hand. He kept a record.'

Matthew, Earl of Ravensden, picked up a few of the sheets, surveyed their contents, crumpled them, and threw them to the ground.

'It's a dead business, now,' he said. 'These writings of his won't interest anyone, and will only remind us of the hurts of this whole affair. Burn them, Iles. Destroy them. Laszlo Horvath is dead. Balthasar Quinton is dead. That's all that matters now.'

With that, he returned to his mutton and his ale.

I looked at the papers again. I was a writer, so the destruction of words on a page was anathema to me. No, I would disobey My Lord in this. I would keep the papers of Balthasar Quinton, the man who might have been Earl of Ravensden.

Perhaps in some future time, others not yet born might find some interest in his story.

CHAPTER TWENTY-NINE

Coronations have been two a farthing in my life.

I have attended no fewer than six, beginning with the joyous reverie that was the crowning of King Charles the Second, miraculously restored to his throne after long years of exile and penury. I was drunk for a week.

From then on, they deteriorated. The crowning of James the Second was a tedious affair, notable only for the ominous spectacle of the Supreme Governor of the Church of England refusing to participate in its Holy Communion because he was a Roman Catholic. That of the joint sovereigns, William and Mary, was awkward: what else could it be, when they were only being crowned because they had just deposed her father? Then came Queen Anne (so dull I have forgotten it), George the First (too German), and, very recently, his present Majesty King George the Second (too much Handel).

But during all of these spectacular enthronements, I have had the same thought, always at the moment when the crown of state is placed upon the royal head, and the royal hands grip the sceptre and orb.

None of you have a blood-right to sit there, adorned with those baubles.

Hence my cynicism towards the great matter of the last forty years, the rival claims of the Jacobites and the Hanoverians: I suppose I am probably the only man in the British Isles who thinks it does not matter a jot which descendant of Davey Rizzio sits upon the throne. But one lesson the last forty years has taught me is that cynicism can easily be misconstrued as disaffection, or even treason, so I have learned to toast King George with appropriate enthusiasm. Just as I would toast King James if he ever managed to organise a decent invasion, which seems unlikely in the light of the alehouse comedies he has commanded to ignominious failure thus far.

Yes, I am probably the only man still living who knows the truth, thanks to the oath *grandmaman* made me swear on her Vulgate Bible on a cold night at Ravensden Abbey, as autumn gave way to winter in that year of 1651. I swore that I would tell no-one else of our secret, and I kept that promise. At first, it was a sort of game between us: what eleven year old does not love a secret that has been shared only with him? But as I grew older, and especially after *grandmaman* died, it became an entirely different business. I realised at once that I could not share the truth with my uncle Tristram, whom I loved and trusted in most other things; but in the 1650s, his loyalties were uncertain, and he was rather too close to the Lord Protector and his spymaster John Thurloe for the comfort of the other members of the House of Quinton. His momentary curiosity about the secret knowledge his mother claimed to possess about the succession to Queen Elizabeth, that day we were all together at Ravensden Abbey, was soon forgotten as more urgent concerns pressed in on him, and in later years, he always seemed to have too much to do, and never pressed me upon the subject.

So no, I could not tell my uncle. I could not tell my brother Charles, the Earl, either, for his loyalty to his King was unquestionable (for very secret reasons that I did not yet understand), so what right did I have to shake it? I certainly could not tell my mother, whose devotion to the memory of the King and Martyr Charles the First was so all-consuming that I dreaded to think what might become of her if she learned the truth. I thought of sharing the burden with my sister Elizabeth, but she was soon married to Venner Garvey, a prominent member of Cromwell's government, while my other sister, my twin Herry, was dead just two years after I learned these truths, before I was grown-up enough to even think of confiding in such a foolish creature as a *girl*. As I grew older, all of my friends were staunch cavaliers, so if I told any of them, they were bound to condemn me out of hand as a madman or worse. And when I finally took a Dutch wife, I could not even confide in her, for Cornelia was an Orangist, and would not have taken kindly to learning that the Prince William she venerated, later England's King William the Third, was descended from a popish Italian lutenist.

So there was nothing for it. Countless times I drew my sword, and risked my life, for the Stuarts, despite the knowledge I possessed. As far as I was concerned, though, the restoration of the monarchy had settled the matter: an event so miraculous, so utterly unlikely until just weeks before it happened, was surely conclusive proof that God wanted Charles Stuart to be King of England, regardless of whose blood flowed in his veins. And when I saw him crowned in Westminster Abbey, and remembering the words my grandfather had written about what the coronation ceremony meant, I knew I would fight and, if necessary, die, for this man.

But even on that glorious day, as we all shouted 'God save the King! May the King live forever!', one thought held sway in my mind.

My father, too, never knew of the secret knowledge that his parents possessed, or so *grandmaman* claimed. James Quinton, ninth Earl of Ravensden for the grand total of one hundred and eighteen days, was a poet-warrior, a dreamer who believed that he was cast in the mould of one of King Arthur's knights, riding out to rid the world of the evil represented by Parliament's great rebellion. Would he really have ridden to his death on Naseby field if he knew that he did so for the grandson of David Rizzio?

That thought is in my mind now, as I set down the last of the ancient papers upon my desk by the window. No, I shall leave this sordid and unseemly writing of 'novels' to the likes of Defoe and Swift, whose gutter-like minds are better suited to it. I am very tired, and in any case, I have no doubt that they would be able to think of a suitable ending to this tale, which I cannot –

The light coming through my window is a peculiar one, creeping through the dark rain clouds that are massing in the west, focusing a narrow shaft of sunlight onto the glass. It illuminates one of my grandfather's papers, which happens to be on top of one of the several piles into which I have sorted them: the paper recounting his meeting with King James, in the wilderness on the border between England and Scotland.

'And at that moment, I will have your unswerving loyalty, My Lord Ravensden? Even though you know what this letter says?'

'You will be my lawful, anointed King, and I will fight for you with every breath left in my body, Your Grace. Even though I know what that letter says. Especially because I know what that letter says.'

I notice something that I missed at first reading, by candlelight on a gloomy autumn day in the muniment room at Ravensden Abbey, when I was eleven years old. There is a slight impression in the margin: some faded writing, so lightly inscribed upon the paper that it must have nearly vanished within a matter of months, let alone years, in marked contrast to the bold, forceful strokes of my grandfather's hand alongside it. An inscription so faint that I must have overlooked it entirely, all those years ago.

I recognise a date: *The fifth day of November, 1628.* Gunpowder treason day: the day on which my brother was born.

I recognise my father's initials: *JQ.*

I recognise the motto of the Quinton family, written in my father's hand: *nihil est quod videtur.*

'Nothing is what it seems.'

HISTORICAL NOTE

Matthew Quinton, eighth Earl of Ravensden, is a fictional character, but both his career and personality are based loosely on a number of the 'sea dogs' of Queen Elizabeth's reign, notably George Clifford, Earl of Cumberland, who set out a number of privateering voyages and commanded warships during several naval expeditions. His career is well described in Richard Spence's book, *The Privateering Earl*. The principal events of this book – the affairs of the 'Invisible Armada' and the Spinola galleys, the killings at Gowrie House, the conspiracy of the Earl of Essex and the Battles of Castlehaven, Kinsale and Sesimbra Bay – and a number of lesser ones (for instance, the treason and execution of Edward Squire, the Spanish galleon at Sligo, and the encounter with the Spanish plate fleet) all took place at the times, and in the ways, that I have described. Inevitably, though, I have injected some elements of poetic licence into each in order to give Earl Matthew and the other principal characters central parts in them. Thus Sir Richard Leveson led the attack on both Castlenipark Fort and the Spanish fleet at Castlehaven, leaving his vice-admiral lying off Kinsale, rather than the other way round; Sir William Monson was Leveson's second-in-command at the Battle of Sesimbra Bay, and carried out the astonishing sortie into the bay in his flagship, the *Garland*; while the admiral who actually commanded at the defeat of the Spinola galleys was Sir Robert Mansel. Similarly, I have taken some minor liberties with the precise timings of some of the events during the Irish campaign of 1601-2. Above all, I am deeply conscious of the fact that I have played fast and loose with the personality and reputation of Sir Richard Leveson, whose boldness and gallantry at the Battle of Castlehaven has been measured, not unreasonably, against the most exacting question of all in naval history, namely, 'What might Nelson have done?'. By way of apology to his descendants, and to the fine city of Wolverhampton, I here reproduce the words upon his splendid memorial in Saint Peter's Church in that city:

Here lyeth the body of Perfection's Glorie
Fame's owne worlde wonder, and the ocean's story.

The right protector, rightful scourge of wrong,
In peace a dove, in war a lyon strong,
Vertues embracer, Vices opposite,
Times chiefest ornament, true valour's Knight.
The all just Heaven, regarding high deserts,
Bereav'd the earth of his devine parts,
Leaving here nought of him but slimy dross
And a continual grief for such a loss.

Readers seeking more detail on the naval history of these years should delve into R B Wernham's magisterial book, *The Return of the Armadas*, although the older account by Sir Julian Corbett, *The Successors of Drake*, still has much to commend it. I also used a number of original sources, especially *The Naval Tracts of Sir William Monson*, published by the Navy Records Society. Regrettably, the Irish campaigns are comparatively little known beyond the borders of the Republic; however, there is a splendid and very well illustrated collection of essays, *The Battle of Kinsale*, edited by Hiram Morgan, although this is quite difficult to get hold of, and a more accessible recent study by Des Ekin, *The Last Armada*. For the history of General Federico Spinola and his galleys, see the article by Randal Gray in *The Mariner's Mirror*, 1978. The clan battle described in Chapter 22 takes place between fictitious septs of two very real clans, but is based quite closely on the Battle of Glen Fruin, fought between the MacGregors and Colquhouns in February 1603 on ground that is now very nearly a stone's throw from the nuclear submarine base at Faslane; here, I drew my inspiration from Nigel Tranter's novel *Children of the Mist*, rather than from any strictly historical work. It is slightly invidious to single out titles from the long list of other books that I consulted prior to, and during, the writing of *The Rage of Fortune*, but special mention should go to Ian Mortimer's marvellous *The Time Traveller's Guide to Elizabethan England*. Nicholas Iles' 'poetry' about the Earl of Ravensden is taken, with appropriate modification where necessary, from *The Legend of Captain Jones* (1631) by David Lloyd, future Dean of Saint Asaph – probably the first work of naval historical fiction to be written by a Welshman!

I have taken a liberty with the record by placing the first meeting of the Earl with his future wife at the chateau of Chambord. This was effectively abandoned by the French royal family for a hundred years after the death of François I in 1547, but for simple narrative logic, I needed the meeting to take place relatively close to Nantes – and my fond memories of Chambord won out over strict historical accuracy. Laszlo Horvath (or, as he would be in strictly correct Magyar, Horvath Laszlo) is a fictional character, but the political and religious make-up of Hungary and Transylvania during this period were as I have described them, and the battles and wars in which I have placed him were real enough; the so-called 'Long War' between the Ottoman Empire and a Christian alliance comprising the Holy Roman Empire, Moldavia, Wallachia and Transylvania lasted from 1591 to 1606. There was a real ship called the *Merhonour* during this period, but readers of the series will recall that the fictional version which I have deployed here 'survived' until the 1660s, when she becomes the command of Earl Matthew's grandson, the eleven year old boy who narrates the story. The young Matthew Quinton is the protagonist of the other books in this series, which are set against the backdrops of the Restoration of the monarchy in 1660 and the Anglo-Dutch wars of that period.

The 'Gowrie House affair' remains one of the abiding mysteries of British history. One of the few certainties is that, on 5 August 1600, James the Sixth, King of Scots, and a party of courtiers went to Gowrie House in Perth at the behest of Alexander, Master of Ruthven, the younger brother of John, third Earl of Gowrie. By mid-afternoon, both Alexander and John were dead, and the King and his apologists insisted that they had made a clumsy attempt upon his life. All sorts of alternative theories circulated during the months and years that followed, but one of the most persistent centred on the notion that a mysterious English ship had been present in the Firth of Tay at the relevant time, perhaps intended to whisk King James to captivity in England. Robert Logan of Restalrig, the shady adventurer who had mysterious dealings with the Earl of Gowrie, was indeed the co-owner of a large private warship on the east coast of England, although in reality, his partner was Lord Willoughby d'Eresby, one of the great soldiers of Elizabethan England (and another of the models for the Earl of Ravensden in this book; for instance, Willoughby went to study at Padua in 1596 in order to recover from his wounds, and undoubtedly met the Earl of Gowrie there, thus providing that element of Matthew Quinton senior's 'back story'). Fast Castle is a real place, and its scanty remains, still perched crazily on the outcrop described in this book, are well worth a distinctly strenuous walk. The castle, which was Logan of Restalrig's property during this period, has always inspired myths and legends, with Sir Walter Scott rechristening it 'Wolf's Crag'. In 1594, Logan entered into a contract with John Napier of Merchiston, later the inventor of logarithms, who was to employ magic to unearth an unnamed and mysterious treasure hidden somewhere in the sea-caves under Fast. Nothing came of Napier's treasure hunt, apart from a falling out between the two contractors; in what appears to have been a mild over-reaction, Napier subsequently forbade the letting of any of his property to anyone named Logan. I owe the notion that the 'Casket Letters' might have been the treasure hidden at Fast Castle to Fred Douglas and his book *Gold at Wolf's Crag? An Historical Investigation* (1971), although Douglas overcooked his thesis somewhat by suggesting that another plausible 'candidate' for the lost treasure of Fast might be none other than the Holy Grail itself. I hope that devotees of Douglas, and the rather more numerous devotees of Dan Brown, will forgive my tongue-in-cheek reference to this theory during the scene in the Fast Castle sea-cave.

The subsequent accession of James the Sixth to the English throne has led many to assume that this was somehow 'inevitable'. Nothing was further from the truth, and I have depicted the furious debates over the succession, the identities of the possible candidates, and the attitudes of leading players like Cecil and Essex, as accurately as I could in a work of fiction. Similarly, the popular perception of James Stuart as a coward and a peacemaker has blinded many people to the undoubted historical fact that, prior to 1603, he appeared to many in England as a belligerent and somewhat unstable warmonger who had personally led armies into battle on several occasions, and who directly threatened to invade England on several others. Thus the possibility of King James invading to assert his rights to the succession seemed very real during this period, and indeed, in 1600 James asked his Parliament for money to fund an army precisely for that purpose. John, Earl of Gowrie, was one of the most prominent critics of this warmongering brinkmanship on the part of the so-called *rex pacificus*.

The question of the degree of foreknowledge of Gowrie's plot, if any, on the part of Robert Cecil, remains an open question, although it is at least worth noting in passing that within a few years, Cecil really was in a relationship with Barbara Ruthven, one of the many sisters of the dead earl and his brother, a relationship alluded to during the moorland meeting of King James and the Earl of Ravensden; and it was Barbara I had in mind as the (unnamed) individual who could have authenticated the Casket Letters for Cecil. Similarly, my account of the 'neutrality' of Broughty Castle during the fight between the *Constant Esperance* and van der Waecken's Dunkirker is based on the unsubstantiated suggestion that Sir James Scrymgeour, the Provost and Constable of Dundee, was secretly in league with the Earl of Gowrie. (Incidentally, van der Waecken was a real character, although I invented this particular cruise of his.) I explore all of these matters in detail in my book *Blood of Kings: the Stuarts, the Ruthvens and the 'Gowrie Conspiracy'* (Ian Allan, 2010), which presents all of the bewildering theories surrounding the 'Gowrie House' affair, provides a tentative explanation of what might really have happened, and stresses an inconvenient but unarguable truth: that King James was in far more real and immediate danger of his life at Perth on 5 August 1600 than he was at Westminster on 5 November 1605.

The paternity of King James the Sixth and First, and the fate and contents of the missing 'Casket Letters', have been debated since the sixteenth century. As I wrote in *Blood of Kings*,

Whispered doubts about the legitimacy of James Stuart were doing the rounds within hours of the child's birth at Edinburgh Castle, if not before...Mary [Queen of Scots] was clearly all too aware of such rumours, and their potentially damaging political consequences. Hence the embarrassing farce on the day of James's birth, 19 June 1566, when Mary's despised and drunken husband was virtually dragged to her bedchamber and made to declare that he was undoubtedly the father of the infant prince... None of it did the queen much good, and when she subsequently blasted what little was left of her reputation by appearing to connive in the murder of her husband, Darnley, and then in short order marrying his suspected murderer, Bothwell, all the whispered suspicions could finally be shouted out loud. Edinburgh graffiti portrayed the queen as a mermaid, a common euphemism for a whore, and a barb from Ovid mysteriously appeared on her wedding night, fastened to the gate of Holyrood Palace:

As the common people say,
Only harlots marry in May...

Like the birth of Prince James Francis Edward Stuart in the summer of 1688, it was politically imperative that the child born to Mary, Queen of Scots, in 1566 should be a healthy son. In the fraught political and religious situation of the day, any alternative – a still birth or a girl – would have been an unmitigated disaster. The legality of female succession was still not entirely clear-cut; as John Knox's tirade against the 'monstrous regiment of women' had demonstrated, many Scots remained deeply uncomfortable about the notion of a female monarch, and certainly had no desire to repeat the experiment. In 1566, anything other than a healthy son would at the very least have triggered speculation about a new husband for the queen, given the obvious precariousness of her marriage to the alcoholic Darnley. At worst, the resultant succession crisis could have triggered a bloody civil war – and although such a war eventually broke out, it only followed Mary's abdication, and a highly unlikely chain of events that no one could possibly have foreseen in the spring and summer of 1566. Therefore...there is a powerful inner logic underpinning the theory of a conspiracy by Mary and certain of her key advisors to pass off a son who might not have been Darnley's as the legitimate son of the King and Queen of Scots...

These dark rumours about King James's true paternity persisted for years. If anything they acquired ever more currency, for as James got older, it became increasingly apparent that he bore little resemblance in personality or physique to either of his supposed parents, Darnley and Queen Mary...If the illegitimacy of King James VI and I really was secret knowledge possessed by the Ruthvens, it might be connected somehow to the undoubted fact that the first Earl of Gowrie [father of the third Earl, killed at Perth on 5 August 1600] *was the last certain owner of the Casket Letters, which were passed to him by the Regent Morton's illegitimate son in 1581 or 1582. These were the mysterious, lost documents that implicated Mary, Queen of Scots, in the murder of her husband Henry, Lord Darnley, King James's legal father. Copies were produced at Mary's first trial in England, shortly after she sought sanctuary there, and their incriminating nature provided some of the justification for shutting her away in a succession of gloomy English castles for twenty years. But copies...do not necessarily give the whole story, certainly not the true story, and the extant copies of the Casket*

Letters do not prove that King James was illegitimate. Argument rages to this day over whether or not the surviving letters are genuine, or clever forgeries produced by Moray's government and based on the manipulation of real letters written by Mary. As far as the paternity of King James is concerned, though, this point is academic. The 'casket' originally contained rather more documents than were presented in public – ten more, to be precise. Although the contents of a couple of the missing documents can be surmised, the rest are lost. There might have been documents that proved or hinted at James's illegitimacy, but if such had existed, the [regimes that ruled Scotland after 1567] would have had good reason to conceal or destroy them. They wanted documents that proved Mary's foreknowledge of the death of Darnley, and might have been perfectly prepared to manufacture them if they could not find suitable proof in her own hand. But they owed their authority and all they possessed to the simple fact that they served James VI, undoubted King of Scots by hereditary right, and any evidence to suggest that the infant to whom they bowed the knee was actually not undoubted king by heredity would at once have threatened their power, if not their very lives.

Regardless of whether or not any evidence of his illegitimacy in the Casket Letters had been destroyed before they came into the first Earl of Gowrie's possession, King James – who presumably only knew the contents of the copies – could not have known this for certain...It is certainly the case that Gowrie refused to sell the Casket Letters to Queen Elizabeth, who was desperate to get hold of them. He might have taken the documents with him when he tried to flee the country by ship from Dundee in 1584: legend has it that when an old house in the town was pulled down, a bundle of old letters in French was found hidden in a chimney.

The Casket Letters are highly unlikely to have been the 'treasure' that drew King James to Gowrie House on 5 August 1600: he would hardly have gone hunting in Falkland Park for four hours if he had even the slightest inkling that the most important documents his mother ever wrote, or else the proofs that he was not the rightful legitimate King of Scots, were within his grasp. But it is just conceivable that at Gowrie House, the Ruthvens sought to blackmail him into agreeing to their demands by threatening to produce the originals of the Casket Letters;

an urn containing ashes, found within a hidden closet of the house when it was demolished in 1807, was inevitably identified as the final repository of the lost documents. Alternatively, the letters could have been produced after James's abduction, or abdication, or murder, to justify the Ruthven coup.

Ultimately, of course, if James Stuart really was the son of David Rizzio, then every monarch of Great Britain since 1603, and subsequently of the United Kingdom – including the present incumbent – has had no right whatsoever to sit upon the throne, as Matthew Quinton suggests in the final chapter.

But that would be another story altogether.

ACKNOWLEDGEMENTS

Ever since I conceived the original idea for the journals of the (younger) Matthew Quinton, I hoped one day to have an opportunity to write a prequel about his namesake, the eighth Earl of Ravensden; and, of course, giving them the same name means that the series title, 'the Journals of Matthew Quinton', can apply to stories about both men. Readers of the previous books in the series will know just how pervasive the influence of his grandfather is for the younger Matthew during his adventures at sea after the Restoration, even to the extent of hearing the occasional (imagined?) ghostly aside from the old sea-dog. I also wanted to correct the still deeply entrenched notion that Elizabeth the First's great war with Spain was all about the Spanish Armada, and that not very much happened after that. In fact, the Armada campaign was near the beginning of the war, not the end, and sixteen years of largely indecisive but often fascinating warfare still lay ahead. So when it was suggested that it would be better for the next two stories about the younger Matthew Quinton during the Anglo-Dutch wars, namely *Death's Bright Angel*, which culminates in the Great Fire of London of 1666, and *The Devil Upon the Wave*, which deals with the Dutch attack on the Medway in 1667, to be published to coincide with the 350th anniversaries of those events, I jumped at the opportunity to be able to write this story in the meantime – especially as it took me back to the period at the very end of the sixteenth century and beginning of the seventeenth that I had both taught for many years and researched in great detail for my non-fiction book *Blood of Kings*, many elements of which provided inspiration, and a substantial amount of detail, for some of the key themes in this story. In the event, unforeseen circumstances greatly delayed the appearance of this book, but I am grateful to my agent, Peter Buckman, and to Jack Butler and Richard Foreman of Endeavour Press, for eventually bringing it into the light of day.

Thanks also to Elizabeth Carr; David Hope; Andrew, Lord Hothfield; and above all, as always, to Wendy, for making another Quinton Journal immeasurably better than it might otherwise have been.

J D Davies

Printed in Great Britain
by Amazon